1993

ALISON —

I HOPE YOU ENJOY THIS.
THE AUTHOR IS AN OLD FRIEND
AND COLLEGE ROOMMATE. IT'S
HER FIRST PUBLISHED BOOK.
MERRY CHRISTMAS WITH LOVE —

Wendy 🎄

THE TV GUIDANCE COUNSELOR

T·H·E
TV GUIDANCE
COUNSELOR

by A.C. LeMieux

TAMBOURINE BOOKS NEW YORK

Library of Congress Cataloging in Publication Data

LeMieux, A. C. (Anne Connelly)
The TV guidance counselor/by A.C. LeMieux.—1st ed. p. cm.
Summary: Sixteen-year-old Michael tries to deal with his parents'
ugly divorce by pursuing his new obsession with photography, until
an accident pushes him to the breaking point.
[1. Divorce—Fiction.   2. Photography—Fiction.   3. Emotional
problems—Fiction.   4. Suicide—Fiction.]   I. Title.
PZ7.L537375Tac   1993   [Fic]—dc20   92-33664   CIP   AC
ISBN 0-688-12402-X
1 3 5 7 9 10 8 6 4 2

First edition

For
Michael, Thomas, James,
Kevin, John, Brian, and
Charles

The author would like to thank
Jenifer A. Nields, M.D.,
Kevin Connelly, Ann Brophy,
and Patricia Reilly Giff
for lending their assistance and support
during the writing of this book.

ONE

I wasn't trying to kill myself the night I jumped into the Mohegan River. At least, I don't think I was. I mean, I didn't stand there on the old swing bridge by Thumm's Market and say to myself, "What you, Michael Madden, are about to do may very likely result in your death. The tide is high, the current's running fast, and the water's colder than a polar bear's butt."

I don't want to think about any of it right now. But Dr. Sherman keeps tossing questions at me. I can't figure out if he's got a method or if he's just playing roulette with my head. He doesn't look much like a doctor. He wears plaid flannel shirts and jeans with ironed creases, and his hair looks molded with some kind of mousse. He kind of looks like a game show host on his day off from "Broken Family Feud." Or maybe "Wheel of Misfortune."

"How did you feel after the divorce, Michael?"

Oh, just dandy, Doc, fine and dandy. Never damn better! What do you think, you stupid bozo shrink? How did I feel? How would you feel?

There's this thing that you're part of for your whole life. It's called a family and it's a living organism. And you're a single cell in this organism and so are your parents and your brother, if you have one, which I don't, and your sister, if you have one, which I do. Each cell has its own nucleus and walls, but all the cells fit together. Then one day, the glue that holds them in place dissolves, and the organism loses its shape. Maybe one of the cells goes spinning off somewhere. The other cells don't know how to relate. What's left is this twitching, incoherent mess. Then the cells start to mutate.

Take my dad—John T. Madden. He used to be Jack. After the divorce, he had all these cards printed up, saying J. THADDEUS MADDEN, WORLD-FAMOUS MARINE PHOTOGRAPHER. Sound like a mid-life identity crisis to you? It does to me, too.

And my mother. About a month after we moved from the big house where I grew up to the rented rathole on the river, she developed a very weird driving habit. All of *a sudden, she refused to make left-hand turns anymore. She'll go eight blocks out of her way to get where she's going only two blocks away, all so she doesn't have to make a left-hand turn.*

My six-year-old sister, Amanda, has turned into a miniature bag lady. Everywhere she goes, she carries this grungy pink duffel bag crammed with her favorite stuff. I mean, everywhere—it's under her chair when she eats, next to the tub when she takes a bath, behind her pillow when she sleeps. Her teacher called Mom about some rule that kids can bring personal stuff only on show-and-tell day. Mom tried to explain to Amanda, but she refused to go to school if she couldn't tote her bag. So they compromised; she can bring it now, but she has to keep it in her cubby.

And I'm the one who winds up in the loony bin. Figure it out if you can. I can't.

There's a sharp pain in my right hand. I look down and see a white-knuckled fist, my fist. I stretch the fingers out slowly and rub the palm to ease the cramping.

"I'm sensing a lot of buried anger here, Michael. Your mother tells me that you two haven't been getting along since the divorce, and that things between you have gotten worse since you moved to the new house. Do you want to talk about how you feel about that?"

Not especially, Doc, no, I don't want to talk about

how I feel. As a matter of fact, I don't want to feel. I've found in my sixteen years that feeling can be very painful.

I look out the window of Dr. Sherman's office. Cars are starting to pull into the parking lot for hospital visiting hours. I wonder if Melissa will come visit me. I haven't seen her in two weeks.

The hospital is way up on Skytop Road. Stunning New England views and all that—very serene, very therapeutic. Off in the distance, behind all the winter-stripped trees, a white sun is getting ready to slip down behind the horizon from a dirty-looking November sky. From up here, the river looks like a long, thin strip of scrap metal.

"You know, Michael, what you're looking for isn't out there." Dr. Sherman interrupts my poetic interlude.

"I'm not looking for anything," I say. It comes out sounding surly.

"Everyone's looking for something," Doc comes back. "Isn't that what the old song says?"

What old song is that, Doc? I think, but I don't really care enough to ask. Everyone's looking for something. It could be true, I guess. But what if you don't have a clue what you're looking for? Or what if in the process of looking for your thing, you really mess up? And mess up not just yourself but somebody else, some innocent bystander?

"The answers aren't out there, Mike," Doc repeats. "You have to look within yourself."

Suddenly I feel irritated. No, I feel more than irritated, I feel really pissed. On the verge of furious.

"What the hell is that supposed to mean? Look within myself. Why would I want to look within myself? There's nothing in there!" I'm shouting now; I can't help it.

"Is that why you tried to kill yourself?" he asks.

"I wasn't trying to kill myself!"

The anger drains away as quickly as it came, leaving this numbness behind it. A deadened feeling. Then the pictures—

The pictures are coming back. They're all still frames, with some lunatic behind the viewfinder who won't stop snapping away. Is the lunatic me? But I'm in all the pictures, even though I'm the one who's looking. It's just like it was that night on the bridge. . . .

Snap click. My father standing in our driveway, handing me his old Nikon F2, just before he took off last August.

Snap click. My mother lying on the couch, staring at the TV in the shack we had to move into.

Snap click. Me and Melissa at the swimming spot up the river—I want to freeze that picture, I want it to stay, but it doesn't.

Snap click. Mr. Dorio, my photography teacher,

11

*kicking me out of class after Ricky pulled that stunt
with my picture of Victoria Kaminsky.*

Snap click. *Melissa in the school parking lot, running
away from me.*

Snap click snap click snap click. *Melissa's getting
smaller and smaller and smaller—but I feel like I'm the
one who's about to disappear.*

Snap click. *My mother and Ricky—in the kitchen.*

Snap click. *The TV Guidance Counselor freaking
out in the parking lot of Thumm's Market, thanks to
the dirty deed that Ricky—then I—just before the car—*

*I squeeze my eyes shut, wish I could squeeze my brain
until I squeezed all the pictures right out of it.*

"*If you weren't trying to kill yourself, Michael, what
were you trying to do?*"

I was trying to get away from—

I was trying to drown out—no, not drown—

I was trying to wash—wash away—

    the pictures—the pain

      what happened

      everything

*Dr. Sherman watches me with this kindness I can't
stand. He pushes a box of Kleenex across his desk. I
can't believe I'm crying.*

If I had to put a date to when my life started rolling
seriously downhill, it might be the last day I saw my

father, right before he blew town to sail in the Royale
Rum Round the World Race.

Ricky and I were at the swimming hole up past the
river bend, north of the parkway. It's way off the beaten
track, out in this wetlands preserve, and it's very private.
Ricky's real name isn't Richard, by the way. It's Roderick Alister Bolton, but don't ever call him that, or Rod,
or especially Roddy. He's not a big guy, but he can
bench-press 220 pounds and he's very sensitive about
his name. There probably aren't a dozen people in the
world who know his whole name. He refused to start
kindergarten until his parents agreed to sign him up as
Ricky.

Ricky and I grew up next door to each other on Old
Mill Road. It's on the outskirts of Eastfield, up by
the country club. Sort of a suburb of the suburbs.
Sometimes I wonder if we would have been friends if
we hadn't happened to wind up as neighbors. Ricky
and I are very different in many respects. But anyway,
we are friends, best friends, more or less. We have
a lot of shared experiences. Like getting sent to the
principal's office together for making Donald Duck
noises during rest time in first grade—very subversive,
huh? And backyard campouts, Little League, building
our tree fort, skating on the golf course pond, escaping
from the cops the Halloween we raided Warren's
Pumpkin Farm—you get the idea.

These days, one of Ricky's primary activities is hassling Victoria Kaminsky, the police chief's daughter. Victoria is your basic gorgeous glamour girl: long, honey-blond hair, a face so perfect it looks airbrushed on the front of her head, not to mention a figure that could inspire a twenty-volume encyclopedia of erotic dreams. She's a real social climber. I wouldn't be surprised if she popped up someday as the other woman who sends some politician's skyrocketing career down the tubes.

Ricky's always had this fixation on Victoria. And you might think he'd be a perfect ladder rung for a high school social climber. His family is rich; they belong to the country club. When Ricky turned sixteen last spring, his folks gave him a brand-new Mustang. And it's not just wealth and stuff. Ricky's also very intelligent—easy A's. To top it off, he's an ace athlete. Last year he was captain of the jayvee hockey team. This year he's playing varsity. He's a great center, good for half a dozen hat tricks a season. All in all, Ricky's definite Ivy League material.

For that matter, I am, too, grade-wise. Or at least I was, until last year. Ricky's probably got a better shot because of the sports—I'm not what you'd call the athletic type. Just because you're tall, people expect you to go out for basketball. It's not that I'm a klutz. I'm just not much for team sports.

So like I said, you might think Ricky had impeccable

credentials according to Victoria's standards. But the thing of it is, Victoria Kaminsky is five feet, eleven inches. Ricky's just about tall enough to whisper sweet nothings into her armpit.

Now, Ricky has the gonads to brazen out a relationship with a taller woman. But when Ricky asked Victoria to dance at Bonny Lippman's birthday party in sixth grade, she said, "I don't dance with midgets. It gives me a stiff neck."

Ricky's never gotten over it. He can't forgive her for squelching him in public, but he can't ignore her. She's too big and too beautiful, and his glands jump into high gear whenever he sees her. Therefore, he hassles her at every available opportunity. He hassles her, she retaliates, and so on. It's escalated into a fairly major feud.

So we were up there swimming that day. I was sitting on a log, toweling off with my T-shirt and thinking it was about time I got moving because my father was supposed to stop by the house to say good-bye. Ricky grabbed the knot at the bottom of the rope that we'd tied to this huge old tree limb that hangs out over the water. He stretched the rope back as far as it would reach, then took a running leap, let out a jungle yodel, and cannonballed into the river. It feels great—a real primal release.

Ricky swam back in, climbed up the bank, and sat

down next to me. Right away, he took his comb out of his pocket and started fooling with his hair. It's a habit of his. Ricky's hair is black and thick, and he spends thirty-five dollars on haircuts. I myself go for the seven-dollar special at Wigclippers Unisex Salon. As Ricky was fixing his coiffure, I noticed a purple ribbon hanging out of his comb pocket. I reached over and tugged. Out came a wet, crumpled, lacy item of women's intimate apparel. Specifically, a brassiere. Ricky made a grab for it, but I wanted to check this out. I held it away.

"Is there something you're not telling me, Rick?" I inquired.

He could tell I wasn't just going to forget about it without an explanation, so he shrugged.

"I snagged it off Kaminsky's clothesline this morning. Thirty-six C. Can you believe it? I think I'm gonna have it bronzed." He went back to combing his hair.

I snorted. "What, and put it in the case with all your other trophies? A little premature, don't you think?"

Ricky was eyeballing the bra.

"Just wait, Madman," he said. Madman is what he calls me. Because of my last name, not because I'm crazy or anything. Or at least, I didn't used to be. "This is the year, I'm telling you. It's gotta happen. It's— whadaya call it—"

"Unlikely?" I suggested.

"Fate. Destiny. Kismet. This is the year Victoria Kaminsky is going to see the light."

I stuck my fist in one of the 36C cups.

"Sure," I said. "I can see it now." I started rubbing the lace. "Magic. A genie'll pop right out and grant you a wish, and you'll say, 'Make Victoria make it with me.' "

Ricky kind of smiled and made another half-lunge, but I stood and pulled it out of reach. I was just getting warmed up.

"Or voodoo. But instead of sticking pins in it, you do this." I kneaded the cup. "Victoria'll be home painting her toenails. Suddenly she'll be overcome. She'll start panting with passion. She'll say, 'Oh, Roderick, I forgive you for the time you put a flaming paper bag of dog crap on my front porch. Come to me now. Fondle me, fond—' "

Ricky dove for the bra, snapped it away, and stuffed it back in his pocket.

"So look who's talking," he said. "Mr. Experience. Not exactly a chip off the old block, are you?"

I felt like he'd suckerpunched me. I got cold all over. It was a low blow and he knew it. I still hadn't gotten used to the idea that my father had cheated on my mother. I guess that's the main reason they got divorced, although it wasn't the only one. Since they split up, he's had a lot of girlfriends. It's no secret or anything and I guess it's legal now, but I didn't like to think about it.

I could tell by the look on Ricky's face that he wished he hadn't said what he said. I put on my T-shirt and headed for the car. Ricky jogged along, kind of hopping as he tried to get his sneakers on.

I opened the door of my mom's old Honda Accord and got in. Ricky got in the other side. He took a deep breath.

"Sorry, Madman. Really."

I shrugged, but I calmed down some. I knew I'd kind of pushed the Victoria thing a bit too far. Plus, I'd called him Roderick.

"It's okay," I said. I turned the car around in the clearing and headed back up the dirt road.

"So—when's he gonna be gone? I mean, really gone?" Ricky asked.

I turned south on North Avenue. "Tomorrow," I said. My voice sounded funny to me, like when you hear yourself on a tape recorder—it's not what it sounds like inside your head.

"Man, I wish I could get my old man off my back for a year," Ricky said. "You can't believe what he wants me to do now. He wants me to start applying to colleges *this* year! Go for early admission and . . ."

Ricky kept talking but I didn't feel like listening, so I tuned out. My father hadn't lived with us for over two years, and the divorce had been final for a year. But still, I saw him on weekends when he wasn't traveling, taking pictures of yachts for fancy sailing magazines.

The Royale Rum Round the World Race is this big-deal international thing—TV coverage, the Goodyear blimp at the start and finish, newspapers, magazines, printed T-shirts. My father was going along on the American boat, *Hex*, as an official photographer. Besides selling his pictures to magazines, he was planning to do a book, one of those coffee-table things too big for a regular bookshelf, very expensive. All about rugged sailors pitting themselves against the challenge of the ocean.

My father's a pretty easygoing guy, a great storyteller, top entertainment at a party. My mother, by contrast, especially since the divorce, is as tight as the strings on a violin. Talking to my dad is a good antidote to her moods; it kind of balances my brain again. But with him really gone, as Ricky put it, things were going to be different. There was a radio on the boat, but it was for emergency use only. I wouldn't be able to just call him up and shoot the breeze. The circumnavigation takes about nine months with long stops in foreign ports between each leg of the race. All in all, I didn't feel great about him going.

When I pulled up in front of my house, I could see my father's red Corvette convertible parked near the garage. My mother and father were standing near the car in some kind of pissed-off face-off. Nothing unusual there. I waited at the foot of the driveway, staring at the FOR SALE sign planted next to our mailbox. The real estate agent had come by the week before to paste a SOLD over it. Every time I looked at that sign, my stomach started churning.

"So, I guess I'll see you later," I said.

Ricky took the hint.

"Yeah. I think I'll get out here. Tell J. Thaddeus I said not to shoot any albatrosses." He got out.

I drove slowly up the driveway, thinking about this science fiction book I'd read, all about parallel universes, and wishing I could slip into one of them where none of it, the divorce and stuff, had ever happened, and let one of my parallel selves come here and deal with this crap.

My father looks like an older, tanner version of me—tall, kind of lanky, with sandy hair that's on the brillo-y side. In the past few years, he's put on a bit of a beer belly. When I looked at him that day, I thought his face seemed kind of puffy. He was wearing his standard outfit, a faded Izod shirt with a boat name and sail number embroidered on it—he gets a lot of those free from guys whose boats he's photographed—khaki slacks, scruffy Topsider deck shoes, and his gold Rolex Submariner watch. He looked like a sailor.

My mother's thirty-seven, five years younger than he is. I guess that's how old she looks. I don't know, I don't think of mothers as being any age, really. She's a pretty good looker, though, compared to some of my friends' mothers. She's, well, trim I guess would describe her. On the petite side. And her dark brown hair has only three gray strands in it. I think they're a by-product of the divorce.

I always used to think my parents looked good together as a couple. Looking at them that day, I could see it wasn't true anymore. They kind of brought out the worst in each other. My mother was standing there looking grim as a homicide detective, eyeballing my father like he was the number-one suspect. It was ugly.

Amanda was riding her pint-sized pink two-wheeler near the garage. She had a plastic, sound-activated daisy in the basket and she was whanging away on her thumb bell, so the flower was going berserk.

I pulled up next to the Corvette, parked, and got out of the car. A big smile swept away my father's frown. He took a step over and held his hand up.

"Hey, Mikey, give me five!"

He kind of overdoes it sometimes with what he thinks is the in thing to do. But I knew he was sincerely happy to see me. I glanced at my mother and tried to gauge the proper degree of enthusiasm for my reaction, to let my dad know I was glad to see him without making my mother think I'd defected to the enemy camp. It's tricky business.

"He's here now, so say good-bye and hit the road, Jack," my mother said. She folded her arms and started tapping her foot.

Amanda took a sudden turn and plowed into the Corvette's front fender.

My father darted my mother one of the special dagger glances that he reserves just for her. Then he swallowed and looked back at Amanda.

"Be careful, sweetheart. I just waxed her." He turned the bike around and sent it rolling in another direction.

My mother snorted. " 'Her?' That's a particularly telling use of the female personal pronoun, Jack."

I remembered the crack she made the first time Dad drove up in the Corvette: "The public ego-masturbation of an aged adolescent. Pathetic." I didn't really see it that way. It's a cool car.

"Give me a break, would you, Caroline?" My father sounded more peeved than he usually allows himself to. "I'm not going to see my kids for almost a year. Do you have to stand here like a warden with a stopwatch?"

"If you were so interested in seeing your kids—" Mom started to retort.

Just then, Amanda drove her bike right between them. She looked up at them both with a fierce scowl on her face. My mother closed her mouth and bit back her words.

I felt an urgent necessity to smooth things over, at least keep the conversation semi-civil. I tried to think of something to say.

"So, Dad, are you looking for someone to take care of your car while you're gone?"

Wrong thing to say.

My mother practically spit nails.

"If you think I'm going to have a sixteen-year-old tooling around town in this—this *death machine*, you're even more irresponsible than I thought!"

Dad blinked a few poison darts at Mom, then rearranged his face into a stiff smile. It was one of those smiles that said "Sorry, son, I would have offered, of course, but I knew your mother the killjoy would never allow it."

"Thanks anyway, sport. I've got someone who's going to look after it for me."

"Debbie? Linda? Or is it Jennifer?" Mom asked, her voice phony sweet.

I could see my father was ready to tell her to blow it out her butt, but he's got a little more emotional control than she does in this kind of discussion. I think he feels it makes him look like the good guy and shows my mother up as a maniac shrew and who could blame him for ditching her.

"It's really none of your damn business anymore, is it?" he said in a tone so acid it could have corroded a tank. Then he turned to me. "Hey, Mikey, I brought you something." He leaned over the side of the car and hauled a cardboard box out of the front seat. Holding it with one arm, he reached in and picked out one of his cameras, his Nikon F2. He handed it to me.

I was speechless. It was one of his favorite cameras.

"There's a couple of lenses for you to fool around with—a wide-angle and a telephoto. I threw a few books in, too, to get you started."

I put the camera back in the box and took the whole thing in my arms. I looked at my dad and he looked at me, and some kind of wordless message passed between us.

Then Amanda broke the spell.

"What about me, Daddy?" she whined.

I could see Mom was on the verge of snapping. "Oh, that's just dandy, Jack, fine and dandy! Now he can follow in your world-famous marine photographer footsteps."

Don't, I was begging her in my head. You don't have to do this, spoil a small thing that's still good. There may be a lot of crap between the two of you, but please don't spill it on this small good thing.

"Where's *my* present?" Amanda cranked the whine up to a wail.

Dad glared at Mom. She glared back. If looks could flay, the two of them would have been standing there stark skinless.

"What's your problem, Caroline?" Dad said.

"*My* problem? *You're* my problem, Jack. And *their* problem. A hand-me-down camera. Isn't that wonderful. Michael can take a picture of your back as you walk right the hell out of his life!"

Amanda was shrieking at full volume, "I want a present, too!"

"Don't cry, sweetie," Dad said. "I promise I'll bring you back a present from every port I stop in, okay?"

My mother picked Amanda up off the bicycle.

"Your promises," she whispered. "Your promises are worth about as much as that 'sure-thing' stock you hocked our life to buy." She trudged up to the house and went inside.

My father dropped his eyes. "Well, I, uh . . . "

I couldn't look at him, either.

"Take care of yourself," I mumbled. "Don't fall overboard."

He cleared his throat. "You take care of yourself, too. And Amanda." He paused, then forced himself to say it: "And your mother."

He gripped my shoulders kind of weakly, then turned, got in his car, and drove away.

TWO

Patty, the night nurse, poked her head in a few minutes ago.

"Everything okay in here?" she asked. "I saw your light come on."

Talk about the walls having ears. Around here, they have eyeballs, too, and big noses for sniffing out your private business. But I was glad for the company, actually. The other bed in my double room has been empty since I was admitted. After I told her about my dream, Patty said I could leave the light on.

It may sound stupid, but I swear I was in a cold sweat when I woke up.

I'm in my old house, the one I grew up in. I'm in the downstairs hall that runs from the front door to the kitchen, trying to go upstairs to my room to get something really important. As I head for the stairs, the hall keeps twisting away from them, like some kind of weird fun-house trick. I wind up in this other room, where our living room should be. Only it's not any room I've ever seen. It's painted neon tangerine. All the furniture and the windows and floorboards are crooked, like Amanda hammered them together. Outside, the dark feels as if it's trying to break through the windows. And the windows themselves kind of leer at me.

Okay, so I'm in this bizarre room, thinking I have to get up to my own bedroom. For some reason, I have no idea what, it's essential. I think, Just put one foot in front of the other and force your way to the stairs. As I try to do this, I realize the walls are starting to pulse in and out as if they're made of rubber, as if the house is gasping for breath. But I'm still looking down at my feet—one step at a time, left foot, right foot, I'm trying to break out of it. I feel the floor start to tremble, then really shake, like an earthquake. It's heaving so much, it practically drives my knee up into my chin. I'm trying to keep my balance, but it's totally dark now. I can't even see my feet anymore—

I never did make it up to my room.

I wish I knew what the important thing was, what I was trying to get.

When I woke up, I was panicked. It's starting to wear off now. But I feel like I've lost my last chance to find that thing, whatever it was. It's about the saddest I've ever felt.

Once the house was sold, everything seemed to happen in fast forward. Mom was anxious to be in the new house—and I use the word *house* loosely—before Amanda and I started school. We moved on Labor Day. So while almost all my friends were partying down at the beach, I was stuck dismantling my life and stuffing it into cardboard boxes, most of which were headed for storage. Who knew when I'd see them again.

I was lying on my bed taking a break, reading one of Dad's photography books—this part about a belief of certain primitive tribes that if someone takes their picture, captures their image, that person has stolen their soul. I was thinking that Ricky would get a kick out of that. All he'd have to do is snap a quick Polaroid of Victoria, and he'd have it made in the shade.

Think of the devil. I heard the back door slam.

"Hey, Madam Madden, Madman here?"

I got up off the bed and put the book in the box of stuff to bring. I went downstairs and wove my way through a maze of boxes in the hall and stood in the kitchen doorway.

Mom was sorting through kitchen junk. She had all her boxes labeled: BRING, STORAGE, TAG SALE. She was kneeling on the floor, emptying a cabinet of pots and pans. Neither Mom nor Ricky noticed me right away.

"So, Madam Madden—" Ricky started to say.

"Ricky, could you do me a favor and get that Dutch oven off the stove and put it in that storage box over there?" Mom interrupted. It wasn't weird for her to boss Ricky around as if he were one of her kids. She's probably fed him half of the dinners he's ever eaten. His parents dine out a lot. They have a live-in maid-cook kind of person, but she doesn't speak much English and Ricky likes companionship when he eats.

If Ricky has a soft spot for any human being in the world, it's probably my mother. I think it goes back to the time he poured a gallon can of black paint into his old man's golf bag the summer after fourth grade. It was right after Mr. Bolton made a big scene at a Little League game, bawling out our coach for putting Ricky in right field instead of on the pitcher's mound.

Anyway, Mr. Bolton is this avid golfer. We could hear him roaring all the way over at our house. A little while later, he phoned to say that Ricky was missing. Mom was the one who found Ricky, holed up out in the small barn she used as a garden shed. I don't know what she said to Ricky, or to his father, but she fixed it. Anyway, that was one time Mr. Bolton didn't haul Ricky down to the barbershop for a wicked crewcut, which was the standard punishment whenever Ricky did something bad. Mr. Bolton's a big-time executive now, but he was in the Navy once. He always talks about running a tight ship. He hasn't done the haircut thing in a while, though, since Ricky started pumping iron. My guess is, he doesn't want to chance losing face if Ricky turns out to be stronger than he is.

"And do me another favor," Mom went on as she dumped a tray of silverware into a BRING box. "Don't call me Madam Madden anymore."

"So what should I call you?" Ricky sounded puzzled. He's called her Madam Madden for years. He nicknames a lot of people. He's the one who came up with "TV Guidance Counselor."

Mom burrowed into another cabinet.

"I'm going back to my maiden name, Ms. Caroline O'Neill. So don't you call me that other thing, or I'll start calling you Roderick Alister Bolton."

"Geez, you don't have to get nasty." He picked a banana out of the fruit bowl on the table and started peeling it. "Hey, I know. How 'bout if I call you Madam Maiden. Get it? Your *maiden* name?"

Mom stood up, dusted off her hands, and shot Ricky one of her dry-as-a-bone looks.

"How come you're changing your name now, when you guys have been divorced for a year?" he asked through a mouthful of banana.

"Because I'm not Mrs. J. Thaddeus Madden anymore. Because I'm tired of living in the past." She chucked a wooden spoon at a box, missed, and swore under her breath. "It's time for a fresh start, a new life."

"Speak for yourself," I muttered.

Now they noticed me.

"What did you say?" The knife tone.

I had to think fast. "I said, 'Can you reach the top shelf?' "

Mom looked confused, but she went for it. "Oh," she said. "I've done those. I used a chair."

Ricky tossed his banana peel in the garbage. "Oh, by the way, Mad—uh, Mrs.—I mean, Ms. O'Neill, my mother said to tell you if you don't want to put that antique rolltop desk into the warehouse, she wouldn't mind storing it for you. Until, you know, you can rent a bigger place. Or if you're gonna sell it at the tag sale, she said . . . "

Like I said, Ricky knows Mom pretty well, well enough to sense her getting irked in a major way before the steam actually comes out of her nostrils. And I myself thought Mrs. Bolton's offer was a little insensitive under the circumstances. Vulturous, you might call it. I knew Mom had been planning to sell the desk because it was worth a wad and we needed the cash. I watched her pride kick in and change her mind on the spot.

"Thank you, Ricky, but you can tell your mother we *are* taking it to the new house with us."

I raised one eyebrow. It's a talent I've cultivated. Mom read the unspoken sarcasm.

"I'll find a place for it!" she snapped.

Ricky was looking definitely uncomfortable, like he was sorry he'd brought it up. He tried to change the subject. It was one of those frying-pan-into-the-fire transitions.

"She also said that she was sorry about the cocktail party they had, you know, about your not being invited, but my old man just happened to run into Mr. Madden and kind of mentioned it, and I thought—I mean, they thought you wouldn't want to—"

Ricky looked at me for help. I was pulling my finger across my neck, signaling "Cut!" Meaning, "Just shut up, stupid!"

Mom walked over to the sink and stood there stiffly, with her back to us. It's not that she's ever been great pals or anything with Mrs. Bolton. But they've always done the neighbor bit, probably more from Ricky and me being friends than from any natural affinity.

The way I pegged it, Mrs. Bolton figured my father was a classier addition to her guest list because of his yachting connections. I think that's what got to my mother—being weighed against my father on the social scale and coming up too light to count.

Ricky had his comb out and was combing his hair like a maniac barber, so I knew he was really upset. I saw Mom take a deep breath, then relax a little. She washed her hands. When she turned around again, she gave Ricky a minuscule smile—an "it's okay, it's not your fault" smile.

"They thought I wouldn't want to be at the same party as Mr. Madden and his latest flame," she finished his sentence. "And they were right. Michael, have you finished packing?"

"More or less," I said. Closer to less, actually. She read my mind.

"How much more is more?"

"I'll get it done, all right?" I thought she was going to take issue with my tone, which was rather peevish. But she let it pass.

"I wish you would," she said after a moment. "I need your help with some heavy things."

"I'll give you a hand, Mad . . . Ms. . . . Uh, I can help you with the heavy stuff," Ricky offered.

I saw Mom's eyes fill with tears before she closed them and nodded. "I'd appreciate that very much, Ricky," she said.

At that point, Amanda came into the kitchen lugging

her pink duffel bag. She had it stuffed so full with Barbies, her favorite Dr. Seuss books, and her blankie that the zipper wouldn't close.

"I'm all packed, Mommy," she said.

Mom's voice was shaky when she answered. "That's wonderful, sweetheart. You're such a big help to me."

.   .   .

So anyway, we moved into the shack on Labor Day. You want to talk about labor—fitting even the minimum of things that we brought into three rooms was like trying to stuff twenty pounds of manure into a shoebox. We probably could have found a bigger place in another part of town, but Mom wanted Amanda and me to stay in our school districts.

Maybe if the house were out in the woods on some gorgeous lake, it might have made a cozy little honeymoon cottage for two people who didn't mind living in each other's laps. For a family of three, well, the word *claustrophobic* comes to mind.

"Look, there's a beautiful view out back, Michael," Mom said. "You love the river. You live right on it now."

Living right *in* it might be more comfortable, I wanted to say. But I guess it wasn't a bad view across the grass and weeds if you blocked out the run-down marina to the left and the sand and gravel storage tanks to the right.

"It's gonna stink at low tide," was all I said.

Ricky helped us move with a U-Haul truck. The last thing in was that damn desk.

"Where do you want this?" I asked Mom, who was trapped in this kind of playpen arrangement formed by the couch, the love seat, and the coffee table.

She looked around and finally pointed to the wall by the front door.

"I guess it has to go there."

"How 'bout the bedroom?" Ricky suggested, wiping the sweat off his forehead with the back of his hand. It had been one of those pressure-cooker days.

"Where, on top of the bed?" I said.

"Just leave it there." Mom sighed. "You can use it for a dresser, Michael, since you'll be sleeping on the couch." She and Amanda were going to share the one bedroom.

All the adrenaline that had fueled the chore of moving was gone, and I could feel weariness moving in like a fog bank coming up the river from Long Island Sound. I was too tired to argue. Ricky and I nudged the desk against the wall.

"That's it—truck's empty," Ricky announced. "Done."

I looked around the combination living/dining room that was now also my bedroom. I looked through the doorway into the tiny kitchen, where boxes were stacked almost to the ceiling.

Done. The word closed around me like a lead body cast.

I knew Mom felt the same way. But she was struggling to put a good face on it, for Amanda's and my sake.

"Well," she said. "I don't know how to thank you, Ricky."

"That's okay. I'm gonna take off now. I gotta get ready for some stupid shindig at the country club my parents are dragging me to."

He scanned the scene. Then he looked at me. He opened his mouth, then closed it again. There was nothing to say, really. Done.

"Thanks a lot, Rick." I shook his hand. It was weird but appropriate, somehow, like a formal change-of-status ceremony. We'd graduated down.

"No problem, Madman."

All this time, Amanda had been crawling through the tunnels between the unpacked boxes. Suddenly she popped out near the couch and started whining. Amanda never used to be such a whiny kid.

"Mommy, I can't go to first grade."

Mom drew a blank. "Why not?"

36

"Because the bus won't know where to find me."
Amanda's chin started to wobble.

Ricky reached down and pulled her ponytail. "Hey,
Mandy Madden, cheer up. You're close enough to
walk now."

Amanda cheered up for a second; then her face
crumpled again.

"Now what?" Mom asked.

"But I *want* to take the bus," she wailed.

Mom picked her up and hugged her.

Ricky waved. "Gotta go. I'll come over early tomorrow so we can get that truck back by nine." He left.

"Don't cry, Amanda," Mom was saying. "I'll walk
you to school every day. It will be fun, I promise. Even
in the rain. You can use your duck umbrella. Please
don't cry, honey." Mom looked at me over Amanda's
shoulder. "She's probably hungry."

"I am, too," I said. I was starving. "What's for dinner?"

Mom shrugged slowly.

"McDonald's?" I suggested.

"I'm a total mess. I wouldn't even go to McDonald's
looking like this," she said. It was true. I'd never seen
her so grungy. "I guess somebody has to go to the store."

I rolled my eyes. Somebody. A euphemism for "Michael, you do it."

"That little market down the street—Thumm's. I

37

know they're expensive, but I think they sell roasted chickens in the deli, don't they?"

I shrugged. "I've never been in it."

"I think they do." Mom leaned over the back of the couch and deposited Amanda next to a stack of blankets. She grabbed her pocketbook from the coffee table and started digging for money while she talked.

"Maybe some potato salad, too. And some things for the morning, milk and bread. Some cereal. Oh, and coffee. And eggs maybe. Oh, and how about peanut butter and jelly and—"

She stopped and counted out the money. A five, eight singles, and $3.50 in quarters. Her shoulders slumped.

"Just get *something*. Do your best. I don't care." She handed me the car keys.

THREE

People. They come in quite a variety. If there is a God who made everyone, and I'm not completely convinced of that, but if there is, I'll say one thing for Him—He must have quite an imagination to have thought up some of the bozos in here.

There's one crazy middle-aged lady named Sally, with long brown hair streaked with gray, who keeps going around to all the other women and girls. She sneaks up behind them with her fingers held out like a pair of scissors. Then she takes their hair and whispers, "Snip, snap, snurp." A real schizo.

It's not funny, but it is, if you know what I mean. The nurses and aides chuckle about it. There's a lot of

gallows humor around here with the staff. Maybe that's
how they can stand working in a loony bin.

Anyway, I think God must have a pretty warped
sense of humor if he thought up Sally Snip Snap Snurp.
Or the TV Guidance Counselor, for that matter.

Thinking about her spreads a sudden chill all over
my body. I haven't asked yet, and nobody's told me if
she's all right. I'm not sure if anyone but Ricky knows
the whole story.

Thumm's Market is in Mohegan Square, right on the
river, along with Thumm's Fish Shop, Thumm's Li-
quor Locker, and Dockside Hardware. It's up the street
from the train station, right at the intersection of River
Road and East Street, where the swing bridge crosses
the Mohegan River. The swing bridge is this metal
contraption that looks like a drawbridge, but to open it,
which they do only once in a while by special appoint-
ment, they need six guys to come out and plug in this
giant turnstile kind of key and manually turn it, like
donkeys, until the bridge swings open sideways. It's
pretty rickety, with that metal grating stuff that hums
when you drive over it, but it's some kind of landmark,
so they're not going to replace it.

Mohegan Square looks old-fashioned, more like an
enormous house than a shopping center. The first floor

has regular storefront windows, but the second and third floors have house windows with dark green shutters. I didn't know it at the time, but the owner and his nephew live in the upstairs apartments.

When I pulled into the small parking lot that day, it was jammed with holiday traffic. While I waited for a Jeep 4 × 4 to load up with groceries and pull out, I read the signs in the windows: LABOR DAY SPECIAL; BEEF TENDERLOIN—$6.99 LB. TRIMMED; FRESH NATIVE CORN ON THE COB—$1.99 DOZ. Way down in the corner was a tiny notice that said PART-TIME HELP WANTED—INQUIRE WITHIN. A silver Porsche tried to steal my parking spot, but I cut it off with a sharp tire-squealing maneuver. I was in no mood to be charitable to a bleached-blond lady driving around in a Porsche.

As you go through the IN door of Thumm's, there's a magazine display on the left, well stocked with commuter-type reading material—the standard weeklies like *Time* and *People*, all the women's magazines, plenty of glossy financial and travel magazines, literary periodicals—everything except the *TV Guides*. Those are in their own racks, right at the registers.

Past the magazine display is the deli. There was a line of three people waiting. I picked up a plastic shopping basket and went over and made it four. Behind the counter, one of the deli workers, a college-age girl, was bustling around like a real worker bee, making sandwiches. By contrast, the other guy moved like molasses. Slow but fluid.

I watched him while I waited. He was eerily thin and really tall, so the white deli apron came down only to the middle of his thighs. Everything about him seemed stretched out—arms, legs, face—like a Silly Putty image pulled the long way. Under his green baseball cap, his hair was so blond it was almost white, and even though he had a light tan, he looked kind of transparent. Around his neck, he wore a cowboy bandanna, and I could see a faint red scar running from the front of one ear up under his hair.

When it was my turn, I pointed to the roasted chickens sizzling in the rotisserie case.

"Can I have one of those?"

He nodded slowly, glided over to the case to snag one, then wrapped it in foil and put it in an insulated paper bag. While he did that, I checked out the big trays of salads and ready-cooked food in the glass case. When he put my chicken bag up on the counter, I pointed to the egg-and-potato salad. It was more expensive than the plain, but I really like egg-and-potato salad. When you have ribs like mine, you're always looking for a little something extra to stick to them.

"And some of that potato salad," I said.

He nodded again, reached for the stacks of plastic

containers, and, taking one of each size, set them up on the counter.

"Half-pound. Pound. Two pounds." He lifted each one to show me as he spoke.

"Uh, a pound, I guess."

Same slo-mo routine. Put the other containers back. Reach down, open case. Grab spoon. Ladle salad. Weigh it. Add some more. Put cover on container. Attach price label. Put it on the counter. Blink. Nod.

"Thanks," I said, putting it in my basket. On an impulse, I turned back. He was waiting as if he had known I had something else to say before I realized it myself.

"The sign for the part-time job—" I started.

He nodded and blinked. "See Uncle Fritz." He pointed to the far wall. Up above the aisles was a framed window. Through it, I saw the top of a white head of hair.

"Up there?" I said. "Uncle Fritz?"

He—you guessed it—nodded and blinked.

"Stairs. Between bread and frozen. Go on up."

I found the narrow staircase and went up the six steps. The door to the small office cubicle was open. The walls inside were plastered with lists, receipts, and newspaper and magazine clippings. On top of a two-drawer file cabinet were a few framed photographs—all black-and-white and all with that ghostly feeling of being fixed forever in the past. There was one of an old-fashioned young couple, a baby portrait of a tiny girl in a frilly dress, another of three young soldiers with their arms around one another's shoulders, grinning and squinting into the sun. But the thing I really noticed was all the books. Not ledger books like you might expect to see in an office—book books. Tons of them. Crammed into every available space.

I stood on the cramped landing and scoped out Uncle Fritz, who was, not surprisingly, reading a book. He sat in an old office chair, leaning over his desk, smiling and nodding to himself. Nodding must run in the family, I thought. He was not a small guy, and not skinny like his nephew, either. His face was very tanned in a reddish way, and craggy, like a rough carving done with big tools, not tiny chisels. He was powerful-looking for an old guy.

I cleared my throat. He looked up and peered at me with these sharp blue eyes between his bifocals and his bushy white eyebrows.

" 'You could not step twice into the same river; for other waters are ever flowing on to you,' " he said. His voice was deep and he spoke kind of melodically, like an actor onstage.

"Excuse me?" I said.

"Heracleitus," he said. He closed his book and patted the cover. "The accumulated wisdom of so many lives in books. Here for the borrowing, since we each have but one life of our own." He smiled. "How can I help you?"

"Oh. Right. I, uh, saw the sign about part-time work, and the tall guy in the deli—"

"My nephew Carl," he told me, nodding.

"Yeah, well, Carl told me to come up here. I'd like to, you know, apply for the job."

"I need someone for afternoons, weekends, some evenings, some holidays," he said. "You're in school?"

I told him I was a junior at Mohegan High.

"Play any sports?" he asked.

Come again? I thought. Exactly how much athletic prowess did a person need to work in a grocery store? Then I realized it probably had to do with the hours, and whether afternoon practices would interfere.

"No," I said. "I'm free afternoons and all. And weekends would be fine."

"Transportation a problem?"

I shook my head. "We just moved in up the street. Next to the marina. I can walk."

He eyeballed me for a minute, not in a nosy or intrusive way, just very thoughtfully—kind of in a measuring way. Maybe he knew the house and figured whoever lived in it really needed the job. Anyway, I guess he decided I measured up to whatever criteria he was using, because he stood and held out his hand.

"Fritz Thumm," he introduced himself formally. I shook his hand. "Michael Madden."

"I need someone to work the register, stock shelves, help Carl in the deli if need be. Five-fifty an hour plus meals. Does this interest you?" he asked.

The work itself didn't particularly interest me when he described it, although after I started, I found it a lot more interesting than I would have expected. But the money definitely interested me.

"Yeah. I mean, yes, sir."

He rummaged around on his desk and came up with a wrinkled application form that he handed to me.

"Can you start tomorrow afternoon, Michael? At three?"

"Uh, sure. Yes. Fine," I stammered. "Do you want me to fill this out now?" I held up the application.

He waved a hand casually. "You can fill it out at home and bring it in tomorrow."

I set down my basket, folded the paper carefully, put it in my back pocket, and grinned. I had a job. I wasn't destitute anymore.

"Thanks a lot, Mr. Thumm," I said.

He shook his head and smiled. "Fritz. We're all friends here."

I felt like singing as I picked up the basket, headed back down the stairs, and started hunting through the aisles for the other groceries Mom wanted. I wasn't paying much attention to prices. I was trying to figure out how long it would take me to save up the down payment for a car if I worked, say, twenty hours a week, and wondering if I could afford the insurance.

The lines were long at all three registers. I picked the middle one, the one with the cashier who looked a little like a freckled, red-haired Marilyn Monroe. She smiled at me as she rang me up.

"Thirty-three seventy-eight," she said.

I dug in my pockets and pulled out my money. My $16.50, including quarters. "Thirty-three seventy-eight," I repeated, trying to stall while I figured out what to do. Right behind me in line was the Porsche lady. She was smirking and rolling her eyes in a can-you-believe-this-idiot way.

"Thirty-three seventy-eight," the cashier confirmed. She blew a bubble with her bubble gum.

I felt acute embarrassment set in like a case of hives.

"I, ah, guess I don't have enough," I mumbled. I looked at the stuff and wondered what I should put back and how long it would take to subtract and what the odds were of a large sinkhole developing right below me and swallowing me through the floor.

Right then, Fritz walked behind the cashier and put a hand on her shoulder.

"Just put the balance on a store charge, Eileen," he said quietly. "Michael works here now." Then he disappeared toward the deli.

What do you suppose makes some people like that— willing to trust to the good in people, take a chance on someone they don't even know?

So I started working at Thumm's Market the next day, the day before school started.

I've always liked grocery stores. There's something comfortable about them, with the aisles all stocked for basic survival. Even if it's gloomy and miserable outside, bright lights are glowing inside so people can read the brand names. The refrigerator cases are humming. And everyone who comes in has a common purpose, which sort of makes for an instant sense of community. If the worst happened, like a nuclear war started, or even if just a monster hurricane came blowing through, I wouldn't mind being stuck in a grocery store.

Thumm's Market is like a miniature supermarket. It's got just about everything but in small quantities, mostly gourmet brands. The meats are prime, the service is personal, and everything costs about twice as much as you'd pay in a regular grocery store. But most of the people who shop there can afford it, no problem.

Fritz put me on the register. He came by a few times to check on how I was doing. About the third time, he smiled. "Interesting, isn't it? Watching the river of humanity flow by?"

It was, actually. It didn't take me long to realize that most customers fall into categories, more or less. You've got your sunshine people, who always smile and have a cheery word for you. You've got your basic mothers, ranging from merely frazzled to borderline hysterical, especially if their kids are grabbing the candy and razor blades off the sundries racks under the *TV Guides*. And your space cadets, who float through, their minds a million miles away, transcending the whole shopping experience while you ring up their herbal tea and Preparation H.

Then there are your chronic cranks, and there's no pleasing them, no matter what you do. You just have to grit your teeth and move them along. Eileen clued me in to them after one blue-haired old lady gave me a really hard time.

"Don't throw my prunes like that, young man— you'll dent the can. Be careful with those dinner rolls. I don't know what's wrong with you young people today. Nobody cares about doing things well anymore." Blah blah blah.

"Sheesh. Picky, huh?" I said as she toddled out the door with her carriage. There was a brief lull in the evening action, no customers.

Eileen blew a bubble and nodded sympathetically. "They can be bad," she said. "You have to keep them in line, let them know not to mess with you."

"What do you mean?" I asked.

Eileen looked around to make sure no one was listening. "Cashier's revenge," she whispered.

I raised an eyebrow. Cashier's revenge?

She winked. "You get them back when you bag their stuff. You smile and say, 'Yes, ma'am, certainly, sir, you're absolutely right.' Then you stick a six-pack of diet ginger ale on top of their Mallomars. Or squeeze their batter-whipped bread. You can even poke a hole in their eggs—through that little opening in the carton, you know? All under cover, inside the bag. Sooner or later, they get the idea."

It sounded a little extreme, but I tucked it in my mental catalog under potentially useful information. "Thanks," I said.

The IN door opened and seven people wearing business clothes raced in.

Eileen groaned. "The six twenty-four commuter express-train gang," she told me. "Watch out for these guys—they're still running at city pace. Just take your time and don't let them rattle you."

And that was when I saw the TV Guidance Counselor for the first time, right in the middle of the 6:24 commuter blitz.

I was doing my best to move people through, to clear up the logjam. But my pace was slow. So the people in my line were getting rather ornery, muttering to one another in voices I was meant to hear: "Why doesn't he go faster?" "What's the problem up there?" and "This always happens to me. When I'm in the biggest hurry, I land in the slowest line." It wasn't doing much for my confidence, first day on the job and all. One guy said, "He must be new. He has to be new. I bet he's new."

No shit, Sherlock, I thought. I looked up for a second to check out the bozo who was putting forth this brilliant hypothesis. And I saw her.

I couldn't put an age on her—somewhere between thirty and fifty, maybe. Her hair was the color of potato peels, pasted to her scalp in tight oily clumps of curls. Her face was pale and pudgy, and her mouth was puckered into a worried frown between marshmallow cheeks. I never saw anyone look so worried. She was wearing one of those school uniform blouses with a round collar and short sleeves, with her arms sticking out like fat bratwurst sausages. And a limp brown skirt that pinched her rolls in the middle and looked like it had been through the wash too many times. You don't see too many ladies dressed like that around Eastfield.

Anyway, without saying "Excuse me" or even looking at anyone, she elbowed her way to the front of my line with this timid determination. A guy in a suit, whose order I was ringing up, just stared. So did I.

She picked a *TV Guide* out of the rack and started reading it. Right then and there. She pored over a page, her watery gray eyes right next to the paper, following her finger down the listings. She turned a few pages and did it again. She flipped slowly to the back and did it a third time, very seriously, as if looking for something very important. I guess she didn't find what she wanted, because she put the magazine back.

At that point, the guy in the suit gave me a look that said, "What's going on here and why aren't you doing something about it?" I shrugged, palms up. What was I supposed to do?

Meanwhile, she tugged on her lip, fingered the rack, and pulled out another *TV Guide*, this one from way in the back. She went through the whole bit again, turning the pages, flipping them. Then she closed it slowly and, very gently, put it back in exactly the same spot she'd taken it from. She elbowed her way back out of my line, still without making eye contact with a single person. She headed over to Eileen's register.

I looked at Eileen. She grinned at me and tapped her head. After that, I was so busy trying to catch up with my customers, I didn't notice where the woman went.

That night, after we closed, I was sitting on a milk

crate in the work area behind the deli—the place where we shrink-wrap produce, put the Sunday *Times* together, and take our breaks. I was eating a sausage-and-pepper grinder while Carl mopped up the deli. Fritz came down from the office after counting the money and making up the bank deposit.

"You survived your initiation very well, Michael," he told me. "Your drawer was only ten cents off."

"Thanks," I said, wiping my chin. While I finished chewing what was in my mouth, I wondered if Fritz would think I was a total busybody if I asked about the weird lady. I decided to chance it because I was really intrigued.

"Hey, Fritz? Who was that lady who was messing with the *TV Guides?* Know who I mean?"

Fritz looked at me thoughtfully, as if contemplating exactly how to respond. "She's one of the wandering souls," he said gently. "How did T. S. Eliot put it? A

> . . . *spirit unappeased and peregrine*
> *Between two worlds* . . ."

He sighed, smiled to himself kind of sadly, then nodded at me.

"Janey Riddley. She causes no harm. You'll see her often." He nodded again, like I was in on some secret now and would know not to bother her.

FOUR

I was sitting in group therapy this morning, thinking, What am I doing here with this bunch of losers? I don't have anything in common with these geeks. I was half listening to this kid Allan. He's your basic slob type, not to be cruel, but he is. I mean, he doesn't even wear deodorant, a fact that I know because we're roommates. They stuck him in with me a few days ago.

He was talking about how one time he ate the last bowl of tapioca pudding in the fridge, then found out his mother was saving it to scarf down herself. He said something that struck a nerve with me, that I could identify with. He said, "My mother's always telling me how selfish I am. One day I screamed at her, 'How can I be selfish when I don't even have a self?' " The amazing thing was, after that he suddenly seemed like a person to me. I mean, I could kind of feel for the guy.

Anyway, for some reason, the whole group thing this morning made me remember this riddle. It's really stupid, but when I was a kid, I got a huge kick out of it. It goes like this:

You're stuck in a closed room with no doors, no windows. You're totally boxed in, in other words. Besides you, the only things in the room are a mirror and a table. How do you get out?

Here's what you do: You look in the mirror, see what you saw, take the saw, saw the table in half. Two halves make a whole; you crawl through the whole and go home.

Whole, hole—get it? Hey, I was in third grade, what do you want?

Somehow it reminds me of being in a psychiatric hospital.

It makes about as much sense as anything else right now.

Things seemed to get better after school started.

First thing I did was go see Mrs. Fattiben, the head guidance counselor, so I could change one of my courses. Ricky calls her Fatty-Bean because he says she looks like a giant, oversoaked lima bean. She does, kind of, stuffed into this white-blouse/pale green cardigan sweater combination she always wears.

I sat there in the guidance office cubicle, watching her across the desk as she went through my file, wondering if she'd always looked that way and what's in a name and maybe if, way back when, she'd married some guy named Mr. Skinniben, she'd look totally different now. She was frowning as if she'd been sucking on a lemon all morning as she read through my record. Every once in a while, her frown would deepen, which made her forehead wrinkle, which made the front of her hair—this helmet of little brown springs that look like she tortures them into submission—move up and down.

"You want to drop Chemistry and take Photography?" She fixed her gunmetal eyes on me through her butterfly glasses with the rhinestones in the corners.

"Yes, ma'am," I said. "I already filled out a course change card." I held it out. She didn't take it. I dropped it on her desk, feeling a little lame.

"You are aware that Photography is a senior elective, open only to those juniors with a three-point-five grade average or better?"

I shrugged one of my ambiguous shrugs, one of my "heh, heh, now that you mention it, maybe I did hear something like that somewhere" shrugs. She flipped through some more papers in my file.

"I see you've moved. Are you living with your father now?"

"No," I said rather coldly. "With my mother. My father's—out of town for a while."

"I see," she said.

Like hell you do, I thought.

Fatty-Bean let her glasses drop off her nose and dangle from their fake pearl rope. She eyeballed me, with her elbows on the desk and her fingertips pressed together making a puffy-handed triangle.

"Michael, the curriculum here at Mohegan is designed to guide each student onto a path into his or her own future. It's a rare student who is able to recognize that path on his or her own. I would prefer to see you continue with Chemistry for your college preparation."

I slumped in the chair. Then, to my amazement, she went on.

"But I would also like to see your other grades back up at the level that I know you are capable of achieving."

I sat up straight, sensing a hint of *Let's Make a Deal* potential.

"I am not unaware of your . . . ah . . . circumstances, of the life difficulties my students sometimes encounter. Photography does fulfill a lab science requirement. Therefore I will allow you to switch courses *on the condition* that you pull your other grades up where they belong."

Yahoo, I shouted mentally. Aloud, I started into the grateful student rap.

"Thank you, Mrs. Fattiben, you won't be sor—"

She cut me off. "Save it, Michael. Show me. I'll allow you to try this on a probationary basis. When the first-term reports come out, if I don't see substantial improvements in other areas, you'll drop Photography, spend the time in proctored study hall, and make up the missing credits in summer school. This is an unearned privilege. See that you earn it."

"Absolutely, ma'am," I babbled. "I won't let you down."

She put her glasses back on and eyeballed me one more time. "Don't let yourself down," she said. She signed my course change card and handed it back. "Take this to the secretary."

.   .   .

At lunchtime, Ricky was saving me a seat. I bought orange juice and potato chips to go with the sandwich I'd brought from home. Economy measures. I worked my way through the crowd, squeezed between the metal chairs, and sat down.

"Old Fatty-Bean give the okay?" Ricky asked.

I nodded and opened my lunch bag.

"Superlative." Ricky gave me a thumbs-up and bit a chunk from his rubbery cheeseburger.

I unwrapped my sandwich. Tuna fish on whole wheat, nice and warm from my locker. I took a bite. Not good.

"How long you suppose this fish has been dead?"

Ricky pushed over one of his extra packets of mayonnaise. "Here, liven up the flavor of dead fish with a little Hellman's."

I squeezed some on, took another bite, and barely gagged it down. "Doesn't help. This couldn't be soggier if the fish was still swimming." I stuffed it back in the bag and hit the potato chips.

Just then, Victoria Kaminsky strolled by with her gaggle of groupies for her daily promenade around the cafeteria, her admiration fix. She was wearing a low-cut tank top and a short denim skirt that was so tight it was practically subcutaneous.

Ricky leered in appreciation and made a grabby, hubba-hubba gesture. Victoria caught him out of the corner of her eye. She did a slow whirl and shot him a look that could chill a volcano.

"Eat dung and die, you little slug."

Then she turned her back on us. It can be a mistake to turn your back on Ricky when you've just finished offending him. Victoria leaned over the table across the aisle to flirt with some jocks. Her pose was needlessly taunting, I thought.

I don't think it was the word *slug* that upset Ricky; I think it was the *little*. He was grinning his "I don't get mad, I get even" grin. He grabbed a packet of mayonnaise, notched one end, positioned it on the edge of our table, and pounded. The mayonnaise squirted out with the force of a lanced boil. Bull's-eye.

Victoria gave a tiny jump at the noise and glanced suspiciously over her shoulder. Then she straightened up and sauntered away, the mayonnaise glistening on her butt like a spectacular glob of phlegm.

Ricky wiggled his eyebrows. "Looks good on her," he said.

.   .   .

When I walked into that photography classroom filled with seniors and 3.5-or-better juniors, I have to admit I was mildly intimidated. I hoped maybe they'd think I was a senior transfer student or something, since I'm not what you'd call a well-known face around Mohegan. I've always kind of blended in with the scenery. I took a seat in the row by the windows, about halfway back.

As the bell rang, the teacher walked into the classroom. He was on the burly side and looked to be about thirtysomething—not quite middle-aged yet. His appearance was a little sloppy; his slacks were wrinkled and his brown beard could have used a trim. He went straight to the chalkboard, picked up a piece of chalk, and started writing his name, talking in a loud, booming voice as he wrote.

"My name is Mr. Dorio." He turned to face us. "In this class, you'll learn the fundamentals—basic principles of photography, how a camera works, and how to use the darkroom. That's the easy part, the technical, more or less mechanical part. The hard part, and it's something I can't really teach you, is developing your eye and your imagination."

He took off his tweed blazer and tossed it on the edge of the desk. It slid to the floor and he left it there. Then he walked around the desk, hitched up his pants, and parked his butt on the desk.

"Okay. This is an elective course. You've all professed a desire to be here. Let's go around. Say your name and tell me why you signed up. You."

He pointed at the girl who was first in my row. I gulped and slumped down in my seat. If he went in order, I'd be fourth.

"My name is Leslie Goldman, and I want to be a Pulitzer Prize–winning photojournalist," she said. Modest ambition, I thought.

Mr. Dorio kept a poker face, nodded, and pointed to the next kid.

61

"I'm Peter Hurley. I'm on the yearbook staff this year, and I want to learn how to develop my own film."

I was starting to panic. I could mention my father, say it ran in the family, but that might set up some kind of expectation, and maybe I'd stink at photography.

I don't know what made me say what I did. It just kind of popped out. Maybe because the kid in front of me had been going on and on about *National Geographic* and a career with travel opportunities, and that reminded me of pictures of naked natives that Ricky and I used to snicker at, and that reminded me of primitive tribes and that book my father had given me—

The finger was pointing at me.

"Uh, Michael Madden," I said. "I want to capture people's souls."

The silence that descended on the classroom was the kind of silence you hear after someone cuts a monster fart. I was afraid to look around, so I looked at Mr. Dorio. He was scrutinizing me intensely. Finally one side of his beard moved, which seemed to be half a smile.

"An aboriginal, if not an original, notion. Well, Michael, so you're interested in portraiture. A word of advice: If you intend to capture people's souls, you better be prepared to treat them with care and respect.

See me after class. I'll lend you a book on Diane Arbus."

I just sat there, stewing in sweat as the finger moved on. I didn't look at anyone until the girl who was sitting across the aisle from me started talking. The instant I heard her voice, I had to look. Her voice was—I don't know how to describe it without sounding like a total moon-eyed idiot. Clear like a flute, but soft, not piercing—kind of breathy. If you can imagine a talking flute made out of cashmere.

"My name is Melissa Ryan, and I don't really have a special reason for taking this course, except I'd like to learn about photography." She sounded shy and apologetic, but underneath was this confidence that you hear from a totally honest person.

"A completely legitimate motive, Melissa. Love of learning." Mr. Dorio gave her a whole smile.

Melissa Ryan. She was gorgeous. Not in a Victoria Kaminsky, Miss America way. More subtle, almost exotic, I thought as I stared at her. Petite, like my mother. Short black hair cut straight all around, bangs across her forehead long enough that she kind of had to peer out from underneath them. Straight nose, not one of those cheerleader button numbers. Really full lower lip, extremely sexy.

She may have felt me staring at her because she

glanced across the aisle at me with these long-lashed big green eyes—a pale jade shade—

I was in love. I mean, chemically speaking. A very visceral sensation, a gut tingler. Mr. Dorio lectured for the rest of the class, passed out textbooks and a bunch of papers—syllabus, darkroom rules and procedures, assignment list for the semester. When the kid in front of Melissa was passing a bunch of papers over his shoulder, he let some drop and they floated down by my shoes. I picked them up and handed them across the aisle. She smiled at me.

"Thanks, Michael," she whispered. I smiled back. I couldn't speak. My own voice was stuck in my throat. She remembered my name.

.   .   .

That night, I was looking at the Diane Arbus book Mr. Dorio had lent me. Mom and Amanda had gone to bed, which was probably just as well, because it wasn't your standard coffee-table material. There were some nudes in it that I could see my mother freaking out about. I mean, she's not the type who thinks you should put fig leaves on Michelangelo's *David* or anything, but these weren't the kind of pictures that you looked at and said, "My, that's a lovely depiction of the human form." Transvestites. Freaks. Outcasts. They were disturbing. Some of the pictures of people in their clothes looked even nuder than the nudes.

But they were amazingly good pictures, if you could stand to look at them. Like the one on the cover, the identical twin girls. Technically perfect. Every stripe in their corduroy dresses, even the pattern on their tights was sharp, clear. I studied their faces—mirror images physically, but not psychologically. It looked to me like one twin thought she got the bum deal, even though everything was supposedly the same. The face of the other seemed more open. There was more light in her eyes. Talk about captured souls.

FIVE

I remember something Diane Arbus said in the introduction to her book, about not being afraid when she was looking through the lens, about feeling like she wasn't vulnerable to danger.

It's true—you do get that feeling, as if the camera is a shield separating you from what you're focusing on, filtering out the reality of it somehow or insulating you from it by transforming it in your brain into an image. After a while, you can even start to see things that way without the camera.

I don't think I ever would have had the nerve to ask Melissa out that first time if I hadn't been looking through my camera.

I hung around the hall before class the next day. As soon as I saw Melissa go in the front door to the classroom, I went in the back and managed to snag a seat next to her.

Mr. Dorio went over some basic stuff and showed us how to load the black-and-white film into our cameras.

"Okay, we have twenty-five minutes left. We're going outside." He wrote on the board:

1. Load film correctly
2. Bracket exposures
3. Fifteen steps between shots

"If you're not sure your film is in right, let me check it. Bracket: When you decide on the proper combination of f-stop and shutter speed according to your camera's light meter, shoot that, then repeat the shot at both higher and lower exposures. Once outside, your camera will not leave your face. You will see the world through your lens for the next twenty-three minutes. Pick a starting point, take your three shots, fifteen steps, then do it again until you've used up the whole roll. Clear? Okay, out."

It must have looked pretty weird to anyone who was watching. Twenty kids with cameras glued to their faces like a herd of nearsighted aliens. Kids were grazing trees, tripping, stumbling. I tried to separate myself from the crowd and paced out my fifteen steps toward the gym, where it just so happened that Victoria Kaminsky's gym class was trotting in from the field, headed for the showers. I got a good shot of her from the rear as she went up the stairs. I figured I could give it to Ricky to add to his collection of Victoria memorabilia. She looked over her shoulder and caught me as I snapped the second shot. I took a step back and clunked heads with Peter Hurley, who was focusing on the same subject.

"Watch it, would ya?" he complained. "This is for the yearbook."

I was about to retort when I heard a laugh behind us. A laugh to match the voice. I turned 180 degrees and there was Melissa.

I lowered my camera, slightly chagrined at having been caught Victoria-stalking.

"I was, ah, bracketing," I said.

"Me, too," Melissa said, and laughed again.

"Did you catch the collision?"

She nodded.

On impulse, I lifted my camera again.

"Say *cheese*."

She ducked a little, then straightened up, wrinkled her nose, and smiled. "Chee-eese."

On further impulse, I blurted out, "Say you'll go out with me Saturday night."

" 'You'll go out with me Saturday night,' " she repeated in a teasing tone that I must say I found completely charming.

"I'd love to. How 'bout eight o'clock?" I held my breath and waited to see if she'd take me seriously. She scoped me out from under her bangs, bit her bottom lip, then nodded real quick, blushed, and turned away to head back into school. I don't recall how I got back to the classroom. I think maybe I flew.

.   .   .

When I got home after work that night about eight-fifteen, Mom was sitting on the couch sorting mail, mostly bills. Amanda was sitting practically inside the TV, watching *The Wizard of Oz* on videocassette. I parked myself at the dining room table since I no longer had the luxury of my own desk—I used the inside of the rolltop for socks and underwear—and started in on my homework.

"Wait, won't wait, wait, wait, next month," Mom was muttering, tossing bills in piles on the coffee table. She flipped a postcard across the room. I picked it up off the floor.

Dear Mike,
*   Tried to call you yesterday, no answer, sorry I*
missed you. Fort Lauderdale's a madhouse, gear-

ing up for the start of the race. Tell your mother
as soon as the book advance comes through, I'll get
some money to her. Miss you, give Amanda a hug
for me.
Love,
    Dad.

I thought it was kind of lousy not to send Amanda a postcard of her own—how long would it have taken to write? I tucked the postcard into my history book and glanced over at the couch, just in time to see Mom rip up the American Express bill and scatter the pieces over her shoulder.

On the TV, Dorothy was clacking those ruby slippers together and chanting on and on about how there was no place like home. Out of the blue, Mom lunged across the coffee table and snapped the tape off so it started rewinding.

"What a crock!" she said. The bitterness in her voice was vicious.

"Mommy, turn it back on! That's the best part." Amanda started to cry.

But Mom was on the warpath.

"Fairy tales, stupid, rotten fairy tales. They teach you to believe in it all. They teach you if you just look hard enough, you'll find the land over the rainbow," she ranted. "But if you make any mistakes, watch out! You'll get thrown to the flying monkeys quicker than a Kansas twister."

I started to feel something in me glaze over, a kind of mental barrier trying to keep the poison in the air from penetrating. She kept going.

"Well, I did the best I could. You tell me what mistakes I made that were so damn terrible that I deserved this! Look at me! I'm thirty-seven—my heart's desire sailed off into the sunset without me. My own backyard got foreclosed on. My life turned to shit!"

Amanda was so shocked to hear Mom use that word, she stopped crying. Both of us sat there gaping while Mom burst into tears, ran into the bedroom, and slammed the door.

I forced my hands to open my Algebra II book while Amanda crept over to the bedroom door and listened at the keyhole for Mom to stop crying.

.   .   .

I worked Saturday from eight to four. It was pretty hectic, the way Saturdays generally are in a grocery store. Just before noon, I heard this tremendous crash from the deli. Carl was standing behind the counter staring at the floor as if some creature from the black lagoon had just crawled out from under the tiles, and a well-dressed lady was staring at him, looking completely put out. Quicker than you could say "hell of a mess," Fritz was down from the office.

"I don't have time to stand around and wait while he makes another platter," the lady fumed. "I have forty people coming at five o'clock—and I hope you don't expect me to pay for that."

Fritz was totally smooth. "Mrs. Milton, I will personally deliver a fresh deli platter to your house by three." He took her by the arm like an usher at a wedding and escorted her over to her shopping cart, nodding and chatting. In less than a minute, Mrs. Milton's round face was beaming like a flashlight with new batteries. After Fritz got Mrs. Milton squared away, he went around the counter and put an arm around Carl's shoulders. Carl's eyelids were blinking like crazy, but they slowed down as Fritz said a few things in his ear.

Eileen leaned over her register between customers. "Poor Carl," she said. "He has to go at his own pace."

"Is he . . ." I didn't know quite how to put it.

Before Eileen could answer, a fresh stampede of customers started unloading their orders.

·   ·   ·

Eileen and I got off work the same time. Carl had two ham and Swisses with honey mustard on marble rye waiting for us. He seemed fully recovered from the

72

splattered platter incident. Eileen and I went outside to sit and eat on the dock behind the store because the weather was so nice. Eileen filled me in.

"My mother used to work here, too. She was working the night of the accident, when they came to tell Fritz. There was an early ice storm, a terrible freak one. It has to be like"—she counted on her fingers—"I don't know, thirty years ago or so. Fritz's wife and daughter were killed, and both of Carl's parents. Carl was about eight. He was the only one who survived."

Eileen took a potato chip from the bag we were sharing and crunched it. "My mother said Carl was in a coma for a long time. Fritz used to go to the hospital and read to him every day."

I couldn't think of a thing to say. I mean, I just couldn't imagine having practically my whole family, messed up as it was, wiped out in one savage smack from fate.

"Does Carl know? Does he realize?" I asked.

"That he's got brain damage?" Eileen said matter-of-factly.

I winced at the phrase. But I guess there was really no softer way to put it.

Eileen sipped from her can of iced tea. "I think he does," she said after a minute. "I was doing French homework on my break once. He was amazed that I could translate this paragraph. I told him it wasn't hard, that he could probably learn it. He said, 'No, my head won't hold it.' "

We sat there chewing, not talking anymore, just watching the riverbanks shrink as the tide came in.

·　　　　·　　　　·

When I got home from work, I noticed immediately that the scruffy, weedy lawn was cut, the cuttings were raked into neat piles down on the edge of the riverbank, and Ricky's car was in the driveway behind Mom's. I was mildly astonished at the idea of Ricky doing yard work. His folks use a lawn service. But then again, I'd seen him go out of his way for my mother over the years, in ways he never would for anyone else. For instance, he used to help her weed her tomatoes sometimes when we were kids. He wouldn't take any money from her, the way I would for chores like that. Mom always made a point of inviting him to dinner when it was spaghetti with her homemade sauce.

I went in the back door. Mom, Amanda, and Ricky were sitting at the kitchen table, which took up about two-thirds of the space in the kitchen, eating cookies and drinking tea. The sight of Ricky with a teacup in his hand was an eyebrow raiser.

"Hey, Madman." He ran his fingers through his hair and gave me a "so I'm drinking tea, wanna make something of it" look.

Hey, not me, I signaled with a shrug. My first pay-check—cashed—was in my pocket, and my first date with Melissa was less than four hours away. Ricky could have sat there swigging infant formula from a baby bottle, and it wouldn't have fazed me in the least.

Amanda was talking about *The Wizard of Oz*. I guess Mom had gotten over her problem with the gap between life and fairy tales, because she seemed very relaxed.

"But why didn't Dorothy turn the hourglass on its side?" Amanda asked. "That would have stopped the bad things from happening."

"It wouldn't have stopped the time from passing, sweetie," Mom told her.

Amanda looked confused. "But the witch said she had as much time left as was in the top of the hour-glass."

I put in my two cents. "What if she'd turned the hourglass upside down? She could have made time go backward and gotten back to Kansas that way."

Amanda's face lit up. "Really?"

Mom flicked me a glance that said "Don't tease your sister." "It wasn't time itself in the hourglass, honey. It was sand, measuring time, like a clock."

"What I could never figure out is why Dorothy didn't use the shoes," Ricky said, munching on a double-fudge chocolate chip cookie. "She knew they were powerful, right? So why didn't she kick the witch in the teeth, boot her right the hell out of Oz?"

Mom smiled at Ricky. "She didn't know how the power worked yet."

"Yeah, but she had nothing to lose by trying. The witch was getting ready to snuff her. She should have tried something. I would have."

I grinned, picturing Ricky doing a Bruce Lee karate kick in the ruby slippers.

"The point of the story was for Dorothy to learn that she had the power inside herself," Mom said. "It wasn't really the shoes at all."

"Oh," Amanda said.

"Good point," Ricky said.

"Can I borrow the car tonight?" I asked.

"Sorry, honey, it broke down again." Mom poured herself another half-cup of tea from the teapot.

My great mood cracked.

"What do you mean? I have plans tonight. Important plans. What's wrong with it?" I exploded.

"Calm down, Michael." She looked surprised at my overreaction. "On the way back from the Laundromat this morning, something started screeching and smoking. It smelled just foul. I barely made it home. Is it something at school? I'm sorry, really. Maybe you can get a ride."

I wasn't interested in her sympathy or her suggestions.

Ricky jumped in. "Don't panic, Madman. I'm not doing anything special. You can hitch a ride with me and—"

"Thanks, but no thanks," I said, cutting him off. I definitely wasn't ready to expose Melissa to Ricky and his crude tendencies. I grabbed the phone off the kitchen wall and stretched the cord as far into the other room as it would go, then took Melissa's phone number out of my wallet and dialed. I had no idea what I was going to say, but I wanted to get it over with.

After three rings, a man answered, "Ryan and Dupres-Ryan residence. May I help you?"

I asked for Melissa and heard him call her to the phone.

"Hello?" Even over the phone, her voice made my pulse skip.

"Uh, Melissa? It's Michael. Madden."

"Oh, hi, Michael. Do you need directions for tonight?"

"Not exactly," I told her. I explained the car situation.

Without missing a beat, she said, "Well, I'll pick you up, then."

"Are you sure? I mean, I feel like a real idiot—"

"Don't be silly," she said. "How do I get to your house?"

Crisis number two! How could I let her see that I lived in a rathole?

"You know where Thumm's Market is? In Mohegan Square by the old swing bridge?"

"Sure, down near the train station, right?"

"Yeah. Can you pick me up in the parking lot?"

This time, there was a moment's puzzled silence before she spoke.

"Sure. Eight o'clock. I'll be there."

When I went back in the kitchen, Mom was starting to clear away the tea things. "All set?" she asked.

"Yep." I rummaged in the refrigerator for something to drink and pulled out a root beer.

Ricky was eyeballing me. "What's the deal, Madman? Hot date?" he asked casually.

"Just a date," I mumbled. For some reason, I didn't want to share anything at all about Melissa—even information. I could tell Ricky's feelings were hurt. He stood up, put his cup and saucer in the sink, and stepped toward the door.

"I'll go check that fan belt," he said to my mother. "If that's what it is, I can pick up a new one and put it on Monday after school."

"Ricky, what can I say but thank you again," Mom said with a smile.

"Yeah, Rick, thanks. Lawn looks great," I said, feeling kind of guilty.

He eyeballed me again, and this time there was something half-hidden in his eyes, some kind of disapproval. "Yeah. Right," he said to me, then turned to Mom. "See you Monday. Thanks for the tea, Caroline."

Excuse me? Caroline? Ricky was out the door and I heard him pop the hood on my mother's car. Come again? I stared at Mom, and she stared back and gave her head what seemed to me to be a defensive toss.

"It's my name," she said.

SIX

I think it's morning, but it's still dark out. Allan's snoring like a troll with bad adenoids in the other bed. Only half-awake, I'm trying to dive back down into this dream. . . .

Melissa and I are on this old-fashioned sailboat, out on the ocean somewhere. I don't know where we are, and I have no idea where we're headed; it doesn't seem to matter. It's a cloudy day, but not cold. In fact, it's sort of balmy; the air itself is almost buoyant. The seas are heaving up and down in slow, gentle swells, waves are breaking over the bow, water is rolling back toward us, *gurgling over us, but it's not threatening in any way. We're not steering; we're just lying together getting carried over the ocean. We're all bundled up in some kind of covers on the deck near the wheel. I'm trying to touch Melissa. I think she's naked, but I can't get through the folds of the blanket. I don't really mind—nothing seems urgent at this point.*

Then something else intrudes—I can't see it, but it's as if something is trying to get my attention. I don't know how I realize it; suddenly I just know there's an important book down below in the cabin. I need to get that book, need to open it, because inside is everything I ever need to know. I want to read it with Melissa.

"Wait here. I'll be right back," I tell her. I start to unwind myself from the blanket, but out of nowhere, the wind is rising, the sky is darkening. The boat's really racing now; water's pouring over us. I can't fight my way against it to get down to the book. It seems like the boat's getting swamped. I think I'm going to be washed away, but I'm not scared—yet.

I'm waking up again. I'm swimming against consciousness because I want to go back to the beginning of the dream and make it come out right. . . .

Too late. My eyes pop open. It's all gone. I wanted to stay and float along forever.

I still haven't heard from Melissa. Not even a get-well card.

I was at the market fifteen minutes early, near closing time. I stood under the streetlight by the parking lot exit and watched last-minute just-gotta-get-three-quick-things shoppers race in. I watched Carl cart the trash out and toss the heavy bags over the top of the big metal bin like they were sacks of cotton. You'd never think someone so skinny could be so strong. He reminded me of some kind of comic book superhero.

Janey Riddley waddled out the door about five of eight. I hadn't seen her go in, so she must have been there for a while. A paunchy silver-haired guy wearing a top-of-the-line jogging suit and gold chains around his beefy neck bulldozed past her and knocked her sideways. She recovered without a visible reaction, but it kind of pissed me off. I almost shouted something like "What's the rush, bud?" or "Slow down, sport." I didn't know why. It reminded me of a playground bully running down a defenseless, nerdy fat kid.

At eight on the nose, a blue Toyota pulled in and drove slowly around, stopping when the headlights had me spotted. I peered through the windshield, then popped into the passenger seat.

"Hi," she said.

"Hi," I said.

"So, where are you taking me?"

"You mean, 'Where are *you* taking *me?*' " A feeble attempt at humor to cover my embarrassment.

She reached across the console and rested her hand on mine. "How about, 'Where are we going?' "

My ego appreciated the diplomacy.

"Want to catch a movie?"

"Sure. Good idea."

We headed up River Road and crossed over the Post Road Bridge into Eastfield Center, a.k.a. downtown.

Downtown is basically a six-block area, a T where Main Street runs into the Post Road. The Saturday night crowds were out and about. We had to park in the field by the performance pavilion on the river, where they hold outdoor concerts and stuff during the summer.

By the time we walked up to the Cinema, the lines for both movies were wrapped around the block.

We looked at each other. "Bad idea," we said at the same time, then burst out laughing.

Without really discussing or deciding, we fell into step together and started to stroll up Main Street. When we crossed the Post Road, Melissa tucked her arm in mine. She kept it there as we walked.

Main Street is very quaint, very picturesque, and very tough on the credit cards if you happen to be shopping. Pricey boutiques, cozy gourmet restaurants, as well as a few venerable old establishments like Darren's Drugstore, which still has an old-fashioned soda fountain, and Brenner Brothers, a three-story book-record-camera-stationery department store.

As we passed a big display window at Brenner Brothers, I stopped. There was a calendar display with all kinds of artsy, expensive calendars tacked up, stacked up, and spread out. Melissa mistook my interest.

"They really start pushing them early, don't they?" she said.

I pointed to the one in the middle, open to a spread with a red, white, and blue spinnaker practically hauling a racing boat right out of the waves. The J. Thaddeus Madden *Full Sail Calendar*.

"That's my father," I said.

Melissa squinted, trying to make out the tiny figures on the boat. "Which one?"

"No, I mean the whole calendar. My father took the pictures."

"Wow. I didn't know your dad was a famous photographer." She sounded impressed. "Is that why you signed up to take photography?"

"I guess. He gave me a camera before—" I stopped. I was going to tell her about the race and all, but for some reason, thinking about it made something in me feel—flat. I couldn't work up the energy to get the words out. I mean, it sounded like a cool thing to have your father doing, theoretically, but it was a major contributing factor to the mess of my life, so—I pushed it out of my mind. "Before school started," I said.

As we hit the top of the block, the garlic-oregano smell of brick oven pizza hit my nose, and a jolt of hunger hit my stomach.

"Want to grab a bite to eat?"

"I'm not hungry, but if you are . . . Are you?" Melissa asked.

"Kind of," I admitted. "I had a sandwich after work, but I skipped dinner. My mother's been into tuna a lot lately. Tonight it was tuna tacos."

Melissa laughed. "Sounds healthy, anyway."

"I don't know. I think I'm starting to grow gills." I caught myself before I made a goofy fish face. I didn't want her to think I was overly juvenile.

Pizza was apparently everyone else's hot idea for the night. We could barely get through the door of Luigi's Brick Oven Pizzeria. In front of the take-out counter, about a dozen people were crowded together, bumping and jostling one another every time a waiter walked by. A hefty guy who looked like the last thing he needed was a pizza shifted back and crunched my foot. It was a good excuse to put my arms around Melissa, though, purely for protection.

"Isn't that a friend of yours at the table by the window?" she said in my ear. "They have an extra seat. We could share."

I looked. Ricky and three other hockey players were scarfing down a deluxe pizza in typically rowdy fashion. Even the prospect of sharing a seat with Melissa wasn't enough to make me want to join them.

"I changed my mind," I said. "I don't think I'm that hungry. Let's get out of here." I ducked behind the cigarette machine before Ricky could see me, and pulled Melissa out the door. She looked a little mystified, but she didn't say anything.

Through the window, I saw Ricky take out his comb and start combing his hair right at the table. See what I mean? Not what you want to expose a girl to on a first date, especially one you'd like to impress.

It didn't occur to me until we were halfway down the block to ask Melissa how she'd known Ricky was a friend of mine.

"I was watching you in the cafeteria the other day," she admitted. I must say, I found the confession flattering. "Can I ask you something?"

"Shoot," I said.

"Why is he always combing his hair? I know girls who do that, but I've never seen a guy do it so much."

I debated whether or not to let her in on Ricky's secret.

"You won't tell anyone? Ricky would kill me if this got around."

"Of course not." And I could tell by her tone that she wouldn't.

I told her about what Mr. Bolton used to do to Ricky as punishment for particularly felonious kid-crimes.

"A real boot-camp buzz cut. And he has these ears that kind of stick out. Victoria Kaminsky used to call him Dumbo. Anyway, I think it traumatized him or something." I thought Melissa might laugh, but she looked shocked.

"That's terrible! What a cruel thing to do. It's like psychological child abuse."

I'd never thought of it like that. I mean, I never razzed him about it because he was my best friend; if it had been some other kid, I might have. But Melissa cared and she didn't even know him. I looked at her and was suddenly really glad that she was so nice. And really, really glad that she was with me.

We ended up wandering back down Main Street, then walking along the riverbank near the pavilion.

We did the fill-in-the-background thing, the *Reader's Digest* condensed autobiography swap. I kept mine to a real minimum. And I asked her a lot of personal questions, which surprised me. With other girls I'd dated, the details didn't matter all that much to me. I didn't much care what their favorite colors were or how many kids were in their families or what they thought about at night before they went to sleep. With Melissa, I wanted to know details. I wanted to know *her*.

"So," I said as we parked ourselves on a bench and sat watching the river lap the reeds. "Are you going to be a lawyer like your parents—defending the rights of the worker bees against the big bosses?"

Melissa shook her head. "I want to be a doctor. A pediatric surgeon."

"Won't you have to dissect stuff in med school?"

She'd been telling me about when she refused to do the dissection labs in biology and almost got suspended because of it. I remembered reading about the whole flap in the school newspaper two years ago, but I didn't realize Melissa had been the one who started it. Her parents helped her prepare her case for the school board. She won, too.

"In college and med school, I'll do it because there's a purpose that makes sense. But it doesn't make any sense to force someone who's going to be a bookkeeper or a . . . a photographer or an English teacher to dissect a real frog. There are perfectly good plastic models they can use to learn what they need to know. I just like things to make sense."

Me, too. Just being with Melissa seemed to clarify things for me. Not to get paranormal about it, but she seemed to have this aura of calm order surrounding her, and it spread to me when I was with her.

When we pulled back into Thumm's parking lot, Melissa pulled into a parking spot away from the street-light and shut off the ignition.

"Are you sure you don't want me to drop you off at your house? It's no trouble, you know."

"This is fine," I said. I wasn't sure what was going to happen next, because as Ricky said, I'm no Mr. Experience. I mean, I've had enough experience to know what to do under normal circumstances with normal girls, but this was different. Melissa was different.

"I've never gone out with an older woman before," I confessed. I was thinking that she was a senior because the frog incident happened two years ago, and biology is a sophomore course.

"I'm not really a senior," she said. "I'm in the accelerated program. So even though I graduate this year, I'm only a junior, age-wise."

"Oh," I said. "Well. I've never gone out with a genius before." I smiled at her and she smiled back. Then I leaned over and our smiles just kind of melted together.

SEVEN

Mom's here for our first session together with Dr. Sherman. Snow flurries are whirling around outside the window. I feel cold. Mom looks incredibly nervous and insecure. I notice that she's got about eight more gray hairs. My fault, I guess. Her hands keep grappling with each other in her lap. I think maybe I should reach over and pat them or something, but I don't. Dr. Sherman gives her a slight nod, like a prearranged signal. She takes a deep breath.

"I don't really know where to start, but before— Well, there's something I wanted to tell you, Michael, and I hope you'll believe I had nothing to do with it because—"

"What?" I cut through the bush she's beating around.

"Your camera is missing. I turned the house upside down, they've looked at Thumm's, your friend Melissa looked at school. I know how much it means to you because your father gave it to you and—" Her words are tumbling out in a rush, but only one word touches me.

"Melissa. You talked to Melissa?" My question seems to hit her like a whip.

"Ricky said I should call her and tell her. . . ." Her voice trails off, and I feel the muscles in my face get hard.

"Why don't you tell Ricky to butt out? Tell Ricky to go screw up someone else's life." As I say it, I know I'm not being totally fair to Ricky. But I'm still pissed off at him. "What did Melissa say?" I can't help asking.

"She said she feels that she deserted you when you needed her," Mom says quietly.

"Tell Melissa it's not her fault, okay? Would you tell her?"

Mom kind of waits before she nods. I get the feeling she may be waiting for me to cut her some slack, absolve her, tell her she's not responsible in any way for what I did. But I don't. I'm not ready to yet. I guess I do blame her for some of what happened. Adults are supposed to know how to handle the crap that life dishes out.

Now Doc puts in his two cents. Actually, with the

price of shrinks, it's probably more like two bucks. "Why don't you call Melissa yourself, Michael?"

I shake my head. Something else I'm not ready to do yet.

Mom sighs. "Anyway, Michael, Ricky said you had your camera at work and maybe you left it there and someone took it. I'm sorry it's gone. I didn't want you to think that I—because your father gave it—" She stops talking and slumps as if defeated by something.

Doc is eyeballing me. "Do you know where it is, Michael?"

I'm tired suddenly. My eyes just want to close, like Dorothy's and her buddies' in the poisoned poppy field outside the Emerald City.

"Where's the camera?" Dr. Sherman prods.

"In the river. I threw it in the river."

When I was a real little kid, I used to do this kind of weird thing. I'd crawl around the house with my head upside-down, imagining what it would be like if people lived on the ceiling instead of the floor. All the angles of the house, the furniture, the moldings, seemed different. The ceiling-as-floor was so clean and uncluttered. Windows upside-down were low to the ground, perfectly placed for a little kid to see out of. Light fixtures bloomed up like fountains. The rugs made it seem like you were in a tent—kind of cozy. It was just a whole different way of looking at something ordinary that made it seem special.

I was home by myself one Saturday around the beginning of October, the first Saturday I'd had off from work. I was hanging around the house, framing shots with my camera. I was practicing setting exposures, not actually taking the pictures, focusing on well-lit things, shadowy things. The Nikon F2 is manual; it has a built-in light meter, but no autofocus or anything. It's a solid, heavy camera, and if you take too long to get set up, you might miss your shot.

So I was lying on the couch, my head hanging half off, and suddenly the upside-down thing I used to do came back to me. I never would have done it if anyone else had been around, but like I said, I was alone and so I just kind of checked it out. The new house, upside down, through my camera. Actually it looked much better that way. As I was working my way toward the dining room table, I noticed some flat stuff was wedged behind the hutch.

I put the camera down and pulled the stuff out—a framed nautical painting that used to hang over our fireplace when we had one, and an oversize black leather portfolio, with a handle, that zipped up on three sides. The kind photographers and artists use. This had to be old because my father hadn't used a portfolio in a long time. Once you make your reputation, you don't need to cart your product all over town begging for assignments—people come to you. Like, for the Royale Rum race, three different magazines cut an advance deal with Dad.

I unzipped it. Inside were large black pages covered with plastic, held in binder rings. And family pictures of us way back when, in the days before Dad made the switch from being a wedding and studio and school-picture photographer to marine photography. Before he started traveling so much.

The photos were mostly five-by-sevens and eight-by-tens. I paged through the portfolio. It wasn't any documentary of our whole life or anything. You know that saying about shoemakers' kids going barefoot? It's like that with photographers' kids. The pictures were clustered around specific occasions: me in my Little League uniform the year we won our division championship; a sequence of Mom gardening, the year she put in the raised beds and the medieval herb garden; two pages of Amanda when she was just born, some of her alone, some with my mother looking as soft and happy as a madonna on a Christmas card.

My father wasn't physically in any of the pictures, but his presence was there, all right. Looking at them, I felt as if I'd had an eye transplant and was seeing what he saw, feeling what he felt when he was seeing it.

I hadn't thought about what life used to be like in a long time. I mean, before my father left, I never bothered to think about what life was like, because it *was* what it was like, more or less. I didn't pay attention to collecting memories of how things were because I didn't know they'd change so drastically. The few times I'd tried to dip into my past recently, to try to sort out how we'd wound up where we were, my brain went fuzzy. Something just wouldn't let me think about it.

Sitting there looking at those pictures, I felt really disoriented trying to get a handle on it all. You've got the past, which is a done deal. You've got the future, which, as far as I can tell, is a crapshoot in a lot of ways. And you've got the present—sort of. I was thinking maybe that's why some people take pictures— to try to freeze and hang on to pieces of life so it can't slip totally away.

I heard Mom's car rumble up the driveway. The muffler was on its last legs. I smacked the portfolio shut and shoved it back behind the hutch along with the painting, wondering why she'd saved it when she hated my father so much.

"Michael, are you home?"

"In here," I yelled, leaping over the back of the couch and grabbing a magazine.

She huffed into the living room with a plastic laundry

basket piled high, and heaved it onto the cushion next to me. Straightening up, she stretched her back out, then looked around, frowned, and put her hands on her hips.

"You didn't get the storm windows up."

I'd totally forgotten she'd asked me to do that.

"It's only the first weekend in October. We'll probably get another warm spell." I tried to make it sound like a well-reasoned, rational decision.

She wasn't buying. "The nights are getting very chilly down here by the water. I can barely afford the electricity bill now, and I certainly can't afford to turn the heat on and have it wasted because— What *did* you do all morning?"

"I was working on homework," I said. It really annoyed me to feel so defensive.

She spotted the camera on the dining room table.

"Homework? Photography, I suppose?" The disapproval in her voice was as thick as putty. "You know, Michael, I'm getting a little fed up with you spending all your free time on photography. You *do* have other responsibilities. You're a member of this family—"

"What's left of it," I muttered.

"What did you say?" The don't-give-me-any-backtalk glare.

Ricky's Mustang pulling around the back of the house saved the situation from getting truly ugly. He barged right in with his customary finesse, looking so cheerful I felt like popping him one.

"Hey, Madman. Hey, Caroline."

"Hi, Ricky," my mother said, reining in her rage.

I gave him a short nod.

Ricky's not stupid; he could tell he'd just walked in on an imminent shit-storm.

"I, uh, just stopped by to see if Madman wanted to go shoot some hoop." He looked back and forth between the two of us, running his fingers through his hair. "We got a game up at school. Dave, Jason, and— but if it's not a good time—"

I felt a little sorry for him. It's embarrassing to walk in on a fight between your friends and their parents.

"Not today, thanks, Rick. I have some stuff I gotta do."

"He has to take some pictures," my mother said, in a tone she might have used if she were saying, "He has to go rob a convenience store."

Ricky took a few steps back toward the kitchen.

"Yeah. Well. Later, then." I caught him aiming a helpless shrug at my mother, as if the two of them were in collusion. Or they both thought I was a hopeless case. Ricky avoided looking at me directly as he left.

I snagged a pair of blue jeans, some clean underwear, and a shirt from the laundry basket. I took my camera into the bathroom for safekeeping while I changed.

Mom was still standing there when I came back into the living room, but she didn't look as mad. Actually she looked kind of uncertain.

"Where are you going?" she asked.

"Out." I brushed past her on my way to the kitchen. I could tell she was trying to reconnect, but I wasn't interested.

"Will you be home for dinner?" she called after me.

"Don't count on it," I muttered.

Melissa and I had made plans to go out that night, but thanks to the altercation, I assumed I was carless again. First thing I did was use the pay phone at the marina to call and let her know about my vehicle situation. But no one was home. And I didn't want to leave a message on her answering machine because I didn't want to chance Melissa calling back and talking to my mother.

I wandered up River Road, crossed over the Post Road Bridge to downtown, picked up a few rolls of film, then hung around Main Street for a while, snapping candids of passersby.

It was funny, the different ways people reacted. Some pretended to ignore me, but self-consciously, as if I might be someone photographing them officially and they could wind up as human interest filler in the local newspaper. Some really hammed it up, made faces, or grinned goofy grins. One junior high wiseacre stuck his finger up his nose. But a few people got really perturbed, as if I really was out to capture their souls, to steal something from them. They put up their hands to block the shot, or turned their frowning faces into their collars.

I figured I should get used to all kinds of reactions if I was going to pursue this as a career. I didn't think Diane Arbus would let a few negative responses stop her.

About five, I called Melissa again. She said she'd meet me at Wong Fat's Golden Pagoda for dinner.

.   .   .

"Does your dad ever take you with him when he's working and traveling?" Melissa asked.

We were sitting on a bench on the town green, eating ice-cream cones after digesting our moo goo gai pan. Somehow the conversation had turned from photography to my father.

"No," I told her. "I was supposed to go to England with him last summer for the Admiral's Cup. But it fell through." I didn't add that it had fallen through because he'd landed a new girlfriend three weeks before the trip. She went in my place. Not that Dad totally dumped me. He just kind of hinted and I bowed out gracefully.

"That must have been disappointing," Melissa said sympathetically. "Oops. Watch that drip."

"Where?"

"Here." She pulled my hand over to her mouth and licked a blob of fudge ripple off the side of my cone.

My heart gave a little thump when she did that. In fact, I got so rattled, I dropped the whole thing on the grass.

Melissa smothered a laugh. "I'm sorry," she apologized immediately. "It's just that you looked exactly like a little boy when that happened." I grinned. She giggled. I cut the giggle off with a kiss.

She pushed me back after a minute. "Michael, we're in a public place." I could see she was blushing by the light of the lantern behind the bench. My heart was hammering now.

"So let's go find a private place," I suggested.

That's what we did.

.   .   .

The next day was the first Sunday I ever worked at the market.

"Things slow way down after lunch, when the bagel crowd's home reading their newspapers," Eileen told me. "I'm leaving at two. You'll be fine."

Around one, Fritz came down from his apartment. He'd been wearing a suit earlier, but now he'd changed into old clothes, with rubber sea boots and a windbreaker. He carried a pair of old sneakers and a white plastic bag that looked like it was full of books, judging from the boxy outlines pressed against it.

"Do you think you can handle the register alone, Michael?" he asked.

"Sure thing, Fritz." I'd picked up a lot of speed. A couple of Saturdays worth of practice will do that for you.

Carl ambled over from the deli with one of his wrapped-up roasted chickens and handed it to Fritz as if it was part of a routine.

"Thank you, Carl. You and Michael will be holding down the fort. You know where to reach me in an emergency."

Carl blinked and nodded. "Sergeant Beitter's number is on the card taped to the wall by the phone," he recited in his solemn way. "You'll be back at five-thirty to close up."

Fritz smiled real gently and patted Carl on the shoulder. "You're a good boy, Carl."

It seemed odd for him to call Carl, who's pushing forty, a boy. But then again, it fit, in a way. Carl does have this kidlike quality about him, kind of innocent and earnest, and like it's a struggle for him to understand some things. Plus, he always wears his green baseball cap. It makes him look younger than he is.

"Why don't you take your break now, Michael, before Eileen leaves?" Fritz suggested. Then he left.

I grabbed a Coke from the soda case and wandered over and looked out the window in the wall behind the deli. Fritz went down the ramp to the floating dock. He got into a small powerboat tied up there, an old wooden one, painted white with a lot of amber varnish work. A real classic. He started up the engine, cast off the dock lines, powered out into the channel, and headed under the swingbridge, upriver.

When my break was over, I went back to my register. Eileen and I talked over and through the occasional customers. Once I'd gotten the hang of cashiering, it wasn't really necessary to pay that close attention. The people and the items moved through like background, especially when it wasn't busy.

"So where's Fritz going?" I asked.

Two cartons of yogurt, a pack of English muffins, and a Sunday *Times*.

"He's got this friend. They were in the war together. Fritz's brother, too."

"Is that the three of them in that picture in Fritz's office?"

A quart of rum raisin Häagen-Dazs, a box of Nilla Wafers, fresh green beans, a package of slivered almonds, a beef tenderloin roast, and a Sunday *Times*.

"Yeah. You've probably seen him with the veterans in the Memorial Day parade. He's the guy in the wheelchair. Fritz takes him out on the boat when the weather's good. He goes to see him every Sunday," Eileen said.

"Was that a bag of books he was bringing?"

Four bagels in white waxed deli paper, a quart of cranberry juice, Tic Tacs, and a Sunday *Times*.

"Probably. Fritz is a total bookaholic. One time I freaked out because my register tape got all jammed on a busy night. Fritz fixed it. Then the next day, he gave me this paperback, *Zen and the Art of Motorcycle Maintenance*."

"What does a jammed register have to do with motor-cycles?"

A roll of Scott tissues, a pound of sliced ham, a loaf of seedless rye bread, a bag of Ruffles, a six-pack of Cel-Ray soda, and a Sunday *Times*.

"I don't know. I haven't gotten around to reading it yet."

A lull came; no customers for fifteen minutes. Eileen went around the foot of her register counter, sat on the bagging shelf, leaned down, and buried her face in her arms.

"What's the matter?" I asked, flexing my arm, which was a tad sore from hoisting all those Sunday *Times*es.

"Oh, nothing. I just wish I were dead, that's all."

"That bad?"

She lifted her head wearily.

"Yes. No. I don't know. I was at this frat party last

night." She sighed. "A keg party. We were playing this game called beer pong. I think I lost."

"You *think* you lost? Aren't you sure?"

"I'm not sure of anything. My memory's a blur. You play with cups of beer on the Ping-Pong table and every time your cup gets hit, you have to chug. I was playing with Robbie Meehan—I think I got killed. The last thing I remember is someone taking away my car keys. Oohhhh." She let out a long groan.

I didn't know exactly what to say.

"I hear tomato juice with a dash of Worcestershire and a raw egg mixed in is good for hangovers," I offered.

Eileen made a gagging noise.

She managed to hang in there until two, but I could see her wilting by the minute under all the makeup she wears. On her way out the door, Carl intercepted her with a bunch of the cut flowers they kept near the produce department. I guess he'd noticed Eileen was under the weather. He pushed the green paper bundle into her hands, then stuck his own hands in his pockets as if he were embarrassed, and looked down at his shoes.

I saw Eileen's eyes get kind of bright. She stood on tiptoe and kissed his cheek.

"Thank you, Carl. You are a gentleman and a sweetheart. Unlike some other guys I know."

She left and Carl grinned and rubbed his cheek, smearing the lipstick mark.

Things were really slow all afternoon. About three-thirty, Ricky strolled through the door.

"Hey, Madman, how's it hangin'?" He got a Dr Pepper from the soda case. I rang him up and he sat down at the end of my register, on the bagging shelf, and popped it open.

"Know why Dr Pepper comes in bottles?" he asked.

I rolled my eyes. Very stale material. "That's not a bottle—it's a can. It would never work."

Ricky checked out the opening and winced. "Very painful thought."

Just then, Janey Riddley waddled in. She walked over to the first register, which was closed, and went into her *TV Guide* routine. I saw Ricky zone in on her activity, and it made me a little nervous.

"She got a bug in her software or something?" He jerked his head in her direction.

"Something like that," I said, but I felt uncomfortable saying it.

She put back a second issue and took out a third.

"Geez, you'd think she was trying to decipher the Rosetta Stone or something."

"Just leave her alone, all right?" I mumbled.

Ricky shrugged his fine-with-me shrug, but he kept

staring. "You know who she looks like? Old Fatty-Bean. Hey, maybe she's a TV Guidance Counselor!"

I had to grin. Ricky's pistol wit strikes again. But I didn't want him to get too cranked up and cause a scene.

"I gotta get back to work." I took a roll of paper towels and a plastic bottle of spray cleaner from underneath my counter and started wiping this sticky spot where a lady's chicken had leaked.

"Well, better you than me. Catch you later." Ricky stood and watched the TV Guidance Counselor shuffle over to the other closed register. "Hey, I'm having trouble with math. Can you look up what time *Sesame Street* is on?"

Janey didn't bat an eyelash. No reaction at all. She just kept flipping carefully through the magazine with her pudgy hands.

Ricky took off, and as I put the cleaning stuff back under my counter, I took out my camera, which I'd started bringing with me pretty much everywhere I went. You never know when you'll see a great shot. Janey was right there, and the temptation was too much for me to resist. I raised it slowly and focused on her face and the *TV Guide*, a good close shot. *Snap click.*

Her head popped up suddenly and she looked straight at me, staring intently. *Snap click.* Then her lips started moving, kind of silently muttering. She put the *TV Guide* back in the rack and went for the door. I felt a little guilty for disturbing her, but I couldn't wait to develop that roll of film and see if the pictures were any good.

EIGHT

What makes you love someone? With Melissa, it started with basic biological attraction. I suppose it did with my parents, too, once upon a time.

With families, I guess you're just born loving them. Maybe that's partly biological, too, programmed right into our genes. Family love is different from romantic love. I was going to say voluntary love, love you choose, but I'm not sure how much choice you actually have in the matter.

Everybody knows the good things about love. But it's really a mixed bag. To tell you the truth, I think love is kind of insidious. It works its way into you, and before you know it, you've developed a dependency. You've gotta have it to be happy.

And boy, watch out if you lose it, because it leaves a hell of a ragged hole when it's gone.

Monday was one of those mild, mellow Indian summer days, a gift from Mother Nature before she clouts you with a New England autumn. When I got up, I congratulated myself for my unintentional foresight in not putting up the storm windows.

Photography was my last class that day.

"Portrait assignments due a week from Friday." Mr. Dorio had to shout above the exit shuffle as the bell finished ringing. "Make sure you and your darkroom partners sign up early so you all have enough time."

"I already signed us up for Wednesday afternoon," Melissa told me as we followed the herd out into the hall.

"Good work, partner," I said.

"Do you want to do each other?" she asked.

I lifted an eyebrow at the suggestion.

"Stop it!" Melissa poked me in the ribs. "I mean the portraits. We could do each other's portrait for the assignment."

"Great," I agreed. "I'll capture your soul. I promise I'll take good care of it."

"Maybe we'll capture each other's souls," she suggested. Coming from Melissa, it didn't sound coy; it sounded like an invitation to paradise.

"Can we do it today? Do you have to work?"

"Uh-uh. Tomorrow and Thursday this week. Today's good. Can I pick the spot?"

"Do you have someplace special in mind?"

I nodded. The river. "I'll stop by my locker and meet you in the parking lot, okay?"

.   .   .

I wouldn't tell her where we were going until we got there. She was a little concerned when she saw the KEEP OUT—ABSOLUTELY NO TRESPASSING sign at the head of the dirt road that leads to the trail down to the swimming hole.

"It's all right. Ricky and I come here all the time. That sign's just to cover their butts in case someone drowns or something," I told her. But to make her feel better, I grabbed a red grease pencil I use in the darkroom to crop prints, hopped out of the passenger seat, and amended the sign to read EXCEPT FOR MICHAEL AND MELISSA.

She laughed as I got back in, and we drove down the dirt road and parked in the clearing.

I shot my roll of film first. When I was done, I grabbed our rope swing. "Want me to pose?"

Melissa was loading her camera, ignoring me. I

ripped off my shirt, pulled back the rope, and swung out over the river. "How about traditional Tarzan?" I yelled.

She looked up. "Michael, what are you doing?"

I swung back in, but my foot hit a slippery spot on the grassy bank as I landed. I let go of the rope and tried to catch my balance. Too late. Splash.

I might have felt like a complete idiot in front of someone else, but Melissa was laughing that laugh and it was doing things to me, so I didn't even care. I wrenched off my sneakers and tossed them up near the tree, then turned and dove under the water.

"Come on in," I invited her when I surfaced for air. "Water's great."

Melissa stopped laughing and looked dubious. She bit her lip.

"Come on," I said, holding out my arms. She was wearing one of those things that's a cross between shorts and a skirt, with a matching sleeveless top. She leaned over and unbuckled her sandals and dropped them next to my sneakers. A warm breeze fluttered over my skin. She stepped down the bank to the water's edge.

"Should I?" she said.

"You should. You really should," I told her. She took my hands and I pulled her out into deeper water. We drifted and floated and swirled in the current. Neither of us surfaced for air much.

Afterward Melissa dropped me off at the market. She teased me a little about it.

"You're so mysterious about where you live. Are you hiding some deep, dark secret, like Bluebeard?"

"Bluebeard's nothing," I told her. "A few dead wives in a closet. My secret is infinitely more sinister."

"What?" She was laughing.

"A sticky little sister who'll smear Twinkie cream all over you, and a mother who'll ply you with tuna fish till you beg for mercy."

"I'm tougher than you think. Why don't you try me?" She was still teasing, but I detected a note of challenge in the question. I deflected it by pretending to take what she said a different way.

"I think I will." I put my arms around her and kissed her. Our clothes were still damp from swimming. It was broad daylight, so I pulled away before the windshield started steaming up. I didn't plan what I said next; it just said itself.

"I love you."

Melissa opened her eyes wide. Her pupils were like the black dots of big twin question marks. I was nervous suddenly, as if I'd stuck my neck out and put myself in a dangerous position. Melissa didn't say anything. I opened the car and got out. She started to drive away, then stopped, backed up, and rolled down her window. She was smiling.

"I love you, too," she said.

. . .

I was starved, so I popped into the market for a roast beef, onion, and Russian dressing on rye. Eileen was working deli.

"What are you so happy about?" she asked. "No, don't tell me. It's gotta be love."

"How can you tell?"

"You're reeking of it." But she smiled.

I went outside and leaned against the railing over the dock, just watching the river flow by as I ate. Carl and Fritz pulled the boat up to the dock while I was there. For someone so gangly, Carl moved pretty gracefully. He was careful and sure with the dock lines. After they tied up, Carl heaved a big cooler off the boat.

"Hey, Carl. Hey, Fritz. Fishing?" An obvious deduction on my part: I could see two rods and a tackle box in the boat. Carl and Fritz went fishing once a week on a slow afternoon or evening, usually Monday or Tuesday.

"Bluefish are running," Carl called up. Then he opened the cooler and showed me the catch. It was full to the brim with big gray blues on ice. He closed it again, hoisted it easily to one shoulder, and started up the dock toward the back entrance of the fish market. Fritz gave me a wave as he followed.

Fritz was kind of a puzzle to me. I didn't know how anyone could have lived through what he had and ever have smiled again. Not that you'd know from hanging around the store that Fritz's life had ever been anything but normal. He was basically cheerful, chatting with customers, fixing any glitches that came up without a complaint. He didn't exactly whistle while he worked, but sometimes he hummed. On the surface, you could call him an outgoing guy.

A lot of times, though, when I went up to the office for something, I caught him poring over some book. I had this feeling that he lived part of his life somewhere else, in a place where what was in books was as real as a loaf of bread.

If Fritz was a puzzle to me, it seemed that I was a bit of a puzzle to Carl. Sometimes when I'd glance at him from the register, or when we worked together in the deli, I'd catch him staring at me as if he were trying to figure out something about me. Or as if I reminded him of someone he knew, but he couldn't quite pinpoint who. It didn't bother me or anything. Actually I enjoyed his company. A nice, quiet contrast to some of my friends—Ricky, for instance.

Carl came back out as I was finishing my last bite of

sandwich. He handed me a large flat package, a plastic bag over white paper.

"Bluefish fillets," he said shyly. "Fresh. Dust with salt and pepper, brush wth olive oil, broil four minutes on each side. If you chop up an onion, sauté it with garlic and two tablespoons of vinegar. It's a nice sauce."

"Thanks a lot, Carl," I said. I wasn't exactly sure why he gave it to me. Maybe I looked hungry because of being skinny. Or maybe he figured, as the shack family, we qualified as poor people and could use the extra food. He was so nice about it, though, that I wasn't about to tell him I was a little off seafood these days.

It was almost dark when I got home. I stuck the fish in the freezer. When I saw the evidence of that night's dinner—a noodle bag and empty cans, tuna, cream of mushroom soup, peas, and Durkee fried onions—I was glad I'd fed myself.

Amanda was standing on a chair at the sink, playing with her Barbie and Ken dolls.

"No, Ken, don't go, don't leave me, please," Amanda said in a high, squeaky voice—that's her version of Barbie.

"Sorry, Barbie, I have to go." Low voice: Ken. "I've got important stuff to do. I'm going on this boat."

Amanda dumped Ken into a Tupperware bowl and

started driving him around in the soapy water. I stood there and watched.

Barbie: "I hate you, Ken. I hope a big storm gets you." Blast of spray from the sink hose. "I hope you fall off the boat and a shark eats you up." Amanda flipped Ken out of the bowl and started pushing the cheese grater toward him.

Amanda, narrator voice: "And here comes the shark."

I couldn't take any more. I wandered out to the living room, where Mom was curled up on the couch, watching *Jeopardy!*

"Oh, Michael, you're home." She sounded glad to see me. She twisted around on the couch, and I could tell she was up for some semi-adult conversation. "We ate early. There's half a casserole in the refrigerator."

"That's okay. I had a sandwich." I opened the roll-top, put my camera inside, and grabbed a clean pair of underwear.

"Oh. Well, how was your day?"

I wasn't in a mood for talking. What I really wanted to do was hibernate in my own room with the door closed and wrap myself up in memories of the afternoon with Melissa. That was, unfortunately, out of the question.

"Did you work? I didn't know you were working Mondays."

I shook my head. "I was out taking pictures. Up by the swimming hole."

"Oh." The pitch of her voice dropped a few whole tones. She paused, and seemed to be trying to figure out how to say something. "Michael, listen, I hope you're not getting too obsessed with this photography thing—"

"What are you talking about?" I could hear the belligerent edge in my voice and tried to soften it. "I'm taking a course in school. It was homework."

I saw her try again, struggle for the right words not to start a fight, but my defenses were up.

"Look, honey, I just mean—well, I just worry that you're getting too wrapped up in this, maybe as a way to avoid dealing with things, or—"

"Or maybe it's the way I choose to deal with things," I said coldly. Look who's talking, was what I felt like saying. Look how you're dealing with things. You're obsessed with hating my father, fixated on tuna fish, and all you do is sit around on the couch and mope. At least Dad had the guts to break out of something that didn't make him happy.

I didn't say all that, of course, I have some sense of self-preservation. Or I did then.

"I'm going to take a shower" is what I said.

NINE

"You know, Michael, if she's autistic—and from the behavior you've described, the isolation in a world of her own, the repetitive routines, the total lack of communication, autism sounds like a strong possibility— it's possible that you're reading more into her TV Guide habit than is actually there. Maybe she's not looking for anything. She may just enjoy the numbers, the arrangement of the pages."

"But you don't know that," I say. "You said everybody's looking for something—are you saying she's nobody? She's somebody, isn't she?" I'm pissed off again. Seems like every time I talk to Dr. Sherman, it happens.

*There's this anger, hibernating inside me. When Doc's
mental poking and prodding wakes it up, I can't make
it go back to sleep. It comes roaring out of its cave. I
hear my voice getting louder. "How do you know what
it's like to be inside her head? Maybe she's looking for
something more important than you or anyone else will
ever know. Maybe even if her brain can't figure it out,
her soul is searching. What the hell do you know about
it?"*

*Doc cocks his head and scopes me out kind of curi-
ously; I can see his wheels are spinning, trying to connect things.*

*"You sound like you have a great deal of empathy for
this woman," he says mildly.*

*Empathy. Putting yourself inside someone else's skin.
Me and the TV Guidance Counselor? Now that's some
food for thought.*

The eye is a lens. Your pupil acts like a lens's diaphragm
aperture—the opening that controls the amount of light
entering the camera. If the camera's not automatic,
you decide where to set the f-stop, controlling the size
of the aperture. You make the opening bigger for low
light conditions, to let in more light. You make it
smaller for bright conditions, to keep out light. The eye
acts automatically. Your pupil closes in response to

bright light; it opens wider in darkness to gather whatever light is available, to help you see. But your brain
is where you experience what you see as seen.

Did you ever notice how with some things, when
you start to do them, you have to think about them,
really direct each part of the action? Like riding a bike.
The more you do it, practice and all, the less you have
to think about it. You run through it a certain number
of times; then something in your brain clicks—says,
"Hey, I've got this down now." You develop coordina-
tion. The thing you're doing goes from being totally
conscious and requiring effort to being unconscious or
subconscious or whatever.

It happens with photography, with learning to use a
camera.

I was starting to build up quite a file of contact sheets.
I kept them all in folders with my prints, in the bottom
drawer of the rolltop desk. I had a thick wad just of
Melissa. Maybe I was going overboard a little, but it
felt great to kind of witness my own skill growing.

My eyes were starting to work differently. I was starting to see things differently. For instance, I was walking
downtown one afternoon, strolling along, cropping
scenes in my head, framing them with my eyes. I saw
a lady, very well dressed, laden with boutique shopping
bags, heading for her Jaguar in the parking lot. There
was a dog sniffing around the garbage cans behind

Wong Fat's Golden Pagoda. Who'd normally notice stuff like that? Or care?

A photographer, that's who. I sensed the potential for an interesting juxtaposition. A symbolic contrast of visual elements. I watched, I waited, this excitement kicked in—then the lady and the dog were in the same frame. Another part of my brain started whirring, saying wait, wait, not yet, the composition's not right. I took a step to shift the angle of view: There was the shot—*snap click!*

I started developing this three-way connection: eyes and brain—camera—the world.

.   .   .

I was sitting in the cafeteria with Ricky one day the next week, cleaning my fifty-millimeter lens. Melissa and I hadn't started sitting together at lunch yet, the way a lot of couples did. The cafeteria's pretty public, and I think we both wanted to shelter our relationship from the comments of our peers. I know I did, anyway. Like a private place apart from the world and all the bozos in it.

Ricky was about halfway through a limp slab of soggy school pizza when I noticed the paper was still on it. They cover the cheese with this thin tissue paper that's supposed to keep it from sticking to the plastic wrap; so the cheese sticks to the paper instead, but the pizza grease makes it kind of transparent. It really blends right in because the cheese is kind of grayish, anyway.

"Hey, Rick, aren't you going to take the paper off your pizza?" I said.

He took another bite and I grimaced on his behalf. "What paper?" he mumbled.

I leaned over and peeled up a corner. "This paper."

Ricky was truly astonished. "When did they start putting paper on the pizza?"

"I hate to tell you, but they always have," I said.

He stared at the pizza in his hand as if worms had come crawling out of it, then squashed it into a ball and dropped it on his tray. He wiped his hands on a napkin, ran his fingers through his hair, and I could see him looking around the room for a diversion to cover his embarrassment.

He zoned in on Victoria, who was sitting at a table across the aisle with one of her sidekicks, Debbie Raymond.

"Watch this. Hey, Victoria."

She looked over lazily.

"I got your message, babe. Sorry, I'm already booked for Saturday night. Maybe some other time," he said, loudly enough to be heard halfway across the cafeteria.

Victoria leaned forward. The front of her shirt scooped open, and I have to admit, it afforded a breathtaking view. Not that I was interested. But I could see

Ricky's hormones hop a few notches, in spite of his basic animosity toward her.

"In your dreams, toad turd," she said. "And in my nightmares." The look she gave him would have withered a lesser ego like a raisin.

Ricky grinned. "I think she loves me." Then he winked at Debbie Raymond, who was eyeballing him with interest. Debbie's fairly pretty, but there's no subtlety about her. She wears too much makeup; she dresses according to the latest party line of the fashion fascists. No originality. I think Victoria hangs around with her because she makes a good foil—not that Victoria really needs one.

"How come you always have to bug her?" I asked Ricky. "Why don't you just let it go?"

"It's a hobby," he said. He was escalating his nonverbal signals to Debbie into more complicated facial expressions—seductive leers and the like. "People need hobbies. Like you, with this photography thing."

Maybe if my mother hadn't been on my case so recently, I wouldn't have reacted so strongly.

"Photography's not a hobby with me. I'm serious about it," I said a little coldly. I gave the lens a last swipe with the lens tissue, then fitted it back on the camera.

Ricky briefly interrupted his activity and flicked me a glance.

"You're just doing it because your old man took off. You carry that camera around with you like some kind of security blanket. It's some kind of psychological substitute thing. Look, she wants me."

"That's bullshit." I wanted to punch him.

He wasn't really listening to me. "No, look. I think she really does. I think I'm gonna ask her to the Junior Harvest Dance at the country club. That'll kill Victoria. She's dying to be seen up there."

"I'm talking about the photography," I said. "And my father. That's a load of crap."

Ricky gave me a "whatever you say, pal, but I think what I think" look and shrugged.

"Fine. So it's crap. My mistake." He changed the subject. "So, what do you think, should I ask Debbie out or what? I heard she's really hot."

"Do whatever you want to do," I said. I was still pissed off.

I forced the frown off my face when Melissa suddenly materialized next to our table.

"Hi," she said to Ricky, then turned to me. "Did you check your work schedule? Are we still on for the darkroom today?"

"Uh, yeah, fine," I said. "I'll get the key from Dorio after last period and meet you down there, okay?"

"Great. See you." She gave me a private smile, Ricky a friendly one, and walked away.

I started to clean up the trash on the table. I could feel Ricky's curiosity.

"You sly dog, you," he said.

I shrugged.

"So, you're spending the afternoon in a *dark room* with Melissa Ryan, the goddess of good grades, defender of frogs, huh? Sounds very cozy."

I was surprised he knew who she was, but I shouldn't have been, with the catalog of women he keeps in his head.

I shrugged again. "We have to work in pairs."

"I bet you do." He smirked. Then I guess he could see that this wasn't something I was going to joke about. "You have a thing going with her?"

"Not a thing, really." I crossed some mental fingers, trying to figure out why I was so reluctant even to talk about Melissa with Ricky. I mean, he was my best friend. "We've just gone out a few times, that's all."

"Superlative. Way to go, Madman." But there wasn't any oomph in his congratulations, and I knew his feelings were hurt.

When Ricky's upset about something, he turns into a bundle of nervous energy. I could see he was getting agitated as he took out his comb, combed his hair, put the comb away, and started scanning the cafeteria.

Victoria was leaning over a trash can, emptying her tray. Ricky has magic reflexes. It's what makes him so good at sports. He picked up the balled-up pizza and went for the shot. It was good!

"Two points." He grinned as Victoria looked down her shirt in total disgust. She tried to fish it out but only poked it farther in. We both scrambled for the exit before she could retaliate, busting our guts laughing.

"One point," I wheezed. "That was a *foul* shot!"

.   .   .

The only time the darkroom is completely dark is when exposed film is transferred from the camera to the developing spool and case. After that, you work with an amber safelight that won't affect the print paper.

The part of the whole process I like best is developing prints, seeing if I caught what I hoped I did on film. It's almost a ritual process—setting up the chemical trays, everything orderly, everything ready for the image to be born.

The enlarger works basically like a slide projector; it projects the negative image onto the print paper, and has a lens you can focus and a timer that sets how long you want the paper exposed to the lighted image. It also has a knob that lets you ride the whole apparatus up and down on a column—the closer it is to the paper, the smaller the picture, and vice versa.

Printing paper looks white, but it's coated with a light-sensitive silver compound. You set the paper on the enlarger platform, called the easel, and strap the edges down flat with the easel bars, like metal rulers. You expose the paper to your negative for X number of seconds. Then the good part starts.

When the exposed paper is in the developer bath, the chemicals in it change the light-exposed silver compound into metallic silver. The picture slowly materializes—like those almost-instant Polaroids, but it's much more impressive in black and white, in the glow of the safelight. It can be a little eerie.

Then you go through the rest of the procedure: stop bath to stop the chemical action of the developer, two fixer baths to get rid of undeveloped and unexposed particles on the paper, wash bath, then into the print dryer.

The week before, Melissa and I had both developed our film and done our contact sheets—eight-by-tens with negative-size prints of every shot on the roll. Printing paper is pretty expensive, and it's hard to tell just from looking at a negative itself whether or not it's worth blowing up. The contact sheets help a lot.

Now we turned the light on to take a good look at the contacts and pick our prints. I thought I had a few good ones of Melissa, and she had a couple of great ones of me. The first two shots on my roll were the ones I took of the TV Guidance Counselor at Thumm's. I leaned over with my magnifying loupe for a closer look at the second one—the one where she was staring right at me—and a chill snaked up my spine. I mean, not to brag, but I thought it had a bit of an Arbus-like quality to it—that breaking through surface appearances to some kind of psychological exposure. The curiosity in her gaze was so intense, it was almost alien.

I straightened up and pointed. "What do you think of that one?"

Melissa squinted at it. "Is that Mrs. Fattiben?"

"Uh-uh." I handed her the loupe.

"Oh. No, it's not. Wow." She kept looking. "Who is she?"

"This lady who comes into the store all the time. There's something wrong with her. Ricky calls her the TV Guidance Counselor."

"Why?" Melissa asked.

"She comes in all the time and checks out the *TV Guides*, then leaves. Never buys one. It's weird. Do you think the lighting's okay?"

"It looks good to me. Make a print," Melissa suggested.

I did, of both shots, the one of her scoping out the *TV Guide* and the one of her scoping out me. When they were dry, Melissa and I stood there, staring at them.

"What do you suppose she's looking for?" Melissa asked softly.

"I don't know." My excitement about the second picture suddenly turned into this sadness, I'm not sure why. I was sad for all the searchers who never find what they're looking for, sad for my father and my mother and Amanda, sad for me. "I don't even know what I'm looking for."

Melissa put her arms around me. "Maybe you're looking too hard. Maybe what you want is closer than you think."

Even Melissa's arms around me didn't hug away the sadness. I mean, I felt like crying. But I didn't want her to think I was a total wimp. What I said came out harder than I intended.

"You mean it's right in my own backyard? Forget it. That Wizard of Oz crap doesn't work in real life."

Melissa dropped her arms and stepped back, as if my words were wasps and they'd stung her.

I put my hand over my eyes and tried to break out of the mood.

"I'm sorry. It's just—I'm sorry," I said. I pulled her back and she let me, but it was like we were holding each other through a heavy curtain.

.   .   .

Saturday Fritz had me on for the two-to-eight shift, so I slept late. Well, if you could call it sleeping. Amanda was watching cartoons and my mother was in a telephone mood. It made for some pretty weird dreams, incorporating Daffy Duck with my mother's side of a conversation with her mother. "I have no clue what he thinks he's looking for, Mother. It obviously isn't a home and a family life." "Thatth deth-picable!" Wabbit season. Duck season. Dad season.

Three toots on a car horn and the kitchen door slamming blew me out of dreamland for good. It was Ricky, and he was psyched about something.

"Madman, great, you're not working. Get dressed quick. The pep rally starts at eleven."

"Don't you believe in telephones?" I mumbled.

"Your line's been busy all morning."

"What time is it?" I pulled the quilt over my head.

Ricky tugged it off. "It's almost nine. Hurry, would ya?"

I rolled over. "I'm not going to the pep rally. I gotta go into work at two."

There was a big pep rally planned for the day, an annual thing they do before the Eastfield/Yardley football game. There's cider and doughnuts, the cheerleaders do their act while the team does warm-ups on the field, and then everyone who's going to the game forms a motorcade over to Yardley, which is the next town east of Eastfield. The game's always held there because Yardley has a stadium. It's an archrival deal, even big-

130

ger than the Thanksgiving game, with alumni showing up and all. The cars are decked out in purple and gold streamers, the Mohegan colors, and everyone honks and screams war cries all the way.

Ricky wouldn't give up. "Geez, it's like a tomb in here. It's not healthy." He pulled back the closed curtains, and sunlight flooded the room. "Come on, this is really important. I need you to take some pictures."

That grabbed my attention. "Of what?"

"You'll see."

When Ricky gets cryptic, it's usually a sign trouble is brewing in his devious brain. "I can't," I said.

"Please, Madman. Do I ask you for many favors?" I groaned. He doesn't, it's true, but guilt trips for purposes of manipulation are supposed to come from parents, not friends. "Look, I'll even pay you. We're talking about chronicling one of the high points in my life. You'll be the official photographer of the event."

When he offered to pay me, I felt pretty cheesy.

"You don't have to pay me." I sat up. "Let me hop in the shower and—"

But Ricky was on the move. "There's no time. I have to get things set before everyone shows up." He grabbed my jeans from the chair where I'd hung them, and flung them at me. "Hustle."

I threw on some clothes, grabbed a banana for breakfast and my camera, waved to my mother, and followed him out the door. He peeled out like an ambulance driver.

"So what's the deal?" I asked as I started to open a fresh roll of film.

"Here. Use color. This occasion calls for Kodak." He pulled a box of film out of his pocket and tossed it on my lap.

"I can't develop this. Color photog—"

"That's okay, I'll get it developed. Just wait, Madman. This'll be a pep rally Mohegan'll never forget."

The rally is held at Mohegan's football field. The team hoists effigies of Yardley players over the goalposts, the cheerleaders whip up the crowd, the team does its drills until it's time to get on the bus. With the perfect weather, there was sure to be a good turnout.

Ricky pulled the car around onto the dirt road behind the field, an old access road that nobody uses since they paved the new parking lot, except for parking—makeout parking.

"In case we have to make a quick getaway." He winked at me.

By now, I must admit, my curiosity was peaking. We got out of the car and Ricky opened the trunk. The first thing he pulled out was a life-size female inflatable rubber doll. I leaned against the car, my eyebrow raised, as he blew it up. It was anatomically correct in every detail.

"Where'd you get that?" I asked.

"Mail order. It wasn't cheap." Next he pulled out a wig of long, straight honey-blond hair and glued it to the doll's head. I was starting to get the picture. Then came a pair of those hairy purple and gold paper things cheerleaders wave around. He tied them to the doll's hands.

"Don't tell me. Victoria's," I said.

Ricky nodded. "Tsk, tsk," he said. "Wouldn't you think with her old man a cop, he'd teach her to lock her car doors?" He was rummaging in the trunk again. He came up with the purple bra he'd copped off the Kaminskys' clothesline. "I knew this would come in handy sooner or later." On it went. The cups were a little wrinkled; the doll wasn't quite as well-endowed as Victoria. Ricky grabbed a few handfuls of dried grass to fill them out.

"And now, the finishing touch." He pulled a purple Magic Marker from his pocket and started writing on the legs in big block letters running from thigh to ankle, one word to a leg: VICTORY AAHHHH!

"What do you think?" Ricky stood the doll up.

I thought it was pretty rude. "What about under-pants?"

Ricky snapped his fingers. "I knew I forgot something. Wait a minute. Here, hold her." He shoved the doll at me. I couldn't look it in the eye.

He started digging around in the trunk. "Bingo!" he shouted a minute later, pulling out an old pair of grungy jockey shorts. Don't ask me what they were doing in his trunk. "These'll have to do."

He pulled them over the rubber legs and they sagged around the rubber butt, so he added a few blobs of Krazy glue. I guess it was better than nothing. But I was beginning to have some reservations about the stunt. "What are you gonna do with it?"

"Watch me." He winked again. He trotted toward the field and I followed with my camera. Beside the goalpost he turned, put his arm around the doll, and grinned.

"Take a few shots before she goes up."

Up? But I snapped a few. Then he went over to the flagpole at the end of the field. He dropped the doll and lowered the flag.

"Here, help me fold this. Careful, Madman, don't let it touch the ground." I had to laugh as I helped him fold Old Glory; I guess the influence of an ex–Navy man for a father can go pretty deep. He laid the triangle on the base of the flagpole. Then he tied the doll to the rope and hoisted away.

"What do you think?" he asked again.

"I think you're a very sick pup," I said, feeling more and more dubious about the wisdom of the whole scheme.

People were starting to come in down at the other end of the field. Real quick, Ricky tied a series of wicked knots in the rope. "Take a shot quick, then let's go around and come in with everyone else. This will have to remain an anonymous gesture of school spirit."

"Like Victoria's not gonna know who did it," I said, focusing on Ricky's victory mascot and taking another picture. Actually I was curious to see what effect different exposures would have on the color, so I bracketed.

"Hey, she'll never be able to prove it," he said as we sprinted to the car.

"What if her old man dusts it for fingerprints or something?"

For a second, Ricky looked doubtful, as if he'd neglected to take that possibility into account. Then he shook his head.

"Nah. My prints aren't on record anywhere. Couldn't match 'em. Besides, what's he gonna book me for? Can you see the headlines? 'Purloined Pom-Poms!' "

We drove back to the main entrance. People were packing in through the gate. No one's attention was on the flagpole yet, because all the action was at the other end of the field.

"You just mill around and take some snaps for me, okay? Thanks a heap, Madman. I owe you one." Ricky grinned, gave me a thumbs-up, and disappeared into the throng.

I took my camera and set to work.

Snap click. The cheerleaders jogging out, Victoria with a smile pasted on her lips but a watchful, suspicious glare in her eyes. She had a pair of pom-poms, although one unhappy-looking sophomore didn't; I guess Victoria had pulled rank.

Snap click. The team, suited up, running onto the field, grunting and hooting.

Snap click. Bleachers full, purple and gold banners waving, everyone standing as the band kicked into "America the Beautiful."

Snap click. The whole crowd going wild and pointing toward the flagpole.

Snap click. Victoria breaking out of a pyramid formation as the crowd started chanting, "Victory—aahhh! Victory—aahhh!"

Snap click. The principal and some teachers struggling with the knots while the doll danced and bobbed, her pom-poms and other things shaking in the breeze.

And Ricky on the sidelines, basking in the glow of one of his finest moments, grinning like a fox in a henhouse.

.   .   .

Mr. Dorio had our portrait portfolios ready to hand back on Monday. He slapped the stack of folders down on his desk, then started pacing up and down the aisles.

"By and large, very few of you gave me what I was looking for with this assignment. And what was that?"

He stopped pacing and waited, but no one ventured an opinion.

"Personal revelation. Something beyond a superficial representation of a face. I've seen mug shots that were more revealing than some of these."

A few kids chuckled nervously, in case that was a joke, but I wasn't sure it was. Mr. Dorio is intensely serious about photography. A bit fanatical, you might say.

"A portrait should reveal some truth—a psychological truth about an individual, a universal truth about humanity," he went on. "It should suggest something, pose a question or answer one. It should tell me something beyond the fact that someone has a wart on his nose. Now, you can achieve this in a number of different ways. Anyone care to hazard a guess as to some of them?"

Leslie Goldman raised her hand. "By the kind of lighting you use?"

"Lighting, good. Shadows might suggest darkness in the soul. Bright sunlight might suggest innocence. What else?"

"How about the setting?" someone else said.

"Setting, another weapon in your arsenal when you go out on a shoot. Take a picture of someone standing on the edge of a cliff—which I'm *not* recommending any of you do. It could give the impression of limitless freedom or of someone psychologically on the edge. What else? Anyone?"

Feet shifted and papers shuffled, but there were no takers.

"How about props? How about costumes? What kind of irony would it imply if I took a picture of Mr. Universe wearing a loincloth, having trouble unshelling a peanut?"

He waited for the laughs to die down.

"Okay. So, you, as a photographer, have tools at your disposal with which you can set up a portrait so it's more than a candid snapshot, more than 'Billy goes to Disney World' in the family album."

He turned and started writing on the board.

"You, the photographer, bring something to the portrait, too. Your *idiosyncratic mode of regard.*"

The class was buzzing a little. I think Mr. Dorio was starting to lose some of the kids. I don't know what the guy behind me was doing, but all of a sudden the chalk in Mr. Dorio's hand was a high-speed projectile whizzing over my head. I heard it crack against the back wall. Total silence. Mr. Dorio's not very tolerant of inattention. He went on talking as if nothing had happened.

"As I was saying, you bring your idiosyncratic mode of regard to every picture you take, your personal way of looking at things. It evolves from your insights about life, the experiences that have shaped your attitudes, your point of view. No one else sees things quite the way you do."

He looked out the window and seemed to be groping for some way to get through to us.

"When you assemble the elements of a photograph in your viewfinder, you make choices—split-second, sometimes subconscious, choices. You frame an image and ideally provide a context for understanding that image and what it means to you. For communicating."

Letting out a slight sigh, he looked around the class to see if his words had connected. I guess he drew some blanks, because his shoulders slumped. Then he took the stack of folders, held one back, and put the rest on the shelf by the door as the bell rang.

"Pick up your folders on the way out. Start thinking about topics for your photo essays. Architectural contact sheets due on Friday. Michael Madden, see me before you leave."

I gulped and looked at Melissa.

"What did you do?" she asked over the school's-out stampede.

"I don't know," I said. I leaned closer to her and sniffed. She was wearing this perfume that made my mouth water.

"Michael!" she whispered, and blushed. "Listen, my parents want to meet you. Can you come for dinner on Saturday?"

"Will it taste as good as you smell?" I asked.

She shook her head at my one-track mind, but smiled. "I promise it won't be tuna fish, anyway."

Melissa left and I stalled for a few moments, waiting for the classroom to clear out before I went up to Mr. Dorio's desk.

"Are you good or are you just lucky?" he asked me.

I raised an eyebrow. I wasn't sure what I was supposed to say. He pulled the second Janey Riddley picture out of my folder.

"This is almost excellent," he said slowly.

Coming from Mr. Dorio, that was practically calling it a masterpiece. Needless to say, but I'll say it anyway, I was very pleased.

He eyeballed it some more; then his beard moved toward a smile.

"You caught it—the moment—a barrier broken through. But the print needs work. I want you to do a test print of multiple exposures to get the exposure perfect. The contrast needs sharpening—what kind of filter did you use?"

"A number two, I think."

"Try a three. And burn in this area here, to bring out the detail in the *TV Guide*. Make sure your enlarger focus is pin sharp. This picture deserves the best darkroom technique you can give it."

I nodded.

"Can you have prints to me by Friday? *Photo Magazine* is sponsoring a student competition. Winning pictures will be printed in the January issue. I want to submit this."

I almost fell over backward. *Photo Magazine* is big time. I could see myself sending off some copies to Dad, slipping in a casual note about how if he needed an assistant on his next assignment . . .

"Uh, sure, yeah. No problem," I stammered.

"Good." Mr. Dorio slipped the print back in my folder and handed it to me. "Good."

I tried not to look too cocky as I took it, but as I left the room, my face almost split from smiling.

TEN

I remember a moment: I don't know why it made an impression on me, but it did. I kind of marked it in my mind at the time. Mom was pregnant with Amanda, so I was nine. Dad wasn't traveling much; he hadn't really gotten into marine photography yet, plus it was winter. We were all just in the house together, puttering around, doing our separate things, but together.

And I remember being happy—and being consciously aware that I was happy—just to be in a normal, regular, more or less Leave It to Beaver *family. It felt very comfortable, very safe, like lying in a hammock stretched between two people who were both holding you up and who would never let you fall.*

After the divorce, it wasn't as if I felt this big swing toward abnormality in my life or anything. I mean, you can get used to almost anything, I suppose.

"Divorce may be common, but I wouldn't call it normal, Michael. At least, not in any ideal sense," Doc comments.

"So whose life is ideal?" I ask. "What are the statistics—something like half the kids in the country have divorced parents. What's the big deal?"

"Maybe it's a bigger deal emotionally than you've allowed yourself to realize. I would expect you to feel angry that your family has split apart."

I don't agree or disagree.

"Well," I say, "maybe it was never meant to be in the first place. Maybe my parents shouldn't have gotten married and had kids at all if they were going to give up after sixteen years."

"Maybe they shouldn't have." He's waiting, one of those pauses that always make me go on and say more than I intend to say.

"Maybe I'm just the by-product of a mistake."

"Is that what you feel like?"

"Yeah, kind of."

"How does it feel?"

Bad, I think. Heavy, like a camel with a lead hump. Sad, with an overlay of guilt.

*"You know that guy who wanted to shave a pound
of flesh off somebody?"* I say out loud.

Doc nods. "Shylock. Shakespeare. The Merchant of
Venice."

*"Yeah, well, that's how my mother looks at me some-
times. Like she wants to carve out the part of me that
I got from my father, half my genes. Like she hates half
of me."*

"Do you know what the judge ruled in The Merchant
of Venice?"

I shake my head.

*"That Shylock couldn't have his pound of flesh unless
he could manage to take it without spilling a drop of
blood."*

I didn't know that.

Going back to my old house was a mistake. I vaguely
suspected it might be before I went, but I talked myself
into it, anyway. Number one, I figured that with Ricky
living right next door, I'd have to go back sooner or
later, so I might as well get the weirdness over with.
Number two, we had an assignment to shoot a roll of
architectural shots. And number three, I kind of wanted
a souvenir, a formal portrait of my lost childhood
home, before the new owners started changing it, digging up gardens, putting up fences, painting it purple—
making it really theirs.

Right after school I rode my bike over. I wanted to take advantage of the late afternoon sunlight. It was a gorgeous day, crisp but not frigid, autumn foliage at its peak and all that. As I rode, I was on autopilot; the way back home was etched so deeply in my brain, I probably could have made it blindfolded. Hockey practice had started, so I didn't have to worry about running into Ricky and seeing him feel sorry for me.

I was pretty relaxed that day. I stopped at the foot of the driveway to scope things out. No one seemed to be home. No major changes in my house's appearance, except for a fancy new swing set in the side yard. I stood there looking for I don't know how long.

The leaves on the gnarly old Japanese cherry tree were crimson and orange, not falling yet. As I watched, my brain did this trick and turned it fluffy pink, the way it is every spring. If you climb into it, it's like sitting in a pink cloud. It was the first tree I ever climbed by myself, and I could practically see this ghost of the old me, ten or twelve years ago, pulling himself up, resting in the V of the twisted trunk. My body was feeling what it felt like to do that, a kind of physical memory.

I snapped back to the present when a tan Country Squire station wagon pulled around me into the driveway. It parked up by the house, and a lady got out and started unloading brown grocery bags while two kids tumbled out—boys, maybe five and seven—and started whooping it up on the lawn, as if they'd been sitting still too long. No one paid any attention to me; not that they would, in that neighborhood. People go for bike rides there all the time because it's so pretty, especially this time of year. I could have been any bike rider stopping for a rest. I could have been invisible.

The two little guys made a beeline for my tree. I watched them swing on the long low limb, then start climbing, and suddenly I was jealous of those kids. I wanted to run over and play with them—I wanted to be seven again and have my father run over and fool around with me—I was mad at him for what he had done to let all this be destroyed for us—I was mad at my mother for letting it happen, too. I missed my father, and—it was very weird—I missed myself, my old self, like a younger brother who had died.

It was too much to feel. I closed my eyes, shut down my brain for a moment. When I opened them again, it was like looking through a filter that flattened every-thing and deadened it. I didn't take any pictures. I just rode away.

I rode and rode, autopilot again, and found myself down at Mohegan Square. I kind of came back to myself and realized I still had this homework to do, so I started taking pictures of the market. I took a few close shots from different angles, then moved back to get some longer ones. I was figuring I'd go to the train station to finish up my roll of film, when I saw the TV Guidance Counselor come out of Thumm's. She was walking the way she always walked, small steps, not looking at her feet or at where she was going, her gaze fixed at a spot on the ground somewhere in front of her. As if she were listening to where she was going instead of looking.

She waited at the corner, not looking up when the light changed; she just seemed to know it was her turn to cross the street.

I don't know what made me do it, but I followed her. She took a right on the street behind Station Street, went past the cleaners, then took another right on a dead-end street near the entrance to the thruway, a street with mostly run-down two-family houses—probably the closest thing Eastfield has to a slum. She went almost to the end and turned in at a small gray house with a chain-link gate between two sections of neatly clipped hedge.

Like a robot, she opened the gate, closed it behind her, went up the front steps and in the front door. I stared, in kind of a trance. A minute later, I saw an older, skinny, gray-haired woman come out the door Janey'd gone in. Her face was expressionless, but in a normal way, as if detachment was a habit with her, not a permanent mental condition. She walked to the gate, got the mail from the mailbox, flipped the red flag down, and went back inside.

I stood there on the corner wondering what the rest of Janey Riddley's life was like.

I wondered if she ever actually watched television.

I wondered if there was some kind of security in her ironclad routine. No surprises, you know? Boring, maybe, but something you could count on.

.　　　.　　　.

When I went into work on Saturday, I gave Fritz a print of one of the market pictures. It was just a quick print I'd dashed off when I did the contact sheets.

"You have a fine eye for composition, Michael," he said. His finger traced one of the angles. "You've given my humble establishment the majesty of a cathedral."

That was an exaggeration, but Fritz really did seem pleased. He smiled at me as if he was proud of me.

"I'm better at portraits," I told him. Then I brought up something I'd been meaning to ask about—more hours. I'd given up on the idea of saving for a car. I was spending a lot on film and printing paper, not to mention dates with Melissa. But I'd seen this flash attachment that would fit my Nikon F2 at the camera store, and I really wanted it. So far, I'd managed to save only about half of the $150 I needed to buy it.

"Hey, Fritz, I was wondering if there's room on the schedule to work some extra hours. Both days on weekends would be fine, if, you know, someone else wants time off. I can cover for them or—if it's possible."

Fritz heard what I was saying between the lines: "I need more cash."

"Let me see what I can work out." He patted my shoulder, then checked out the print again. "I must run right over to the hardware store and get a frame for this fine piece of art. Thank you, Michael."

I went kind of red. "Well, I don't know if I'd call it art."

"What is art, Michael, but a human spirit meeting creation and resonating in harmony to create something new?" Fritz said.

"Yeah, I guess so," I said vaguely, trying to figure out what he meant.

He took off to get the frame for my art.

As I counted out the money in my drawer, I thought about what Fritz had said. My mind started meandering around the spirit thing. How do you define "human spirit"? A spark of energy that's the difference between alive and kicking or six feet under? A ghostly outline of a person that stretches as you grow? Is it the soul that primitive tribes think you're stealing if you take their picture? I started wondering if human spirit was conscious, conscious in a separate way from everyday consciousness. Can you get to the point where the two consciousnesses intersect, like a person waking up from a coma? Maybe spirit has a lot more to do with who someone really is than you'd think.

Anyway, that day the thought passed through my mind that photography was working on me as much as I was working on it. I was getting much more proficient technically. A few times when I saw an incredible shot coming, something kicked through me—a rush, an energy that almost hummed. I thought maybe that was what Fritz meant when he talked about spirit resonating.

As I was leaving work that afternoon, Carl handed me a brown bag. I peeked inside and saw four two-pound deli containers filled with different salads—egg-and-potato, three-bean, chicken salad, and coleslaw.

"I make new ones on Sunday morning," he said.

"Thanks, Carl." I patted my stomach. "I'm gonna weight three hundred pounds if I keep working here."

He chuckled, the first time I ever actually saw him laugh.

.   .   .

"What's that?" Mom asked as I put the bag on the table.

"Food from the deli," I told her.

"Oh, Michael. I feel so awful that you have to spend your hard-earned money—" she started to say.

"It's okay, it was free. Carl gave it to me."

I saw my mother go stiff. "I don't need anyone's charity," she said. She grabbed the bag and stuffed it on top of the already overflowing kitchen trash can.

"What are you doing? It's good food! Besides, Carl was just going to toss it." I couldn't understand what she was getting so huffy about. As far as I was concerned, food was food.

"Great. Just great. I certainly don't need anyone's unsalable leftovers." She was close to foaming at the mouth.

Somehow I managed to keep my own mouth shut. I was going over to Melissa's for dinner, anyway.

"Whatever." I shrugged and went to get ready.

.   .   .

Melissa lives on Mohegan Point, down on the Sound. The Point was once a peninsula, but the hurricane of '38 broke through to the creek, washing out the old road, and turning it into an island, at high tide, anyway. Now you reach it by crossing a narrow stone bridge. There's only one road, which winds all the way around the perimeter of The Point, so all the houses are waterfront properties. Melissa's house wasn't one of the really ritzy ones, the kind you find listed in the back of the Sunday *Times Magazine,* in what my mother refers to as "the real estate porn section." But it was very, very nice, in a tastefully modern way.

With both Melissa's parents being lawyers and with her being an only child and such a spectacular one at that, I really expected to get grilled over dinner. It didn't turn out that way at all. The only thing grilled was the teriyaki shrimp appetizer, and that was as close as anything came to tuna fish, too.

If I had to pick a word to describe the evening and the household, I think *harmonious* might come close. The food, the decor, which was understated but not sterile, the conversation—everything complemented everything else. Melissa's parents seemed so in tune with each other that they sometimes finished the other's thoughts, not in an interrupting way, more in a "know how you feel, feel the same" way.

After dinner, Mrs. Dupres-Ryan shooed us off. "Your father and I'll do the dishes, honey."

"Come on, let's go upstairs and listen to music or something," Melissa said.

I followed her, thinking to myself, Upstairs? As in, bedroom? If you don't ask, how will you know? So I asked.

"Your bedroom? Your parents don't mind if you bring a guy up to your bedroom?"

Melissa looked a little surprised. "Why should they mind? They trust me."

She must have followed my train of thought through to the station. "And I trust *you*," she added.

She didn't need to say any more. I was on my best behavior. Not that I wasn't tempted, but I didn't want to be the one to betray all that trust. Melissa and I had plenty of time. We'd go to college—if I kept my grades up, maybe the same college—we could live in married students' housing and I'd support her through med school—

I pushed *that* train of thought onto a sidetrack as soon as I realized how serious it sounded.

Melissa's room wasn't your typical frilly girlish room. Not that I'd been in a lot of girls' rooms, but I knew the stereotype: pink, ruffles, flowers, eighty ka-zillion stuffed animals. Her walls were painted soft gray. The curtains were lace, more sophisticated than sweet. The furniture was that white stuff with the gold trim, but she had only two stuffed animals, a worn-out old chimpanzee and a white bulldog. There was an expensive-looking telescope by one window. And over her desk, the wall was tiled with those corkboard tiles, but there were no rock stars or movie stars pinned up on it. There was a peaceful-looking poster of an indoor courtyard from the Isabella Stewart Gardner Museum, another one of scruffy ballet shoes, and five eight-by-tens of me!

"Oh." Melissa blushed when she realized they were there and that I'd noticed them.

I grinned. "Great decor," I told her. "You have wonderful taste."

She put on a classical tape. We sat on the floor and spent about an hour looking through the telescope. Melissa could name just about every star I pointed out.

"I don't want to overstay my welcome," I said when I noticed her clock said 10:13. I stood to stretch my legs.

Melissa nodded. I strolled over to her bulletin board for a last gander at the portraits. There was one I especially liked from that afternoon at the river—a shot of me from the waist up, shirtless, smiling as if I didn't have a care in the world.

"Why don't you take that one," Melissa offered.

"Are you sure?"

"It's okay. I have another print of it."

We grinned in unison.

"An original Melissa Ryan portrait. This could be valuable someday. Maybe you should sign it."

"It's valuable now, to me. Anyway, you're the one who's going to be famous. I overheard Mr. Dorio talking to Mrs. Fattiben."

I rolled my eyes. "Fatty-Bean was probably checking up on me. I practically had to promise to hand over my firstborn son to get into the course."

"Well," Melissa said, "Mr. Dorio said you were his most promising student."

I blew on my knuckles and polished an imaginary medal on my chest.

Melissa gave me a little shove and laughed. I caught her and pulled her close.

"I'm developing other talents, too," I said. I proceeded to demonstrate, but I ended up pulling away before she did. I really did want her to be able to trust me.

Downstairs, I thanked her parents. They were sitting together on one of the couches in the living room, with their heads bent over a wad of legal papers. Her father had his arm around her mother's shoulders. It was nice to see a married couple who liked each other.

.   .   .

I got home about eleven. I went in through the kitchen and automatically opened the refrigerator as I passed it. Inside were Carl's four salads. I guessed my mother had come to her senses. Either that or the tuna fish was getting to her, too.

Mom was lying on the couch—my bed—watching television. Nothing unusual there. I yawned, hoping she'd take the hint, but she didn't. Just the opposite, in fact. She straightened up and patted the cushion next to her.

"How was it?" she asked, and gave me a big smile.

"Great," I said. "Teriyaki shrimp, fillet of beef with

155

peppercorn sauce, roasted potatoes with some kind of herbs, watercress salad, and chocolate mousse parfaits for dessert."

I sat down and burped for punctuation.

"Oh," she said. I guess her tone could have been called deflated. Something told me I should have kept my big mouth shut.

I slipped the picture Melissa had given me into one of my notebooks in a pile on the floor next to the couch.

"Sorry I didn't bring home a doggie bag," I offered, trying to compensate for making her feel bad.

Conversational mistake number two got me the ice-cube treatment. I sighed and tuned in to the news. The sportscast was winding down.

And suddenly there he was, in glorious, slightly green color, J. Thaddeus Madden, standing next to a reporter.

"And here in Palma, Majorca, the festivities to cele-brate the end of the first leg of the Royale Rum Round the World Race have commenced. The winner of the first leg is the American boat *Hex*," the reporter an-nounced.

In the background, I could see the boat tied up to the dock, which looked as if it were about to sink from the number of people on it—sailors, newspeople, and hordes of the boat groupies Dad calls "racer chasers."

Dad looked tanned, windblown, and like his quest for happiness had paid off in spades.

"With me is J. Thaddeus Madden, world-famous marine photographer, a member of the *Hex* crew." The camera got jostled and it pulled back as it steadied, just in time to reveal a very voluptuous blonde, maybe in her twenties, sneak her head under my father's arm, then reach up and pour a glass of champagne over his hair.

"Tell me, J.—is that what people call you, J?"

Mom suddenly broke out of her stunned-doe-in-the-road trance.

"Bastard! That's what I call you, you son of a—" She was in a frenzy, almost falling off the couch, pushing buttons on the remote control. The TV went black.

"Hey," I shouted. I wanted to see the rest of it. I leaned over the coffee table and snapped the television back on.

"A little rough weather, but the lads pulled together," Dad was saying to the moronic grinning nods of the bozo with the microphone.

Mom stepped past me with frozen calm. She grabbed the cord and pulled the plug. I couldn't say anything, because she was glaring at me with this intense hatred I'd never seen her aim at anyone but my father.

. . .

Usually at night, I imagine myself to sleep. I mean, I think about something, put myself in a scene, and kind of watch my own bedtime story inside my head until I drift off. Lately it was mostly stories of me and Melissa.

That night, though, I was really agitated, and thinking about Melissa didn't calm me down. It wound me up even more, scratched this itch of a need to see her until it felt like an open sore. It was way too late to call, but I was going crazy. Finally, about three in the morning, I couldn't stand it anymore. I got up, got dressed, grabbed my jacket, and slipped out the back door. It wasn't rational, but I really felt that seeing Melissa was the only thing that could fix me.

If I'd been thinking clearly, I might have taken my bike; it's about two and a half miles from my house to the Ryans'. Instead, I just started walking. The moon was up, not full, but enough to make the night seem friendly. I went past the market, over the railroad tracks, and headed down Mohegan Point Road for the second time that night. I wasn't thinking anymore, just walking, as if a giant magnet were pulling me along.

Once I got there, the reality of it kind of hit me and I got a little nervous. I hoped no one would see me and mistake me for a prowler, although technically that's what I was, I guess.

Next to the rhododendron bush in Melissa's front

yard, I stopped, feeling a little stupid. I mean, if I couldn't call her, I sure as hell couldn't march up and ring the front doorbell. But the need was bigger than anything else, so I picked up a few pieces of gravel from the driveway and edged around the house till I was under her window. Her light went on as the third pebble hit the glass.

"Melissa, it's me," I whispered, as loudly as I could, once I saw her face. I stepped back on the grass so she could see me in the circle of light from the garage spotlight. She didn't answer, just disappeared. I retreated into the shadows, not having a clue what to do next. I waited.

A few minutes later, I heard the back door open and heaved a sigh of relief. Melissa walked across the lawn. I walked to meet her. She was wearing a bulky sweater over a flannel nightgown and sneakers on her feet. Her expression was questioning, but not angry.

"Michael? What is it? What's wrong?"

Now that I was with her, things didn't seem so wrong. Everything that was bothering me—my mother, my father, the whole situation—started to subside.

"Tell me," Melissa was urging.

I pulled her near and closed my eyes and stood still, holding her until there was nothing in my head, no thoughts, no worries. Only the two of us, standing on the grass, under the moon, in the middle of the night.

"I'm okay now," I whispered. "I just needed to see you." I kissed her. "I love you."

Then I turned and sprinted off.

ELEVEN

"Hey, Doc, why don't you ever have me look at ink blobs or play shrink games?" I ask. I don't feel like having a heavy session today. I'm not up for emotional dredging. I'd rather take a nap, but they don't let you sleep during the day around here. Roger, one of the psychiatric aides on the ward, said sleeping during the day can be a sign of depression. I don't see why a little nap is any big deal. Still, I don't really have the energy to buck the system.

"Would you like to try some free association?" Doc asks casually, but with a gleam in his eye. He may have a trick up his sleeve. "You know how it works? I say a word; you say the first thing that—"

"Right, right. Supposed to free things stuck in the subconscious." I may be a wacko, Doc, but I'm not a moron.

He scans his notes for a minute, then picks up a pad and pen.

"Photographer."

"My father."

He notes my answer.

"Photograph."

"Camera."

"Lens."

"Um, focus."

"Vision."

"Sight."

"Eye."

"Detached retina."

He's been going along very smoothly, but that answer pulls him up short. "Detached retina?"

"Yeah, I had one once. Freshman year. I was at a hockey game and Ricky got off a slap shot—it went over the cage, over the Plexiglas—and popped me right in the eye. I saw flashes of light every time I moved my eye."

Flashes of light. I start to see the TV Guidance Counselor again, right after I took the first flash shot. I wonder what she thought she was seeing. . . .

I give my head a little shake to dislodge the image.

Doc's waiting.

"God," I say. "I thought I was catching glimpses of God."

He smiles. "I see. Well, then. Detached."

Detached. Attached. You get too attached and you risk losing something. You get too detached and you float away; there's nothing to anchor you, to ground you. You keep trying to find the balance, but in the end, you wind up not caring one way or the other. It's just too hard.

"I see," Doc says.

I jump a little. I didn't realize I'd said that out loud.

"Sometimes quitting is the easiest thing to do," Doc goes on. I sense an attempt to lead me somewhere else.

"I didn't say I quit."

He accepts that, shuffles a few papers, then zings one out of the blue.

"I guess that's what your father did when the responsibilities of marriage and parenthood got too difficult. He quit trying. He stopped caring."

"He cares about me and Amanda!" The comment really pisses me off.

Doc gives me a that-might-be-debatable look.

"Do you hate him for leaving?"

I'm sputtering. "Of course I don't—how can you hate your own father? Anyway, he couldn't take it if he thought I hated him."

163

"Do you mean he's too weak to stand it if you hate him?"

"I didn't say that."

"So you turn all that hatred on yourself."

"I didn't say that!"

I'm totally confused. "All right, you want me to say it? I'll say it. I hate the son of a bitch for walking out, for letting us end up like this."

Doc pushes the Kleenex over.

I don't understand how the conversation got turned around to this. I don't understand what it has to do with everything else. But I feel like somebody's lifted an anvil off my chest.

Melissa didn't mention my nocturnal visit specifically when I saw her in class on Monday. All she said was, "Are you okay?" I told her I was fine. I felt fine, as if I'd vented some steam from the pressure cooker.

Nobody was around when I got home from school. Mom had given me the silent treatment since our fight, so when I heard the car pull in the driveway, I kind of held my breath. The back door slammed and Amanda came running into the dining room, where I was working on an English report due the Friday before.

"Michael, Michael, look what I got!" She looked happier than a pig in a mud puddle as she held up this very fancy sweat suit, pink with sequins and lace all over it. Definitely not bargain basement merchandise. "And I got socks to match and fancy barrettes and a new jacket, too."

The door banged shut again, followed by the sound of rustling paper bags. Lots of them. Mom came in and dumped an enormous armload of shopping bags on the other end of the table. She was smiling normally, so I guess she'd forgiven me. But looking at all that stuff made me a little nervous.

"What's the occasion?" I tried to sound casual.

"No occasion. We needed some things." She was emptying the bags and starting to sort stuff into piles. "Just a little shopping."

I raised my eyebrow. Calling that mound a little shopping was like calling the Taj Mahal a little cottage. She slid a shoebox down the table toward me.

"Here, honey. New sneakers. You've been needing them."

It was true, I did, but it wasn't like the soles on my old ones were flapping off or anything. I opened the box and peeked at the price tag: 169 bucks. I swallowed hard.

"What's the matter? I had to go to three places to find your size. Don't you like them? The salesman said all the boys your age—"

"They're very nice." That wasn't it. I shook my head. "But—"

I closed my mouth when I saw it coming, the mood swing toward the ugly side of hysterical.

"If *your* father can go gallivanting off around the world, showering in champagne with some little blond bimbo, living *the* life, I think we're entitled to some decent clothes."

Her voice gained in volume as she picked up steam.

"I've lost my home, I've lost my husband, I've lost most of my friends who used to be *our* friends. I'm *not* going to lose my self-respect."

Amanda was standing there hugging her new sweat suit.

Don't say it, you'll be sor-ree, a warning voice was singsonging in my head. But my internal brakes weren't strong enough to halt the remark.

"You're going to lose something else when the bills for all this stuff come in—your credit rating."

Mom's hand slashed through the air, but I blocked the slap with my forearm. She stood there, looking at me as if I were a convicted felon. Then tears welled up in her eyes, and she ran into the bedroom and slammed the door. I felt lower than a snake's navel.

"How come you always fight with Mommy?" Amanda said. She sounded sadder than any six-year-old kid should ever sound.

I had been staying away from the house as much as I could, because it was just too depressing to hang around. Fritz had given me some more hours during the week, which meant that most nights I got a decent dinner. I felt a little guilty about leaving Amanda to the mercy of the tuna cans, but I couldn't help it. Some days I stayed late, helping Carl mop up the deli. Though Carl doesn't say a lot, he has a very restful presence. Nonjudgmental. He just let me be.

That last Tuesday in October, Fritz came down the aisle where I was stocking the soup section.

"Michael, it's a perfect afternoon for fishing. But I have a mountain of paperwork that demands my attention. Would you like to go with Carl?"

"Yeah, sure, Fritz," I said. "But there're five more cartons out back and—"

Fritz dismissed them with a wave of his hand. "They can wait. This may be the last chance this season. When the water turns cold, the bluefish migrate. Just finish what you've begun here. Carl's waiting in the deli."

So we went, Carl and I. He lent me a jacket and a pair of rubber boots to wear. As we headed down the river, toward the mouth of the Sound, a flock of Canada geese flew overhead in V formation, honking signals to one another as they worked their way south. The sun was getting low, tinting the sky this pale, peaceful pink. I was totally relaxed. Carl seemed to be, too, as if he was in his own element.

I hadn't spent much time on the water in years. My father used to take me out on the Sound a lot, on this old Sunfish we had, before he got hooked into the big-time sailing league. I hadn't even realized I'd missed it, being on a boat.

Carl spoke up as if he'd tuned right in to what was on my mind. "I like boats."

"Me, too," I said.

He stepped aside and motioned for me to take over the controls. I steered us under the railroad bridge, keeping to the middle of the channel, then under the span of I-95, between huge concrete supports. The riverbanks seemed to slide by in slow motion, probably a combination of the tidal current, which was running against us, and being with Carl, the way he is.

"My father's on a boat," I said out of the blue, surprising myself. "He's sailing around the world."

"Your father's gone?" Carl said.

"Yeah. My father's gone." Usually I tried not to think about it. When I was forced to, it was most often in the context of an argument with my mother, so I'd be feeling mad. But that day, I just felt this quiet, swelling sadness.

Carl opened the tackle box and baited our hooks with pieces of fish, telling me how you had to use wire leaders for bluefish because their teeth are so sharp and they feed in frenzies, like sharks. Then he shot me a look tinged with anxiety.

"Don't fall overboard," he said.

His words resonated in my mind like a weird echo, like déjà vu. Then I remembcred. That was the last thing I said to my father before he left.

The tide was coming in fast—I could tell by the way the current pulled the lobster-pot buoys under, toward the river inlet. Carl scanned the horizon, then pointed at an area where a bunch of terns were wheeling over the water. I saw one dive down and come up with a small silver fish in its beak.

"Over thcre," Carl said softly. "Nice and slow."

I throttled down and headed over. As we got closer, I could see there was a roiling rough patch on the otherwise glassy surface of the water. It traveled slowly toward the mouth of the river like a miniaturc storm system. We circled the spot.

"The blues herd the bunkers toward the shallower water," Carl whispered. He reached across me and cut the engine as we drifted down on the patch.

All around the boat, little bunkers were popping up out of the water, doing evasive maneuvers. I felt kind of bad for them. They'd probably just been swimming

169

around on this peaceful afternoon, minding their own bunker business, when all of a sudden—watch out— red alert—survival struggle. I felt like I was doing them a favor, going after the blues.

We cast our lines and waited. A minute later, Carl spoke.

"My father's gone, too," he said. Then he patted me on the shoulder, in a kind of awkward imitation of the way Fritz does.

.　　　　.　　　　.

Once the hockey season starts, most of the varsity players eat together at the same table every day. It's some kind of team spirit, jock-bonding thing. They're a fairly rowdy bunch—Ring Ding slap-shot games, stuff like that. Since Ricky had made varsity, he was kind of obligated to sit with them. But it was okay with me, because Melissa and I had started to eat lunch together as our relationship intensified; it just happened naturally.

I hadn't been seeing much of Ricky at all, as a matter of fact. I hadn't really talked to him since giving him the film from the pep rally. He was keeping a fairly low profile at school. There'd been a lot of official rumblings over the P.A., requests for information leading to the apprehension of the culprit, an assembly about appropriate displays of school spirit. I'd been a little

worried about my part in the incident, taking the pictures. I had a feeling if Mr. Dorio knew, he might have
disapproved. I'd asked Ricky to keep the pictures to
himself, at least until the whole thing blew over. Everyone knew who had done it, but no one fingered Ricky
to the authorities. I was sure Victoria knew, too, but so
far she hadn't avenged herself. She was ignoring Ricky
totally, which seemed a bit ominous. I couldn't see her
letting it slide.

I wasn't exactly avoiding Ricky—now that we didn't
live next door to each other, we'd sort of drifted apart.
He'd stopped by the house a few times since the rally,
but I hadn't been around. I knew only because Mom
mentioned it, rubbing my nose in it a little when he
did her a favor, like putting up the storm windows.
He'd called, too, but I'd been pretty busy with photography and Melissa and work, so I hadn't called him
back.

The day after I went fishing with Carl, I was fooling
around with my camera in the cafeteria, doing this
mock shoot for advertising or fashion. Melissa was my
model. My unwilling model.

"Michael, would you put that thing down, please?"

I moved in for a close-up on a spoonful of yogurt
touching lips. Very sensuous.

"That's perfect. Love it. Could you turn your head
a little to the right?"

"Would you cut it out, please? I'm trying to talk to you."

She was getting irked, I could tell, but I kept going; I don't know why.

"I'm listening. Talk to me, baby." I kept clicking away.

"No you're not. Just stop. Stop, okay? You are *really* starting to get carried away with this."

Kids at nearby tables were looking over, and some of them were laughing. I guess I was just in a perverse mood and taking it out on Melissa. I hammed it up even more, slid off my chair onto one knee.

"Can you give me a little more anger? You're so sexy when you're angry."

Apparently that snapped the last straw of Melissa's patience. She stood up, almost knocking me over, and grabbed her books.

"Okay, okay, I'll stop." I blocked her way and she sat back down. "I'm sorry. Look, there's not even any film in it, see?" I opened the empty camera and showed her.

She frowned, shook her head, but finally smiled a tiny smile, like she guessed she'd tolerate me. Then she looked over my shoulder and smiled at someone else. I twisted around to see who. Ricky was standing there, running his fingers through his hair.

"So, Madman, been pretty busy lately, huh?"

"Yeah, pretty busy." I was uncomfortable. Feeling guilty, maybe. "Hey, thanks for putting up those storm windows for my mother. You don't have to do all that stuff, you know."

"Yeah. Well. Someone has to," he said in a somewhat pointed way. "But anyway, listen. Debbie and I are going to the Halloween Dance together this Saturday, and I thought maybe we could, you know, go together if you guys are going. Double or something. Whadaya say?"

It took me by surprise. I didn't even know he'd started going out with Debbie Raymond. I shot a quick glance at Melissa, who was smiling in a very friendly yeah-why-not kind of way. Before she could say anything, I cut her off.

"Geez, Rick, we'd really like to, but, uh, we have to go to this other thing that night. Some other time, though."

Ricky looked pissed off, and even more, he looked hurt. "Yeah, sure. Some other time." He walked away.

I could sense Melissa's disapproving stare without even looking.

" 'Go to this other thing'?" she echoed in my ear. "What's the matter with you?"

"Nothing. I just don't want to double with them, all right?" I knew I sounded ornery, but I just didn't want to do it.

"Michael, we need to talk," Melissa said quietly.

"Fine. I'm all ears," I mumbled. I started fiddling with the ASA setting on my camera.

She stared hard at me for a moment, then shook her head, frowning. "Where *are* you?"

I looked up, over my shoulder, all around. "In the cafeteria?"

"You know that's not what I mean."

I didn't want to think about what she meant. She didn't say anything else, just kept looking at me until I couldn't stand the questioning silence anymore.

"So what *do* you mean?" I asked.

She flinched a little at my voice, which sounded kind of hard, I guess, but she didn't back down.

"I know you're having problems with your family—"

"There's no problem," I cut her off. "My parents are divorced, remember? There *is* no family."

"You have a mother and a sister whom I've never even met, and I'd like to, by the way."

"Sure. Whatever. Sometime."

Melissa closed her eyes, and her face tightened up. "I can't stand it when you do this."

"What am I doing?"

"You're keeping me out. Whenever something's bothering you, you retreat into this . . . I don't know where you go. Inside yourself. And you won't let any-

174

one in. Not me, not your friends. I thought Ricky was your best friend."

I really wanted her to stop pushing the issue because it was getting me pissed off and I couldn't stand being mad at her.

"Look, Melissa, I know you're scientifically oriented and all, but there's nothing anybody can do about what's bothering me, and I don't want to dissect it, okay? I mean, what's the point?"

"Michael, I only want to help—"

"Don't help me, all right? Just love me." I got up and left her sitting there. I could feel myself getting ready to boil over, and I didn't want to take it out on her any more than I already had. And I couldn't stand any more of the let's-talk-about-it stuff.

The whole cafeteria turned and looked as she yelled after me:

"I *do* love you, you idiot. *That's* the point!"

.   .   .

Thursday and Friday that week I worked until closing. Friday afternoon and evening, traffic through the registers was nonstop. My mind wasn't on what I was doing. I don't know where it was, to tell you the truth. I overcharged a lady almost a hundred bucks for some steaks by hitting $99.90 instead of $9.99. I wouldn't

175

even have noticed that it was odd for her to owe $112.89 for six items if she hadn't made a little joke about the price of beef. She was very nice about the mistake; some people wouldn't have been.

Anyway, I was totally beat by the end of the night and was actually glad Melissa and I hadn't made plans to go out. After I closed out my register drawer and gave it to Fritz to count, I went to get my coat from the back. I was so exhausted, I wasn't even planning to stay and eat. But Carl had a meatball grinder and a paper plateful of egg-and-potato salad waiting for me, so I sat on a milk crate and took it.

As I ate, I watched Carl putting together a deli platter, one of his super-duper ones with cold cuts, cheese, and grapes in the middle. If I hadn't been so tired, I would have realized it was odd for Carl to be doing that after the store was closed. He kept looking over at me while he arranged slices of roast beef, ham, turkey, salami, and American and Swiss cheese in circular patterns on the foil tray.

Fritz came down from the office and handed me my paycheck envelope.

"You have things on your mind these days, Michael?" he asked very kindly.

"Yeah, I guess. Does it show?" I tried to smile.

"Your drawer was off by seventeen dollars tonight,"

he told me, not in a mean or angry way, more like concerned.

"Shi— I mean, shoot. I'm really sorry, Fritz. Was it short? You can take it out of my paycheck."

He patted my shoulder. "Not to worry. It happens now and then. Everyone gets tired. Why don't you take tomorrow off?"

"Are you sure?" I asked. "It's Halloween—it might get kind of crazy in here. People stocking up on candy."

"I'm sure." He nodded, turned to go, then paused and turned back. "You're a good boy, Michael."

A warm feeling washed over me. Somehow it was incredibly reassuring to hear Fritz say that, I don't know why.

I did feel a little better after I ate. As I was putting on my coat, Carl brought over the super-duper deli platter, all wrapped up in cellophane, and handed it to me.

"Special order," he said. "Never came to pick it up. You take it home." He nodded and blinked.

I think he was a little too slow to put it together that I'd watched him make up the whole thing after we closed, and knew it couldn't be a special order. But he wasn't too slow to try to make it seem like he wasn't doing me a special favor, so I wouldn't feel like a beggar or something. My mother might have had a point with her pride, but Carl was just so . . . so giving about it that I would have felt like a total crumb not taking it. As Ricky would say, Carl's not a rocket scientist, but when it comes to reading people's moods and feelings, he's a hell of a lot more talented than many people I know.

"Thanks a lot, Carl." I looked through the cellophane; it really was artfully arranged, for cold cuts. "You do beautiful work."

He blinked, nodded, and then smiled very shyly.

I was almost home when I realized that now, with a lot of the leaves gone from the trees, I could see the top floor of the market from where I lived. Silhouetted against one of the windows was Carl's spidery-thin shadow, looking out. I didn't know if he could still see me, but I waved.

.   .   .

The next day, Mom seemed to have thawed out from our latest argument. She even thanked me for bringing home the cold cuts, which I'd slipped into the refrigerator without telling her. She didn't complain when I said I was going out for the morning to shoot a few rolls of film.

What I actually did was cash my paycheck at the market and go downtown to the camera store for that flash attachment. I ended up spending more than I intended to, because I got a case for it, some lens filters, and a special kind of high-contrast printing paper I wanted to experiment with in the darkroom.

I got back around midafternoon. The house was all straightened, the dishes were done for a change, and I could hear the vacuum cleaner running in the bedroom. A big pot of beef stew was simmering on the stove. Things seemed kind of . . . normal. Homey. I thought it might be a good sign, like maybe we were finally starting to adjust.

While I unpacked the flash on the coffee table and put in the battery, Amanda hopped around in her Halloween costume. She was a pink bunny.

"Take my picture," she ordered. She crouched in a bunny pose and I took a few shots. Then I had this inspiration: I thought it might be an interesting juxtaposition if I superimposed the little girl/bunny costume picture with the picture I had of Victoria in her gym suit, the one I took that day we practiced bracketing. I hadn't done any fancy darkroom stuff like montages yet. I made Amanda pose some more, so I'd have enough to work with.

As Amanda hammed it up, Mom worked her way out into the living room. She switched off the vacuum cleaner near the couch and bent down to pick up a pile of my things, schoolbooks, mostly.

"Michael, how can I vacuum with your things all

over the floor?" she asked, but only with mild exasperation. It was something she might have said in the old days.

I focused on her and set the exposure. *Snap click.*

"Don't vacuum," I said. "It's an unnatural act."

"What?" she said. I snapped another shot.

"Nature abhors a vacuum." I caught her again as she chuckled. A picture of the Mom I used to know and get along with.

As she picked up some of the packing material from my new stuff, a slight frown crossed her face. She noticed the flash.

"Was that expensive?" she asked.

A shade of potential disapproval in her tone activated my defensive shields. "I paid for it with my own money."

She pursed her lips. "Honey, do you think it's wise to spend a lot of money on camera equipment when there are so many things we need?"

It just popped out before I could put a lid on it: "I need this more than I need a pair of $169 sneakers."

I matched her glare, even though I was thinking, You idiot, why don't you ever keep your big mouth shut? You want to borrow the car tonight—apologize, you dope, you.

Too late. She dropped my stuff back on the floor.

On impact, the print of myself that Melissa had given me slipped out of my notebook. Amanda hopped right on it.

"Look, Mommy, Michael's naked!" she squealed.

Mom snatched the picture before I could grab it. There was nothing left to do but brazen it out.

"Who took this picture?" Voice—liquid nitrogen, minus 200 degrees.

"A friend of mine."

"This Melissa person?" She sneered Melissa's name. "What kind of girl is she, taking nude pictures of you?"

"It's not what you think," I said through gritted teeth. "I was wearing pants. We were swimming. So don't go insulting her, because she's, she's . . ." I closed my eyes. I didn't want this conversation, these angry tones touching Melissa.

"If she's so wonderful, why haven't you brought her home and introduced her to your family?"

Maybe if the question hadn't been full of nasty innuendos, I wouldn't have been so quick on the draw.

"Why do you think?" I said. I couldn't believe how mean I sounded. And all the while, in the back of my head, I was amazed that I was engaged in one of those face-offs that I absolutely hated.

Without another word, Mom ripped the picture in half, then in half again, and again. With each rip, I felt something in me shred, until there was nothing left to feel anything. Mom dropped the pieces of me on the floor and stalked off to the bedroom. I sat there, numb.

Amanda looked like she was going to throw up. She crawled over, picked up the pieces, and handed them to me without a word. Then she went and knelt next to the bedroom door, knocking very softly.

I walked outside, holding the ripped picture fragments in one hand, my camera in the other. I wandered down to the river's edge. The water level was about halfway down. The outgoing tide had left a small brown pool of water on a ledge of the muddy bank. Tiny wind ripples skated across it. I wasn't wearing my jacket, but I didn't notice the cold.

I let the picture pieces fall from my hand. They floated down into the tidal pool, then drifted slowly apart, spread out—here a nose, there an ear, a small jagged square of fractured smile. Slowly I raised my camera. *Snap click.* Portrait of Michael Madden literally coming apart at the seams. *Snap click.* I waited to feel something. *Snap click.* It didn't happen.

TWELVE

I got Escorted Grounds Privileges a few days ago; it's a nuthouse promotion. It means the staff is reasonably sure I'm not going to do anything drastic like throw myself in the path of a moving snowblower or something. I can go anywhere on the grounds, inside or out, with another patient who has EGP or better, or with any staff person or an approved visitor. Next step is Unescorted Grounds, then Weekend Pass—probably this weekend, Doc says. He says I've made a lot of progress. Toward what, I have no idea.

Anyway, I went out for a walk after lunch with Ellie, this girl who's here because she pigs out, then sticks her finger down her throat to regurgitate, because her parents boss her around too much and expect her to be perfect like her older sister. We hiked up to the highest point on the grounds. You look down and you see "life out there" or "the real world" and you're watching, outside of it for the time being. I have to admit, it's restful stepping outside the mainstream for a spell.

From up here, the town, the houses, the river, the train tracks—everything is miniaturized. You feel as if you could just reach out and move things around, like Playskool Village pieces. It's a different perspective.

"Your friend sounds like kind of a jerk," Ellie says shyly, and kicks a stone. It's interesting about group— some days, everyone's picking on you and telling you to get your act together; other days, they all seem to be on your side.

"Yeah, I guess he does," I say. I haven't described Ricky in the most glowing terms.

"So why would you hang around with a jerk?"

I shrug. I've asked myself that question more than once lately. I don't know. Maybe I kind of admire the way he refuses to be defeated by things. He takes life head-on. Like a bulldozer, sometimes.

"You just have to know Ricky," I say finally, by way of an answer. I guess I'm not as mad at him as I was.

The varsity hockey team at Mohegan has its own special initiation for rookies. The new guys never know exactly when it's coming—usually after the weather's gotten good and cold—but all rookies know for sure it's coming. It's a toned-down version of what I hear happens to first-year guys in the NHL, but it's bad enough. Though the coaches don't actually condone it, they wink and look the other way. Ricky was the first rookie to get it this season.

Hockey practice is over at the Wonderworld of Ice rink on the Post Road between Eastfield and Yardley. What happens is, the old guys, seniors mostly, gang up after practice and jump one new guy in the locker room. They hold him down, shave a strip down the middle of his skull, strip him bare-butt naked, slap on a glob of Deep Heet—this hot ointment the trainers use on muscle pulls. Anyway, they slap it on his privates, then throw him out the locker-room emergency exit, out in the cold. The rookie has to sprint once around the whole building and come in the front door, where the rest of the team is waiting to escort him to the showers.

If you ask me, it's a pretty barbaric ritual, but like I said, I'm not much for the team thing. That kind of mentality is part of the reason.

A lot of times, the seniors will tip off the cheerleaders

when there's going to be a Rookie Razing, as they call it. They think it's funny to have a squad of cheering, squealing girls there when they boot the poor guy's butt out into the cold.

Even without the word of witnesses, everyone in school knew right away that Ricky had been razed, because of the Mohegan Hockey Mohawk—the bald strip running from his forehead to the back of his neck. He went around school kind of sheepishly all morning; I think the hair thing bothered him more than it might another guy because of his background. But it's kind of a badge of courage, too, like a varsity letter. It says, "I'm tough; I survived." Razed rookies get a lot of attention. And Ricky's not averse to that kind of attention, the sports star stuff.

So Ricky was okay. Until lunchtime.

Melissa and I were in line getting lunch when the hockey jocks came in as a group, Ricky included. They headed down the middle aisle toward their usual table, laughing, backslapping Ricky, being their normal rowdy selves. I saw them all stop short and look at the back wall of the cafeteria.

I looked and saw what had stopped them.

Victoria, Debbie, and a couple of other cheerleaders had unrolled this huge paper sign and were taping it to the wall. It said RODERICK ALISTER BOLTON—PUNY PECKER. There were some very rude illustrations.

I saw Ricky go beet red, even his bald strip.

"What's the matter?" Melissa asked. I blocked her way so she wouldn't see the rude illustrations.

The hockey jocks started right in on Ricky.

"Hey, Bolton, you got a brother named Roderick?"

"No, man, it's him—Rick, Rod-*rick!*"

"You've gotta be kidding. Roderick?"

"Your middle name is Alister?"

"Oh, Roderick, Roderick."

It got worse. Guys started coming up with the predictable rhymes—Rod-*rick*, puny— You get the idea. Ricky looked ready to burst a blood vessel, but there was really nothing he could do. He had to tough it out. Victoria had this look of vicious triumph on her face. She'd sure exacted her revenge for Ricky's pep rally stunt. I wondered how she'd found out his real name. He'd managed to keep it a secret for a lot of years.

Across the cafeteria I caught Ricky's eye. I shrugged and smiled to try and let him know I was on his side. He looked away, as if having a friendly witness to his humiliation made him feel worse, somehow.

"Come on, let's get out of here," I said, and steered Melissa toward the hall. It was too painful to watch.

.   .   .

Melissa and I met at the public library that night. We were supposedly doing homework, and she was working on a physics report. I just wanted the excuse to be with her. I had a bunch of photography books I was looking at.

I'd brought a folder of prints with me, a whole portfolio of Melissa Ryan—some from the river, some from dates we'd gone on, and some candids I'd snapped at school when she wasn't looking. She didn't react the way I expected her to.

"Don't you like them?"

She was frowning. "Of course I do, Michael. I mean, they're really good pictures. But . . ." She chewed her lip and looked kind of disturbed.

"But what?"

"I don't know. It makes me feel a little weird, that's all."

"What do you mean, weird?" To tell the truth, I was mildly annoyed. "You could be a model, you know. I could do your portfolio and—"

"Stop it." Now she sounded annoyed. "I don't want to be your model. I'm a person, not a subject."

"I know that. But you can be both. Some of the greatest photographers in the world were in love with their subjects. Look at Alfred Stieglitz and Georgia O'Keeffe." I pushed a book across the table to show her.

"I don't want to look at them." She closed the book

hard enough that a guy working at a nearby cubicle said, "Shhh."

I put my hands over hers.

"I don't want to fight with you," I whispered. "Don't be mad. Please."

She let out a slow sigh.

"I'm not mad. But maybe you could be a little less intense about the whole thing. It's all you ever think about."

"Look," I said. "Mr. Dorio says we have to learn not only to focus the camera but to focus ourselves on working hard, if we want to get good. I want to get good."

"He talks about balance, too," Melissa shot back. "A picture should be balanced. Well, I think a life should be balanced."

We sat there in disagreement. Stalemate. It felt lousy.

.   .   .

Melissa's parents pulled her out of school for a few days the next week to go on college interviews. I tried not to think what it would be like next year, with her away at school and me still stuck here. That Wednesday, Ricky limped over to where I was sitting at lunch, and pulled up a chair.

"Hey, what happened?" I asked.

He grimaced as he sat. "I did something to my knee last night at practice. Ligament. Just pulled, not torn. But I'm off skates for a little while."

He looked kind of down, and I wondered if the guys on the team had been giving him a real rough time about his name. I noticed Debbie was sitting with Victoria, too, so I assumed that fledgling relationship had crashed. All in all, Ricky looked a tad forlorn.

"So," he said through a mouthful of watery chili. "Where's the woman?"

"Melissa? Away until tomorrow. Checking out colleges." I drained the last drops from my milk carton and crumpled it. Things with Melissa had been less than sublime lately. She wanted to talk about my problems, but as far as I was concerned, there was nothing to say. And there wasn't a damn thing I could do about them.

Ricky looked at a loss as to what to say next.

"So, you busy this afternoon? Wanna go do something?"

"I have to work in the darkroom," I told him. I hesitated a second, then went ahead and invited him along. "You can hang out, if you want."

He gave a kind of ambiguous shrug. "Sure. Okay. Whatever," he said.

"I'll be up there at three-thirty. Just knock if the

door's locked and the red light is on." I guess I was feeling guilty about making myself so scarce lately.

.   .   .

I had a few prints I wanted to work on—the ripped portrait in the tidal pool, and the montage of Amanda in her Halloween costume with Victoria in her gym suit. The tidal pool one came out well, but it was a pretty strong image and fairly personal; I wasn't sure I wanted to put it in my portfolio. My first try at the montage, the composition was really unbalanced. My second try, the composition was better, but the exposures were wrong.

Ricky was yammering on about a scheme he was cooking up, while I put the negative of Amanda back in the enlarger for a third try.

When I'm setting the focus on the enlarger, I use an old exposed piece of print paper. It looks white, but it's no good for printing. Then when I'm ready to do the actual print, I slip a new piece out of the lightproof envelope and into place. I did that first with the Amanda picture, then put the Victoria negative back into the enlarger and reexposed the same paper.

"I'm serious, Madman. We'd make a mint," Ricky was saying. He was sounding like his old irrepressible self.

I slipped the exposed paper out of the easel and into the first chemical bath, the developer. I stirred, waiting for the double image to appear.

"Look, I'll drill the hole into the girls' locker room and take care of having everything printed up. All you have to do is take the pictures and develop them. They don't even have to be that great. You know, artistically. Every guy in school will buy one."

I wasn't paying too much attention to Ricky's rambling. I was trying to figure out how to adjust the exposure. "Too washed out," I muttered.

"We'll call it *Jockettes in the Locker Room*."

I put the print in the fixer and stepped back to the enlarger. I repeated the exposure sequence and swished the chemical around.

"I bet we could charge ten bucks apiece."

This print was too dark, I could tell already.

"So, whadaya say?"

"Geez, would you give it a rest? You know, you're like a pit bull with his choppers clamped on some poor guy's leg. You just won't let go." I was irritated about having to do the print for the fifth time.

"Are you saying no?"

"I'm saying forget it, Rick. That's not how I want to make my name in photography—with a sleazy calendar."

"Well, it wouldn't be the sleaziest thing a photographer's ever done," Ricky muttered. There was a hidden barb in the remark that really got me. I called him on it.

"What the hell is that supposed to mean?"

Ricky stuck his chin out. "I think dumping your wife and kids and going sailing around the world while they can barely survive is a pretty sleazy move."

My jaw tightened. "Yeah? Well, I think it's none of your damn business." I stared him down. He backed off.

"Sorry," he said. But his tone was tense.

"Forget it." So was mine.

I did another double exposure and popped it into the developer. Behind me, I could hear Ricky fiddling around with stuff. I was beginning to be sorry I'd invited him.

"Don't break anything, would ya? If you do, I have to pay for it," I said.

"I won't. Hey, Madman, look at this!"

"What?" This print was definitely better than the others, but I was beginning to wonder how I felt about pairing Amanda with Victoria. It felt kind of like pimping my little sister.

I turned around. Ricky had switched on the enlarger light and was fooling around with my piece of test paper, rolling it so that Victoria's anatomy was grossly distorted.

"Watch it—you'll burn the negative if you leave the light on without the timer." He was really starting to get on my nerves.

"Okay, but just wait a sec. If you hold the paper like this, will the picture come out this way?"

I looked over his shoulder. The way he was holding the paper, kind of humped in the middle, Victoria looked like the biggest lard-butt I'd ever seen. I had to laugh.

"I don't know," I said. "Maybe."

"Can we try it? Just once?" he asked.

I guess I felt that Ricky deserved a little private revenge after Victoria's public slaughter of his ego.

"Okay. Move over."

I set the timer, took a fresh piece of paper, and held it the way Ricky had held the other one.

"Push that button."

He did.

The enlarger light went back on, exposed the distorted image for the time I'd set, then clicked off. I stuck the paper in the developer and watched the doctored and not very flattering portrait come into being.

"All right!" Ricky's eyes gleamed redly in the glow of the safelight.

When I finished the processing, I handed him the dried print. "Add it to your private collection. Listen, Rick, I've still got a lot of work to do—" I hinted.

"Say no more, Madman. I'm outta here. See you tomorrow." He took the print and left.

THIRTEEN

"How did it hit you when Melissa said she saw you as breaking up into little pieces?" Doc wants to know.

"How about, like a sledgehammer?" Heh, heh, joke, Doc. Or maybe not. If I was breaking up into pieces before, like she said, I was pulverized after.

When I think back, though, that's not exactly true. I mean, I heard what she was saying, that she wanted us to quit seeing each other. And I knew, in a theoretical way, that I was devastated. But something didn't connect. The feelings I should have been feeling, I just wasn't.

Thinking about the way I felt—or didn't feel—reminds me of this Melville story we read in my English *class last year, "Bartleby the Scrivener." Bartleby worked for a lawyer. One day his boss told him to do something, and Bartleby said, "I would prefer not to." No matter what the boss said, that's all Bartleby would answer: "I would prefer not to." So the boss fired him. Bartleby wouldn't leave. He preferred not to. So the boss packed up the whole office and moved to another building. One day the new tenant of the old office came to see him, because Bartleby was still sitting there, refusing to budge, saying, "I would prefer not to." Not rudely, not obnoxiously—he was a totally mild-man-nered-gentleman type of guy. Finally they hauled Bartleby's butt off to jail. And he died. I never really got the point of the story, but I really like that line.*

Would you like to talk, Michael? I would prefer not to. Would you like to feel, Michael? No thanks, I'd prefer not to. Do you want to live, Michael? I think maybe I'd prefer not to—

Did I say that?

When I got home from the darkroom that night, it was late. Mom was sitting at the kitchen table, going through classified ads, circling notices in the help-wanted section. She looked about as tired as I'd ever seen her look. It was a relief, though, to see her addressing our financial situation in a realistic way for a change.

"Did you work tonight?" She glanced up as I dumped my stuff on the counter and started unwrapping the meatball grinder I'd picked up on the way home.

"Uh-uh. Darkroom," I said. Carl had really piled up the grinder for me. It was very messy, so I grabbed a plate and a knife and chopped it in thirds.

Mom sighed. "How can someone do what I've done for seventeen years and come out without any marketable skills? I don't take shorthand, but I can mesh four schedules and get everyone where they need to be, on time, wearing clean, matching socks. Doesn't that count for something?"

"Organizational skills?" I said through a mouthful of meatball.

Mom gave me a small smile.

Amanda came zipping through the doorway during a TV commercial. "What's that smell? Spaghetti?"

"You had dinner, Amanda," Mom said a bit sharply.

"I hate tuna fish. I don't care if it's good, cheap protein." Amanda scowled. "I'm never eating it again."

I thought Mom was going to holler at Amanda, but she didn't.

"I hate it, too. As soon as I get a job, we'll never eat it again. I promise."

Amanda was looking kind of longingly at my dinner. I got out two more plates, and gave one piece to her and one to Mom.

"Yeah!" Amanda shouted, and dove into her portion.

I was closest to the phone when it rang, so I picked it up. An overseas operator told me to hold for an international call. Then I heard Dad's voice, thin and tinny through echoing static. He sounded as if he were talking from the bottom of a deep well on some other planet.

"Michael, is that you?"

"Yeah," I said. Mom was looking at me with mild interest. "Where are you?"

"Still in Palma. We're getting ready for the start of the next leg down to Cape Town, South Africa, and I just wanted to touch base."

My throat tightened. He was going even farther away then he was already, and I suddenly felt each mile of distance like a small tug on a torture rack, stretching something in me toward a breaking point. I tried not to think about it, but it kind of hit me all at once, as I listened to him yak on about how after Cape Town, they'd be off to Hobart, Tasmania, and how tough that leg would be, with force-nine gales, the roaring forties, the Southern Ocean, icebergs. . . .

Mom was starting to get a suspicious look on her face.

"Is Amanda there?" Dad asked. "Can you put her on the phone?"

"Amanda, want to talk to Dad?" I said.

"No." That was it. Just say no. I had to admire the kid.

But Mom, meanwhile, had leapt up from her chair and was advancing on the phone with blood in her eyes.

"Give me that!" She yanked the receiver out of my hand before I even had a chance to say good-bye.

"Where's the money you promised? Your kids are getting sick of Tuna Helper seven times a week."

I didn't want to hear it. I went for the nearest exit, abandoned ship.

.   .   .

A bunch of kids were crowded around the social activities bulletin board when I got to school the next morning. They were laughing and pointing. I didn't realize right away what they were looking at. Then I saw the row of legal-size fliers stretching down the corridor wall. They looked like photocopies of a black-and-white photograph. A knot of anxiety twisted my gut. I skirted the crowd to move in for a closer look.

There she was, Victoria Kaminsky, in the doctored lard-butt picture Ricky had talked me into printing. He must have pasted it onto a longer sheet of paper. Underneath the photo, in bold black print, were the words CAUTION—WIDE LOAD—HEAVY TRAFFIC. There were arrows pointing to the obvious target.

I couldn't believe he'd done it. Not only had he done it, he'd overdone it in typical Ricky Bolton style. I started down the hall, snatching every one, and heaved a sigh of relief when I got to the end. Until I went around the corner and through the fire doors, that is. Two rows, both sides of the hall, one taped to every locker, all the way down to the gym. I leaned against the wall and groaned as the bell rang.

.   .   .

Photography was my third class that day. I'd told my homeroom teacher I was feeling sick—which wasn't far from true—and gotten excused to go to the nurse. I used the opportunity to take down any fliers that were still up. But kids had already snagged a lot of them, and I assumed they were floating around school.

The photography classroom was conspicuously silent when I got there. Melissa, back from her college-inspecting trip, wouldn't look at me.

Mr. Dorio was pacing the front of the room, holding a copy of Ricky's flier in his hand. His beard was set in this dangerous-looking little smile. His eyes weren't smiling. I knew Mr. Dorio knew it was my picture, because the original was in my portfolio and he remembers whose stuff is whose. Finally he spoke.

"Anyone care to comment on this?"

No one cared to comment. Least of all, me.

"No? Allow me, then. Technically it's on the sloppy side. Poor contrast—the image is grainy. But there's something else very wrong with this picture. What?"

Walt Kelly put up his hand. Mr. Dorio gave him a curt nod.

"I think maybe the photographer used the wrong kind of lens or something, like a wide-angle lens."

The few snickers that escaped were quickly squelched by one look from Mr. Dorio.

"This print was manipulated in the darkroom," he said in a monotone.

Leslie Goldman raised her hand. "But, Mr. Dorio, aren't you allowed to do that? Like burning in and—"

He cut her off.

"Darkroom manipulation can be a legitimate tool. It depends on the photographer's intentions. What do you think this photographer's intentions were? To illuminate some subtle truth? Or to hurt someone, to ridicule?" He fixed a stare on me. "Diane Arbus captured souls on film. In return, she put her own on the line. Gave back. She did not mock."

He crumpled the paper in his hand, tossed it in the trash with disgust, then jerked his thumb at the door.

"Michael Madden: Out!" he spat.

The words hit me like bullets. I was too stunned to be embarrassed at that point. I grabbed blindly for my books and somehow got out of the classroom.

I cornered Ricky at lunch.

"Geez, lighten up, would ya? We're talking about a few copies here, not a mass murder."

"A few? A few?" I was literally spitting mad.

He took a nervous step back. "Say it, don't spray it, huh? Okay. Not a few. Two hundred. But Victoria had it coming to her after what she did."

"What about what *you* did? The doll and the flag-pole—anyway, that's beside the point. I gave you that picture for your own private sick enjoyment." People were looking, so I lowered my voice.

Ricky eyeballed me. "So, you gonna sue me for copyright violation or what?" he drawled.

I couldn't believe he was being so casual. Maybe I wouldn't have cared so much if it was something else besides my photography. But he'd totally screwed me up with Mr. Dorio. He'd made me look like an idiot in front of the whole class. Including Melissa.

"You really are a hemorrhoidal butt-hole, you know that?" I had to walk away before I twisted his head right off his neck.

After school, I rushed to find Melissa, to set things straight with her. She was almost to her car, walking like she was in a huge hurry, when I went out the door. I shouted across the parking lot.

"Melissa!"

She didn't turn around.

"Melissa!" I broke into a sprint.

"Melissa." I stood in front of the car door so she couldn't open it. The expression on her face scared me. Like she'd come to some decision and it wasn't a happy one. I launched into a garbled explanation.

"Hey, Ricky was the one—I mean, I did the print, but I had no idea he was going to—"

I wasn't getting through. She looked over my shoulder, past me, not at me.

"It's not that," she said.

"What, then? What is it?" A horrible thought occurred to me. "Is it someone else?"

"No." She shook her head and finally looked me in the eye. "Well, maybe, in a way. You. You seem like someone else lately."

"What?" I stared at her.

She frowned, as if trying hard to find the right words. "You've changed. It's like you're closing up, and soon even I won't be able to get in."

"What are you talking about?"

"I'm talking about the way we never do anything with friends—we're always alone. It's like you want me to be this separate thing, cut off from the rest of your life. I still haven't met your family. And I get the feeling you don't want me to."

"You're not missing anything," I muttered. I cringed when I saw her response to that.

"Look, Michael. I try and picture you at night and I can't, because I don't even know where you live. I've tried—I've tried—" She was getting upset. "I did a lot of thinking while I was away. I feel shut out of what's going on with you. I thought I loved you. But right now, I don't even feel like I know you. And with the photography . . ." She said it as if she hated it almost as much as my mother did. "You use your camera to put up a . . . a barricade between you and the world. Between you and your own feelings."

"What are you talking about?" I said again.

"I'm talking about this." She pulled a print out of her binder and handed it to me. It was the pieces-in-the-water picture I'd taken of the one she had given me from her bulletin board, the one my mother had ripped up.

"This fell out of your folder when you left class today."

Relief flooded through me. I thought I could explain.

"You think I ripped up the picture you— I didn't rip it. I had this fight with my mother and she—but don't take it personally. . . ." I was blabbering like an idiot, trying to straighten things out.

Melissa wasn't buying.

"It's not the picture being ripped. It's what you did with it. If this is what you feel like right now, I can't handle it."

My stomach clenched like a fist. "So what are you saying?"

"I'm saying I think we should take a break from each other for a while. I'm saying there are things you need to figure out, and I think you need help to do it and I'm not—I'm not— I can't give you the help you need." She was crying now.

I tried to put my arms around her, but she pushed me away.

"I can't stand by and watch you come apart in little ripped-up pieces—I just can't—" Her voice broke.

She turned and walked away from the car.

"Where are you going?" I yelled after her.

She didn't look back, just shook her head and started running toward the gym doors.

FOURTEEN

. . . spirit unappeased and peregrine
Between two worlds . . .

*Those are the words Fritz quoted to me that first day at
work when I asked about the TV Guidance Counselor.
I found them in this book he sent me in the mail yesterday,* Four Quartets, *by T. S. Eliot. I'm not what you'd
call an ardent fan of poetry; a lot of it's too hard to figure
out. Too obscure. But I'm working my way through this
book because I have a feeling Fritz wants me to know
something that's in it.*

I didn't know what peregrine *meant, so I asked Patty,
the night nurse. She dug up a dictionary for me. Pere-*

grine: wandering. The dictionary didn't list unappeased, *but it had* appease: *to satisfy.*

*Unsatisfied and wandering. That's sort of how I feel
right now. This place is like some kind of limbo between
the world I stepped out of and the world I'll be going
back to. Or maybe limbo is a state of mind.*

I wasn't sure if Mr. Dorio had kicked me out of class
for just one day or for good, so I got myself to school
early on Friday and went to talk to him. He was sitting at
his desk reading a magazine; the classroom was empty. I
took a step inside and stopped, having no idea what I
should say. I mean, I could explain about Ricky, but
I didn't want him to think I was trying to weasel out of
all the blame, by ratting on a friend. I stood there and
waited until he sensed my presence and looked up.
The anger was gone, but I could read the personal
disappointment in his eyes. The moment stretched out
until I couldn't take it anymore. I just said it.

"I'm sorry, Mr. Dorio."

He eyeballed me a little longer. Finally, he dipped
his head, which I took to mean he accepted my apology.

"Don't ever pull a stunt like that again. You foul
your own talent."

I shook my head, nodded, and shook my head again,
figuring he'd sort it out. Then I turned and made my
escape.

I didn't see Melissa at lunch. I'd been too upset to call her the night before, plus I thought maybe overnight she'd reconsider, given a little time to think. Apparently not. In Photography that afternoon, she took the farthest seat from mine she could find. After about a dozen tries to catch her eye, I gave up. I almost wished Mr. Dorio *had* kicked me out of class for good, because sitting in that room with Melissa giving me the freeze was excruciating.

.   .   .

Over the weekend, I tried to call her. After four attempts with Mr. Ryan saying she wasn't available, Melissa's mother got on the phone.

"Michael, I'm very uncomfortable lying. Melissa doesn't want to talk to you right now. She asked me to tell you not to call again, please." Her voice was very kind, but I felt like someone had stuck a vacuum cleaner down my throat and sucked all the air from my lungs. I couldn't speak.

"Why don't you give it some time, Michael? Maybe things will work out." The pity in her voice made me feel even worse. It wasn't the kind of remark that filled a person with confidence for the future.

The whole next week went by in a blur. I wasn't talking to Ricky. Melissa wasn't talking to me. Pretty much both of the above applied to me and my mother.

At work, Fritz was very quiet. Not that he was normally a motor-mouth, but he seemed preoccupied. Kind of tucked into himself, not connecting with people the way he usually did. Carl hovered around him a lot, as if he was keeping an eye on him. I asked Carl if Fritz was all right, if he was sick or something.

"The bluefish are gone. The leaves are gone," was how he answered me. "The cold is coming." As if that explained it.

The weather was on the grim side, overcast, heavy, and gray. It wasn't helping my spirits much, either. I was basically plodding along, just going through the motions.

Our photography assignment didn't excite me too much—still life. First-term reports were due out, and I had a feeling old Fatty-Bean was going to bust my butt into study hall. I'd brought my grades up some, but not as high as they used to be. All in all, I was feeling like a total failure. And I was too weary to try to fix it.

Saturday I worked a double shift at the market. I was exhausted by the time I strolled up the driveway, and for some reason, Ricky's car being parked there didn't register. I went in the kitchen door. And stared.

Ricky was standing, leaning against the kitchen counter, with his arms around my mother. She had her head resting on his shoulder. It was one of those frozen moments when every detail seems distinct, every outline of every thing seems etched in the air.

I put my hands up to my face with an imaginary camera. *Snap click.*

"Makes a real nice picture," I said, and smiled about the nastiest smile my lips have ever cracked.

Mom gave a start and disengaged. She looked at me very coldly.

"Have you gotten so wrapped up with that camera of yours that you can't see straight?"

"Listen, Madman, you have no idea—" Ricky started to say, but I wasn't listening. Something inside me was taking over, something ugly, boiling up, about to explode.

"I have no idea why my best friend is standing here rubbing bodies with my mother. I know you guys have always had a close relationship, but don't you think this is carrying it too far?"

"Shut up, you idiot!" Ricky sprang across the kitchen in two steps. He shoved me in the chest so hard, I thought my left lung was collapsing. I grabbed his shirt, swung him around, and shoved him back through the doorway. He stuck his foot behind my leg. I went down on my back with a thud and pulled him with me. My head hit the bottom of the railing with such a bang, I saw fireworks. We did a bone-crunching double somersault down the stairs.

The adrenaline rush of fury gave me power I didn't normally have.

"You lowlife scumbag!" I yanked Ricky around and scrambled to get a knee in his gut, to hold him while I beat the crap out of him. He got me a good one, square in the eye.

Mom was on the porch, screaming, "Stop it! Stop it!"

I swung my fist toward his jaw, missed, and felt his nose give as my knuckles connected. A small geyser of blood spurted out. I was winding up for another punch, but he flipped me over.

"You're—so—damn—stupid!" Ricky punctuated each word by slamming my shoulders against the ground. He was huffing and wheezing, and the blood from his nose was dripping all over me. I tried to worm out of his grip, tried to get an arm free so I could knock his teeth down his throat.

"You don't know jack-shit about it," I grunted. "You want to be the man of this house? Go on, go ahead." I heaved my whole body and caught him off balance. But he whipped around behind me and got me in an iron headlock. He squeezed so hard, my head felt like it was going to explode.

"Don't be a total jerk-off." His breath was coming out in short, gurgling snorts. He just held on till I stopped moving.

I could see Mom in a crumpled heap on the steps, with her head in her lap, and hear her sobs. All of my rage drained away suddenly, and I went limp.

"It's not—we weren't—" Ricky was losing steam, too. He let go of me and pushed me away. "Who the hell is she supposed to lean on, huh? First your old man dumps her, takes off, and you—you might as well have taken off, too. Who helped her pack? Who fixed the car and mowed the lawn and put up the damn storm windows? Who even talks to her like she's a person? Huh? Huh?"

He spat, dragged himself up, and staggered over to his car.

I just lay there, looking up into the moonless black night. By the time I hauled myself in, Mom must have gone to bed.

.   .   .

The next day, Sunday, was bleak. Raw and rainy, November with a vengeance. Mom and I weren't talking; what else was new? I was stiff all over, and when I checked out the mirror, I saw Ricky had left his mark—one hell of a shiner. I stood there looking at myself. Man of the family. Right. Well, I obviously hadn't filled the bill. I might have felt guilty except that I just didn't care.

I went to the market at eleven. I was scheduled to work till closing time at six.

Eileen was alone in the deli when I got there, and Ruth, one of the other part-time cashiers, was alone on the middle register. Eileen's eyes got big when she took in my battle scars, but she didn't say anything.

"Where's Carl?" I asked as I hung up my coat.

She tossed me a cheese danish. I caught it and took a bite.

"Upstairs. He and Fritz'll be gone most of the day. Ruth leaves at two." She cast another glance at my eye, which was puffy, purple, and half-closed. "You be okay on the register if I cover the deli?"

I nodded. "Where are they going?"

"To the cemetery."

I raised my good eyebrow. "Not a great day for it." As if there was ever a good day to go to a cemetery.

"It's the anniversary of the accident," she said. "They go every year before Thanksgiving."

I guess that explained Fritz's going into emotional hibernation the past week. The upstairs door opened, and Carl and Fritz came down. They were both wearing suits, ties, and overcoats. Fritz had on a tweed fedora and carried an umbrella. For once, Carl wasn't wearing his baseball cap. He looked, if possible, paler than usual, and somewhat dazed, out of it. Haunted, you might say.

"I think it will be a very slow afternoon," Fritz said quietly. "Michael, your drawer is up in the office. It's not locked. You two can hold down the fort until we return?"

"Sure thing, Fritz," Eileen told him. "Have a—"

She'd been going to say "nice time," I think, then realized it wasn't quite the right thing to say.

"Safe trip," I finished for her.

Fritz nodded. "Thank you. Come, Carl."

They left.

I got my drawer, opened my register, and processed the orders of the Sunday *Times*/on-the-way-home-from-church crowd, which was definitely sparser than usual, probably because of the lousy weather. I was thinking about Fritz and Carl out there in the grave-yard. Dismal is how I felt. One way or another, life was really a killer. It passed through my mind that maybe it wasn't worth the bother.

After lunch, business was totally dead. Ruth left. I hooked up my flash, figuring I might as well knock off the still-life assignment while I had a whole produce department handy for props. I snagged a zucchini, some scallions, and some tomatoes, and started arranging them on the empty register counter near the front window.

I was piling up my vegetables, knocking them down, halfheartedly trying to come up with some arrangement that, if it didn't suggest some hidden meaning, at least looked okay, when Ricky came through the door. His nose looked like a miniature eggplant.

I looked at him and felt nothing. It was like I was looking at a total stranger. He stood there, running his fingers through his hair. I basically ignored him and kept piling and unpiling vegetables.

"Colder than a witch's tit out there," he said.

I didn't say anything.

"It wasn't what you were thinking, Madman," he said after a minute.

You have no clue what I was thinking, I thought.

"I may be a lowlife, but I'm not that low."

I still didn't say anything. What was there to say? Ricky sighed, but he didn't budge. I could see he was determined to tell his side of the story. I wasn't about to help him out.

"Did Caro—your mother tell you why I was there?"

He waited for an answer. I finally shook my head. The scallions weren't cooperating at all. I left my register, went back to the produce aisle, grabbed a bunch of radishes, a head of cauliflower, some carrots, and a lemon. Ricky was standing there when I returned.

"I stopped by the house looking for you. I knew you were still mad about those fliers and—anyway, Amanda needed a ride to some kid's house, some slumber party thing. Your mother's car crapped out again, so I gave

Amanda a ride. On the way, she asked me to buy her some Burger King because she was hungry. I figured if the kid hadn't eaten, Caroline probably hadn't, either. So I brought her back a burger and some fries. And she started crying. I didn't know what to do. That's all. We just stood there. That's when you came in. That's all it was."

I looked through the viewfinder at my pile of vegetables. Still something missing. And the lemon was wrong.

"Something vertical," I mumbled, and went back for a bunch of celery.

Ricky had dug in his heels. He was waiting for some kind of response from me. I could tell he wasn't going to leave until he got it. I knew he was telling the truth and I'd been way out of line with those cracks I'd made the night before. The thing of it was, I just didn't care anymore. About anything.

"Forget it," I said.

Still, he didn't go away. I kept fiddling with the vegetables, but I could feel his restlessness. He was charged up, sparking like a live wire. He combed his hair, fiddled with the sundries racks, his eyes darting all around.

"Geez, neither sleet nor rain keeps her from making her appointed rounds, huh?" he said suddenly.

I glanced up and saw the TV Guidance Counselor

coming across the parking lot. I decided to ditch the carrots.

"I bet I know what'd stop her," he said.

Maybe if I hadn't been so depressed, I might have tuned in to the undertone in Ricky's voice. Like when he used to get a brainstorm on mischief night. Not malicious so much as impulsive.

But I just picked up the carrots and headed for produce again. When I got back to my register, Ricky was stuffing a stack of *TV Guides* under the counter. He'd already removed them from the other two registers.

"Put 'em back, you idiot," I started to say, but it was too late. Janey Riddley approached the first empty rack. A look of confusion crossed her face. In jerky, nervous steps, she started to come to my register and the second empty rack, saw it, stopped in midstep, then raced for the register by the window.

Suddenly I was mesmerized by the contorted expressions on her face. Automatically I raised my camera.

Snap click. Portrait of confusion—of loss—total disorientation. As the first flash went off, she freaked. Spinning, she whacked over my pile of vegetables. Her hands clawed at her face as if the flash had burned her skin. But I couldn't stop.

Snap click. She reeled out the door, squawking like a crow hit by a napalm bomb.

My hands let go of the camera. I heard it smash—saw the headlights through the window—heard the brakes screech as she spun head-on into the car.

Snap click. My head was doing it all by itself. I watched the frames like a nightmare slide show:

Eileen rushing over from the deli, running outside.

Ricky, panicked, stuffing the *TV Guides* back in their racks, spotting my camera on the floor, shoving it under my register.

Eileen punching in the emergency number on the wall phone in the deli.

The first red and blue flashing lights peeling into the parking lot.

More flashing lights, red ones—the ambulance.

And the TV Guidance Counselor, finally still, being placed on a stretcher.

.   .   .

Fritz and Carl pulled in as the last police car left. The police had asked questions. Eileen did all of the talking. I said I hadn't seen what happened. Ricky seemed to have disappeared.

"There was an accident?" Fritz said, frowning in deep concern.

I closed my eyes.

Eileen told him the same story she'd told the police—that she was slicing ham and ran out when she

219

heard the brakes screech. I didn't know what she'd actually seen from the deli, or if she was covering for me.

"I guess she just lost it and ran in front of the car that was pulling in."

I opened my eyes. Carl was looking at me.

"You should go rest," he said.

Fritz gave me a quizzical once-over that made me think he suspected there might be more to the story. I mean, he'd been watching the TV Guidance Counselor for a lot of years, and she'd never run in front of a car before.

But all he said was, "Carl, would you please change and do the deli? Eileen, you can take over the register. Michael, you can take the rest of the day off."

He and Carl went upstairs. Ricky reappeared. He poked his head around the last aisle, then made a bee-line for the register. He had a shopping cart full of random stuff, as if he'd just won one of those shopping sprees—all you can grab in ten minutes.

Eileen looked at him like he was a total nut case, but she started ringing things up.

I retrieved my camera from under the register. It rattled inside, as if something was broken. My arms and legs felt heavy—my head felt heavy—I barely had the energy to get my coat.

"That's $67.23," Eileen said to Ricky as I headed for the door.

"Hey, wait, Madman." Ricky fumbled with his wallet, slapped some bills on the counter, and charged out behind me.

"What about your change?" Eileen called after him. "And your groceries?"

"Wait up, Madman." Ricky huffed up behind me and grabbed my arm. I shook it off and kept walking across the parking lot.

"Mike, come on. Get in the car. I'll take you home."

I ignored him and kept walking toward the bridge— I don't know why.

"Fine," he finally shouted. "You're on your own, pal."

I heard his car door slam, then the shriek of tires as he tore off.

I walked out to the middle of the swing bridge and just stood there, watching the water level rise as the tide flowed in. The gray sky gradually blackened. The tide turned. An icy drizzle was beating down on my head. The camera was frozen to my hands. The streetlights went on, over on River Road. The market lights went off. Once I glanced up at Carl's apartment and saw him standing in the window. The next time I looked, he was gone. Every once in a while, a car hummed over the metal grating of the bridge, and blinding lights washed over me, then moved on.

I guess I was there for a couple of hours before I felt something rise inside me, like some furious beast in my gut, throwing its head back and getting ready to howl its throat raw.

The crazy pictures started again—*snap click snap click*—my life passing in front of my eyes? With sound effects roaring in my brain.

My mother. *Get off my back and get a life, would ya?*

Ricky. *Some friend—just take your meat and beat it, pal.*

Melissa. *Don't leave me, please don't*—the beast broke down in sobs.

And my father. Maybe if he wasn't off sailing the seven seas—maybe if he was here where he belonged, none of this—

Screw maybe, the beast shrieked. *Screw him. All he left you was a lousy camera.*

I lifted the camera over my head and hurled it. It arced out, then down, disappearing in the darkness before I heard the distant splash. Gone. As easy as that.

The beast was silent.

My body was alone. So alone it almost seemed like even I wasn't there.

Something was pulling me up, lifting my feet onto the guardrail.
There was nothing to go back to—
There was nothing to go forward to—
Nothing, really, to hold on to—
So I just let go—

FIFTEEN

Melissa's here. In the lounge at the end of the ward. I was sitting on the plaid couch, looking out the window, watching this cardinal flit from one hemlock tree to another in low swoops. He was the only spot of color in the whole landscape. I didn't realize Melissa was here until she sat on the end of the couch.

Other patients are scattered around, playing cards, watching television. A few are chatting with their visitors. Melissa's biting her lip and looking kind of sick herself.

"Hi," I say.

"Hi," she says. She unzips her coat but doesn't take it off. She's holding a rolled-up magazine in her hand.

"How are you?" I ask.

"Well, you know, okay. Fine. I'm fine."

Sally sidles up to Melissa. She holds out her scissor fingers and takes some strands of Melissa's hair between them.

"Snip, snap, snurp," she whispers.

Melissa sits still as a statue and looks at me for help.

"It's okay. Sally wants to be a hairdresser when she graduates. Hey, Sally, go give someone else a haircut, okay?"

Sally glides off and Melissa relaxes a little. She looks around the room, then back at me.

"Michael, I'm—I'm sorry—"

I cut her off with a wave of my hand. I'm starting to feel a little choked up, just with her being here, and I don't trust myself to say anything.

She sighs. "Well, um . . . Oh, Mr. Dorio said to say hi."

I nod.

"He was really upset, not just because of what you—you know—did. The bridge. He said something about hoping that lending you that Diane Arbus book hadn't been a mistake, sending you in the wrong direction."

"Why would he think that?" I'm confused. What does the book have to do with it?

"Well, because she was kind of a model for your

photography and she killed herself. You knew that, didn't you?"

No. I didn't know Diane Arbus had killed herself. She's dead? I feel something in me, a little current, a kind of spirit-to-spirit connection, die, too. I'd kind of hoped I might get to meet her someday, ask her some questions. Death suddenly seems deader than I've ever thought about it being.

"Mr. Dorio asked me to give you this."

"Huh?" I tune back in to see Melissa holding out a copy of Photo Magazine.

"The new issue. Your picture's in it. You won first prize in the portrait category."

I don't take the magazine. I suck in my gut like the wind's just been knocked out of me. My hands start to shake. In the month at the hospital, I haven't been able to bring myself to find out what happened to the TV Guidance Counselor. Doc and I have talked about her some, but I haven't told him exactly what happened that day. . . .

"Michael, what's wrong?" Melissa's looking very alarmed. Out of the corner of my eye, I see Roger the aide eyeballing us. I force myself to calm down.

"Do you know if she's okay?" I say the words very slowly and carefully.

Melissa dips her head, lets out a tiny sigh, and smiles. And nods.

226

"I think she's fine. I was in Thumm's last week and I saw her—I knew who she was from the pictures. She had her arm in a sling, so she was having some trouble with the TV Guides. But she was doing what you said she always does."

The relief is like a rain shower after a long, very dry spell. I let it soak into me for a minute.

Melissa lifts her eyebrows questioningly and holds out the magazine again. I take it and set it down on the end table. She bites her lip and looks like she's searching for something else to say.

"Do you think you'll go back to photography class?" she asks.

I look around the room at the other patients, thinking how much my view of them has changed in the past month. At first I'd seen them as a bunch of wackos. Now I kind of see them more as injured spirits. Some great material for a photographer. But I'm not interested in capturing any of their souls; I just want to try to hang on to my own.

"I think I'm going to give it a rest for a while," I say.

We sit there looking at each other for a few moments. Finally Melissa holds her hands, palms up, in a what's-next gesture.

I swallow. "I get out of here next week. Can I—can I call you?"

She smiles a tiny smile. "Yes," she says. "Call me."

It was Carl who pulled me out of the river. He was watching me as I stood on the bridge. I don't remember any of it, after the letting go. But Doc Sherman told me that Carl had been sitting out in the boat, watching, waiting, keeping a vigil. "Your self-appointed guardian angel," Doc called Carl. So he was ready when I went.

"You were damn lucky, Michael," Doc said. "Most stories like this don't have happy endings. They just have endings."

SIXTEEN

Mom will be here to pick me up in an hour. For good. I'm having my last in-patient session. After this, I'll see Doc once a week for a while.

"You know, Michael, every journey of a thousand miles begins with one step."

Very profound. A Doc Sherman original?

He's starting to be able to read me. "It's an old Chinese proverb," he says, smiling.

"Oh. Like, 'Man who fart in church must sit in his own pew'?" I say. But joking, not in a hostile way or anything. Actually I've been feeling good all day, ever since I woke up.

"So what would you like to talk about?" Doc settles back in his chair. He seems relaxed.

I shrug. We've pretty much hashed out all the big things.

"Well, I had this weird dream last night. I don't remember all the details, but the TV Guidance Counselor was in it."

Doc gives an encouraging nod.

"I think she might be dead. I'm not sure how I know—she doesn't look dead or anything; she's standing, with her eyes open. Waiting. She's waiting. But anyway, we're standing on the platform of the train station. Then old Fatty-Bean comes up the platform steps and goes over to her, and they're standing there looking at each other like long-lost twins. Fatty-Bean takes off her glasses—these rhinestone-studded deals— and gives them to Janey. Janey puts them on, and all of a sudden, she smiles. Then Fatty-Bean points to the platform. There's this yellow brick path on it."

"The Wizard of Oz?"

"Yeah. So a train pulls in and Janey follows the path over, and the doors open and she gets on. And it pulls out. That's it."

Doc smiles. "The glasses are an interesting symbol. She's able to see in a new way, find the path, the direction she needs to follow. The train could be heading into the future."

"Yeah. I guess that fits."

"But you think she might be dead, you said."

I nod.

"Death in a dream often symbolizes change, not necessarily literal death. A person doesn't have to die to experience a rebirth."

"I guess," I say.

Doc taps his pencil on his desk. Then he looks up at me. "If she is dead, it sounds like death is a release, a freeing, in the dream. Do you think of death that way?" he asks.

"I don't know," I say. "Maybe. In some cases."

He nods, as if acknowledging that as a legitimate point of view.

"It's a pretty final step, though," he adds casually.

So Mom came to pick me up and I went home for good. I'd been home the weekend before, out on a pass, and it had gone pretty well. Actually, as I walked through the door of the rathole, it had felt like home for the first time. The place where I was supposed to be living.

Mom was kind of nervous in the car. The ride took a while because of all the detours to avoid left-hand turns. But I didn't mind. The holiday decorations were up around town. Good cheer and all that. And we had a pretty decent chat.

"I talked to your father again," Mom said.

"Yeah?" I was on my guard. She'd gotten ahold of him on the boat right after I jumped off the bridge, and I'd gathered it hadn't been a pleasant conversation. He was in the middle of the ocean and there was nothing he could do.

"They just got into Cape Town. He said he's dropping out of the race, coming back."

"He doesn't have to come on account of me," I said.

"Well, no, not just that. He had an accident. Not serious, but . . ."

I could see her debating whether or not to tell me.

"He fell through a hatch and tore something in his groin. He may need surgery. He said he's getting too old—ocean racing is for young men." Mom nodded to herself and I read her mind. Fitting retribution, a groin injury. It was okay. She was entitled to feel it. But I didn't have to.

"When he gets back, Michael, if you want to try living with him for a while, if you think you'd rather or . . ." Her words trailed off.

I remembered what Ricky had said about the camera being a substitute for my father. It might have been true then. I didn't think it was anymore. It seemed like as far as that went, I'd gotten rid of something when I chucked the camera off the bridge. Something it felt good to be free of. Something I didn't need anymore.

"I'll see," I said. Then out of nowhere, I blurted it out: "Do you hate him?"

I saw her fingers tighten on the steering wheel for a second, then relax again. She half smiled.

"No. No, I don't think you can love someone as much as I loved him and wind up totally hating him."

"Yeah." I stared at the traffic light and watched it turn green.

"Oh, by the way, I sold the rolltop," Mom told me.

"You're kidding." I was very surprised. I knew it was kind of a symbol of something to her.

"I put all your pictures and things in a box. I was very careful with them." She sounded anxious.

"Thanks," I said.

"An antiques dealer gave me a very good price. It'll hold us until your father gets some money to us. And pay for the word-processing course I signed up for." She glanced at me to check my reaction.

"That's good. That's really good," I said.

.   .   .

Amanda wasn't there when we got home, but her coloring stuff was spread out all over the dining room table. A red and green paper chain, a picture of a lopsided snowman. And a drawing of a wobbly-looking boat in the water, with three people in a corner of the page and one person on the deck of the boat. She'd drawn a blue

233

line, like a river, connecting the three to the one. I guess she was still working things out in her own way. Her pink duffel bag was on the floor beside the table, which meant she hadn't dragged it with her. That seemed like a good sign.

As I unpacked my own duffel bag and started to put my stuff in the drawers of a small dresser that was where the desk used to be, I came across the *Photo Magazine* Melissa had brought to the hospital. I hadn't opened it yet. I opened it then.

There was Janey Riddley, looking at me—a look that seemed to say "Do I know you? Do you know me?" On impulse, I grabbed our *TV Guide* off the couch and took both magazines over to the dining room table. With Amanda's safety scissors, I cut out the picture, then used her glue stick to paste it in the middle of the *TV Guide*. It fit perfectly on the page.

I was feeling kind of restless. Mom was moving around the room very carefully, trying to stay out of my way, I could tell.

"I think I'm going out for a walk, okay?" I said.

She hesitated a second, then said, "Sure. Dinner's at five-thirty. If I'm not here when you get back, I'm just picking up Amanda."

On my way out, I tucked the *TV Guide* into my coat pocket.

As I went toward the door, I had a moment of panic,

this feeling that once I was by myself, I might vanish. But it passed. Actually, as soon as I got used to it, it felt great to be really alone for the first time in a month. Nobody eyeballing me, checking up on me.

It was cold, but the sun was shining. As I walked, I saw all these familiar things: the marina, glimpses of the river through the buildings, street signs. But I was also noticing other things, details—a squirrel stopping short on the sidewalk when he heard a car approach, thinking whatever squirrels think when they sense a hint of danger, then darting back to the safety of his tree. A small rainbow in an oil slick by the curb of the road. A few tufts of brown grass poking through a patch of crusty snow. I was just seeing them, taking them in as they were. My eyes weren't searching for an angle; my brain wasn't trying to fit them into a properly composed shot. Same with the people I passed. It was amazing how different everything looked.

All of a sudden, I became conscious of me, if that makes any sense. Me, Michael Madden, looking at this stuff and these people, me walking out there in the big old world. It was funny, I almost felt the need for an introduction—to say to myself, "Nice to meet you, Madman." Which I didn't do: I didn't want someone to see me talking to myself and stick me back with Sally Snip Snap Snurp.

I just kind of smiled to myself and kept walking. I

didn't pay much attention to where I was going, until I realized I was standing in front of the house that I'd watched the TV Guidance Counselor go in that day. I put my hand in my pocket. The magazine I'd pasted up was there. I opened the mailbox and slipped the *TV Guide* in. I don't think I did it for her as much as for me.

I was walking back up River Road when I heard a car slow down beside me. It gave a little honk. I turned and saw Ricky's Mustang. I stepped to the curb and leaned over as he rolled down the window.

"Hey, Madman. Ms. Mom said you were out for a stroll. I just stopped by . . . you know . . ." Ricky seemed to be groping for words. "How're you doing?"

"I'm okay," I said. I was looking at his head. It was covered with bristly black stubble, like he'd recently graduated from boot camp. His ears didn't look as bad as they used to; maybe his head had grown into them. I remembered one of the things Victoria used to say to him way back when, after a scalping at the barbershop: "What'd you do? Get your head stuck in a pencil sharpener?"

He caught me scoping out his skull and grinned, kind of sheepishly.

"That stupid Mohegan Mohawk. I shaved it. I figured I'd give the whole thing a fresh start."

He ran his hand over the stubble and looked me in

the eye. I read the apology there. I wondered if there might not be a touch of personal penance involved in Ricky's shaving his own head. Well, good, if there was, I thought.

"So, you want a lift?" he asked.

I shook my head. "No thanks. I want to stop by the market."

Ricky bobbed his head. "Well, I'll see you. Right?" He waited for an answer.

"Right," I said.

When I got to Thumm's, I went straight to the deli, where Carl was mixing up a big batch of seafood salad. He froze when he saw me, as if unsure how to react. I stuck out my hand. Slowly he wiped the mayonnaise off his and stretched his arm toward me. We shook.

"Thanks, Carl. For everything," I said.

He blinked and nodded, squeezing my hand so tight, my fingers practically creaked. Then he glanced up at the office window. I did, too, just in time to make eye contact with Fritz. His eyebrows drew together in a funny kind of frown, not angry, not puzzled, more like deeply distressed.

He came right down to the deli and looked at me for a long moment, the way he did that day I applied for the job. Out of nowhere, his eyes got watery and he put his arms around me, hugging me like I was a long-lost son come home. My own eyes prickled, I have to admit. After a minute, he stepped back and shook his head.

"Ah, Michael," he said. "Sometimes I don't have the right words. But the book—" He gave a little do-you-know-what-I'm-trying-to-say wave of his hand.

"Thanks for sending it, Fritz. It's pretty meaty." I'd read the whole thing through from start to finish and was on my second go-around. Some things you just can't get all at once, I guess.

Fritz gave me a solemn nod, then started to quote from the last quartet.

"*At the source of the longest river . . .*"

"*All manner of thing shall be well*" Carl finished for him. Then he stood there looking as surprised as if he'd just pulled a rabbit out of his baseball cap.

Fritz looked astonished, and delighted, too. He smiled, clapped one hand on Carl's shoulder and the other hand on mine. The three of us stood there, grinning like fools.

Fritz told me I could come back to work whenever I was ready, if I wanted to. I wasn't sure yet when that would be. I thanked him again and said I'd let him know. Fritz went back up to the office. I started to leave. On my way out, Carl called after me.

"If you get hungry, you come here."

I gave him a yes-sir salute.

When I got outside, I didn't go straight home. My

feet took me slowly toward the swing bridge. As I walked, my head was filled with thoughts about everything that had happened, that had led up to—

I mean, maybe I wasn't thinking about killing myself that night I jumped in the river. But the thing of it is, I came close to doing it. And no matter what you're looking for, even if you don't know what it is, if you check out—either by mistake or on purpose—how are you going to find it?

Maybe the TV Guidance Counselor doesn't know what she's looking for; maybe she does and she'll never tell and we'll never know. But there's something about her I kind of admire. I think it might be her perseverance. Fatty-Bean talked about guiding students onto a path into the future. In a funny way, I feel like my path's going to be guided more by something I learned from Janey Riddley than by any course I've taken in school. I'm not sure exactly how, but I have time to figure it out.

So I was walking and thinking these thoughts, and all of a sudden I stopped and looked over my shoulder. I'd walked all the way across the bridge.

INDUSTRIAL
AND
COMMERCIAL
WIRING

KENNARD C. GRAHAM

Electrical Engineer;
Consultant, Apprenticeship Instruction
Material Laboratory
of Bureau of Trade and Industry,
California State
Department of Education

AMERICAN TECHNICAL SOCIETY · CHICAGO

THE COVER
The cover photo illustrates an installation
using material and methods typical
of both Industrial and Commercial applications.
Courtesy of General Cable Corp.

PREFACE TO THE SECOND EDITION

This book has been rewritten to reflect the latest developments in the electrical field; covering new techniques and materials, and incorporating the latest additions and changes in the National Electrical Code.

As in the first edition, this book uses the practical approach to the problems of Industrial and Commercial wiring. In conformance with the National Electrical Code, principles are brought out through the application of rules to specific Installation projects. The project method of teaching, found so effective in the first edition, is again utilized with new examples planned for concise explanation of the projects.

The beginning of this volume deals with methods and materials peculiar to the industrial and commercial field. The subject of lighting, starting with basic lighting terms and principles, and discussing incandescent, fluorescent and mercury vapor lighting is covered along with the subject of lighting design as applied to both industrial and commercial applications. Principles learned in the first chapters are applied immediately to the design of various lighting and wiring installations.

The subject of motors is given a thorough coverage. Beginning with various types and operating conditions, wiring, overcurrent protection, controls and safety precautions are discussed making use of practical examples to demonstrate the code requirements and principles of installation.

A new chapter is devoted to Commercial and Industrial calculations which makes use of newly devised procedures which greatly simplify the necessary computations for an installation. Much of the tedious figuring is eliminated, allowing quicker solutions to problems with greater accuracy.

The Publishers

CONTENTS

Contents

Contents

loop system—Loop system with bus-ties—Bus-tie conductors—Limiters, Circuit breakers, and switches—Network systems—Cable and conduit — Shielding — Stress cone — Potheads — Circuit protection — Motors.

Chapter One

Industrial and Commercial Wiring Methods

Comparison with Residential Wiring

Commercial and industrial wiring methods are no different basically from those for residential installations, but the general run of problems varies somewhat from that met with in the simpler type of construction. Operations are usually on a much larger scale, a greater number of workmen being employed on a given project, heavier conductors, switchgear, and panelboards being required.

The element of expense receives particular attention, calling for mass production methods in handling materials, utilization of labor saving devices that would not pay for themselves on smaller jobs, use of manufactured accessory items, and careful planning throughout. This chapter describes some of the tools, materials and practices found in commercial and industrial operations. Fundamental steps in the bending of conduit, installing of conductors, soldering, splicing and connecting, are set forth in the book, *Interior Electric Wiring—Residential,* by the same author.

Note: The terms "Code" or "NEC" when used in this text, refer to the National Electrical Code.

INSTALLING CONDUIT

Determining Location of Runs

When a single line of conduit is to be installed between two points, for example between switchboard and panelboard location, the first consideration is to select the exact path for the run. In some cases, it is necessary only to choose a direct line, especially when the work is to be concealed in the building structure. Quite often, however, conduit remains exposed in shop or manufacturing areas. In

1

such case, angular lines of conduit have an unsightly appearance. The usual practice is to install exposed conduits parallel to walls or at right angles to them, as the particular case may require, employing elbows or pull boxes for changing direction.

The path, when determined, will consist of one or more straight lines between two or more points. In order to lay out these routes a chalk line is often employed, the line being drawn taut and then snapped sharply to mark a straight line upon the surface. Another method which may be advantageous where the surface is so uneven that a line cannot be snapped, is the use of a surveyor's transit. One man sights the telescope, the other marks points along the way with crayon or chalk.

Trapeze Hangers

After the path has been marked out, methods for placing the conduit should be considered. Where it is of large size, the weight factor becomes important. With small conduits, such as used in residential work, a single workman can install the run from a stepladder, moving it along as the work progresses. With heavy conduits, such procedure is impractical. It is necessary, first, to install supports. For single runs of conduit, one-hole straps are often used to conserve labor. The straps are installed loosely, then the conduit is slipped into place. After it is screwed to the next length, the straps are tightened.

Where several conduits are run parallel, trapeze hangers like the one shown at the left in Fig. 1 are employed, rather than straps. The trapeze consists of two long bolts and a supporting bar. The bolts, threaded at either end, are first installed in the ceiling. When they are in place, the cross member is fastened to them by means of nuts and washers as shown in the figure. These hangers are placed at

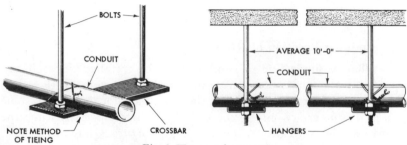

Fig. 1. Trapeze hangers

intervals of 10' or more, as indicated at the right in Fig. 1, the spacing depending upon the size of conduit.

The code does not specify how close together supports must be, simply stating that raceways shall be securely fastened in place. In any case, there must be a sufficient number of hangers so the weight of conduit and conductors will not impose undue strain upon fastenings. When the hangers have been installed, conduits are laid from hanger to hanger, coupling two or more lengths together if necessary.

After a run of conduit is completed, it must be fastened to the supporting bar. This may* be accomplished with pipe straps, patented fasteners, plumber's tape, or galvanized iron wire. The pipe-strap or fastener methods are expensive, and are considered unnecessary in most cases. The weight is carried by the cross bar and the sole purpose of additional fastening is to prevent shifting of the conduit. The usual method is to employ the soft iron wire, passing it around conduit and supporting bar in one diagonal direction, then in the other diagonal direction, as indicated in Fig. 1. The ends are twisted together to prevent unwinding.

It is sometimes convenient, where there are two or more parallel conduits, to work on the various runs at the same time, screwing all lengths tight before going on to the next hanger. When there are a great number of conduits, double trapeze hangers are often employed. The left illustration in Fig. 2 shows a hanger of this type. It is better from the standpoint of appearance, as well as from that of accessibility, to use a double or even a triple trapeze rather than a single wide hanger.

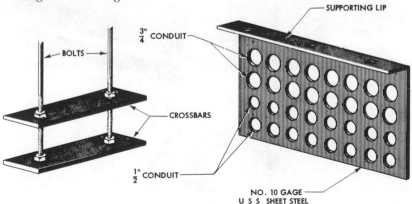

Fig. 2. Double trapeze and punched hanger

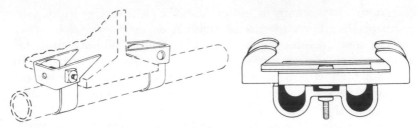

Fig. 3. Clamps for steel beams
Courtesy of the Thomas and Betts Co., Inc.

Other Types of Hangers

The punched hanger, which has become quite popular, is shown at the right in Fig. 2. It is suitable especially for a large number of small conduits, making a neat, compact installation. The one in the figure is arranged for four rows of conduit, the upper ones being ¾" and the two lower ones ½". The metal is No. 10 gage USS sheet steel, and the holes are made on a punch press.

Where necessary to support conduits on steel beams, trapeze hangers may be employed, but the labor of fastening is so great that patented devices, such as shown in Fig. 3, are often called upon. There are several varieties, all of them depending upon a clamping type of support instead of screws or bolts. Brackets, like that shown at the left in Fig. 4, are used for horizontal rows of conduit installed

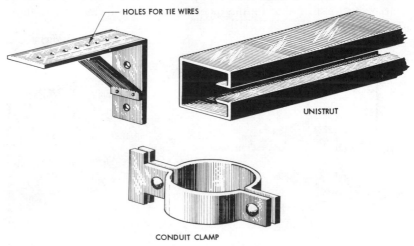

Fig. 4. Other methods for supporting conduit

along a wall. Conduit runs are placed on them in the same way as on ceiling trapeze units. Multiple brackets are employed where necessary. The punched hanger is equally serviceable for wall mounting of conduits up to 2″ in diameter.

Fig. 5. Mobile scaffold
Courtesy of the Up-Right Scaffolds Div. of Up-Right Inc.

Another method of supporting conduits includes Unistrut and conduit clamps, as indicated at the right and bottom of the illustration. Unistrut is a patented device consisting of a partially closed channel of square cross section as indicated at the right in the figure. The pipe clamp is a sheet metal hanging device which is inserted into the channel, and which is held tightly to the conduit by a clamping screw. For supporting vertical rows of conduit, Unistrut channel offers many advantages over the pipe-strap method.

Conduits installed in concrete slabs should be tied to reinforcing steel in order to prevent movement during pouring operations, and they should be supported at intervals to keep them at an even level. If permitted to sag, water pockets may form and insulation trouble may develop later on.

Scaffolds

The use of stepladders becomes impractical when installing large sizes of conduit. Scaffolds are usually employed for the purpose.

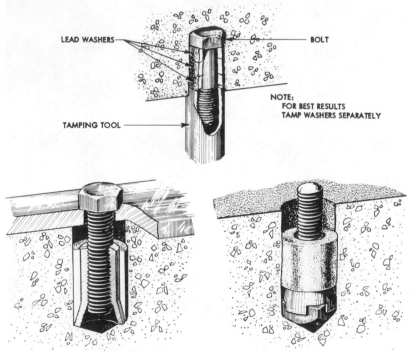

Fig. 6. Lead-expansion devices

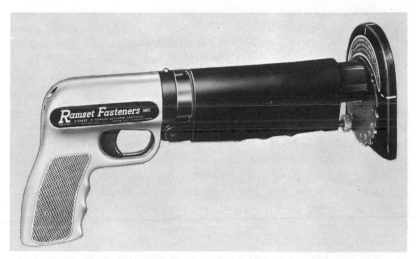

Fig. 7. Fastening device using explosive cartridge
Courtesy of Ramset Fasteners Inc.

Where mechanics from several trades are working in a particular area, it is customary to erect fixed scaffolds. But where the installation consists of long runs of conduit, the mobile type shown in Fig. 5 is more practicable. When the scaffold has been moved to the desired location, its wheels are locked so it cannot move out of place under strains imposed by those working above.

Fastenings

For supporting objects on concrete or masonry, some form of expansion anchor is usually employed. There are a number of such devices, most of them depending upon the holding power of lead which has been expanded into the bolt hole. The general principle governing these devices is illustrated at the left in Fig. 6. Two common types are shown at the right.

Manual Installation. In order to install a bolt, a hole slightly larger than the head of the bolt is made with a star drill. The bolt is inserted, the lead washers placed on its shank, and a tamping tool is hammered against the lead. As the lead is forced into the hole, it spreads out to fill crevices at the sides. When properly installed, the device can withstand a pull equal to any load which the material of the bolt itself can safely carry. Objects may be fastened to the bolt after it is in place by means of nuts and washers.

Where a nut is required in the ceiling, a screw anchor is installed instead of a bolt. The screw anchor consists of a nut set into a lead holder. When tamped down, the lead holder expands into the hole grasping the nut firmly so that a bolt may be screwed into it.

Powder-Actuated Tool. A rapid method for installing small bolts in walls and ceiling, or for fastening conduit straps, is by means of an explosion device. Fig. 7 shows one of these units. By means of this tool, screws or other fastening devices may be set into the concrete without drilling holes. It makes use of a small-calibre blank cartridge to shoot the hanging device into place when the trigger of the "gun" is pulled. Ominous warnings accompanied these tools when first put into operation, but serious results failed to materialize. Safety shields and other improvements have made them quite safe in the hands of skilled workmen.

This tool may be used also to install small bolts in steel beams or channels. The pressure created by the explosion of the cartridge is sufficient to force a hardened supporting pin into the metal object. A somewhat longer cartridge is used for this purpose than for attaching to concrete or masonry.

Concrete Slab. In concrete work, metal inserts like the one at the left in Fig. 8, are placed on the wooden deck before concrete is poured. When the decking is stripped, the inserts offer a convenient means for supporting hangers below. This application is shown at the right in the figure. Unistrut, Kindorf, and similar patented supporting materials, may be cast in place in this way for attaching conduits to walls or ceilings.

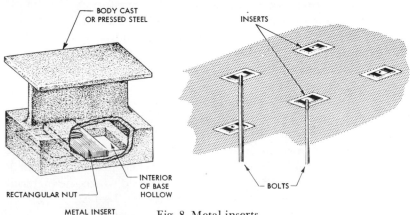

Fig. 8. Metal inserts

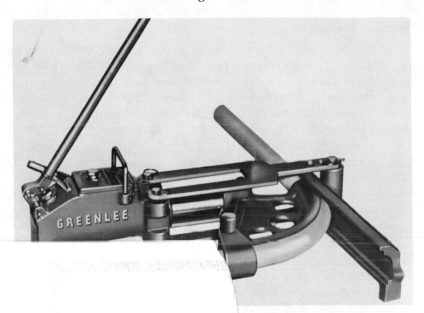

bender

Courtesy of Greenlee Tool Co.

ools and Materials

re at all times for his own
ty. This is particularly true
tools. Where a concrete or
ts may occur even when the
in the normally correct posi-
hand that the wall or ceiling
not emerge from the other
directly behind or above the

e possibility of injury from
s is most important in work-
ild brace himself when pull-
no danger of tumbling in
loose during a heavy pull.
survey the working area for
ird others working nearby.
ition where material is be-
ies.

Bending Conduit

While hickeys may be used with small sizes of conduit, just as in residential installations, larger sizes are shaped by means of mechanical devices like the one illustrated in Fig. 9. This is a hydraulic bender which consists of a triangular supporting device, a set of conduit shoes, and a piston which is actuated by a hydraulic pump.

The conduit is marked at the point where the bend is to start, allowing sufficient total length so it can be made with ample radius. The proper shoe is installed on the piston, the conduit is inserted in the supporting device, and the handle of the pump is operated. The shoe presses the conduit against two stationary shoes, causing it to bend. Then pressure is released to permit moving the conduit, and another portion of the bend is made. This operation is repeated as often as necessary until a smooth bend is produced. The triangular supporting element is adjustable to suit different bending radii.

Although manufacturer's literature provides detailed instruc-

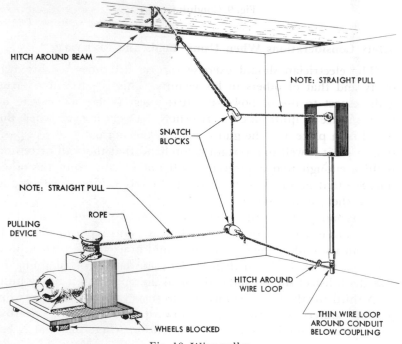

Fig. 10. Wire puller

tions on the method of handling the device, a certain amount of personal experience is required before the wireman becomes expert. The best plan, at first, is to go slowly, not taking too great a bend at one time, moving the conduit back again to increase the degree of curvature if necessary. If bent too sharply at one point, the conduit tends to flatten and to show ridges where the edges of the shoe press into it. Similar machines are employed for bending electrical metallic tubing. With one of these hydraulic units, it is possible to make exactly duplicate bends for conduits which are to be run parallel with one another.

Horizontal Runs

After the conduit is fastened in place, the conductors may be installed. For pulling heavy conductors, a steel fish tape is first inserted and a rope drawn through the conduit. If the conductors are heavy or the runs long, it is impractical to draw in by hand power

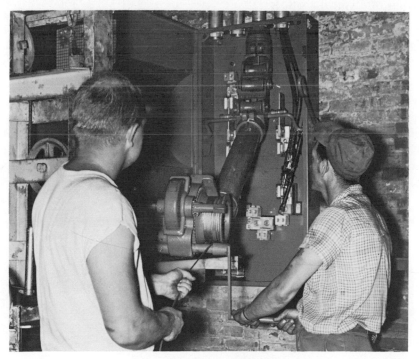

Fig. 11. Modern cable puller

Courtesy Greenlee Tool Co.

alone. Where the installation consists of a single run of conduit, a block and tackle may be rigged up. But this method is slow and laborious. If there are a number of runs, it is wise to make use of a pulling device.

There are a number of such machines on the market, one of the best consisting of a mechanical winch with an electric motor, as illustrated in Fig. 10. In use, it is braced, as shown in the figure, and a pair of snatch blocks are employed to carry the pulling rope from the end of the conduit to the rotating drum.

A few turns of rope are wound around the drum, and the motor is started drawing the conductors through the conduit run. It will be seen from the illustration that a straight pull is obtained at the end of the conduit and also at the winch. Thus, a steady and direct application of power is provided. If the other end of the run is out of sight and easy hearing, it is well to have signal bells, a pair of signal lights, or an intercom telephone line connecting the feed-in location and the winch.

A popular unit of this kind, which is obtainable through an electrical supply house, is illustrated in Fig. 11. In practice, this winch also is often driven by an electric motor.

Reel Holders

Electrical conductors are shipped on wooden or metal reels. These reels may be set up on improvised horses or jacks with a piece of conduit through the center, or they can be mounted on a portable rack, as shown at the left in Fig. 12. Where considerable

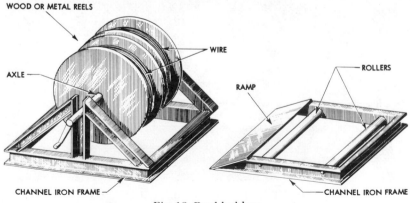

WOOD OR METAL REELS

WIRE

AXLE

RAMP

ROLLERS

CHANNEL IRON FRAME

CHANNEL IRON FRAME

Fig. 12. Reel holders

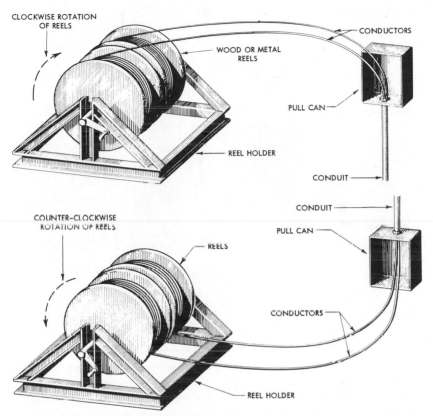

Fig. 13. Feeding conductors in conduit

wire pulling is to be done, a unit of this kind is a valuable time saver. Another device sometimes used for the purpose is a reel roller shown in the right-hand illustration. No "axle" pipe is needed, the reel turning on steel rollers which contact its outer circumference.

Vertical Runs

When installing conductors in vertical conduits of high buildings, it is wise to take advantage of gravity feeding the wires from above, as in the upper illustration of Fig. 13. The reels should be so arranged that conductors pass from the top. With the conduit on the right, as shown, the reels will turn in a clockwise direction. In cases where it is more convenient to feed conductors from below, the wire should pass from the bottom of the reel as shown in the

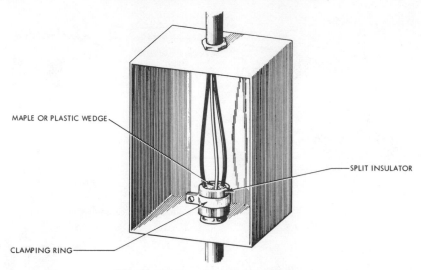

MAPLE OR PLASTIC WEDGE

SPLIT INSULATOR

CLAMPING RING

Fig. 14. Wedge-type clamping device

lower illustration. With the conduit at the right, the reels will turn in a counterclockwise direction. With heavy conductors, it is necessary to provide some means for braking the reel as wire is unwound. If this is not done, the weight of free conductor may cause the reel to spin out of control, and to dump the whole length of wire or cable down the conduit run. Some manufactured reel holders are provided with means for braking the reel with a hand lever and a friction shoe which presses against the outer circumference. For

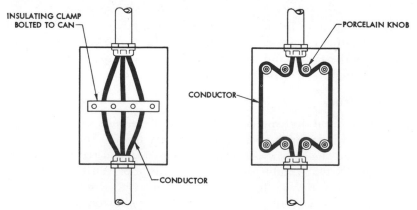

INSULATING CLAMP BOLTED TO CAN

PORCELAIN KNOB

CONDUCTOR

CONDUCTOR

Fig. 15. Other methods of supporting conductors

temporary setups, a plank may be arranged to provide such friction, or a restraining rope may be used. It is wise, also, to make sure the conductor will not slip free suddenly, and go plunging down the conduit when the end winding on the reel has been reached.

Conductors in vertical raceways should be supported at intervals not exceeding those prescribed by the NEC. The code provides that cables shall be supported by clamping devices employing insulating wedges, Fig. 14, or by other means. Where conductors are installed in wire shafts or other raceways in which it is impractical to use the wedge type of support, insulating clamps are mounted in junction boxes as shown at the left in Fig. 15. In some cases, the method shown at the right is employed, the wire being deflected horizontally to pass around insulating knobs.

Attaching Wires to Pulling Rope

The manner of fastening conductors to the pulling rope is rather important. With small wires, it is necessary only to remove insulation and to wrap the wire around the fish steel. With large, stranded conductors, it would be wasteful of material and labor to do so. A popular scheme is to drill a hole in each cable a few inches back from the end and to pass a soft iron wire through the hole as indicated in the top illustration of Fig. 16. The ends of these wires are twisted together and fastened to the pulling rope. Tape is

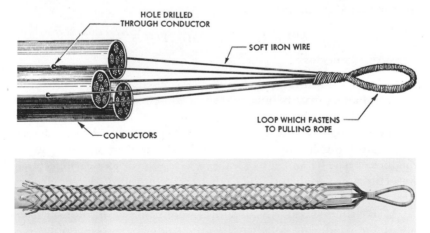

Fig. 16. Attaching wires to pulling rope

Courtesy of Kellems Company

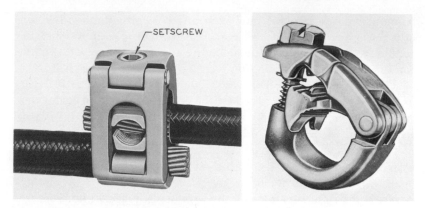

Fig. 17. Pressure connectors
Courtesy of the Thomas and Betts Co., Inc.

wound over the connection to prevent snagging as the wires are drawn in.

Another plan is to use a Kellems cable grip, shown in the bottom illustration. This device consists of a cylinder made of woven steel or bronze wires. Its open end is slipped over the cable assembly and the loop at the other end is attached to the pulling rope. When a strain is imposed on the rope, the basket weave causes the device to grip the conductors tightly. The nature of this clamping action is such that the greater the strain on the pulling rope, the tighter the hold on the conductors.

SPLICING CONDUCTORS

Pressure Connectors

Unless an approved splicing device is used, the NEC provides that conductors shall be first spliced or joined so as to be mechanically and electrically secure. That is, they shall be twisted together or wrapped tightly with copper wire. Then they shall be soldered with a fusible metal or alloy, or shall be brazed or welded. Small conductors may be joined by means of wire nuts or screw connectors. But with large conductors, the Code phrase *approved splicing device* means some form of pressure connector.

At one time, practically all splices were made with solder. Heating of the conductor, incidental to the soldering process, often resulted in damage to conductor insulation. For this reason, among others, the pressure connector was developed. The standard device utilizes compression established by a nut or a setscrew. Samples of both types are shown in Fig. 17. The insulation is stripped back a sufficient distance for insertion into the connector. The nut or setscrew is then tightened by a wrench until the conductors are pressed tightly together. When the operation is completed, the joint is covered with insulating material. These devices are used for connecting wires to switches or to lugs. Right-angle taps may be made with the proper type of device.

Pressure Machines

Hydraulic pressure is often employed in fastening lugs or connectors to conductors. After the conductor is inserted into the lug, hydraulic pressure causes a plunger to squeeze the metal of the lug and the metal of the conductor together, forming a union which appears almost as solid as if welded. Fig. 18 shows a tool which performs a similar operation without the use of hydraulic pressure, the crimpings or indentations being formed by rollers which press the two metals together.

Thermit Welding

Another scheme which is used where conditions permit, is pre-

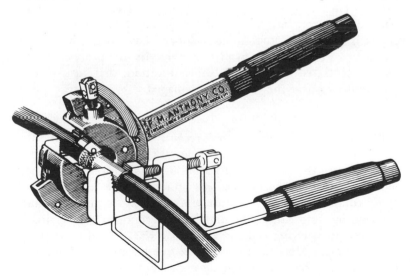

Fig. 18. Compression machine
Courtesy of F. M. Anthony Company

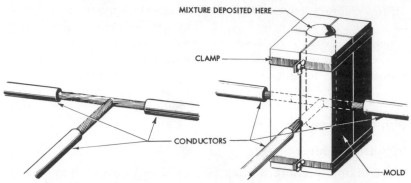

Fig. 19. Welding with thermit mixture

sented in Fig. 19. If a tap is to be formed on a conductor, as indicated in the left-hand illustration, the main conductor and the tap conductor are inserted into a mold lined with asbestos, as shown at the right. A charge of thermit mixture is poured into a hole at the top of the mold, the powder filling the space indicated by dotted outline in the figure.

The thermit mixture consists of powdered copper-oxide, powdered aluminum, and a quantity of flash powder. The powder is ignited by a match or a spark-producing device. It flares momentarily, combustion lasting only a few seconds. When the mold is removed, it is found that molten copper has fused with the two conductors, welding them firmly together. In this process, the heat is so concentrated and of such short duration, that insulation on the conductors near the joint is undamaged.

Plastic and Similar Conduit

Plastic, polyvinyl conduit has recently been introduced in the electrical trade. One type is known as PVC (polyvinyl chloride). It is made in two thicknesses, thinwall and standard, the former being made in sizes up to and including 2″ trade size, the latter up to 4″. Plastic couplings, box connectors, and elbows are also obtainable.

Couplings and fittings on lightweight conduits are secured by means of quick-drying cement. The material is readily bent with the aid of heat. Metallic outlet boxes can be used, enclosures and devices being grounded where necessary by a separate conductor. Heavier plastic conduit is furnished with standard size threads and couplings.

"Under Section 347 of NEC, this material cannot be used underground without a 2" concrete envelope, unless able to withstand continuous (earth) loading. Provisions of this section apply also to: fiber, asbestos cement, and soapstone conduits.

These raceways shall be not less than 24" below grade, and where the voltage exceeds 600, shall be encased in 2" of concrete. They may be used in concrete walls, floors, and ceiling, but are not permitted above ground outdoors, in hazardous locations, or in concealed spaces of combustible construction."

Mineral Insulated Cable

The material shown in Fig. 20 is known as mineral-insulated-metallic cable, designated by the Code as type MI. One or more electrical conductors are enclosed in a liquid-tight, gas-tight metallic tube, separated from each other and from the wall of the tube by highly compressed insulating powder. The illustration also shows the special gland-type fittings that must be used with the cable.

The Code states that type MI cable can be used for services, feeders, and branch circuits in exposed or concealed work, in dry or wet locations. It may be exposed to the weather, embedded in plaster, masonry, or concrete, and run underground. It may be exposed to oil, gasoline, or other materials that do not have a deteriorating effect on the metal sheath. MI cable is rather expensive, as compared with ordinary wiring, but where extremely severe conditions prevail, it is sometimes the only possible method that can be employed. This material also finds applications where space is highly limited, especially in alteration work.

DUCT SYSTEMS

General Nature

A method of wiring that finds wide application today may be classified under the general heading of duct systems. The term, as used here, includes underfloor raceway, cellular metal raceway, wireways, and busways. Each one has its particular field of application. But they have certain points in common, under provisions of the code. None of these systems are permitted in a hazardous location, a commercial garage, a storage-battery room, or where exposed to corrosive vapors. All four systems are made of metal. One form of underfloor raceway made of fiber has limited application.

It is necessary, first, to decide upon the location and layout of runs, as in conduit installations. More care is required in the actual placing of ducts because they must be maintained level. Those installed on ceilings or walls are supported with bolts or brackets. These above-floor systems cannot be effectively concealed, but must

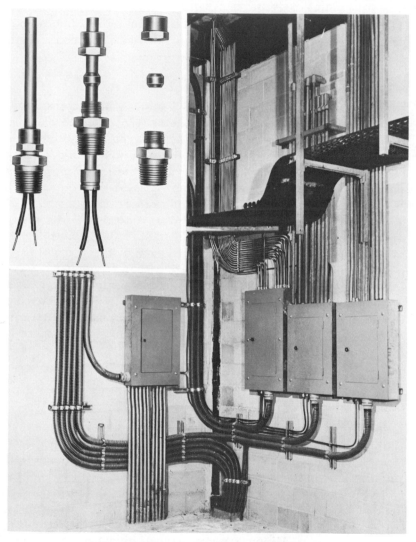

Fig. 20. MI cable installation and fittings

Courtesy of General Cable Co.

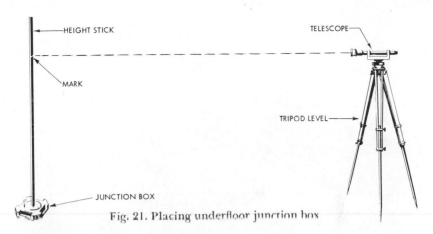

Fig. 21. Placing underfloor junction box

be run exposed except where they pass through dry walls or partitions at right angles to them. They are permitted above luminous ceilings where readily accessible through removal of glass or plastic sheets.

Underfloor Metallic Raceway

After the directions of the runs have been laid out, the locations of junction boxes must be determined. Junction boxes are placed accurately and leveled to the correct height with the aid of a surveyors transit or a tripod level, as indicated in Fig. 21. After the finished floor height is obtained from architectural plans, the telescope is set and the rod or height stick is marked so that junction boxes may be adjusted to this height. When the bottom of the stick is at the correct level, the mark on the stick will coincide with the cross hairs in the telescope.

The box is placed, and leveled with the aid of a spirit level. The stick is then held vertically upright upon the upper surface of the box. The height is increased or decreased by means of the adjusting screws until correct. The box is then checked carefully with the spirit level, making such adjustments as required before grouting with cement to hold it in place.

While the cement is hardening, supporting saddles, illustrated at the left in Fig. 22, are attached to the rough concrete floor at intervals of about 5'. They are fastened by rawl plugs, powder-actuated screws, or other available means. The saddle consists of the stationary base portion, and a movable part which can be moved

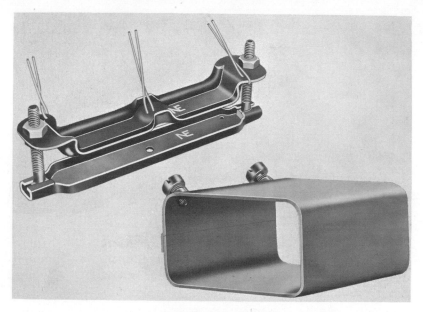

Fig. 22. Saddle and coupling
Courtesy of National Electric Products Corp.

up or down by adjusting nuts at either end.

With saddles in place, 10' lengths of raceway are laid upon them, and extended from one junction box to another. Where the distance is greater than 10', a coupling, illustrated at the right in the figure, is inserted. When runs are in position, they should be fastened to saddles by means of tie wires. Then they should be leveled throughout the whole length with the aid of the height stick, ducts being raised or lowered by means of saddle adjusting nuts.

Fig. 23 shows an underfloor duct installation. As noted in the figure, underfloor duct systems are usually run in multiple, one section being for lights, a second for telephone, and perhaps a third for power. The junction boxes are designed so that each class of circuit is completely isolated from other classes, but all are accessible from the top.

Ducts may be connected to panelboards by special fittings and conduit. In other than office locations the Code requires that raceways not over 4″ in width shall be covered by not less than ¾″ of concrete or wood. If more than 4″ in width, or if separation between ducts is less than ½″, they must be covered with concrete to a depth

Fig. 23. Underfloor duct installation
Courtesy of National Electric Products Corp.

of not less than 1½″. The Code limits the size of the largest conductor to No. 0, and raceway fill to 40 percent of cross-sectional area. Splices and taps must be made only in junction boxes.

The Code provides further that ducts shall be laid in straight lines, and that a marker or fitting shall be installed in the floor at a point where a duct line ends. After concrete has been poured outlet hubs may be located by measurement, by marker screws which have been inserted for the purpose, or by use of a magnetic device. When the desired outlet points have been found, the concrete is punched through with a hammer, and outlet caps are removed to give access to the duct. Circuit and feeder wires are then pulled in.

Cellular Metal Raceway

As shown in the illustration of Fig. 24, this type of duct is similar in many respects to underfloor duct. Cellular duct, however, is

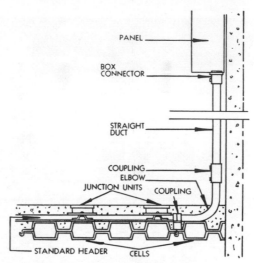

Fig. 24. Cellular floor installation
Courtesy of General Electric Co.

a structural building member, being laid by structural iron workers from steel beam to steel beam. When electrical, plumbing, and other trades work is completed, concrete is poured on top of the duct as indicated in the figure. Certain duct cells are assigned for the electrical installation. They are connected together, and to the panelboards, by means of headers.

Where connections to panelboards are made above the floor, a standard header is used. Where below the floor, a ceiling header is employed. Special tools are called upon to make holes in ducts for insertion of receptacle outlets, conduit taps, or for other purposes. The lefthand illustration in Fig. 25 shows the connection of a standard header to a panelboard. At the right is a cross-sectional view of the connection between a ceiling header and a panelboard which has been installed in a partition below.

Code requirements with respect to this type of installation parallel those for underfloor duct systems in regard to limitations on use, size of conductors, and percentage of fill. As with underfloor duct, splices and taps can be made only in junction boxes or header access units.

Precast Ducts

Tile or precast concrete ducts are quite similar to underfloor

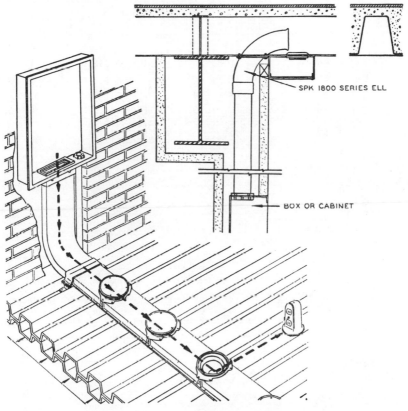

Fig. 25. Connecting to cells
Courtesy of General Electric Co.

metallic raceway. Access headers are of metal. The same Code rules apply to it as to other such raceways.

Wireways

Wireways are sheetmetal troughs with hinged or removable covers, for housing electrical wires and cables. Their use is limited in the same way as the underfloor systems. They are not allowed in hoistways. Troughs must be supported at distances not exceeding 5', unless specially approved supports are employed. In no case may the distance between supports exceed 10'.

The largest conductor permitted by the Code is No. 500,000 CM. Not more than 30 conductors, except control or signal circuits,

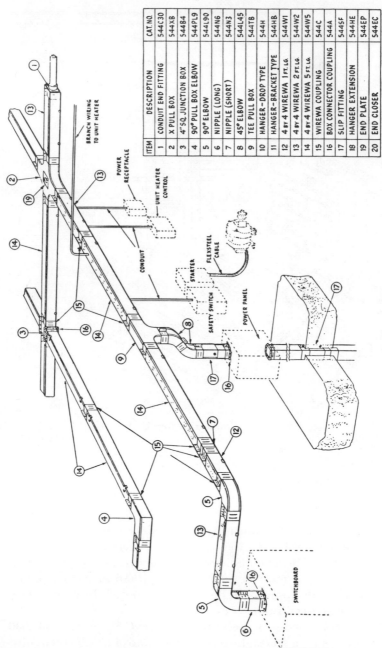

ITEM	DESCRIPTION	CAT. NO
1	CONDUIT END FITTING	544C30
2	X PULL BOX	544X8
3	4" SQ. JUNCTION BOX	544B4
4	90° PULL BOX ELBOW	544PL9
5	90° ELBOW	544L90
6	NIPPLE (LONG)	544N6
7	NIPPLE (SHORT)	544N3
8	45° ELBOW	544L45
9	TEE PULL BOX	544TB
10	HANGER – DROP TYPE	544H
11	HANGER – BRACKET TYPE	544HB
12	4 BY 4 WIREWA 1 FT. LG	544W1
13	4 BY 4 WIREWA 2 FT. LG	544W2
14	4 BY 4 WIREWA 5 FT. LG	544W5
15	WIREWA COUPLING	544C
16	BOX CONNECTOR COUPLING	544A
17	SLIP FITTING	544SF
18	HANGER EXTENSION	544HE
19	END PLATE	544EP
20	END CLOSER	544EC

Fig. 26. Wireway installation

Courtesy of National Electric Products Corp.

are permitted in any cross section of wireway and the sum of cross-sectional areas of conductors must not exceed 20 percent of the interior cross-sectional area. Conductors, together with splices and taps, shall not fill the wireway to more than 75 percent of its area. Extensions from wireways are made with rigid or flexible metal conduit, electrical metallic tubing, surface metal raceway, or armored cable.

Adjacent sections of wireway are connected by means of bolts and nuts, or by special sheetmetal couplings. Wireways are manufactured with various fittings to suit particular requirements of installation. Some of these are shown in Fig. 27. A complete wireway installation is shown in Fig. 26.

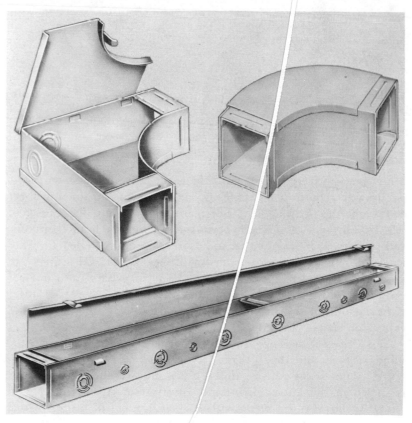

Fig. 27. Wireway fittings

Courtesy of National Electric Products Corp.

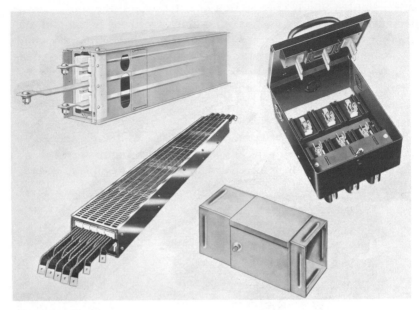

Fig. 28. Busway units
Courtesy of National Electric Products Corp.

Busways

A comparatively recent addition to duct methods of wiring is the busway or busduct system. Copper bus bars are enclosed in sheet metal housings or troughs as shown in the lower left illustration of Fig. 28. This type of wiring is permitted for feeders, branch circuits, and services. It is supplied in standard 10' lengths joined together with bolts, compression washers, and heavy nuts. Housings are fastened by means of metal plates and screws. Where the run is of considerable length, expansion joints such as the one in the lower right illustration of Fig. 28 are employed because of different rates of expansion of steel and copper.

Two types of busways are used as feeders or branch circuits; the standard type, and the "plug-in" type shown at the upper left in Fig. 28. One of the plug-in units, a disconnect switch in this case, is shown in the upper right-hand illustration. As in the case of wireways, busways are made with a great number of fittings which are suited to particular requirements of application. Fig. 29 shows a typical busway installation.

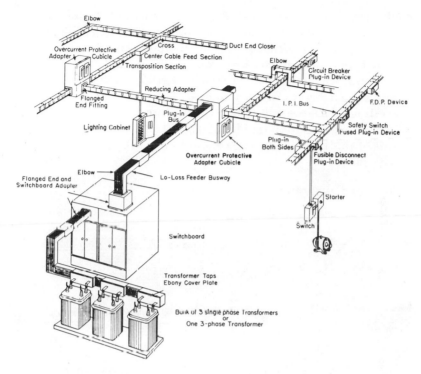

Fig. 29. Busway installation

Courtesy of National Electric Products Corp.

Under the Code, its use is subject to the limitations applying to underfloor raceway, and also to a prohibition with respect to damp locations or hoistways. Busways must be supported at intervals not exceeding 5', except that special approval may permit the distance to be increased to not over 10'. If the allowable current rating of a busway used as a feeder does not correspond to a standard rating of overcurrent device, the next higher rating, not exceeding 150 percent of that of the busway, may be used.

Branches from busways shall be made with busways or rigid or flexible metal conduit, electrical metallic tubing, surface metal raceway, armored cable, or with suitable cord assemblies approved for hard usage. Cords may be used only for portable equipment, or for the purpose of facilitating interchange of units of stationary equipment. Overcurrent protection may be omitted at points where busways are reduced in size, provided the smaller busway does not extend more than 50', and provided it has a current rating at least one-third the rating or setting of the overcurrent device which protects the larger conductor. A further limitation is that the busway shall not come into contact with combustible material.

Busways which are used as branch circuits, and which are designed so that loads can be connected at any point, shall not, in general, be of a greater length, expressed in feet, than three times the ampere rating of the branch circuit. Thus, a 15-ampere branch circuit of this type should not be longer than 45', and a 20-ampere circuit, 60'.

Ventilated Cableways

Raceways such as those illustrated in Fig. 30 have a somewhat

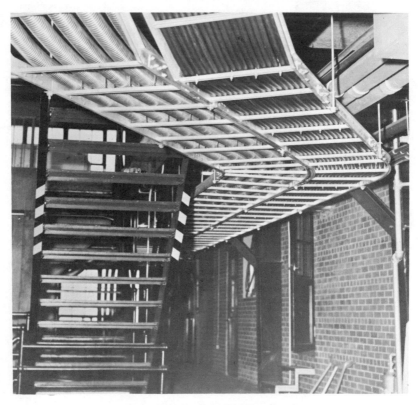

Fig. 30. Ventilated cableways
Courtesy of Husky Division of **Burndy Corp.**

more limited application than busways.

"Under NEC 318, they may be used only to support: MI, aluminum-sheathed, metal-clad, non-metallic sheathed, service-entrance, UF, and factory-assembled cables approved for such use. Details relative to spacing between individual cables are provided in the section."

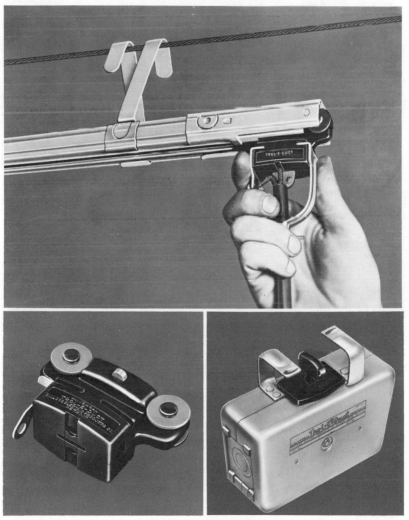

Fig. 31. Trolley devices
Courtesy of Bulldog Electric Products Co.

Fig. 32. Trolley duct installation
Courtesy of Bulldog Electric Products Co.

Trolley Type Duct Systems

Trolley systems come under the general heading of busways. Two of the more prominent systems are covered by the trade names "Trol-E-Duct" and "Trolley-Closur." Both make use of a semiclosed channel which has contact bars along the sides as shown at the top of Fig. 31. The lower left-hand illustration shows a portable trolley unit, and the lower right-hand one, a fixed type. A complete installation is shown in Fig. 32.

Trolley systems are employed in offices for connecting tabulating machines and other apparatus whose locations may be altered frequently. They are used in industrial applications for hanging light fixtures whose locations are not permanently fixed, and for connecting small portable tools which may be shifted along a bench or from one part of the establishment to another as needed.

"Recent Code Changes—

NEC section 410–26 now states that in an assembly of end-to-end fixtures, branch circuit conductors within 3″ of a ballast shall be

Type RHH AWG or equivalent, such conductors being approved for temperature of 90° Centigrade. NEC 210–6(a) allows mogul-base sockets operating at 151 to 300 volts to ground to be installed in commercial locations, provided that they are at least 8 ft. from the floor and do not include a switch integral with the fixture. Formerly, this rule applied only to industrial locations. This section also permits electrical discharge fixtures which operate between these voltage limitations to be mounted less than 8 ft from the floor.

Attention should be called to the fact that Type ALS aluminum-sheathed cable is approved for general feeder and circuit wiring, not including services, hazardous locations, or direct burial in the earth. Table 310-12 now lists a new conductor, Type THWN, which has an outer braid of nylon. The term "armored-cable" has been changed to "metal-clad cable," of which there are two general types, AC and MC. The outer covering of Type MC may be aluminum, bronze, or suitable alloy."

REVIEW QUESTIONS

1. What set of rules is referred to here by the term "Code"?
2. What is the first consideration in planning a conduit run?
3. Name the simplest type hanger for parallel conduit runs.
4. Name one other kind of hanger.
5. Are stepladders commonly used when installing heavy runs of conduit?
6. Name a common powder-actuated tool.
7. What device is useful for supporting conduits from a concrete ceiling?
8. How should reels of heavy conductors be supported when in use?
9. What force should be taken advantage of when installing heavy cables in vertical conduits?
10. Name a common type of device used to support heavy conductors in vertical raceways.
11. Name the patented device commonly used when pulling heavy conductors through conduit.
12. How are connectors usually fastened to large conductors?
13. What instrument is most useful for leveling runs of underfloor duct?
14. How are couplings fastened to plastic conduit?
15. Would MI cable be permitted in a hot location?
16. What kind of headers must be used with a precast concrete duct system?
17. Is "wireway" simply another name for busway?
18. What is the largest size of conductor permitted in a cellular floor raceway?
19. Trolley duct is basically similar to what other type of wiring?
20. What types of non-metallic conduit are used for underground runs?

Chapter Two

Electric Lamps

Introduction

Lighting installations are designed primarily to furnish a substitute for natural illumination. Although artificial lighting may never quite equal Nature's product, electric lamp development is bringing the two closer together, step by step.

The three most common types of lamps are: incandescent, fluorescent, and mercury vapor. The incandescent is often preferred to the others because the color of its light more nearly approximates that of daylight. Fluorescent lamps are superior to incandescent in some respects, but are decidedly inferior with regard to color. Mercury units have the least desirable color qualities of the three.

Through corrective measures, as will be seen later, color defects of both fluorescent and mercury lamps have been partially eliminated. Before discussing the various types in detail, however, it will be necessary to consider certain fundamental principles applying to light obtained from every possible source.

BASIC CONSIDERATIONS

Candlepower

The first important lighting term is candlepower, the standard for lighting intensity. It represents the strength of light given off in a horizontal direction by a source of light known as the International Candle. Fig. 1 illustrates use of the term. The International Candle is manufactured according to rigid standards as to size, type of wick, and composition of wax. The ordinary wax candle has approximately one candlepower.

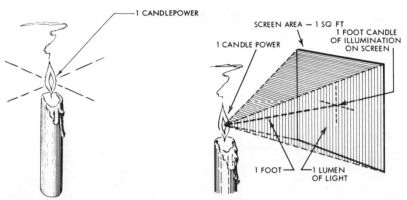

Fig. 1. The international candle   Fig. 2. The foot-candle and the lumen

The Foot-candle and the Lumen

The term candlepower refers to the strength of illumination present at the light source. But common observation shows that illu- ·mination weakens, or decreases, as one moves away from the source. The intensity of light at a distance from the source is expressed in foot-candles or in lumens. The two terms are closely related.

Fig. 2 represents a surface whose area is 1 sq ft, and which is part of a large sphere. Every point on this screen is exactly 1 ft from the center of the candle flame. The *strength* of the illumination on this surface is said to be 1 foot-candle, and the *amount* of light is said to be 1 lumen.

The difference between the two terms will be made clear with the aid of Fig. 3.

It is well to think of each lumen as a pyramid of light which spreads outward from a point source. In the figure, the surface to be lighted is at a distance of 2′ from the candle, while the location of the smaller one used in Fig. 2 is indicated by dotted outline.

The area now lighted by a single lumen of light is equal to 4 sq ft, the base of the pyramid having increased in size according to the square of the distance from the candle. That is, its area at a distance of 2′ is equal to 2 × 2 or 4 times what it was at a distance of 1 ft. Thus a single lumen is now spread over an area four times as great as in Fig. 2, and its new value can be only ¼ lumen per sq ft.

If the screen were placed at a distance of 3′ from the candle flame, the illumination per sq ft would amount to only ⅑ lumen.

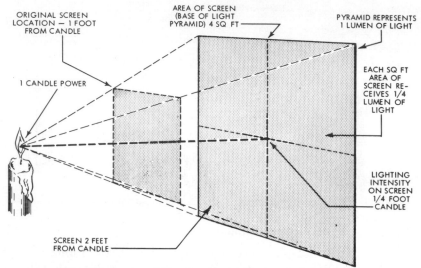

Fig. 3. Intensity of illumination varies inversely as square
of distance

This value is arrived at as follows: The square of the distance equals 3 × 3, or 9. Since the lumen is now spread over 9 sq ft, the value per sq ft must equal ⅑ lumen. The rule covering this fact may be stated: Lighting intensity varies inversely as the square of the distance from the source.

Reflectors used with lamps are so designed as to prevent the lumens from spreading out, and to concentrate them within a given area. The output of an electric lamp is rated on the number of lumens which it can produce. Thus, a lamp whose filament produces 1000 lumens, all of which is directed onto an area of 100 sq ft, will deliver 10 lumens to each sq ft. And, since each lumen per sq ft is equal to one foot-candle intensity, the strength of illumination would be 10 foot-candles. This subject will be discussed in detail later on.

Foot-lambert

Another term which has become increasingly important as foot-candle intensities have become greater is the foot-lambert, which is the unit of brightness. It is particularly useful in the study of glare and contrast. The brightness of any surface is gaged by the amount of light that it directs into the eye. For example, if a wall is illuminated to an intensity of 40 lumens to the sq ft, and it reflects 20 lumens into the eye of a clerk sitting at a desk, the brightness of the wall is said to be 20 foot-lamberts.

INCANDESCENT LAMPS

Types

The underlying structure of the incandescent lamp has not changed a great deal despite the fact that there are now hundreds of types designed to suit a great variety of lighting needs. One noteworthy fact is the constantly decreasing size of the bulb for a given wattage lamp. Another is the change from the original clear glass globe to the standard inside frosted globe in order to reduce objectionable glare from a bare filament. Yet, it still consists of but three essential parts: filament, enclosing globe, and base.

Fig. 4. Lamp bases

Lamp Sockets

General use lamps in sizes up to 300 watts are furnished with medium screw bases, Fig. 4. Those from 300 watts up are equipped with mogul screw bases; while very large lamps, those from 1500 watts up, are furnished with mogul bi-post bases. Lumiline lamps have metal contact discs at either end, so that special sockets are required. Smaller screw type sockets, designated as intermediate, candelabra, and miniature, are employed on smaller sizes which are used mostly for decorative purposes.

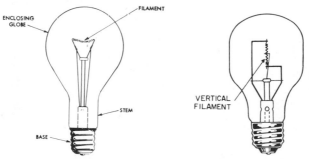

Fig. 5. Lamps with horizontal (*left*) and axial filaments (*right*).

Lamp Filaments

Filaments may be straight, coiled, or doubly-coiled. Their composition has changed throughout the years, from carbon to tantalum, to tungsten. Most filaments are mounted horizontally, as in Fig. 5A, but a recent variation is to mount the filament axially, as in Fig. 5B. The latter construction permits better control of the lumen output.

Lamp Bulbs

Incandescent lamps are classified as type *B* or type *C*. The type *B* lamp is evacuated so that its filament operates in an approximate vacuum, while the type *C* bulb is filled with inert gas.

Lamp bulbs are made in several shapes as indicated in Fig. 6. The bulb shown at *A* is a general use type commonly found in sizes

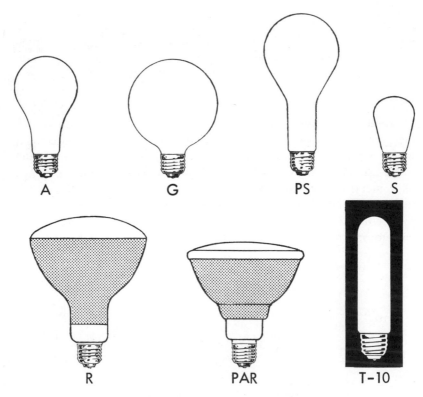

A   G   PS   S

R   PAR   T-10

Fig. 6. Incandescent lamp bulbs

Courtesy of General Electric Co.

of 100 watts or less. *G* is round, or globular, *PS* is pear shaped, *S* is straight sided, *R* is a reflector lamp, *PAR* is parabolic, and *T* is tubular.

The most common types of glass enclosure are; *inside frosted, blue daylight, bowl enameled,* and *silvered bowl.* The *inside frosted* is the one commonly found in the home. The *blue daylight* is used for special applications. The *bowl enameled* is employed with larger sizes to reduce glare, and the *silvered bowl* is found in larger sizes where it is desired to throw the greater part of the light upward.

The number used in connection with the type letter for designating incandescent lamps, is determined by the bulb diameter in ⅛'s of an inch. Thus, the T8 lamp is 1" (eight ⅛'s) in diameter, and the P52 is 6½" (fifty-two ⅛'s) in diameter.

The type *PAR* bulb is called a "projector" unit, and is designed for outdoor use, such as the lighting of yards and gardens. A similar bulb, the type *R,* is designed only for indoor use. It is known as a "reflector" unit. A new series of reflector lamps is designed to radiate the filament heat upward, through the back of the lamp, while the light is directed downward. They are known as "cool-beam" lamps, and are used in meat cases or similar locations.

Fig. 7. The Quartzline lamp
Courtesy of General Electric Co.

A Special Incandescent Lamp

A recent development in this field is the quartzline unit, Fig. 7, which combines extremely small size with tremendous lumen output. The bulb contains a small quantity of iodine, which acts to prevent volatilized tungsten from blackening the inside of the tube. The iodine actually causes the tungsten to be redeposited on the filament while the lamp is in operation.

FLUORESCENT LAMPS

Principle of Operation

The fluorescent lamp, Fig. 8, first appeared in 1938. It consists

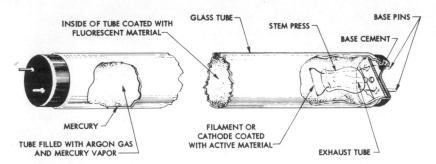

Fig. 8. Construction of a fluorescent lamp

of a glass tube which contains a small quantity of mercury. There is a filament at either end of the tube. The flow of current heats the filaments, and vaporizes the mercury. When an arc is established through the tube from one filament to the other, invisible ultra-violet light rays are created. These rays strike against the particles of phosphor material with which the wall of the tube is coated, causing it to give off visible light.

Types of Tubes

The original form of tube is called the preheat lamp. The filaments heat a few seconds after the switch is turned on, before the lamp starts to burn. Many preheat lamps are still used, but three other general types have been developed.

The rapid start is similar to the preheat lamp, but there are important structural differences, especially in the filaments. They are more rugged, and preheat only momentarily until the arc strikes. The instant start lamp has filaments which are not preheated, the arc striking across the tube the instant the switch is thrown. The slimline lamp has no filaments, but only cylindrical metal cathodes. It is called the "cold cathode" tube.

The simplified sketches of Fig. 9 will help explain the operation of the tube circuits. Complete circuits of various fluorescent tubes may be found in the Appendix.

Fig. 9A deals with the preheat lamp. Current flows from supply wire *1* to tube filament *F1,* then through starter *S* to filament *F2,* to ballast inductance *B,* and through it to supply wire *2.* Starter switch *S* breaks the circuit after the filaments have heated a sufficient length of time. The sudden interruption of current through

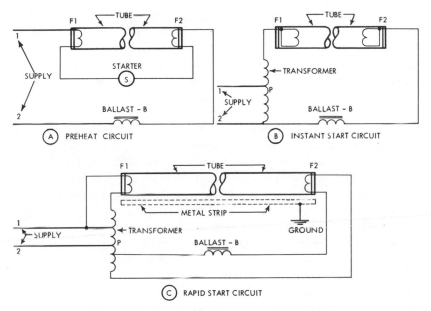

Fig. 9. The three basic fluorescent lamp circuits

the many turns of wire in ballast *B* generates a high voltage which causes an arc to flash across the tube from *F1* to *F2*, starting the lamp. After the arc has struck, it keeps the filaments hot so that they continue to give off electrons.

In addition to helping start the tube, the ballast performs an important service during normal operation. Without this inductance in the circuit, a fluorescent lamp would burn out within a few seconds after starting because an electric arc is unstable. Current flow would increase rapidly until the metallic filaments were entirely consumed. The inductance of the ballast supplies the necessary stabilizing influence.

Fig. 9B illustrates the circuit for an instant start lamp. No starter is present in this arrangement, but there is a ballast *B* and a transformer *P*. When the switch is turned on, the high voltage transformer causes a spark discharge between *F1* and *F2*, thereby vaporizing the mercury and placing the tube in operation. The arc itself excites the filaments so that they give off electrons without necessity for them being preheated. Note that the filaments are not connected in a "local" circuit, as are those of the preheat tube. In fact, the ends of each filament are short-circuited upon one another inside the tube. Here, as with all fluorescent tubes, the ballast acts so as to control the arc.

Fig. 9C shows the circuit for a rapid start tube. It combines features of both the preheat unit and the instant start lamp, because it has preheated filaments and a transformer. Three defects of the other units are overcome, however.

The main difficulty experienced with the preheat lamp is the fact that it does not start until some time after the circuit switch makes contact. Also, the starter provides an additional source of trouble. With the instant start lamp, the voltage generated in the transformer must be high enough to establish a spark from one end of a cold tube to the other. This high voltage tends to destroy the transformer, unless it is of expensive design, and especially if the tube circuit becomes open through removal of a lamp, or otherwise.

The rapid start lamp employs sturdy filaments which need to be preheated only momentarily before they produce a great number of electrons, so that its transformer does not have to create an extremely high voltage to strike an arc through the tube. The lamp starts up within a second or less of the time contact is made by the circuit switch. It will be observed that the filaments remain heated throughout the whole period of use.

The grounded metal strip indicated by a dotted line in Fig. 9C is essential to proper starting of the tube. This strip, not more than 1″ from the tube, and about 1″ in width, extends from *F1* to *F2*. A capacitive discharge between it and the filaments helps vaporize mercury inside the tube, so that the arc strikes quickly. If the strip is not grounded, so as to complete the capacitive circuit, trouble is usually experienced in starting.

Lead-lag Circuits

Two lamps are usually arranged in lead-lag, or tulamp, circuits to improve power factor of the load, one lamp having a capacitor in series with it. The capacitor makes the current through its lamp lead (start before) that in the "uncorrected," or lag, lamp. Such arrangements are employed with all three basic types: preheat, instant start, and rapid start. Special ballasts are required in every case.

In the preheat lead-lag circuit, the life of the lead lamp tends to be less than that of the lag lamp because it often starts before its filament is hot enough. If a damaged lead lamp is not removed immediately, in the instant start circuit, the transformer may be damaged. For this reason, the circuit is often arranged so that the lamps start in sequence (one before the other), and operate in series. Failure of one lamp, in such case, does not result in transformer trouble. Rapid start circuits are also arranged for sequence starting and series operation.

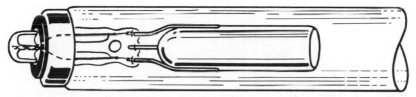

Fig. 10. Slimline tube

Courtesy of General Electric Co.

Other Common Types of Fluorescent Lamps

The slimline, or cold cathode lamp, Fig. 10, employs a circuit like the instant start. A relatively expensive transformer is incorporated in the ballast element. Its voltage is high enough to draw a large quantity of electrons out of the cathode, and thus to establish a steady arc as soon as the circuit switch makes contact.

The trigger start arrangement is similar to that of the preheat lamp. Filaments are heated when a starting button is depressed. Line voltage is generally high enough to establish an arc. When the button is released, a resistor ballast is inserted and the filament circuit is opened at the same time. Because the tubes are small, the lamp continues to operate.

High-output lamps require more current than the comparable standard lamps, and give about 40 percent more light. Super-hi and Power-groove lamps require even higher values of current, but produce comparatively greater lighting output. All of these lamps work on the rapid start principle. The circline tube once used the trigger start circuit, but it has now been adapted to rapid start.

Special Types of Fluorescent Lamps

A lamp which is just emerging from the development stage is the panel, or labyrinth lamp, Fig. 11, whose lighting surface has a waffle pattern. It is a glass block approximately 1 ft square, and $1\frac{1}{2}''$ thick. A labyrinth passage which extends from one terminal to the other, is between 4 and 5 ft long. Each panel is equipped with

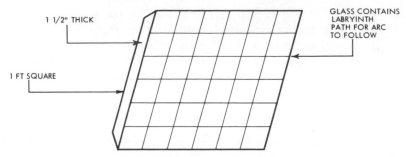

1 1/2" THICK

GLASS CONTAINS
LABRYINTH
PATH FOR ARC
TO FOLLOW

1 FT SQUARE

Fig. 11. Panel fluorescent lamp

standard terminals so that it may be used singly, if desired, or in a group which provides a lighted ceiling or a lighted wall.

An aperture lamp is similar to the ordinary fluorescent tube, but the greater portion of the tube cylinder is rendered opaque so that a light beam emerges from only about one-twelfth of the circumference.

Tube Bases

Tube bases, Fig. 12, are equipped with four types of contacts: bipin, four pin, single pin, and recessed double contact. There are three sizes of bipin bases: miniature, used with small lamps; medium, used with average sizes; and mogul, used with large ones. The four pin type is employed only on the circline tube at present, but may also appear on the panel lamp. Slimline lamps have a single pin base, and high output tubes have the recessed double contact base.

Effect of Low Temperature

Low temperatures affect the starting of fluorescent tubes, and reduce their light output. For this reason, they were not employed successfully out of doors until special measures were adopted. Since the appearance of glass or plastic covers to entrap the heat and protect the lamps from drafts, their use in such locations has been widely extended. This is true especially of the newer high output tubes. With special ballasts, they can even be employed in zero or sub-zero locations such as refrigerating rooms.

Today, fluorescent tubes are often found in outdoor electric signs, in service stations, and in street lighting electroliers. In general, however, slimline tubes are not recommended for low temperature work.

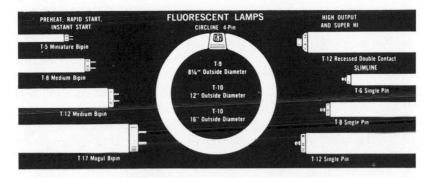

Fig. 12. Tube bases of fluorescent lamps
Courtesy of Westinghouse Electric Corp.

Interchanging Fluorescent Lamps

The fact that preheat, rapid start, and instant start lamps may all have medium bipin bases, does not mean that one lamp may be interchanged in all cases with one of the other types. Instant start lamps, because of their short-circuited filaments, must never be substituted for either of the others. Also, neither of the other two lamps should be substituted for an instant start.

Although a rapid start lamp serves quite well in place of a preheat lamp, the reverse is not true. The filament of the preheat lamp will not hold up under the heavy current required by the rapid start circuit.

SPECIAL OPERATING CONDITIONS

Dimming Incandescent Lamps

The lumen output of an incandescent lamp may be altered as desired, from maximum value to zero, by adjusting the voltage across its terminals. The simplest method is to insert a variable resistor in series with the unit. This method is inefficient, however, because power which is normally converted into light by the filament of the lamp must be absorbed by the material of which the resistor is composed.

Another disadvantage is that heat developed in the process may prove objectionable. Thus, where the dimming unit is installed in a wall outlet box, the increased temperature may damage insulation on supply conductors. When a single lamp of moderate size is concerned, heat may not represent an important factor, but when a number of lighting outlets are involved, the rise in temperature may be great enough to require special provisions for ventilating the controller.

If a series reactor is substituted for the resistor, the amount of heat generated in the controller will be considerably less, because the voltage induced in the turns of the reactor winding will oppose circuit voltage. Thus, its value will be lowered without consumption of a great deal of power. In comparison with the resistive controller, the reactor's principal short-coming is that lamp voltage is varied in a certain definite number of steps rather than in a continuously smooth sequence.

An autotransformer dimmer is more satisfactory than either of the others. This unit develops little heat during normal operation, but it suffers the same defect as the reactive type with respect to the definite number of voltage steps. In practice, the device is considered quite acceptable.

The output of fluorescent lamps is not so easily regulated as that of incandescents. This problem will be taken up in the next chapter, in connection with glare and contrast.

Flashing Incandescent Lamps

Incandescent lamps are readily adaptable to flashing or cycling operation. The life of small and moderate sizes used in such applications, is not affected. Fluorescent lamps present certain difficulties that will be explained as mentioned above.

MERCURY LAMPS AND SODIUM VAPOR LAMPS

Mercury Lamps

The left-hand illustration of Fig. 13 shows a tubular mercury lamp which has a double-wall enclosing globe. The inner bulb is made of quartz, the outer one of ordinary bulb glass. The outer bulb shields the inner from effects of varying temperatures and drafts. The inner one contains an arc chamber with two main electrodes and a starting electrode. It holds a quantity of liquid mercury and a small amount of argon gas.

The gas starts the arc when a high voltage is imposed across the electrodes. This arc stream gives off very little illumination, but creates heat sufficient to vaporize the mercury. As the mercury vapor expands, it fills the tube to form a conducting path from one main electrode to the other. When current flows through the vapor, a light of intense brilliancy is developed. This lamp is quite efficient as compared to an incandescent unit. Although the 400-watt

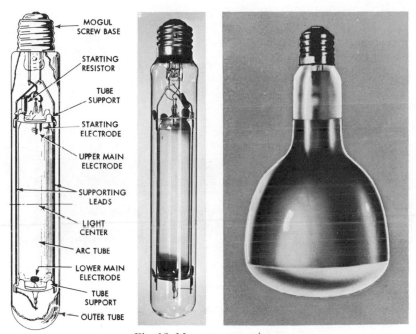

Fig. 13. Mercury-vapor lamps

Courtesy of General Electric Co.

lamp shown in the middle of Fig. 13 is perhaps the most popular, they are made also in 1,000-watt and 3,000-watt sizes.

Light produced by the mercury arc contains no red rays, making it unsuitable for applications in which color must be recognized or maintained. It was common practice, therefore, to group mercury and incandescent lamps for the purpose of adding these rays. Color-improved mercury lamps are now manufactured. The outer globe is coated with material that fluoresces to produce the needed colors. The light is similar to that from combinations of mercury and incandescents. One of these lamps is shown at the right in Fig. 13.

A disadvantage of the mercury lamp is that it takes four to eight minutes to attain operating brilliancy. If turned off, either intentionally or accidentally, the same period of time must elapse before it relights. Auxiliary ballasts are required for supplying the high starting voltage.

Sodium-Vapor Lamps

Fig. 14 shows the sodium-vapor lamp which is similar in princi-

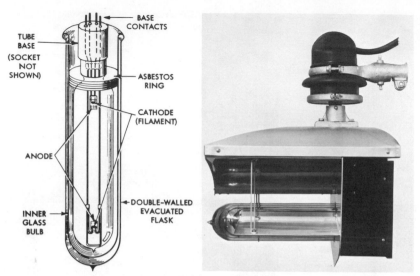

Fig. 14. Sodium-vapor lamp
Courtesy of General Electric Co.

ple to the mercury-vapor. As indicated in the left-hand illustration, it has dual enclosing globes, the inner containing a quantity of the metal sodium and a small amount of neon gas. At starting, the gas acts as the sole conductor until the sodium becomes vaporized in the heat created by the arc. When the vapor begins to conduct, it gives off a golden yellow light which is suitable only for outdoor areas. Where color distinguishing is of importance, this light will not be acceptable. A unit similar to the one shown at the right in Fig. 14, is excellent for such locations as street crossings, where the primary consideration is visibility. Unlike the mercury lamp, the sodium-vapor lamp restarts at once if momentarily turned off.

REVIEW QUESTIONS

　　1. What term refers to lighting intensity at the source?
　　2. What is a lumen?
　　3. What term defines intensity of light striking upon a surface?
　　4. Name the unit of brightness.
　　5. Is it correct to say that lighting intensity varies directly as the distance from the source?
　　6. What type of socket is found on a 500 watt incandescent lamp?
　　7. Are most incandescent lamp filaments mounted vertically?
　　8. What term designates the PAR bulb?

9. Name the three general types of fluorescent lamps.
10. Does the construction of the slimline lamp resemble that of the rapid start lamp?
11. Can the instant start lamp be used in a rapid start circuit?
12. Can a rapid start lamp be used in an instant start circuit?
13. May rapid start and preheat lamps be used interchangeably?
14. What other term describes the slimline lamp?
15. What is the advantage of using the tulamp circuit?
16. Is the quartzline a fluorescent lamp?
17. What other term is often used for a tulamp circuit?
18. Is the arc voltage maintained constant as a fluorescent lamp is dimmed?
19. Does the mercury lamp start immediately after the circuit is broken for an instant?
20. Is the sodium-vapor lamp preheated by a filament?

Chapter Three

Modern Lighting Practice

Factual Background

Electrical fixture practice, in the beginning, was the offspring of gaslighting methods. Light sockets were installed upon extensions from the old gaspipes, using the original enclosing globes, if any. Often, since the only purpose of the original globe was to prevent air currents from tearing fragile gas mantles, it was dispensed with altogether.

As brighter and higher-powered lamp filaments were produced, their intense glow proved annoying to the eye, so that measures for shielding were adopted. Translucent enclosures proved satisfactory, and also deep reflectors. Progress in design of both types gradually resulted in more efficient and better looking units.

The old gaslight fixtures had to be mounted on exposed surfaces for reasons of safety. Electrical installations continued this practice, even though the basic cause was no longer present. In the course of time, cove lighting, and wholly or partially concealed lighting sources were employed on special occasions. Manufacturers experimented with units that reflected some of the light onto the ceiling instead of directing it straight down, but the over-all design of lighting fixtures was more or less fixed.

Advent of the fluorescent tube in 1938 served to shock the industry into action. The long, cylindrical light source was not adapted to conventional enclosing globes, and the higher intensities of illumination now readily available, brought about a new concept of the whole problem. Under the leadership of the Illuminating Engineering Society, the truth became widely accepted that a lighting system should provide the right kind of light at exactly the right spot.

50

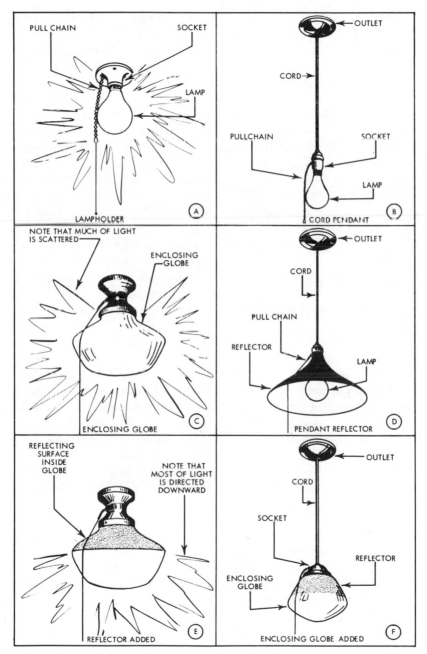

Fig. 1. Early lighting units

The changed ideas which appeared along with the fluorescent tube, carried over into the incandescent field. Today, the general public demands much more of a lighting source. Recessed lighting has found broad application. Luminous ceilings are seen in offices, stores, and more recently, in homes. Also, the color-corrected mercury lamp has proven quite satisfactory for many commercial and industrial applications. Architects have come to view lighting equipment as part of each master plan, rather than a necessary inclusion that has to be suffered. This chapter presents the essential features of modern lighting systems.

Surface and Pendant Fixture

Early incandescent lighting outlets consisted of a socket mounted directly upon the ceiling, or dangling from a cord pendant, Fig. 1A and B. In both cases, light radiated in all possible directions, much of it being absorbed by dark ceiling and wall surfaces. Presently, a frosted enclosing globe was used in connection with the ceiling outlet, and a plain reflector was applied to the pendant, views C and D, Fig. 1. The enclosing globe reduced objectionable glare, while the reflector partially shielded the eye from the bright filament, and directed much of the light downward onto the working plane.

Through the process of gradual improvement, reflectors were incorporated into enclosing globes, and enclosing globes were added to the simple reflector. The reflector inside the enclosing globe, Fig. 1E, reflected much of the light downward, and the enclosing globe, Fig. 1F, shielded the eye from direct glare. Today, both types are fundamentally the same as earlier units, although they have changed considerably in detail. Ceiling and wall fixtures have become more efficient and outwardly pleasing to the eye. The pendant fixture is not usually suspended on a cord, but is hung from the outlet box by means of a chain or a stem.

Light Patterns

Attention was directed, in the course of time, to the more efficient use of light created by a fixture. By then, the lighting fixture had come to be known as a "luminaire." Pendants were still quite popular in the high-ceilinged rooms of that period, but they were changing in form. Architects realized that more light could be directed onto the working plane by painting walls and ceilings with light-colored paint which reflected more lumens than darker hues. Luminaire manufacturers began experimenting with reflector arrangements that would spread lumens over a greater area, and thus soften troublesome glare. Their combined efforts resulted in lighting units which offered a variety of distribution patterns, as illustrated in Fig. 2.

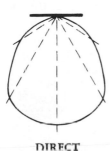

DIRECT
0-10% upward, 90-100% downward

SEMI-DIRECT
10-40% upward, 60-90% downward

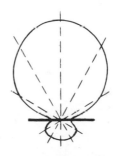

GENERAL DIFFUSE
40-60% upward, 40-60% downward

SEMI-INDIRECT
60-90% upward, 10-40% downward

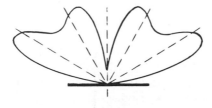

INDIRECT
90-100% upward, 0-10% downward

Fig. 2. Patterns of light distribution for standard types of luminaires
Courtesy of Sunbeam Lighting Co.

A luminaire that sends 90 to 100 percent of the light downward is termed a direct-lighting unit. The simple reflector falls within this class. One that sends down only 60 to 90 percent of its light is termed semi-direct. If only 40 to 60 percent is downward, and the remainder upward, it is called general-diffusing, or direct-indirect. Where 60 to 90 percent of illumination is upward, and the remainder down, the unit is said to be semi-direct, and where all the light is projected upward, it is termed indirect. Some of these types are illustrated in Fig. 3.

Fig. 3. Pendant Incandescent luminaires (A) Direct lighting unit
(B) General-diffusing luminaire (C) Luminaire suitable for
either indirect or semi-direct lighting

The one to be selected for a particular application is determined by the result desired. In high-bay factory locations where workmen's eyes are not subjected to glare, direct lighting is satisfactory. It is also useful in small stores or offices that seldom need artificial light, and other such places where moderate lighting intensities are not objectionable. Semi-direct units are suitable for passageways in which shadows are undesirable, but where most of the light is needed on the floor. General-diffuse lighting imparts a more even illumination which is often desirable in offices and stores. Semi-indirect luminaires create an even distribution that is highly pleasing to the average person. Indirect lighting, wherein the whole ceiling takes on the character of a reflector, is extremely easy on the eye, and practically free of shadows.

Fluorescent Lighting

The early fluorescent unit consisted of a bare tube mounted upon a narrow rectangular box, and fastened directly to wall or ceiling. The fact that source intensity was so much lower than that of an incandescent globe, made shielding less imperative. Most people experienced no discomfort in gazing at the bare tube. Sometimes, reflectors that were designed to concentrate more lumens onto the working area, introduced glare from bright reflecting surfaces, and shielding was required. In general, however, enclosing

Fig. 4. End to end fluorescent units
Courtesy of General Electric Co.

globes were seldom employed in connection with surface-mounted fluorescent lamps.

Incandescent lighting arrangements for large offices and stores usually consist of luminaires, ceiling type or stem-hung as the case may be, located at corners of evenly-spaced squares of ceiling area. This plan has been found necessary in order to create a reasonably even distribution of light. It soon became evident that a like procedure could not be followed in the placing of tubular luminaires. The tube is in a line-source of illumination which projects lumens at right angles to the length of the tube, whereas the incandescent lamp is a point source which projects light in a more or less circular pattern. Fluorescent lamps, therefore, supply an even pattern of light in these locations, only when installed in continuous rows. Lines of end-to-end fluorescent units, Fig. 4, appeared shortly in commercial establishments.

Where high ceilings prevailed, as in supermarkets, these rows were hung on long pendant stems, Fig. 5A, or on chains. A popular method, illustrated in the figure, has been to fasten individual luminaires to a supporting channel, such as Unistrut or Kindorf preparatory to suspending them. Under NEC rules applying to end-to-end assemblies, a line of fixtures can be supplied by a circuit which enters at one end of a run and carries through to the other. Some channels are approved for use as raceways, in addition to furnishing support.

Egg-crate and similar types of louvered shielding, illustrated in Fig. 5B, are often provided to spare the eyes from reflector glare. Supporting stems for these installations are often equipped with ball, or swivel, joints at the ceiling to insure even distribution of weight and to allow for side sway. Less frequently, and usually in earthquake regions, the stems are also jointed at the bottom to permit end sway.

A surface type fluorescent luminaire, Fig. 5C, which is 2 ft wide and either 4 ft or 8 ft long is particularly suitable for small offices. This unit, of shallow construction, sometimes has translucent sides. It is equipped with a plastic cover for diffusing the light.

A type similar to this unit in appearance, but which is suspended from the ceiling on short stems, is the "floating panel" luminaire. It, too, is frequently installed in small offices. When such a panel is expanded for use in a larger area, by joining several standard luminaires, the effect resembles that of the luminous

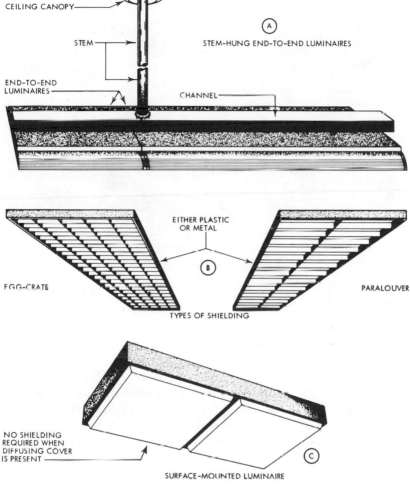

CEILING CANOPY

STEM

END-TO-END LUMINAIRES

CHANNEL

(A)

STEM-HUNG END-TO-END LUMINAIRES

EITHER PLASTIC OR METAL

(B)

EGG-CRATE

PARALOUVER

TYPES OF SHIELDING

NO SHIELDING REQUIRED WHEN DIFFUSING COVER IS PRESENT

(C)

SURFACE-MOUNTED LUMINAIRE

Fig. 5. Supporting and shielding of fluorescent luminaires

ceiling, which will be discussed later on.

Recessed Incandescent Lights

The first real departure from surface-mounted luminaires is represented by the recessed incandescent units, some of which are illustrated in Fig. 6. They are manufactured in a variety of shapes and sizes, depending upon the application for which they are in-

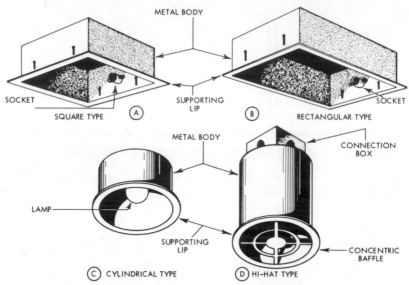

METAL BODY

SOCKET

SUPPORTING LIP

SOCKET

SQUARE TYPE (A) (B) RECTANGULAR TYPE

METAL BODY

CONNECTION BOX

LAMP

SUPPORTING LIP

CONCENTRIC BAFFLE

(C) CYLINDRICAL TYPE (D) HI-HAT TYPE

Fig. 6. Recessed incandescent luminaires

tended. Figure 6A, B, C shows square, cylindrical, and rectangular luminaires. The original ones were designed to fit between two standard ceiling joists.

This form of device is installed flush with the ceiling, and secured by hanger lips or strips attached to structural ceiling members. With an opalescent glass or a plastic cover, the light is thrown straight down in a narrow cone which has but little side "spill." If a prismatic lens cover is employed, light rays may be diverted sidewise to form a larger cone of distribution. Glare is minimized, but dark ceiling spots between the outlets prove annoying in some applications.

The cylindrical "high-hat" luminaire, Fig. 6D, is often combined with an R type lamp to give a concentrated beam for illuminating particular objects. Similar luminaires are employed for spot and accent lighting in stores, cocktail bars, and theaters. When so used, they are generally provided with concentric or circular-disc baffles which protect the eye from lamp and reflector glare. They are sometimes termed "downlights."

Recessed Fluorescent Lights

Recessed fluorescent luminaires, called *troffers,* came soon after the recessed incandescent unit. They are usually arranged end-to-

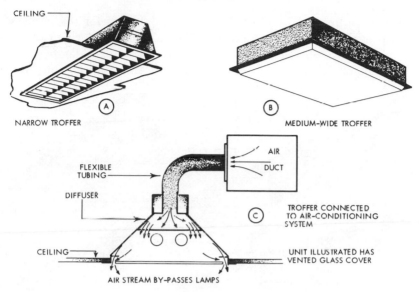

CEILING

Ⓐ
NARROW TROFFER

Ⓑ
MEDIUM-WIDE TROFFER

FLEXIBLE
TUBING

AIR
DUCT

DIFFUSER

Ⓒ

TROFFER CONNECTED
TO AIR-CONDITIONING
SYSTEM

CEILING

UNIT ILLUSTRATED HAS
VENTED GLASS COVER

AIR STREAM BY-PASSES LAMPS

Fig. 7. Fluorescent troffers

end, and furnished with louvered shielding. Sometimes they have opalescent glass or plastic covers which produce a lighted panel effect. The first troffers, Fig. 7A, were about 12″ wide, also dimensioned to fit between standard ceiling joists, but the 24″ type, Fig. 7B, is currently popular, especially for office lighting.

Troffers 4 ft wide and 8 ft long are found in stores where they are used with louvered or plastic ceiling cover to highlight a particular display, or section of the room. When several of these units are joined together, they provide the equivalent of the luminous ceiling, which will be discussed in the next section.

As shown in Fig. 7C, troffers are sometimes combined with air-conditioning apparatus. Air drawn in at the sides of the unit, from the room below, passes around the inner shell to a flexible tube which connects to an air-conditioning duct. Heat from the room and from the ballast of the troffer, is carried off in this manner. It may be observed that air does not flow across the lamps. If it were to do so, trouble might be experienced in operation of the fluorescent tubes.

LUMINOUS CEILINGS

General Features

A notable feature of modern commercial architecture is the

lowered ceiling height. One of the primary reasons for the trend is
the progressive mechanization of office equipment. Mechanical devices are driven by electric motors, which radiate considerable heat
while in operation. Air ducts and blowers are required for with-

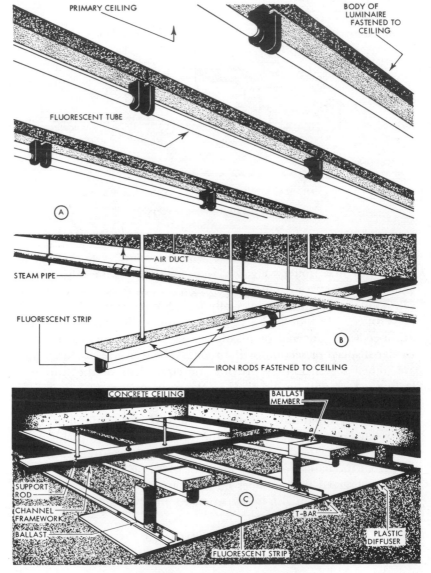

Fig. 8. Strip lighting above ceiling

drawal of excess heat, in order that personnel may have a reasonably comfortable place to work. Since this equipment requires a great deal of room, the logical solution is to lower ceilings for the purpose.

This procedure has been followed throughout the whole country, a plenum space being provided above the visible ceiling to house not only air-conditioning apparatus, but the electrical luminaires, water, gas, and steam pipes, sprinkler heads, sound equipment, telephone cables, and other facilities. Acoustical baffles are sometimes placed here, too, because plenum chambers are often subject to hollow reverberation, and to magnification of incidental noise, such as ballast hum.

Air may be drawn into the plenum from the room below in a manner similar to that discussed in connection with troffers, or through special ventilating openings. The latter is the usual plan, but many others have been tried. One scheme called for evacuating the air through holes in acoustical tiles which are often placed between luminous ceiling elements to deaden sound originating in the room itself. This particular method did not prove very successful.

Lower ceiling heights made the use of recessed incandescent luminaires impracticable. It doomed also, every kind of pendant fixture. Narrow troffers were unsatisfactory in this situation, unless the rows were very close together. Through a process of elimination, the luminous ceiling came into being. There are two general types, the louvered and the translucent (light shines through). Some manufacturers use the term "translighted" to cover both types.

Arrangement of Luminaires

Lighting units are in most cases single fluorescent strips which are mounted in a number of ways, depending on the particular conditions met with in each individual installation. Position of air ducts and other equipment largely dictates the method to be followed.

Figure 8A shows a simple plan, the lighting strips being attached directly to the concrete surface of the primary ceiling. This scheme is often impractical because of interference from other elements or apparatus. Consideration of it, however, will serve to bring out other factors worth mentioning at this time.

One point is the matter of spacing the end-to-end rows. If, in a large room the strips were installed on the surface of the visible ceiling, they would have to be spaced evenly in order to give a symmetrical appearance. Even though more light were required in a certain area, for example directly above a line of desks close to a wall, the architect would not likely agree to uneven spacing for accomplishing the purpose. But, since light sources above the ceiling are not in direct view, their spacing can be varied to suit the condition, without danger of creating an unsymmetrical layout.

Another advantage is that lighting intensity in certain spots may be varied at will through substitution of other luminaires directly above them. Here, too, the desired result may be gained without spoiling the general appearance of the room. The substituted units may be of different size or shape from others in the room but this fact is effectively concealed.

In Fig. 8B, the strips are fastened to stems which drop them far enough to clear ducts and pipes. The end-to-end luminaires are often mounted upon a piece of channel iron, or on one of the patented channels. Circuit wires are connected at one end of the strip, and run through to the other, as explained earlier. Luminaires should not be lowered to a point where individual bright spots are created on the plastic material, or where lines of brightness are visible from below.

Figure 8C illustrates a method commonly employed on large installations. Luminaires fastened together as in view B, are attached to a channel-iron framework, which is suspended from the primary ceiling at the most convenient distance for clearing obstructions. Ballasts are not placed inside the body of the luminaire, but are attached to vertical members, where they are accessible for quick replacement. They also remain cooler in this open position. The vertical members are fastened to a network of T-bars which support plastic or glass surface material. The plenum, as well as ducts and pipes, are often painted glossy white to provide good reflection. A luminous ceiling is shown in Fig. 9.

Translucent Materials

The material which forms the diffusing ceiling may be glass or plastic, customarily the latter. Where glass is used, it is often prismatic, and designed to create a desired pattern of illumination directly underneath. The two common types of plastic are vinyl and acrylic, their names being abbreviations of their chemical formulas. Vinyl usually comes in rolls, while acrylic material is generally supplied in sheets or panels.

Fig. 9. Luminous ceiling

Courtesy of General Electric Co.

Louver Ceilings

The problems connected with installation of louver ceilings are much the same as in the diffusing type. Placing of luminaires is much the same, and the mounting of the supporting structures. Louvers are often clipped onto U-bars instead of T-bars, however. Louvers are made in a variety of patterns and materials. Some have large cells on the order of the familiar egg-crate used with troffers. Others have small cells whose dimensions are as small as ½". They are composed of sheet steel, plastic, and aluminum.

Incandescent luminaires are sometimes employed in particular areas, with this type of ceiling, reflector lamps providing brilliant highlights where desired. As with the highhat units mentioned earlier, this kind of lighting is often found in show windows, particularly in jewelry stores.

The bare lamps can be seen, looking directly upward from below, but where the layout is skillfully designed, the height of luminaires above the louver surface, and the size of openings in the louver, are such that lamps are not visible to the casual observer. One trouble with louver installations is that bright lamp filaments cause annoying reflection from glass, enameled, or painted work surfaces directly underneath.

OTHER PHASES OF MODERN LIGHTING

Foot-candle Intensities

The matter of foot-candle levels required for efficient performance of various tasks has received a great deal of attention. Until the past few years, however, recommendations were based upon trial and error. Through experiments conducted at the University of Michigan under the sponsorship of the Illuminating Engineering Society, scientific values have been determined.

They are, generally, much higher than older standards. Thus, for difficult office work, the older value was 50 foot-candles, but the new recommendation is 150 foot-candles. For exacting machine work, in factories, the older standard was 100 foot-candles, whereas the new one is 500 foot-candles. In numerous tests based upon the recent findings, improvements in worker efficiency and decrease in eye fatigue have been noted.

Glare and Contrast

Increased lighting intensities have brought greater attention to the problem of glare and contrast. Glare is unwanted light. Expressed in another way, glare is light which is uncomfortable to the eye. Direct glare is that which comes directly from the light source. Reflected glare is that which comes from a lighted surface.

The original incandescent lamp caused annoyance on account of filament brilliance. Frosting the inside of the globe diffused, or scattered, the light from the filament so that the objectionable quality was removed. Reflectors proved the next source of discomfort, their glossy surfaces reflecting bright rays into the eye.

Fluorescent lamps were considered free of glare because of their low surface brilliance. As reflectors were added for the purpose of controlling light distribution, however, the old trouble appeared. It became customary to provide the luminaires with 45° shielding.

The reflectors were so designed that anyone viewing them from an angle of 45° or less, Fig. 10, would be unable to see the bright areas. In those cases where the shape of the unit did not permit such

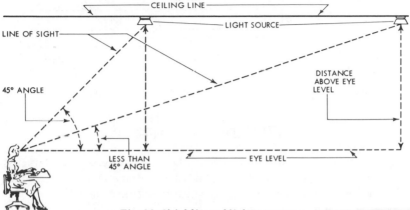

Fig. 10. Shielding of light source

shielding, baffles were incorporated to provide both lengthwise and crosswise protection. Troffers which did not have a diffusing cover were treated in the same manner. It might be added here, that incandescent luminaires which contain bright lamps, must also be shielded within the 45° zone. This is usually done with concentric baffles. Tests show that with any type of lighting, reflected brightness is seldom noticed where intensities exceed 50 foot-candles.

Closely allied to the subject of glare is that of contrast. If the brightness of a ceiling is 100 foot-lamberts and that of an adjacent wall is 20 foot-lamberts, contrast between the two degrees of brightness is annoying to the eye in much the same way as glare. Lighting experts feel that the contrast ratio between lighted areas which are normally within range of the eye at the same time, should not be higher than 3 to 1. In the example stated above, the brightness of the wall should be increased, by adding lumens from a special source, to 33 or more foot-candles.

Dimming

The brightness of fluorescent lamps, whether preheat, rapid start, or instant start, can be decreased to some extent through reduction of circuit voltage. The method is not recommended, however, because the degree of control is very small, and when the lamp is turned off, it will not restart at the lowered voltage setting.

When equipped with a special ballast, the brightness of preheat lamps may be readily controlled, especially the 40-watt, rapid start

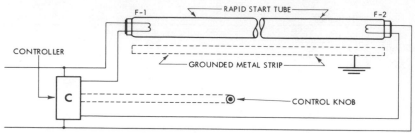

Fig. 11. Simplified dimming circuit

type. The circuit, illustrated in Fig. 11, is so arranged that filaments *F1* and *F2* are supplied with their normal voltage at all times, while the voltage supplied to the arc is varied by controller *C*.

Controller *C* may take any one of several forms. An electronic variety, which has two Thyratron tubes, provides a smooth dimming range of about 100 to 1. A potentiometer, or variable resistor, is employed to adjust the grid voltage of the tubes so that current will flow during only a portion of each cycle.

Such a device is capable of handling a single lamp, a whole circuit, or even a feeder which supplies two or more circuits, depending on the capacity of the unit. The control potentiometer, since it requires a very small current at a low voltage, may be placed some distance away from the lamps if desired. Thus, it could be in the manager's office of a nightclub, or in the projection booth of a movie theatre.

Another form of controller for providing a smooth variation of lighting intensity is the variable autotransformer. A third form has a series inductance. It is only about one-half as effective as the other types. Neither of these units allows control from such a remote distance as the electronic type. A fourth controller includes a magnetic amplifier and a dry rectifier unit. Results with this device are comparable to those obtainable with the electronic unit. Dimming is widely employed in theaters, restaurants, and places of public assembly. It is also used in stores, offices, and conference rooms for the purpose of what is termed "mood" control, the intensity of the light being altered to suit a desired emotional mood.

Flashing

Until recently, fluorescent lamps were not adapted for use in flashing signs. Filaments deteriorated rapidly in this kind of service so that the life of a lamp was greatly reduced. By inserting a dimming type ballast, however, which maintains filaments at a constant temperature while the arc is turned on and off, flashing signs of this sort have become popular.

Color

Color has become an important element in commercial lighting. Incandescent hues may be readily varied to suit special requirements through the medium of tinted globes or screens. The color of other forms of lighting is not so readily manipulated. As mentioned earlier, steps have been taken to remedy color defects in both fluorescent and mercury lamps. This is true, particularly, of the fluorescent tube.

The rapid start lamp is obtainable in a number of shades of white, as well as in other colors. It is listed as cool white, deluxe cool white, warm white, deluxe warm white, white, daylight, soft white, cool green, blue, pink, red, and yellow, the latter being the insect-repellent lamp. Lumen output is sacrificed to some extent in varying the natural color of the source.

Differences between the several whites will be presented briefly. Cool white is blue-white that contains no yellow or red rays. Deluxe cool white contains some yellow and red, but more blue-white than an incandescent lamp. Warm white gives an orange tinted white glow, but does not contain much yellow or red. Deluxe warm white is slightly pinkish. White lies between cool white and warm white. Daylight contains more blue than the cool white lamp. The soft white tube emphasizes the reds.

Showcase, Display, and Show Window Lighting

The nature of some merchandise requires that it be placed in lighted showcases. The portable showcase of Fig. 12A is essentially all glass. Lighting is accomplished by one or more narrow reflector lamps placed along the upper rear edge of the interior. Either incandescent or fluorescent lamps may be used, both types being shown in the figure. Wiring to the lamp is carried up from the base in small diameter brass tubing which is approved for such applications.

When a fluorescent tube is used, the ballast is placed underneath the lower shelf as indicated. Incandescent showcase lamps sometimes have self-contained reflectors. The reflector lamp usually has

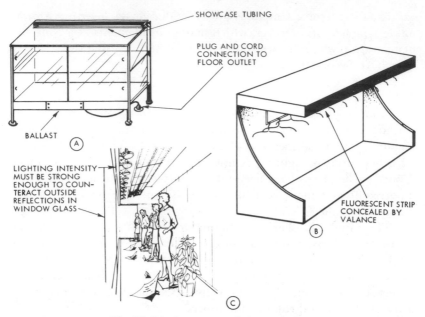

SHOWCASE TUBING

PLUG AND CORD
CONNECTION TO
FLOOR OUTLET

BALLAST
(A)

LIGHTING INTENSITY
MUST BE STRONG
ENOUGH TO COUN-
TERACT OUTSIDE
REFLECTIONS IN
WINDOW GLASS

FLUORESCENT STRIP
CONCEALED BY
VALANCE
(B)

(C)

Fig. 12. Display cases and show window

a spring fastened to its center contact so that it will remain tight
in the socket when turned to the most effective position for lighting
the material.

A wall case is illustrated in Fig. 12B. End-to-end fluorescent
strips are commonly employed for lighting these units, the luminaires being concealed behind a valance. Shelves are frequently
lighted in this matter also, the valance supported on brackets extending out from the top of the shelving.

The show window of Fig. 12C offers difficult lighting problems.
High intensities of illumination are required, especially in daytime,
to combat reflections of objects located outside the window. Since
high lighting intensities require high wattage, some method for
carrying off the heat must be provided. Fluorescent ballasts are usually located remotely from the show window luminaires, in a place
where their heat can be more readily dissipated. The cool-beam
reflector lamp, mentioned in Chapter 2, is one of the popular incandescent lamps for this sort of application.

Color receives a great deal of attention in this connection, along
with flashing and, in certain particular cases, dimming for mood
control. Dimming can be employed quite effectively at night, when

the problem of outside reflections is much less severe.

High-frequency Lighting

Although a supply frequency of 60 cycles is standard throughout the nation, fluorescent lamps operate more efficiently, producing more light for a given input, at frequencies around 400 cycles. There are numerous reasons why it would be impractical for utility companies to deliver current at the higher frequency, but it has been found advantageous in many instances, to generate such current locally.

Under high-cycle operation, the efficiency of the lamps themselves is increased because of the lower percentage of electrode losses. The greater saving, however, is in the lamp ballasts which are about ⅓ as heavy as 60-cycle ballasts, and which consequently produce less heat. In some installations, where small capacitors are used alone, the saving in ballast weight may run as large as 90 percent.

Higher frequencies have been tried with good results, some as great as 840 cycles. Such extremely high values are obtained by way of motor-generator converters. The general run of high-cycle applications is based upon a frequency of approximately 400 cycles. Either motor-generator converters or magnetic frequency multipliers are suitable. It is widely accepted that the best potential for the 400-cycle system is in the neighborhood of 600 volts. With center-tapped windings on the generator or multiplier, voltage to ground may be held within the 300-volt limitation of the NEC.

The lead-lag principle is adhered to in order to maintain a reasonably high power factor. Inductive ballasts are included in one-half the ballasts, and capacitors in the other half. When it is desired to use capacitor ballasts for all lamps, lumped inductance must be provided in the supply feeder or in the generator itself.

Saving in ballast cost is more than offset, as a rule, by the expense of conversion apparatus. It has been found in some plants, that reduction in over-all ballast heat makes it possible to reduce the size of air-conditioning apparatus to a point where savings here make the whole installation economically worth while.

INDUSTRIAL LIGHTING

Comparison with Commercial Lighting

The problem of illuminating industrial plants is not different

Fig. 13. Mercury lighting in a steel mill
Courtesy of General Electric Co.

basically from that encountered with commercial establishments. Details vary, however, according to the nature of the particular location. For example, a foundry may have a low general average lighting intensity; a machine shop may need a background intensity of 30 to 40 foot-candles, and high intensity spot lighting over special machines; an electronics factory, where small parts are assembled at long tables, may require an even distribution of 150 foot-candles. In other words, the problems connected with industrial lighting are highly individualized.

Required Types of Industrial Luminaires

The kind of lighting for a given occupancy is frequently dictated by the physical character of the surroundings. Thus, in a high-bay machine shop, mercury lamps at the roof level, or suspended on stems, Fig. 13, according to the distance from the floor, could provide either a moderate background intensity or a high average value of illumination. In the former case, luminaires could be high up

Fig. 14. Fluorescent lighting in a machine shop
Courtesy of General Electric Co.

and far apart; in the latter instance, they would be lower, closer together.

With a flat roof or ceiling in a modern factory building, the machine shop could be illuminated at high average foot-candle intensity with either fluorescent or mercury luminaires, the roof or ceiling being painted white to improve reflecting qualities. If the electronics factory were under a high-arched roof, the lighting problem could be solved through the use of end-to-end fluorescent luminaires suspended above the tables at a convenient height, the rows being spaced so as to avoid shadows.

The present trend emphasizes an even and rather high foot-candle value in most industrial areas, Fig. 14, rather than dependence on spot lighting for individual machines. There are no rules, however, that can be applied strictly in every case. Thus, in a high-bay shop where mercury lights would be used ordinarily to provide all necessary illumination, the presence of traveling cranes might introduce disturbing shadows which could only be avoided through individual lighting of heavy machines underneath the runways.

Auxiliary Industrial Locations

Storerooms, warehouses, receiving and shipping departments will be illuminated to a degree which depends to a large extent upon the nature of materials stored or handled. The foot-candle level in a rough casting warehouse might be fairly low, while that in a storeroom devoted to small electronic parts would be moderately high. If the goods were stored in open bays and racks throughout the building, an even general distribution would be desirable. Where parts were stored in bins that had narrow aisles between them, luminaires could be suspended over the aisles.

Factory office requirements resemble those in commercial establishments, except that appearance is not so important. Higher ceilings make practical the use of pendant or recessed luminaires. Footcandle values will depend on the sort of clerical work done there. A testing laboratory must have a fairly high over-all lighting intensity, and a drafting room must have something on the order of 200 footcandles for best results.

Rest and lounging rooms, especially those for women employees, are treated like similar commercial locations, more attention being given to the factor of appearance. Cover lighting, use of color, and perhaps dimming may be included.

Safety Considerations in Lighting Practice

One of the primary concerns of NEC rules governing minimum lighting intensities is the matter of safety, both to the general public and to employees of the occupancy involved. The prescribed minimums are usually adequate, but upon occasion they prove rather low. In this regard, a value of $\frac{1}{2}$ watt per sq ft for halls and corridors may or may not be sufficient, depending upon local conditions.

Thus, passageways or stairs leading to storage rooms in commercial and industrial locations should be illuminated to a point consistent with lighting intensity of surrounding areas. If the general level is 100 foot-candles, for example, a workman coming suddenly upon a $\frac{1}{2}$-foot-candle stairway may find the contrast almost as great as if entering a place that is in total darkness.

OUTDOOR APPLICATIONS

Area Lighting

Outdoor lighting includes the surface illumination of areas such as neighborhood parking lots, shopping centers, or thoroughfares, and the floodlighting of buildings or signboards. The first of these types will be considered in this section.

Area lighting is usually accomplished with the help of poles or towers, luminaires being mounted in groups to project light in selected directions. For play fields, the light is aimed at right angles to boundary lines; for large parking lots, having poles arranged at corners of evenly spaced squares, the light is distributed in all four directions.

Incandescent lighting is still found in connection with sports areas, but fluorescent and mercury lighting have forged ahead in most other locations. The fluorescent tube is not suited for projection of light any considerable distance. Its use is limited therefore to situations in which light is needed within a small radius of the foot of the pole. Street intersections are representative of this application, lamps being shielded from the weather by plastic or glass enclosing globes.

Mercury lighting has proven excellent for parking lots in big shopping centers, Fig. 15. Relatively few poles are required, since

Fig. 15. Mercury lighted shopping center
Courtesy of General Electric Co.

they may be spaced up to 200 ft apart, depending on their height. Luminaires may be obtained in varying styles to suit particular needs. Some are designed to project a light beam in one general direction, while others are made to spread light throughout a complete circle around the pole.

Towers are used where the supporting structure must be quite high, or where a great number of lamps is grouped at one location. Poles are used more often. They are made of steel or aluminum. Circuits, run to the poles in conduit or approved cable, are often controlled by light sensitive photoelectric cells which operate magnetic contactors.

Quartz-iodine incandescent lamps which have a relatively small luminaire, entered this field recently. These are mounted on poles in the same way as mercury units. This lamp is burned in a horizontal, or nearly horizontal position.

Floodlighting of Structures

The methods for lighting vertical signboards and facades of buildings have undergone changes too, through improvements in lighting equipment. Signboards, formerly illuminated by incandescent floodlights or sign reflectors alone, are now lighted by a wide choice of luminaires. Fluorescent lamps are used in many cases. The newer aperture type fluorescent tube which emits a narrow beam of light, has been applied to this service.

Facade lighting is still done to some extent by standard incandescent units, but the mercury lamp has proven more economical. The latest entry in the field is the quartz-iodine lamp, which is also highly satisfactory.

REVIEW QUESTIONS

1. What percentage of a direct lighting unit's output is in a downward direction?
2. In what sort of factory location is direct-incandescent lighting satisfactory?
3. A tube represents what kind of fundamental light source?
4. Egg-crate shielding is used on surface fluorescent luminaires to shield the eyes from what kind of glare?
5. What is a common name for recessed fluorescent luminaires?
6. What is the most notable feature of modern commercial architecture?
7. Why are surface incandescent luminaires usually spaced evenly?

8. What members actually support the plastic material in a luminous ceiling installation?

9. What may be said generally of the newer footcandle intensities?

10. State the meaning of the term "diffused."

11. Surface luminaires are usually shielded within what minimum angle?

12. What should be the maximum ratio between brightness of surfaces visible at the same time?

13. Are dimming ballasts used with instant-start lamps?

14. Is the life of a fluorescent lamp in a modern electric sign considerably shortened by this kind of service?

15. High intensities of lighting are required in show windows to combat what type of reflections?

16. The most common frequency for high-frequency lighting is about what value?

17. What principle is called upon to maintain a reasonably high power factor in circuits devoted to fluorescent lamps?

18. Are mercury lamps unsuited for high-bay machine shops?

19. Are fluorescent lamps adapted for use in parking lots of big shopping centers?

20. What type of incandescent lighting is being successfully adapted to the lighting of parking centers?

Chapter Four

Lighting Design

Foreword

Determination of lighting requirements for a given office, store or factory is covered by the phrase "lighting design." The term includes estimates of the number and kind of luminaires, their spacing, and the size of lamps to be installed in them. Certain facts apply to every project, however large or small, while others refer solely to the particular equipment used in a specific case. The manner of solving the various problems will be set forth in this chapter.

Difficulty of Applying Basic Rule

The distance rule given in Chapter 2 states that intensity of illumination varies inversely as the square of the distance from a source of light. This formula can be used successfully only where the source is isolated from everything else, as for example a candle

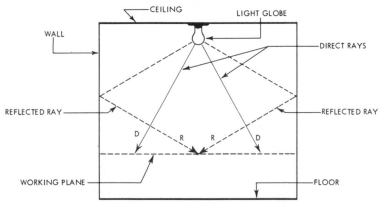

Fig. 1. Reflection complicates distance rule

76

flame in the open air. In the practical business of lighting an enclosed area, such as a room, the source is not isolated, but is surrounded by the ceiling and walls, all of which reflect light rays, as in Fig. 1.

The direct light rays, *D*, would provide at the working level, an intensity that might be calculated from the distance formula if the candlepower of the lamp were known. But reflected rays, *R*, also provide illumination at the working level, so that the calculation becomes of no value. It may be stated, therefore, that the distance rule for calculating lighting intensity is unworkable in practical situations.

Lumen Method

Most lighting calculations are made today by the lumen method. The basis for this procedure is a table of data supplied by the lamp manufacturers. Such a listing gives the number of lumens produced by each lamp. For example, Table 1 shows that a 100-watt,

Watts	Volts	Bulb Shape	Bulb Finish & Color	Base	Initial Lumens	Rated Life (hrs.)
INSIDE FROST LAMPS. Burning position—ANY, except as noted.						
15	120	A-15	I. F.	Med.	142	1,200
25	120	A-19	I. F.	Med.	266	1,000
40	120	A-19	I. F.	Med.	470	1,000
50	120	A-19	I. F.	Med.	665	1,000
60	120	A-19	I. F.	Med.	840	1,000
75	120	A-19	I. F.	Med.	1,150	750
100	120	A-21	I. F.	Med.	1,640	750
100	120, 125	A-19	I. F.	Med.	1,750	750
100	115–125	A-23	I. F.	Med.		750
150	120	A-23	I. F.	Med.	2,700	750
150	120	PS-25	I. F.	Med.	2,640	750
200	120	PS-25	I. F.	Med.	3,820	750
200	120	PS-30	I. F.	Med.	3,720	750
300	120	PS-30	I. F.	Med.	6,000	750
300	120	PS-35	I. F.	Mog.	5,750	1,000
500	120	PS-40	I. F.	Mog.	9,900	1,000
750	120	PS-52	I. F.	Mog.	16,700	1,000
1000	120	PS-52	I. F.	Mog.	23,300	1,000
1500	120	PS-52	I. F.	Mog.	33,000	1,000

Table I. Incandescent lamps

Courtesy of General Electric Co.

type A-21 incandescent lamp has a rated output of 1640 lumens. Starting with this fact, it is possible to learn in advance how many footcandles of light will be found on the working plane of a room whose dimensions are stated, when this lamp is employed in a certain luminaire. The reverse problem may also be worked out, beginning with the desired intensity on the working plane, and carrying through the various steps to the size of lamp that will be needed. The process is altogether systematic.

Before turning to practical examples of commercial and industrial lighting installations, it is necessary to consider some important terms which are used in making calculations. One of them is "Coefficient of Utilization," abbreviated "CU."

Coefficient of Utilization

Table II deals with the proportion of total lamp lumens which manages to reach the working plane. This imaginary plane or level

NO	STYLE	TYPE	D.B.	M.F.	R.R.	80% 50%	80% 30%	70% 50%	70% 30%	50% 50%	50% 30%	30% 30%	30% 10%
			FLOOR REF.						10%				
			CEILING REF.			80%		70%		50%		30%	
			WALL REF.			50%	30%	50%	30%	50%	30%	30%	10%
			D.B.	M.F.	R.R.				COEFFICIENT OF UTILIZATION				
6F		Indirect Incand. Comm'l 750 W.	1.2	G.7	2.5	.34	.32	.33	.32	.32	.31		
				M.63	3.	.36	.34	.32	.32	.31	.31		
				P.55	4.	.39	.37	.35	.34	.32	.32		
					5.	.43	.40	.38	.37	.35	.34		
10R		Rec. Incand. Comm'l. 500 W.	.8	G.75	2.5	.62	.60	.62	.60	.60	.59		
				M.65	3.	.64	.62	.63	.61	.62	.60		
				P.55	4.	.65	.63	.65	.63	.63	.62		
					5.	.66	.65	.66	.64	.64	.63		
8T		Troffer Fluor Comm'l 4T-48"	1.	G.75	2.5	.53	.50	.52	.50	.51	.49		
				M.70	3.	.55	.52	.54	.52	.54	.51		
				P.60	4.	.56	.55	.56	.54	.55	.53		
					5.	.58	.58	.57	.56	.56	.55		
15M		Direct. Mercury Indust. 1000 W.	1.	G.75	2.5			.75	.71	.73	.70	.68	.66
				M.65	3.			.78	.74	.76	.73	.72	.69
				P.55	4.			.81	.78	.79	.77	.76	.74
					5.			.83	.81	.82	.80	.78	.77
19F		Gen. Dif. Fluor. Indust. 2PG 96"	1.	G.7	2.5			.64	.60	.60	.56	.53	.51
				M.63	3.			.67	.63	.63	.59	.55	.54
				P.55	4.			.70	.67	.65	.63	.59	.57
					5.			.73	.70	.68	.65	.61	.60

DB—Distance between = multiplier x mounting Height
MF—Maintenance Factor - Good - Medium - Poor
RR—Room Ratio

Table II. Coefficient of utilization (CU)

Courtesy of General Electric Co.

is usually taken at 3 ft from the floor in a store or an office. It is worth noting that the luminaire itself, regardless of how efficient it may be in the matter of reflecting light rays, absorbs some of the lumen output of the lamp.

The CU factor is affected by the amount of reflection to be expected from ceiling, walls, and floors, light-colored surfaces absorbing fewer lumens than darker. Tables such as II, here, show different CU ratings for different reflecting values of ceiling, wall, and floor.

Thus, commercial ceiling reflectance is estimated to vary from 50 percent to 80 percent, while that of an industrial ceiling varies from 30 percent to 70 percent. Similarly, commercial wall reflectance is shown as varying from 30 percent to 50 percent, and industrial from 10 percent to 50 percent. Floors, in both cases, show values ranging from 10 percent to 30 percent. It may appear strange that reflectance of the floor should be considered at all in determining intensity of light on the working plane. However, light rays falling thereon are reflected upward again to the ceiling and to other objects in the room, reaching the working plane finally through multiple reflection. The value of 10 percent is commonly used for all locations, unless some special feature is present, such as a highly polished surface.

The size of the room is important, too, because the quantity of light which strikes the walls, and the amount reflected back into a room depends on its width relative to its length. Wall reflection in a room 20 ft wide and 60 ft long will have a greater general effect than that in a room which is 40 ft wide and 60 ft long. This im-

LUMINAIRE HEIGHT—40% LT. DN.					
WIDTH FT.	LENGTH FT.	11'	12'	13'	15'
40	40	2.4	2.1	1.9	1.6
	60	2.8	2.5	2.3	1.9
	80	3.1	2.8	2.5	2.1
	100	3.4	3.0	2.7	2.3
	120	3.5	3.2	2.9	2.4
50	50	2.9	2.6	2.4	2.0
	70	3.4	3.1	2.8	2.3
	100	3.9	3.5	3.2	2.7
	140	4.3	3.9	3.5	2.9
	170	4.5	4.1	3.7	3.1

CEILING HEIGHT—LESS THAN 40% DN.					
WIDTH FT.	LENGTH FT.	15'	16 1/2'	18'	21'
40	40	2.4	2.1	1.9	1.6
	60	2.8	2.5	2.3	1.9
	80	3.1	2.8	2.5	2.1
	100	3.4	3.0	2.7	2.3
	120	3.5	3.2	2.9	2.4
50	50	2.9	2.6	2.4	2.0
	70	3.4	3.1	2.8	2.3
	100	3.9	3.5	3.2	2.7
	140	4.3	3.9	3.5	2.9
	170	4.5	4.1	3.7	3.1

Table III. Room ratio (RR)

Courtesy of General Electric Co.

portant factor is taken care of in a Room Ratio Table which supplies numerical values to be used in connection with the CU table. The abbreviation for this term is "RR." A portion of the Room Ratio Table is shown in Table III. The complete table is included in the Appendix.

Spacing of luminaires also affects CU, the distance between them depending upon the height above the floor. This distance is normally the same as the mounting height. With recessed types, however, the spacing of adjacent units may vary from .5 of mounting height for a downlight, to .9 for a troffer. In some cases, the ratio of spacing to mounting height may be greater than 1, but it is seldom more than 1.2.

Shielding Media for Panels	Floor 10% Reflectance* Ceiling 80% Reflectance Walls 50% 30% Room Ratio Coefficient of Utilization	
	Room Ratio	Coefficient of Utilization
Diffusing plastic panels, usually acrylic or vinyl	0.6	.19	.14
	0.8	.26	.20
	1.0	.32	.25
	1.25	.38	.31
	1.5	.43	.39
	2.0	.50	.43
	2.5	.55	.49
	3.0	.58	.53
	4.0	.62	.59
	5.0	.67	.63
Clear, configurated glass or plastic brightness-controlling panels	0.6	.22	.17
	0.8	.29	.24
	1.0	.35	.29
	1.25	.42	.35
	1.5	.46	.40
	2.0	.53	.46
	2.5	.57	.52
	3.0	.61	.56
	4.0	.65	.61
	5.0	.68	.64

Maintenance Factors for Panels:
Good—0.65, Med.—0.55, Poor—0.45

Shielding Media for Louvers	Floor 10% Reflectance* Ceiling 80% Reflectance Walls 50% 30% Room Ratio Coefficient of Utilization	
	Room Ratio	Coefficient of Utilization
Small - Scale translucent plastic louvers providing 45° shielding	0.6	.20	.14
	0.8	.26	.20
	1.0	.31	.25
	1.25	.37	.31
	1.5	.42	.35
	2.0	.48	.41
	2.5	.53	.47
	3.0	.56	.51
	4.0	.60	.56
	5.0	.63	.59
Small-scale white-enameled metal louvers providing 45° shielding	0.6	.19	.14
	0.8	.25	.19
	1.0	.30	.24
	1.25	.35	.29
	1.5	.40	.33
	2.0	.46	.40
	2.5	.50	.45
	3.0	.53	.48
	4.0	.57	.53
	5.0	.60	.57

Maintenance Factors for Louvers:
Good—0.70, Med.—0.65, Poor—0.55

Table IV. Coefficients of utilization for luminous and louver ceilings
Courtesy of General Electric Co.

CU values for luminous ceilings, Table IV, are somewhat easier to apply. They are based, primarily, on a reflectance of 80 percent, because plenums are invariably painted, as mentioned in the preceding chapter. CU ratings for louver ceilings are slightly different than for the plastic diffusing type. Floor and wall reflectances are the same as for standard commercial units and locations.

Maintenance Factor

Another term necessary to lighting calculations is "Maintenance Factor," abbreviated "MF." It deals with reduction in light which comes through use. Gradual deterioration of the lamp filaments, dust accumulation, and the sort of care received by the equipment, are the essential elements. Illuminating Engineering Society publications treat MF on the basis of three divisions: Good, Medium, and Poor. If the atmosphere in the room is clean, luminaires frequently dusted, and lamps are replaced systematically, the MF is deemed Good. If the atmosphere is smoky, but units are given reasonable care, the MF is deemed Medium. If the atmosphere is quite dirty, and fixtures receive only haphazard attention, the MF is deemed Poor.

MF is listed in the CU table with each type of luminaire, ranging from 50 percent in the worst examples to 85 percent in the best. It can never be equal to 100 percent because of decrease in lumen output of the lamps themselves in the course of normal operation. In any case, application of the MF factor during a lighting calculation, always reduces the effective value of CU.

MF for luminous ceilings varies from 0.65 for Good, to 0.55 for Medium, to 0.45 for Poor. Those for louver ceilings range from 0.7 for Good, to 0.65 for Medium, to 0.55 for Poor.

APPLIED LIGHTING CALCULATIONS

Project 1—Incandescent Pendants

The dining room in Fig. 2 is 40 ft wide and 42 ft long. Although recommended foot-candle intensities have increased greatly, requirements for this kind of occupancy have remained much the same. Old practices are still followed, because lighting in restaurants and nightclubs is based upon atmospheric considerations rather than

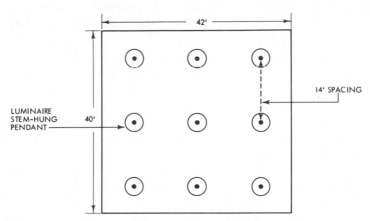

Fig. 2. Hotel dining room with 9 luminaires arranged in a pattern of squares

on sharpness of vision. The owners have requested lighting on the tables equal to about 15 foot-candles, and have selected indirect incandescent luminaire No. 6F, mounted on a 3-ft stem. Cove lighting is to be employed along the walls, for decorative purposes, but it will be of such low value that its overall effect may be ignored.

The floor area is: 40 ft × 42 ft, or 1680 sq ft, and the amount of light needed to provide 15 foot-candles per sq ft is: 1680 × 15, or 25,200 net lumens. Walls and ceiling, which is 15 ft high, are surfaced with white acoustical plaster.

Referring to the RR table, the room ratio for a space 40 ft by 42 ft is slightly more than for one 40 ft by 40 ft, or about 2.5. Note that the 15-ft column of the table on the right is used, because less than 40 percent of the lumens are sent downward. The CU table gives a value of .34 for the No. 6F type of luminaire, and states MF values of .7, .63, and .55 for Good, Medium, and Poor, respectively. In this sort of establishment, dust is likely to collect, and lamps are usually changed until they burn out. Maintenance, therefore, must be considered Poor, and the value .55 selected. The corrected rating of CU, then, equals: .55 × .34, or .19. The total number of lumens must be not less than: 25,200/.19, or 132,500.

The CU table shows that the distance between luminaires should not be greater than 1.2 times mounting height. Since the units are 12 ft from the floor, the spacing should not be greater than 1.2 × 12 ft, or 14.4 ft. In order to obtain a perfectly even distribution of lighting, the distance between the wall and the nearest line of fixtures should be equal to one-half that between lines of fixtures. It may be seen in Fig. 2, that the lengthwise arrangement is perfect for a spacing of 14 ft between units in the row, because there is one-half this distance, or 7 ft remaining at either end wall.

The width of the room does not permit quite as good an arrangement, because, for the same spacing between rows, the distance to either side wall is only 6 ft. To provide more space from the wall, the distance between rows could be reduced to 13 ft 6 in without any particular harm. However, the change is hardly worth considering, here, especially since cove lighting is present. In general, the square arrangement of Fig. 2 should not be departed from in laying out a group of incandescent pendants.

There are three rows of three each, or a total of 9 luminaires. Each lamp must contribute at least: 132,500/9, or 14,720 lumens. Table I shows the nearest standard lamp to be a 750-watt, PS 52,

NATURE OF VISUAL TASK	F.C.
OFFICES	
CLERICAL TYPING	100
ACCOUNTING	150
SCHOOLS	
EASY READING	30
CLASSROOMS	70
AUDITORIUMS	30
FACTORIES—SHOPS	
DRAFTING	200
BENCH WORK	50
MACHINE, MEDIUM	100
MACHINE, FINE	500
GRINDING	1000
STORES	
MERCHANDISING	100
SHOWCASES	200

Table V. Recommended foot-candle intensities

From National Electric Code

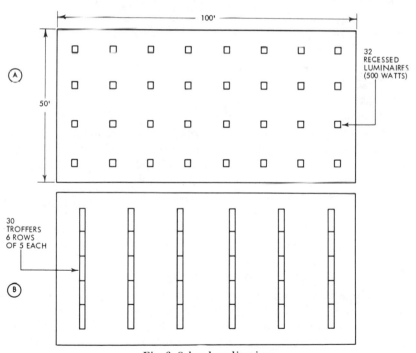

Fig. 3. School auditorium

inside frost type, which has an output of 16,700 lumens. These lamps will produce: 16,700/14,720 × 15 foot-candles, or 17 foot-candles, which is quite acceptable.

A word of advice might be timely at this point. Always obtain the manufacturer's data applying to the particular luminaire that is to be used. The lamp tables given here are from a standard lamp manufacturer, and the RR table is a condensation of a standard form which is reprinted whole in the Appendix. The CU table, however, is made up of luminaires taken from more than one source.

Project 2—Recessed Luminaires

The auditorium, Fig. 3, is 50 ft wide and 100 ft long, with a 15 ft ceiling. White acoustical tile is used on walls and ceiling. In Fig. 3A, the room is lighted with recessed incandescent luminaires. The floor area is: 50 ft × 100 ft, or 5000 sq ft. The amount of light to provide 30 foot-candles per Table V equals: 5000 × 30, or 150,000 lumens.

The RR table shows a room ratio of 2.7. Carrying this value to the No. 10R luminaire in the CU table, the CU rating is found to be .63. Maintenance in school properties is consistently good, so that the MF factor of .75 will be selected. The corrected CU factor is: .75 × .63, or .47. The required amount of lighting equals: 150,000/.47, or 320,000 lumens.

The CU table states that the distance between centers of luminaires should not be greater than .8 × mounting height, or .8 × 15 ft, which is 12 ft. The most even square arrangement, as indicated in Fig. 3A for luminaires approximately this far apart, gives 8 rows of 4 each, or 4 rows of 8 each, depending upon the observers point of view, a total of 32 luminaires.

Each lamp must produce: 320,000/32, or 10,000 lumens. Table I indicates that a 500-watt, inside frost, type PS 40 lamp has a rated output of 9,900 lumens, which makes it precisely correct for this installation.

If it were decided to substitute troffers for the incandescent system, and a four-lamp, 48-in, rapid start, glass covered unit were agreed upon, the calculations would be carried out in much the same way. The No. 8T troffer would be selected, its CU factor being .54, and the MF factor .75. The corrected value of CU becomes: .75 × .54, or .41. The amount of light that must be supplied is: 150,000/.41, or 366,000 lumens.

TYPE	BULB	WATTS (Nominal)	LENGTH	INITIAL LUMENS		AMPS
				Cool White	Deluxe CW	
RAPID START	T12	40	48"	3100		.425
INSTANT START	T12	40	48"	2650	2050	.425
PRE-HEAT	T17	90	60"	5300	3900	1.52
SLIM-LINE	T12	74	96"	5600	4100	.425
POWER GROOVE	PC17	215	96"	15000	11000	1.5

Table VI. A selection of fluorescent lamps

Courtesy of General Electric Co.

The maximum distance between centers, from the CU table, is equal to mounting height, or 15 ft. The arrangement of Fig. 3B is worth trying. There are six rows of five troffers each, a total of 30 units. Since each has four lamps, the number of tubes is 120. Each tube will have to provide: 366,000/120, or 3050 lumens. Table III lists a rapid start tube which produces 3100 lumens, and thus makes it acceptable here.

Project 3—Luminous and Louver Ceiling—Store Details

The store illustrated in Fig. 4 is 50 ft wide and 106 ft long. The

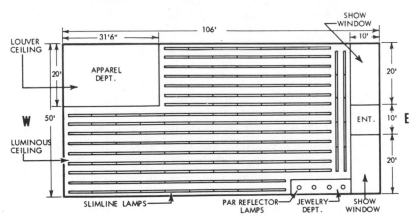

Fig. 4. Modern store building with luminous and louver ceiling

primary ceiling height is 16 ft, the finish height 12 ft. Show windows and a 10-ft entrance cover the front, or East end of the building. The main section is lighted by a plastic luminous ceiling, except for the Northwest corner, which is devoted to a women's apparel department, and which has a louver ceiling. A jewelry department, in the Southeast corner is especially illuminated by downlights.

The plastic ceiling will give 100 foot-candles of lighting intensity to that portion which it covers. The women's apparel section is illuminated by open louvers to an intensity of 200 foot-candles, and the jewelry department, particularly the display case area, is lighted to an intensity of 350 to 400 foot-candles. Each phase of the problem will be treated in turn.

The area beneath the plastic ceiling is 4070 sq ft, that under the louvers is 630 sq ft, that of the jewelry department is 100 sq ft, while show windows and entrance take up 500 sq ft. Since the show windows are outside the main body of the store, the room ratio will be determined on the basis of the dimensions: 50 ft by 96 ft.

The light required for the main ceiling is equal to: 4070 × 100, or 407,000 net lumens. The RR rating for a room 50 ft by 96 ft is 3.6. This dimension is not listed in Table III, so it had to be calculated by the formula:

$$RR = \frac{\text{Width} \times \text{Length}}{(MH - 3)(\text{Width} + \text{Length})}$$

Applying the formula here:

$$RR = \frac{50 \times 96}{(12 - 3)(50 + 96)} = 3.6$$

Table IV lists a CU rating of .60 for such a room with MH (mounting height) of 12 ft. In this sort of occupancy, it is not safe to assume a maintenance condition better than Medium, for which the table shows a value of .55. The corrected CU rating becomes: .55 × .6, or .33. The total amount of lighting to be supplied, therefore, must not be less than: 407,000/.33, or 1,235,000 lumens.

Note—Use this formula only with left portion of Table III.

Specifications ask for 96-in, Deluxe Cool White Slimline lamps. Table VI gives a rating of 4100 lumens for this lamp. The number required is: 1,235,000/4100, or about 301. It is a good plan, at this time, to make a fixture layout. Numerous alternatives for arranging the fluorescent strips, present themselves. There are three separate portions of the main ceiling: one from the apparel section to the front of the store, the second from the West wall to the East end of the room, and the narrow portion of shorter length that extends from the West wall to the jewelry department.

Strips above the first mentioned section could be arranged either lengthwise or crosswise, while those in the remainder of the ceiling are arranged lengthwise. It is quite apparent that the ones in the 5-ft wide section next to the jewelry department must be arranged lengthwise if the main body of the ceiling is laid out in this manner. After due thought, it is decided to use a lengthwise pattern insofar as possible.

The next problem is to decide upon how many rows of luminaires, and what type. With so many lamps, the number of rows of single-tube units would be excessive, and the hanging expense almost double that for a two-lamp fixture. The distance between rows of the two-lamp units should not be greater than the distance from the finish ceiling to the primary ceiling, which is 4 ft. And, since part of the lamps will be somewhat lower, in order to clear ducts and piping, the distance between rows will have to lie somewhere between 3 ft and 4 ft.

The main section is the full length of the room, or 96 ft. Luminaires are slightly longer than 8 ft, so that 11 of them can be placed in a single row. Area of this section, leaving out the narrow strip adjacent to the jewelry department, is equal to: 25 × 96, or 2400 sq ft. Net lumens to provide 100 foot-candles of lighting can not be less than: 2400 × 100, or 240,000 lumens. Useful output per lamp is equal to the corrected CU factor times rated lamp lumens: .33 × 4100, or 1353 net lumens. The number of lamps needed for the area must be: 240,000/1353, or 177. With 22 lamps per row of 11 luminaires, the number of rows should be equal to: 177/22, or approximately 8.

Proceeding on this basis, the plan of Fig. 4 is arrived at, the final result showing a total of 16 parallel rows: 7 with 11 luminaires each, 7 with 7 each, and 2 with 9 each. There are also two crosswise rows of 5 each at the East end of the room. The spacing, center to center between rows, is 3 ft-4 in. In all, 154 luminaires are needed, with 308 lamps.

The area of the apparel corner is 630 sq ft, and the desired foot-candle intensity is 200, so that the required lighting amounts to: 630 × 200, or 126,000 net lumens. Small-scale, translucent plastic louvers are specified. Although the dimensions of the space are small, the area is part of the large room, so that the original value of RR, 3.6, will apply. There are only two walls, however, making it necessary to use the 30 percent wall reflectance column.

88   *Industrial and Commercial Wiring*

Ceiling	80%		70%		50%		30%	
Walls	50%	30%	50%	30%	50%	30%	30%	10%
Room Ratio	Multiplying Factor							
0.6	1.03	1.02	1.03	1.02	1.02	1.02	1.01	1.00
0.8	1.04	1.02	1.04	1.02	1.03	1.02	1.01	1.01
1.0	1.05	1.03	1.04	1.03	1.04	1.02	1.02	1.01
1.25	1.06	1.04	1.05	1.04	1.04	1.03	1.02	1.01
1.5	1.07	1.06	1.07	1.05	1.05	1.04	1.02	1.02
2.0	1.09	1.07	1.08	1.06	1.05	1.04	1.03	1.02
2.5	1.10	1.08	1.09	1.08	1.07	1.05	1.04	1.03
3.0	1.12	1.10	1.10	1.09	1.08	1.06	1.04	1.03
4.0	1.14	1.12	1.12	1.10	1.08	1.07	1.04	1.04
5.0	1.15	1.13	1.13	1.11	1.09	1.08	1.05	1.04

Table VII. Multiplication factors for 30% floor reflectance
Courtesy of General Electric Co.

Table IV lists a CU rating of .54 for such an area which has 80 percent ceiling and 30 percent wall reflectances. Assigning the Medium MF of .65, the corrected value of CU becomes: .65 × .54, or .35. Yet another factor is involved here, the matter of floor luminosity. Calculations up to this time have been founded upon 10 percent floor reflectance, which is normal for most locations. But in this department, the floor is highly polished, so that its reflectance may be taken at 30 percent.

Table VII shows that the CU estimate should be multiplied by 1.11, the true value of CU becoming: 1.11 × .36, or .40. Specifications

Watts	Volts	Ordering Abbreviation	Bulb Shape	Bulb Finish & Color	Approx. Initial Total Lumens	Rated Life (hrs.)
CLEAR PAR LAMPS. Burning position—ANY. Heat-Resistant Glass.						
200	120	200PAR46/3NSP	PAR-46	Narrow Spot	2,250	2,000
200	120	200PAR46/3MFL	PAR-46	Med. Flood	2,250	2,000
300	120	300PAR56/NSP	PAR-56	Narrow Spot	3,720	2,000
300	120	300PAR56/MFL	PAR-56	Med. Flood	3,720	2,000
300	120	300PAR56/WFL	PAR-56	Wide Flood	3,720	2,000
500	120	500PAR64/NSP	PAR-64	Narrow Spot	6,500	2,000
500	120	500PAR64/MFL	PAR-64	Med. Flood	6,500	2,000
500	120	500PAR64/WFL	PAR-64	Wide Flood	6,500	2,000

Table VIII. A selection of reflector lamps
Courtesy of General Electric Co.

200-300 AND 500 WATT PAR LAMPS.

- Minimum Footcandles (useful light Limit)
- Maximum Footcandles (on beam Axis)
- Mounting distance

LAMP	MAXIMUM FOOTCANDLES	LIGHTED AREA LENGTH	WIDTH	MINIMUM FOOTCANDLES
200-W PAR46/NSP	368	4-FT.	3 FT.	36
200-W PAR46/MFL	124	7 FT.	3½ FT.	12
300-W PAR56/NSP	788	3½ FT.	2½ FT.	72
300-W PAR56/MFL	260	6 FT.	3½ FT.	24
300-W PAR56/WFL	116	11½ FT.	5½ FT.	12
500-W PAR65/NSP	1208	3½ FT.	2 FT.	104
500-W PAR64/MFL	468	6 FT.	3½ FT.	52
500-W PAR64/WFL	128	12½ FT.	6 FT.	16

Comparison Data for 10-Foot Mounting Distance.

Table IX. Spot areas of PAR lamps

Courtesy of General Electric Co.

state that one third of the illumination here shall be incandescent, and two thirds fluorescent, with as little glare as possible from the glossy floor.

Under this condition, the amount of light supplied by incandescent lamps must be: ⅓ × 126,000, or 42,000 net lumens. That of the fluorescent lamps must be the remainder, or 84,000 net lumens. The total quantity of incandescent light will be equal to: 42,000/.4, or 105,000 lumens, while the fluorescent component is: 84,000/.4, or 210,000 lumens.

Although glare is much less troublesome where the intensity of illumination exceeds 50 foot-candles, the warning given in the specifications merits some attention. As a precaution, the incandescent lighting will be furnished by reflector lamps that throw their light upward onto the plenum ceiling. Table VIII lists a 500-watt reflector lamp with a rating of 6500 lumens. The number required to produce 105,000 lumens is: 105,000/6500, or 16.

Examination of specifications reveals that 96-in, Cool White Power Groove lamps will be accepted for the location. Table VI gives a rating of 15,000 lumens for this tube. The number of them to create 210,000 lumens will be: 210,000/15,000, or 14 tubes. Single-tube luminaires, arranged in 7 rows of 2 each can be fastened directly to the plenum ceiling, making sure that no ducts or pipes interfere with them. The 16 incandescent lamps may be spread out as evenly as possible, underneath them.

The third problem concerns the jewelry department. Parabolic reflector lamps may be used here, the 500-watt PAR64/MFL being chosen from Table VIII to provide from 350 to 400 foot-candles at counter height. The reason this lamp is selected, may be learned from Table IX.

This type of reflector lamp projects the rays in parallel lines, so that a confined spot of high intensity is produced. The table shows that the rays from this lamp, when it is mounted 10 ft above the area to be lighted, make a bright spot whose dimensions are approximately $3\frac{1}{2}$ ft by 6 ft. Four lamps will be employed, the spacing between centers, 5 ft. The confined, overlapping beams will provide an intensity within the specified range, or somewhat greater than this when the lamps are new. Carpenters will construct a suitable valance to shield the bright lamps from direct view.

Show windows, according to the specifications, are to be illuminated to an intensity of 500 foot-candles, using Cool Beam reflector lamps. The 300-watt PAR56/MFL type listed in Table VIII, falls within this class. Each window has an area of 200 sq ft, requiring: 200 × 500, or 100,000 lumens. Since the lamps are rated at 3720 lumens, the number per window is equal to: 100,000/3720, or 27. The entrance passage offers no difficulties, specifications stating that it is to be lighted with 10, 150-watt downlights.

Project 4—Industrial Location—Mercury or Fluorescent Lighting

The building of Fig. 5 is to be lighted with an intensity of

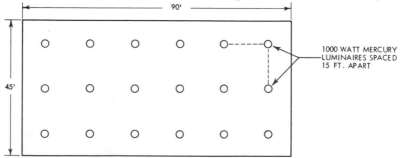

Fig. 5. Industrial location using mercury luminaires

approximately 120 foot-candles. Either mercury or fluorescent lighting is satisfactory, depending upon relative cost. Dimensions of the building are 45 ft by 90 ft, by 19 ft high. Mercury lighting will be considered first.

The area, Fig. 5, is: 45 ft × 90 ft, or 4050 sq ft. For an intensity of 120 foot-candles, the amount of light must be: 4050 × 120, which is 486,000 net lumens. In order to reduce danger of glare, it is decided that mercury lamps should not be closer than 15 ft to the floor. Ceiling, wall, and floor reflectances are taken at: 70 percent, 30 percent, and 10 percent respectively. The RR table does not list a room with these dimensions. Therefore, the value must be calculated, as explained earlier. This rating is equal to:

$$\frac{45 \times 90}{(15 - 3)(45 + 90)}, \text{ or } 2.5.$$

A type 15M mercury luminaire selected from Table X will be tried with a 1000-watt lamp. Referring the RR factor to the proper column in Table II, the CU factor is given as .71. Since maintenance in this particular location is good, the MF will be chosen as .75, giving a corrected CU value of: .75 × .71, or .53. The total number of lumens necessary here must equal: 486,000/.53, which rounds out to 917,000.

Color improved lamps are requested for this operation, the H1000 of Table X being selected. This unit has an initial output of 51,000 lumens. The number required will be: 917,000/51,000, or

TYPE	BULB	WATTS	LENGTH	INITIAL LUMENS		SERVICE
				Vert.	Horiz.	
H175	CLEAR	175	8 1/4"	7000	6650	Indoor Outdoor
H400	CLEAR	400	11 1/2"	21000	20000	Indoor Outdoor
H400	COLOR IMP.	400	11 1/2"	20500	19500	Indoor Outdoor
H700	CLEAR	700	14 5/16"	36500	34600	Indoor Outdoor
H1000	CLEAR	1000	15 1/16"	54000	---	Indoor
H1000	COLOR IMP.	1000	15 1/16"	51000	---	Indoor

Table X. A selection of Mercury lamps

Courtesy of General Electric Co.

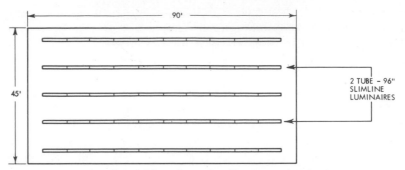

Fig. 6. Industrial location using fluorescent luminaires

18, permitting an even layout, Fig. 5, of 3 rows which have 6 luminaires each, and which are spaced 15 ft apart. For an even distribution of light, the table designates a spacing that does not exceed mounting height. Since the mounting height is 15 ft, the tentative spacing is satisfactory.

A comparative arrangement of fluorescent luminaires will now be made. A No. 19F, two-tube industrial unit will be selected. This type of fixture can be mounted within 12 ft of the floor without introducing glare trouble. Proceeding as before, a rating of 3.3 is calculated for a mounting height of 12 ft. Table II lists a CU value of .64 for this unit, and a Good MF of .7, making the corrected CU value: .7 × .64, or .45. The total amount of lighting supplied can not be less than: 486,000/.45, or 1,080,000 lumens.

This luminaire is equipped with two Power Groove tubes. Table VI lists a rating of 11,000 lumens for the 96-in Deluxe Cool White lamp deemed suitable for the location. The total number of lamps equals: 1,080,000/11,000, which is 98, requiring 49 fixtures.

Before deciding upon a definite number, it is well to investigate possible layouts. It would be possible to install 11 luminaires in a lengthwise row, or 5 in a crosswise row. After some trial and error attempts, it is apparent that the best plan is to use 5 rows of 10 luminaires each, Fig. 6, making a total of 50 units. This amounts to 1 more than the calculated number, so that lighting intensity will be slightly greater than the necessary value.

Project 5—Area Lighting of a Neighborhood Parking Lot

The lot, Fig. 7, which is to be lighted with mercury luminaires, measures 80 ft on a side. Usual practice calls for an intensity of 2 foot-

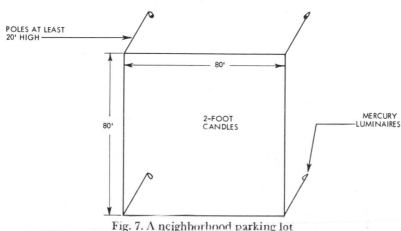

Fig. 7. A neighborhood parking lot

candles. It is impractical to perform step-by-step calculations as with interior locations, because there is no roof structure from which to hang evenly spaced luminaires. Also, the number of poles must be kept to a minimum.

Tests in which standard lamps and fixtures are employed, show that about .05 watt of mercury lighting is required to produce 1 foot-candle of illumination, .06 watt of fluorescent lighting, and .15 watt of incandescent lighting. For 2 foot-candles, in the present instance, .1 watt of mercury lighting is needed. The area is: 80 ft × 80 ft, or 6400 sq ft, so that necessary lamp wattage must be: 6400 × .1, or 640 watts.

The height of the four poles at the corners of the lot should be not less than 1/4 the distance between lights, or 20 ft. Each lamp must contribute 1/4 × 640 watts, or 160 watts. Referring to Table X, the nearest standard mercury lamp is the H175 clear, which is rated at 175 watts, the value being close enough to the required wattage of 160. The luminaire is an M250 in the manufacturer's catalogue.

The shopping center of Fig. 8 is 500 ft square. It is to be lighted with mercury lamps. Such areas are usually illuminated to an intensity of 5 watts per sq ft. Allowing .05 watt per foot-candle, the power needed for 5 watts is: 5 × .05 watt, or .25 watt per sq ft. The total power is equal to: .25 × 250,000, or 62,500 watts. It is proposed to use 1000-watt lamps in No. M1000 luminaires. The required number can not be less than: 62,500/1000, which is 62.5 lamps. This result should be changed to the nearest larger even number, which is 64.

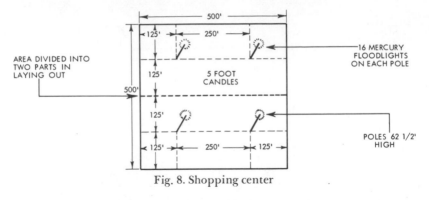

Fig. 8. Shopping center

Large areas should be divided into equal spaces with poles along the center line of each. As an aid toward dividing the area and spacing the poles, it must be remembered that the distance between poles should be approximately four times the height of a pole which height, for ease of maintenance, should not greatly exceed 60 ft. If the plan of Fig. 8 is carried out, the poles will be 62.5 high, 250 ft apart, and one-half that distance from a pole to the edge of the space. Since there are 64 lamps on four poles, or 16 apiece, each group of lamps may be arranged in a square or, preferably, circular pattern at the top of the pole.

Project 6—Flood Lighting a Vertical Surface

Floodlighting differs from both general lighting and area lighting with respect to method of calculation. The procedure is based upon data which must be supplied by the manufacturer of the particular floodlighting equipment which is to be used. The most important factors are beam lumens, and beam spread.

The building facade, Fig. 9A is to be illuminated to about 10 foot-candles from a distance of 50 ft, using 1000-watt incandescent floodlighting equipment. No. F84 floodlights with 1000-watt lamps appear satisfactory. The manufacturer's data states that beam lumens are 6400, beam spread 30 degrees horizontal and vertical, with beam efficiency of .45. The term beam lumens means the total number of lumens in the projected beam. Beam efficiency refers to the proportion of this beam which is actually confined to the main cone of light.

The effect of beam spread can be learned with the help of Fig. 9B. A vertical line is drawn, representing a distance of 50 ft to any

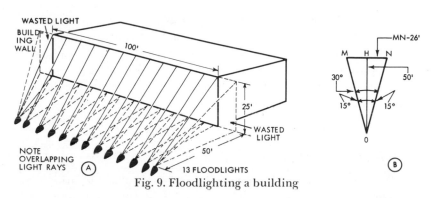

Fig. 9. Floodlighting a building

convenient scale. From the lower end, *O*, of the line, an angle of 30 degrees is laid out with a protractor, 15 degrees on each side as shown. A horizontal line is drawn through the upper end *H*, at right angles to the vertical line, and the sides of the angle are continued to meet it, forming the triangle *OMN*. The line *MN* is measured, and compared with the length of *OH*, which represents 50 ft. *MN* is found to measure approximately 26 ft. In the present case, both vertical and horizontal beam spread is 30 degrees. More often, they are different, so that a triangle must be drawn separately for each one.

It is necessary, first, to check the result against the vertical height of the surface which is to be lighted. The beam spread is equal to 26 ft, and the vertical height of the target surface is 25 ft, an acceptable comparison. The next step is to determine how many floodlights are needed, making use of the formula: Number of

$$\text{lamps} = \frac{\text{Length} \times \text{Width} \times \text{Foot-candles}}{\text{Beam lumens} \times \text{Efficiency} \times \text{MF}}.$$ MF, the mainte-

nance factor, is generally .75. Applying the formula to the facts,

$$\text{Lamps} = \frac{100 \times 25 \times 10}{6400 \times .45 \times .75} = 11.6, \text{ or } 12.$$

One further consideration must be noted. The distance between floodlights should not be greater than one-half the horizontal beam spread, which is one-half of 26 ft, or 13 ft. If the length of the wall is divided into twelve equal spaces, floodlights will be 8 ft-6 in apart, which satisfies the requirement. The reason that floodlights must be so spaced is that intensity of a spot formed on the target area by a beam of light decreases from the center to its edge. Overlapping of spots becomes necessary, therefore, to overcome the tendency for separate bright spots to appear instead of a uniform brilliance.

Since the line of floodlights is divided into twelve equal spaces, with a unit at each division, there will be 13 of them instead of 12. The effective value of lighting produced, nevertheless, is equal to only that of 12 floodlights, one-half of the light from the two end ones being wasted as indicated in Fig. 9A.

LIGHTING BRANCH CIRCUITS

Comparison with Dwellings

Branch circuits for commercial and industrial locations are treated by NEC on much the same basis as those for residential applications. The 15-amp general lighting circuit and the 20-amp utility circuit use No. 14 type R, or equivalent conductor for lighting, the circuit being protected by a 15-amp fuse or circuit breaker because the allowable carrying capacity of the wire, under NEC rules, is 15 amps. The utility circuit uses No. 12 wire, which is protected by a 20-amp fuse because the carrying capacity of the conductor is 20 amps.

Detailed circuit calculations will not be taken up until a later chapter. For the present, it is sufficient to note that these circuits are furnished with overload devices whose ratings are not greater than the carrying capacity of the circuit wires. Two additional lighting circuits are allowed in non-dwelling occupancies, provided that only heavy duty lampholders are connected to them, the 30-amp circuit and the 50-amp circuit. In most cases other than dwellings, No. 12 is the smallest conductor used on lighting circuits because of the need to limit voltage drop.

Industrial practice is similar to commercial in this regard, except that 30-amp and 50-amp circuits are more common. One reason is the widespread use of mercury luminaires in manufacturing plants. In sizes larger than 100 watts, these lamps are equipped with mogul sockets, which come within the code definition of heavy duty lampholders.

Phase and Voltage

The nature of the power supply should also be mentioned at this time. In single-family residences, the service is always single-phase, usually 115-230-volt, three-wire, from which either two-wire or three-wire circuits may be run to points of distribution. Three-phase, four-wire, 120-208-volt, so-called network systems, are sometimes employed in large apartment houses. Today, this form of circuit, or a similar one, is the rule in commercial and industrial buildings. A popular variation is the 277-480-volt system used with heavy fluorescent lamp loads.

REVIEW QUESTIONS

1. What method is used for most lighting calculations?
2. What term indicates the proportion of total lamp lumens which reach the working plane?
3. State the height of the working plane in an office.
4. What is the average value of ceiling reflectance in an industrial location?
5. What is the average value of floor reflectance?
6. RR is the abbreviation of what term?
7. What is the maximum spacing ratio with respect to mounting height?
8. What is the standard value of reflectance for a plenum cavity?
9. MF deals with reduction in light which comes through what?
10. State the three classes of MF.
11. What is the first calculation usually made for an area which is to be lighted?
12. By what factor is the first CU rating multiplied in order to obtain the corrected value of CU?
13. What general arrangement is best when laying out a group of incandescent pendants?
14. Area must be multiplied by what number in order to obtain net lumens?
15. What is the maximum permissible distance between rows of fluorescent strips in a luminous ceiling?
16. What is the nature of light rays projected by a PAR lamp?
17. To what intensity is the usual neighborhood parking lot illuminated?
18. How much power is required to produce 1 foot-candle intensity in a parking area, using mercury lamps?
19. In floodlighting, what beam characteristic is equally as important as beam lumens?
20. Should the distance between floodlights be equal to the beam spread?

Chapter Five

Wiring for Motors

Required Knowledge

The inside wireman must be familiar with outward characteristics of motors in order to intelligently carry out the work of connecting them. It is unnecessary, however, for him to have a technical knowledge of windings and internal details equal to that of the motor-shop electrician. He should be able to recognize and to distinguish between the numerous types from information recorded on the motor nameplate. And from this data, he should be capable of deciding what materials and methods are best suited to the particular task.

In order to be thus competent, he must understand factors which control the matter of wire size, circuit fusing, motor protection, controllers, and starting methods. He must know the meaning of code letters found on nameplates, and standard markings for motor lead wires. As part of his mental equipment, he must also be acquainted with code requirements for hermetic motors, group installations, and machine tools. Among other things, he must be reasonably well informed with regard to cranes, elevators and escalators, IBM machine wiring, and the underlying principles of carrier-system remote control devices. The present chapter seeks to impart this information.

Kinds of Motors

Today, alternating current induction motors practically monopolize the electric-drive field. They are manufactured in single-phase, two-phase, and three-phase, although the two-phase type is seldom encountered. Direct-current units, still very scarce, have enjoyed a revival in some branches of industry where their stable variable speed qualities are highly important. The printing trade has always preferred direct-current. Recently, the electronically-controlled direct-current motor has become an essential element in closed-cycle operations connected with automation.

Single-phase motors are found only in relatively small sizes, usually less than 1 hp. Common types are: repulsion, repulsion-start, and capacitor split-phase, particularly the latter two. Except in special cases, the nominal operating speed is 1800 rpm. They are widely used for portable and semi-portable refrigerating equipment such as ice-cream cabinets, as well as for conveyors, blowers, or other air-conditioning units.

Three-phase motors appear in all sizes and speeds, from 1 hp or less to 1000 hp or more, and at speeds from 3600 down to 600 rpm or less; the slower speeds being with the very large sizes. As with single-phase, the 1800 rpm is the most popular 60-cycle type. Most are standard, constant duty, squirrel-cage motors, but there is a great variety such as: high-torque, brush-shifting variable speed, intermittent duty, and wound-rotor.

The usual current frequency in this country is 60 cycles, and the usual voltages 230, 440, 550, and 2300. The supply potential may vary somewhat from these amounts, but manufacturers customarily guarantee their motors to operate satisfactorily on circuits whose voltages differ not more than 10 percent from the value stamped on the nameplate. Thus, a 220-volt motor may be used successfully on a 208-volt circuit. It should be mentioned, however, that a 208-volt motor is now available for network systems.

ESSENTIAL TERMS

Motor Nameplate

The best place to start is with a simple nameplate, Fig. 1. Every motor, according to the NEC, must be equipped with a

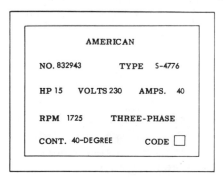

AMERICAN		
NO. 832943	TYPE	S-4776
HP 15	VOLTS 230	AMPS. 40
RPM 1725	THREE-PHASE	
CONT. 40-DEGREE	CODE ☐	

Fig. 1. Motor nameplate

nameplate that gives the maker's name, the rating in volts and amperes, the normal full-load speed, and the interval during which it can operate at full load, starting cold, before reaching its rated maximum temperature. All motors, except those for driving arc welding generators and hermetic units are marked in horsepower. If the motor has a built-in protective device, this fact must be stated on the nameplate. Those for sizes ½ hp or larger, with the exception of the polyphase wound-rotor type, must be marked with a code letter.

The most important notations for the wireman are: *HP, Volts, Amps, Phase, Duty,* and *Code Letter.* The horsepower rating is necessary in determining circuit switch size for all motors over 2 hp. The current rating is required in the selection of an over-current device.

Ambient Temperature

The normal temperature of a random location is taken to be 40 degrees Centigrade, which is equal to 104 degrees Fahrenheit. This is called the ambient temperature. The notation, *"40-degree"*, refers to the maximum temperature rise above the level of ambient temperature, that will occur while the motor is operating at full load. Since this is a 40-degree unit, it will not heat beyond the point: 40 degrees + 40 degrees, or 80 degrees, Centigrade.

Insulation on the windings deteriorates rapidly if this maximum temperature is exceeded. For example, if the motor were used in a location where the thermometer showed an ambient temperature of 50 degrees Centigrade, the insulation would fail if the unit were operated at full load for a considerable length of time.

There is also a standard 50-degree motor whose insulation is of a somewhat better grade that can withstand higher temperatures. Such a unit may operate at 90 degrees Centigrade, under full load conditions, without suffering insulation damage.

Duty

The term *"Continuous"* stands for "Continuous Duty." This means that the motor can be operated steadily at full load, even twenty-four hours a day if necessary. Besides continuous duty motors, there are intermittent types rated at 5-min, 15-min, 30-min, and 60-min. They can be operated at full load only the stated length of time before reaching the maximum allowable temperature, which is usually 55 degrees above the ambient value. An equally long rest period is usually in order before the motor can again be operated at full load. Cranes and hoists are often supplied with such units.

Code Letters

The *Code* letter shows locked-rotor current of the motor. This is the amount of current that will flow into stator windings when the rotor is blocked so that it cannot turn. Under this condition, the motor will draw a current several times as large as the running value. Consider, for example, the motor whose nameplate is shown in Fig. 1. Normal full load current is 40 amps. If the rotor is held fast while lead wires are connected to the supply line, a current of more than 200 amps could flow, the actual amount depending upon the electrical nature of the windings.

These electrical characteristics are expressed by the code letter stamped on the nameplate. Table 430-7(b) of the NEC (*See App.*) lists code letters from **A** to **V**, inclusive. Under locked-rotor conditions, a motor with letter **A** will draw a certain percentage of normal current, one having letter **B** will draw a larger percentage of normal current, one with letter **M** very much more, and so on. An important NEC table which is to be discussed later on, groups these code letters as follows: **A**, alone; **B, C, D,** and **E; F, G, H,** and all other letters to **V** inclusive.

The code letters have such individual values that if the motor of Fig. 1 has the letter **A** on its nameplate, its locked-rotor current will not be greater than 120 amps, which is 300 percent of normal. With one of the letters from **B** to **E** inclusive, the locked rotor current will not exceed 200 amps, or 500 percent of normal. With one of the remaining letters, the locked rotor current will be 240 amps or more, which means 600 percent of normal, or greater. For standard squirrel-cage induction motors, this value of 600 percent may be accepted as maximum.

The practical importance of locked-current ratings will now be explained. At the instant of starting an induction motor behaves as if its rotor were actually unable to turn. Even though its shaft is perfectly free in the bearings, it hesitates for a moment while drawing a current equal to the locked-rotor value. This term, then, expresses the instantaneous starting current of the motor under consideration.

METHODS FOR STARTING

Need for Starting Methods

A large percentage of squirrel-cage induction motors have windings that draw 600 percent of normal current if connected directly to the supply wires. If the motor is of small size, for example 2 hp and a normal full load current of 6 amps, the initial surge of current does not exceed 36 amps. This amount is not large enough to strain the capacity of the power company's supply transformer, especially when the higher current persists for only a short space of time. With a motor as large as that in Fig. 1, however, and a load which takes a half minute to accelerate, the effect might prove quite disturbing to supply equipment.

For this reason, power companies usually prohibit connection of motors larger than 5 hp without some means for limiting current inrush. There is another inducement for cutting down starting current, this time from the owner's viewpoint. The sudden heavy flow of current may shock the motor and its driven machinery to such an extent that constant repetition over a period of time will result in costly damage.

Features Common to all Starting Methods

All starting procedures are based upon application of a reduced voltage to the motor terminals. The reduction in voltage produces a lower starting torque than would be obtainable at full line voltage. The term *"torque"* means "turning effort." Torque causes a motor to start from rest, and to carry its load. Since it is created by the action of current which flows in the stator winding, it will certainly be less when the current flow decreases because of reduced voltage.

Tests have proven that torque for a given motor, varies as the square of the voltage. For example, if full line voltage is 200, and it is lowered to say 100 volts by one means or another, the torque at this reduced voltage would compare with that at full line voltage as: 100 squared/200 squared, which is equal to: 10,000/40,000, or $\frac{1}{4}$ as much.

The starting torque of an average squirrel-cage induction motor with full voltage impressed on its windings is about 150 percent of normal full-load torque. If the voltage is reduced to one-half, the maximum starting torque becomes: $\frac{1}{4} \times 150$, or $37\frac{1}{2}$ percent of full-load value. The required turning effort is dependent upon the nature of the load. When a motor drives a fan or blower, very little torque is needed to move the rotor, because the starting load is practically zero. As the propeller speeds up, and thus agitates the air, the load gradually increases.

An air compressor with an unloading device that permits the drive motor to come up to speed before meeting with resistance, is another easily started machine. Here, the weight of the pistons and crankshaft offer the only opposition during the accelerating process. Starting conditions, generally, are more severe than this, but in most cases, somewhat less than full-load torque is sufficient to set the machine in motion.

Older equipment sometimes offered a choice of four starting voltages over a range covering from 85 percent to 40 percent. Modern starters provide three voltage selections: 80 percent of normal, 65 percent, and 50 percent. The percentage of across-the-line starting torque offered by the three steps, as calculated by the preceding formula, are: 64 percent, 42 percent, and 25 percent, respectively. In terms of full-load torque, these values become: .64 × 150 percent, .42 × 150 percent, and .25 × 150 percent, or 96 percent, 63 percent, and 37½ percent, respectively.

Series-Resistance Method

The first plan likely to occur to one for reducing starting current, is to insert resistors in series with the supply wires, as in Fig. 2. This principle is used by a well-known manufacturer. The arrange-

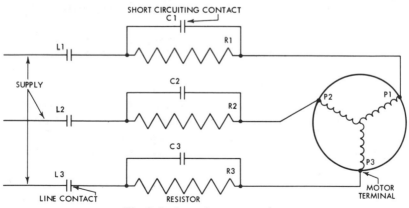

Fig. 2. Series-resistance starting

ment of Fig. 2 consists of three elements, the main contactor with three contacts, *L1, L2,* and *L3;* the resistor bank *R1, R2,* and *R3,* together with contacts *C1, C2,* and *C3,* and the motor which has terminals *P1, P2,* and *P3.*

Supply wires are connected to *L1, L2,* and *L3.* Resistor *R1* is in series with *L1* and motor terminal *P1. R2* is in series with *P2,* and *R3* with *P3.* When the main contacts close, current passes from the supply wires through the resistors to the motor terminals. The resistors limit the flow of current, while the voltage across the motor terminals becomes less than that between line wires. The rotor begins to accelerate, and after a certain interval whose length is governed by a timing device, contacts *C1, C2,* and *C3* close, short-circuiting the resistors, and presenting full line voltage to the motor terminals.

If the resistors are of such value that the voltage at motor terminals is 80 percent of normal, the starting torque will be 64 percent of full-load value, while the current taken from the line wires is 80 percent of the across-the-line value. With the 15-hp motor of Fig. 1, this current will amount to: .8 × 240 amps, or 192 amps. If the starting voltage at the motor terminals is 65 percent, and the resulting torque 63 percent of full-load, the current taken from the line will be: .65 × 240 amps, or 156 amps. Again, if the starting voltage is limited to 50 percent, and the resulting torque 37½ percent of full-load, the current from the supply wires is: .5 × 240 amps, or 120 amps. To sum up these results, the motor exerts 96 percent of normal torque for a line current input of 192 amps, 63 percent for a line current of 156 amps, and 37½ percent for a line current of 120 amps.

The voltage at the motor terminals depends, of course, on the value of the series resistance which is employed. Note that the change from starting to running position is made here without opening the circuit between supply wires and motor terminals. For this reason, the series-resistance unit is said to be a closed-transfer starter. Before going on, it should be stated that the commercial type resistance starter often uses but two resistors. The one between *L2* and *P2* is omitted, thus simplifying the equipment, but still accomplishing the same purpose.

Series-Reactance Method

The series-reactance starter of Fig. 3 is quite similar to the

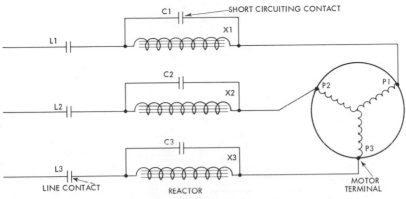

Fig. 3. Series-reactance starting

series-resistance unit; reactors being substituted for resistors. The principle is the same, and the relative values of currents and starting torques are the same. The series-reactance starter also falls within the closed-transfer classification. One important defect is that reactors disrupt the power factor of the supply system. The term *power factor* will be discussed later in the chapter.

Auto-Transformer Method

The auto-transformer starter of Fig. 4 includes a main contactor, two other sets of contacts, and two auto-transformers. At starting, one end of the winding from auto-transformer *T1* is connected to the wire from *L1*, by means of contact *S1*. The other end of

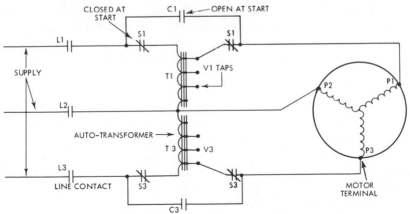

Fig. 4. Auto-transformer starting

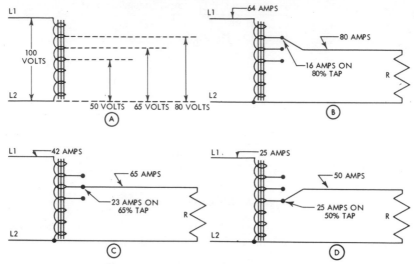

Fig. 5. Principle of the autotransformer

T1 is attached to the wire from *L2*. One of the *V1* taps on the winding of *T1* is connected to motor terminal *P1*. One side of contact *C1* is attached to the wire from *L1*, the other side to the wire from *V1* to *P1*.

Auto-transformer *T3* is connected in a similar way, one end going to *S3*, the other to *L2*. Its tap, *V3*, is attached to a wire from motor terminal *P3*. The left side of contact *C3* runs to the wire from *L3*, the other side to the wire from *V3* to *P3*. Contacts *S1* and *S3* remain closed during the starting period, while *C1* and *C3* remain open, auto-transformers *T1* and *T3* furnishing a reduced voltage to motor terminals. After the rotor has accelerated to a certain point, the timing device operates, and contacts *S1* and *S3* open, thus interrupting current flow to the motor. An instant later, contacts *C1* and *C2* close, so that full line voltage is applied to motor terminals.

Since it is necessary to open the circuit to the motor during the change from starting to running positions, the auto-transformer starter is classed as an open-transfer device. Opening and reclosing the circuit causes a temporary reduction in rotor momentum, and then a sudden increase. The resulting shock strains both motor and driven machinery, an undesirable effect that is not encountered with either resistance or reactance starting. In this respect, these types

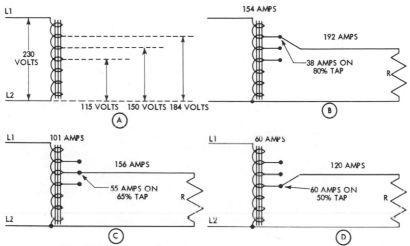

Fig. 6. Voltages and currents in auto-transformer starter

are considered superior to the auto-transformer, but the latter offers so many other advantages that it is the form most widely used today.

One of its principal recommendations is that the current taken from line wires during the starting interval is much lower than with the other methods. Before making a comparison with the aid of the 15 hp motor of Fig. 1, it is well to review briefly the principle of the auto-transformer.

An auto-transformer has a single winding that is connected across line wires *L1* and *L2*, Fig. 5A. If the line voltage is 100 volts, and tap wires are brought out at points which include 80 percent, 65 percent, and 50 percent of the turns from *L1* to *L2*, the voltages from taps to wire *L2* are: 80 volts, 65 volts, and 50 volts, in that order.

In Fig. 5B, a non-inductive resistance of 1 ohm is connected between wire *L2* and the 80 percent tap. The current flowing through *R* is 80 amps, 16 amps being supplied by transformer action, while 64 amps flow from the line wires. If the load is connected to the 65 percent tap, Fig. 5C, current through *R* drops to 65 amps, of which 23 amps are supplied by transformer action and 42 by the line wires. When *R* is connected between the 50 percent tap and wire *L2*, current drops to 50 amps, of which 25 amps are supplied by transformation and 25 amps by line wires.

Fig. 6A is similar to Fig. 5A except that the line voltage has

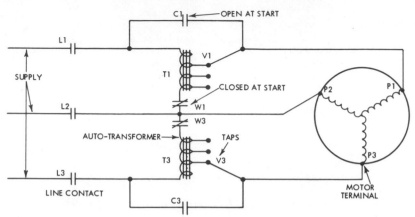

Fig. 7. Auto-transformer-reactor starter

been changed to 230 volts. Tap voltages are now 184 volts, 150 volts, and 115 volts. Referring back to the motor of Fig. 1, it may be recalled that the across-the-line current at starting was 240 amps. If the motor is connected to the 80 percent tap, the starting current through the windings becomes: .8 × 240 amps, or 192 amps, as in Fig. 6B. Applying the same ratios as those illustrated in Fig. 5B, the current supplied by transformation is 38 amps, and that by the line wires, 154 amps.

On the 65 percent tap, Fig. 6C, current through the windings is reduced to 156 amps, of which 55 amps are supplied by transformation, and the remainder, 101 amps, by the line wires. With the 50 percent tap, current through the motor falls to 20 amps, Fig. 6D, 60 amps coming by way of transformation, and 60 amps from the line.

These results are slightly optimistic, because a magnetizing current of about 10 amps is also carried by the line wires. Upon making the necessary adjustment, it is seen that the motor draws a line current of 164 amps while exerting a starting torque equal to 96 percent of full-load. On the 65 percent tap, a line current of 111 amps provides a turning effort equal to 63 percent of normal, while on the 50 percent tap, a line current of 70 amps results in a starting torque which is 37½ percent of normal.

When these results are compared with those obtained with series-resistance and series-reactance starters, it is obvious that the auto-transformer starter causes far less strain on supply equipment. It is

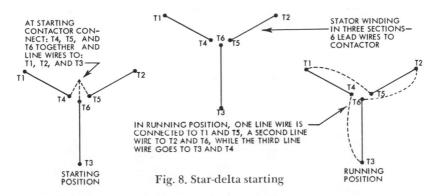

AT STARTING CONTACTOR CONNECT: T4, T5, AND T6 TOGETHER AND LINE WIRES TO: T1, T2, AND T3

STATOR WINDING IN THREE SECTIONS— 6 LEAD WIRES TO CONTACTOR

IN RUNNING POSITION, ONE LINE WIRE IS CONNECTED TO T1 AND T5, A SECOND LINE WIRE TO T2 AND T6, WHILE THE THIRD LINE WIRE GOES TO T3 AND T4

STARTING POSITION

RUNNING POSITION

Fig. 8. Star-delta starting

more efficient, too, because it is not burdened with the power loss consumed in series resistors.

Combination Starting Method

In order to avoid the shock incident to the change from starting to running positions when using an auto-transformer starter, the circuit illustrated in Fig. 7 has been devised. It is similar to Fig. 4, except that the S contacts have been omitted, and a new set of W contacts have been installed. The procedure at starting is exactly the same as with the standard auto-transformer arrangement. When the motor has accelerated to the right speed, however, contacts W1 and W3 open, disconnecting one end of each auto-transformer.

Motor current is not interrupted, but a portion of auto-transformer T1 remains in series with motor terminal P1, serving as a reactor, and a portion of T3 remains in series with P3. Current through the windings increases, and the rotor gains speed. Then, contacts C1 and C3 close to short-circuit the reactor windings, and to apply full voltage to the motor terminals. Thus, a closed-transfer occurs between starting and running positions, and the equipment is not subjected to shock. This method is used in special cases, particularly with large units.

Star-Delta Method

The star-delta scheme of Fig. 8 is infrequently employed, and only in special situations. Six lead wires from the windings are brought out to a contactor which groups them into a star, or Y, pattern for starting, and a delta pattern for running. The change from starting to running position is, of course, an open-transfer

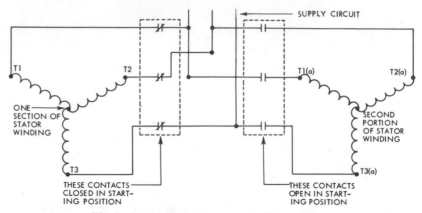

Fig. 9. Arrangement for part winding starting

type. The line current at start is reduced to about 58 percent of across-the-line value, while the torque is only about 50 percent of full-load torque.

Incremental Starting Method

In Fig. 9, the stator winding has two circuits. Only one of them is connected to supply wires at starting. As the rotor gains speed, the other circuit is connected. Thus, the change from starting to running positions is of the closed-transfer type.

Standard 230-volt induction motors generally have two-circuit windings so that they may be reconnected when necessary, for 460-volt service. If the supply is 440 volts, however, and it is desired to use part-winding starting, the motor will need a stator especially wound for the purpose.

Should the 15-hp motor of Fig. 1 be adapted to incremental starting, and one of its two stator windings be connected to the supply wires, it would draw a current of approximately 130 amps, while producing a torque equal to 75 percent of full-load value.

Starting Wound-Rotor, High-Reactance Squirrel-Cage, and Direct Current Motors

The ordinary squirrel-cage induction motor has a low-resistance bar winding on the rotor. If it were possible to greatly increase the resistance of this winding during the starting period, methods for limiting the flow of supply current would be unnecessary. This fact is taken advantage of in the wound-rotor unit of Fig. 10. Its stator

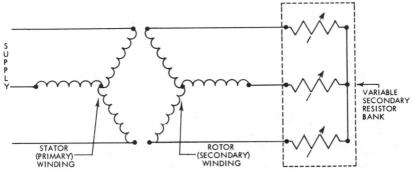

Fig. 10. Schematic diagram of a wound-rotor motor

winding is identical with that of a squirrel-cage motor, and the rotor has a similar winding. Through the aid of slip-rings, an adjustable resistor bank is connected in circuit with the rotor winding. The resistance is relatively high at starting, but as the rotor speeds up resistance is gradually reduced until its value is nil in the full-speed position. The same arrangement may be employed to provide speed control during normal operation, the rotor slowing down as resistance is cut into circuit. Starting torque as high as 150 percent of full-load torque may be obtained with a current inrush of between 150 and 200 percent.

The rotor resistance of a high-reactance induction motor is much higher than that of an ordinary squirrel-cage unit. When the motor terminals are connected directly to supply wires, the inrush of current at starting is only one-half to two-thirds that of the standard motor. It finds application for elevator, crane, hoist, and like service where it would be impractical to insert a starting device. In the so-called "line-start" motor, whose squirrel-cage winding is of peculiar and more expensive design, rotor resistance at starting is much greater than after normal speed is attained.

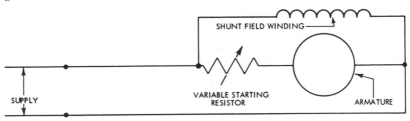

Fig. 11. Schematic diagram of a direct-current motor

Starting characteristics of direct-current motors resemble those of the wound-rotor induction motor. A resistor is connected in the armature circuit, as illustrated in Fig. 11, but it is gradually cut out as the armature comes up to speed. A starting torque of 150 percent of normal is obtainable with a current inrush of approximately the same amount.

CIRCUIT REQUIREMENTS

National Electrical Code

Motor circuit wiring must conform to provisions of the National Electrical Code. The wireman should have a copy at hand. For purpose of quick reference, however, some of the most important NEC tables are reprinted here, in the Appendix. Presence of such tables is indicated by the notation, "(*See App.*)". Reference to less frequently used tables is made by the notation, "(*See NEC*)". Rules governing motor installations are concentrated in Article 430 of NEC, but there are comparatively minor groupings for particular applications in: Article 500 Hazards; Article 610, Cranes and Hoists; Article 620, Elevators; and Article 670, Machine Tools.

Conductors

The NEC provides that branch-circuit conductors supplying a single, continuous-duty motor, shall have a carrying capacity not less than 125 percent of the motor full-load current rating. One reason for the added 25 percent is to allow a heating margin for the high, but short duration, starting current. Another is to provide for the small percentage of overload which the continuous-duty motor is designed to withstand. Smaller circuit conductors are permitted with intermittent-duty motors, under strict code limitations, but all motors are deemed continuous-duty unless the nature of the driven load is such that continuous operation is impossible.

In the case of the 15 hp motor of Fig. 1, whose running current is 40 amps, the supply conductors must have a carrying capacity of at least: 1.25 × 40 amps, or 50 amps. Assuming that Type R conductors are used, the nearest size listed in NEC Table 310-12 (*See App.*) is No. 6, which has a carrying capacity of 55 amps.

Disconnecting Means

Every motor larger than 1/8 hp must have a disconnecting means.

It shall be a motor-circuit switch, rated in horsepower, or a circuit breaker. There are two principal exceptions. First, motors rated at 2 hp or less, 300 volts or less, may be disconnected by a general-use switch whose ampere rating is not less than twice full-load current rating. The second main exception concerns motors exceeding 50 hp. Here, the disconnecting means can be a general-use switch rated in amperes, or an isolating switch.

Applying this code rule to the 15 hp example, a motor-circuit switch rated at not less than 15 hp must be employed. The switch must be within sight of the device which controls operation of the motor, or else it must be arranged for locking in the open position. It must disconnect all ungrounded supply conductors from both motor and controller, and it must have a continuous carrying capacity of at least 115 percent of the nameplate current rating of the motor. The term "within sight" as used in the NEC, means visible, and not more than 50 ft distant.

Motor Controller

A controller is a switch or other device normally employed for starting and stopping a motor. In some cases, the disconnecting means may serve as the controller, or it may be in the same enclosure as the controller. The controller must be horsepower rated, the only important exception being one for motors of 2 hp or less, the provision worded exactly as in the case of the disconnect switch.

Unless the controller is also the disconnecting means, it need not open all supply conductors, but only a sufficient number to interrupt flow of current to the motor. When not within sight of the motor which it controls, it should be locked; otherwise, a switch that will prevent starting of the motor must be placed within sight of the motor location. An auto-transformer starter used to control the familiar 15-hp motor would be required to open only two of the circuit wires.

Branch-Circuit Overcurrent Protection

The branch-circuit overcurrent device must be able to carry the starting current of the motor. Overcurrent devices are either fuses or circuit breakers, Fig. 12. A fuse will not blow immediately unless subjected to a current equal to 200 percent or more of its rating. Circuit breakers are of two kinds, instantaneous-trip, and time-delay. The former are used only with direct-current motors. The latter may

Fig. 12. Fused switch and circuit breaker
Courtesy of General Electric Co.

have either a magnetic or a thermal tripping mechanism, the thermal type being more common in small or medium-size classes.

NEC Tables 430-152 and 430-153 (*See App.*) list maximum allowable ratings or settings of branch-circuit protective devices, the first dealing with those having code letters, the second with all others. As mentioned earlier, all new alternating-current motors ½-hp and larger, except polyphase wound-rotor motors, must have a code letter stamped on the nameplate. A great many were manufactured, however, before the code rule went into effect. Table 430–152 relates to them, as well as high-reactance, wound-rotor, and direct-current motors.

The fuse and circuit breaker ratings are expressed in percent of full-load current. Table 430–152 lists them in two sections, the upper one referring to all single-phase motors and to polyphase squirrel-cage or synchronous motors which are full-voltage-, resistor-, or reactor-starting. The lower portion deals with squirrel-cage and synchronous motors with auto-transformer starting.

In all cases, motors with code letter **A** have both fuse and circuit breaker ratings of 150 percent, because the maximum starting current to be expected with a motor of this kind is 200 percent of normal. The ratings for auto-transformer starting are, generally, lower than the others.

If the 15 hp example motor had a code letter **A**, its maximum circuit protection would be either a 60-amp fuse or a 60-amp circuit breaker, since its full-load current is 40 amps. With a code letter **B** to **E**, and across-the-line-, or resistor-, or reactor-starting, the maximum fuse rating would be 100 amps, the maximum circuit breaker rating 100 amps (nearest standard rating to 80 amps, which is called for—see NEC 240–6). For a letter from **F** to **V**, the maximum permissible fuse would be 125-amp (nearest standard rating to 120-amp), and the circuit breaker 100-amp.

Under auto-transformer starting, for a code letter from **B** to **E**, the largest fuse would be 80-amp, the circuit breaker 100-amp (nearest standard rating to 80-amp). With a code letter from **F** to **V**, the fuse rating could not exceed 100-amp, the circuit breaker 100-amp (nearest standard rating to 80-amp).

Turning to NEC Table 430–153, if the 15 hp motor did not have a code letter, it would be handled on the same basis as an **F** to **V** motor in the other table, with but one exception. With an auto-transformer starter, the maximum fuse rating would be 80-amp instead of 100-amp. This is true because the table makes a distinction between motors drawing more than 30 amps, as compared to those drawing 30 amps or less.

It was stated at the beginning of this section that the branch-circuit overcurrent device must be able to carry the starting current of the motor. In some cases, the maximum allowable fuse is not large enough. Thus, under across-the-line starting, a motor with code letter **H** may draw 700 percent of full-load current, and the 300 percent fuse will blow. NEC Section 430–52 makes provision for such conditions, stating that the fuse size may be increased, where necessary, but that it may never exceed 400 percent of full-load current. The purpose behind all these restrictions is to insure that the rating of branch-circuit protective devices is as small as practicable.

It will be recalled that lighting circuits are fused according to the carrying capacity of the branch-circuit conductor. This is certainly not true of the motor branch-circuit. The conductor used with the 15-hp motor, for example, is No. 6 Type R, which has a carrying capacity of 55 amps. Yet, the fuse in the circuit switch may be as large as 125 amps. The situation is basically undesirable, but the only alternative would be to demand a wire having the same carrying capacity as the fuse rating. This requirement would impose

Fig. 13. Motor switch with thermal overload device

such a burden upon the public that it could not be permitted. The next section will show, however, that the condition is not quite so bad as it may appear.

Overcurrent Protection

An alternative term for this section is, "motor running overcurrent protection." It is intended, primarily, to safeguard the motor windings. The NEC provides that continuous-duty motors shall be guarded against running overcurrent by an approved means. There are a few unimportant exceptions: small high-impedance motors such as electric clocks; a motor which is part of an approved assembly which has built-in safety controls, an oil-burner for example, and a manually-started portable motor of 1 hp or less that is within sight of the controller.

All other motors must be protected by an overcurrent device, Fig. 13, which is responsive to motor current. It may be a separate unit, rated at not more than 125 percent of full-load current in the case of 40-degree or hermetic motors, and not more than 115 percent of full-load current for all other types. This latter rule applies, of course, to the 50-degree motor. The overcurrent device may be a thermal protector integral with the motor, and which acts to interrupt current flow when a dangerous condition arises. Temperature detectors embedded in the windings may be employed with motors larger than 1500 hp. Motors in service which is basically short-time duration, are considered protected against overcurrent by the branch-circuit overcurrent fuse or circuit breaker.

In the case of the 15-hp example motor, the rating of an overcurrent unit cannot be greater than: 1.25 × 40 amps, or 50 amps. This value is acceptable only if the motor is a 40-degree or a hermetic type. If the motor were 50-degree, the overcurrent protector should not be rated higher than: 1.15 × 40 amps, or 46 amps. The NEC permits a slight variance in these ratings.

There are two general types of overcurrent units: adjustable, and non-adjustable. The overcurrent setting of the first type may be changed by means of a screw or a nut; the setting of the second cannot be altered. As with fuses, the latter are supplied in a number of standard sizes. Although the adjustable type must be set at the 125 percent or the 115 percent point, as the case may be, the nearest higher standard non-adjustable rating is acceptable if there is no exact standard size.

NEC 430–34 imposes a definite limit on the amount of variation, however. The device for a 40-degree or a hermetic motor cannot exceed 140 percent of full-load current, and that of other types 130 percent. Returning for a moment to the 15-hp motor, if there were no standard 50-amp non-adjustable overcurrent device, a substitute one having a rating not exceeding: 1.4 × 40 amps, or 56 amps in the first case, or 1.3 × 40 amps, which is 52 amps, in the second. The NEC also states that the smallest acceptable rating of an overcurrent device is 115 percent of full-load current.

A few additional observations are in order. The overcurrent devices may be part of the motor controller. Under certain conditions of manual operation, the overcurrent units may be shunted out during the starting period. Thermal devices which are not capable of handling short-circuit currents, must be preceded by fuses or circuit breakers rated at not over 400 percent of motor full-load current. The code states that, after tripping, an overcurrent device must not allow the motor to restart automatically if there is any danger of injury to persons. The number of units required for motors used on various supply systems is governed by Table 430–37 (*See NEC*).

At the end of the foregoing section, it was said that lack of circuit protection was not so bad as it may have seemed. Since the current which can flow through the conductor, under normal operation, is limited to 125 percent of full-load motor current, and since the carrying capacity of the circuit conductor is also 125 percent, overloading of the wire is not likely to occur. The only possibility of higher current flow is through the happening of a ground or a short-circuit at a point between disconnect switch and running-overcurrent device. In this case, the current will be far greater than full-load value, and the branch-circuit fuse or circuit breaker will act. For this reason, branch-circuit protection is sometimes called, "short-circuit and ground fault protection."

USE OF NEC TABLE 430–146

Content of Table

It is unnecessary to perform all the above calculations in order to find allowable branch-circuit and running-overcurrent protection. NEC Table 430–146 (*See App.*) presents these values on the basis of full-load motor current. The first column lists currents from 1 to 500 amps, while columns 2 and 3 give maximum ratings of running-overcurrent protective devices for the 40-degree and hermetic motors. Column 2 states ratings for non-adjustable units, column 3 for adjustable ones. Remaining columns, 4 to 7 inclusive, are concerned with branch-circuit protection.

Each of these branch-circuit columns has two sections, fuses being indicated at the left, circuit breakers at the right. Column 4 deals with single-phase, squirrel-cage, and synchronous motors which start across-the-line, or with resistor-, or with reactor-starters. It applies to all such motors having code letters **F** to **V**, and to those without code letters. Column 5 supplies ratings for use with the same classes of motors and starters, but with code letters **B** to **E**. It also includes auto-transformer-started motors having code letters **F** to **V**, and non-code motors drawing not more than 30 amps. High-reactance motors drawing 30 amps or less are also covered.

Column 6 treats of squirrel-cage and synchronous motors using auto-transformer starters, and having code letters **B** to **E**. It includes non-code-letter motors of these types, and also high-reactance motors, which draw more than 30 amps. Column 7 is confined to motors with code letter **A**, direct-current motors and wound-rotor motors. A headnote to the table states that ratings for branch-circuit protection may be taken from the table, but that running-overcurrent values must be based upon current value stamped on the motor nameplate.

There is a practical reason for this rule, which is NEC 430–6 (a). Drawings or sketches showing horsepowers of motors are in the hands of the electrician while the job is still in the rough stage. In order for him to decide upon the size of wire and conduit, circuit switch, and branch-circuit protective devices, he must depend upon current ratings taken from NEC Table 430–150 (*See App.*), because the actual motors are not yet available. When it comes time to install running-overcurrent units, however, the equipment is already in place.

Another headnote explains that ratings shown in columns 2 and 3 are to be reduced by 8 percent for motors other than 40-degree and hermetic types. This factor is used because 115 percent is 8 percent less than, or 92 percent of, 125 percent. That is, $115 = .92 \times 125$. The table will now be employed in connection with some practical examples of motor wiring. Single-line diagrams are used to show motor-circuit elements, including wire, conduit, and equipment.

Wiring a 5 HP, Three-Phase, 230-Volt, Squirrel Cage, Induction Motor

The nameplate of the 5 hp motor, Fig. 14, shows it to be a 40-degree type with code letter **D**. The current stamped on the name-

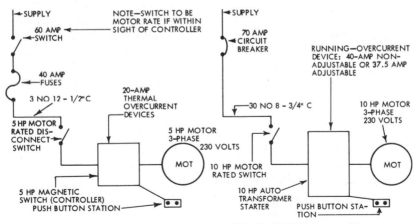

Fig. 14. 5 HP motor with magnetic switch

Fig. 15. 10 HP motor with auto-transformer starter

plate is 15 amps, which checks with the value given in Table 430–150 (*See App.*). Current carrying capacity of the conductors must not be less than: 1.25 × 15 amps, or 18.75 amps. Type R wire is to be used, and the nearest size listed in Table 310–12 (*See App.*) is No. 12, whose rating is 20 amps. Three conductors are necessary. Table 1, NEC Chapter 9 shows that 3 No. 12 Type R wires may be installed in ½-in conduit.

Checking requirements for a 15-amp motor current in column 1 of Table 430–146, the rating of a non-adjustable overcurrent device is found to be 20 amps, an adjustable one 18.75 amps. Across-the-line starting is customary for 5 hp, three-phase motors. Column 5 of the table, which includes full-voltage starting of motors with code letters **B** to **E**, gives either a 40-amp fuse or a 30-amp circuit breaker for branch-circuit protection. The fuse will be chosen here, with a 60-amp switch. The disconnect switch must be horsepower-rated because it is in excess of 2 hp, and the magnetic switch, which serves as controller here, must also be horsepower-rated.

Wiring a 10 HP, Three-Phase, 230-Volt, Squirrel-Cage, Induction Motor

The motor of Fig. 15 is not immediately available for examination. Drawings state that it is 10 hp, started with an auto-transformer starter, and wired with Type RHW conductors. Table 430–150 gives a current rating of 27 amps for a 10-hp, 230-volt motor. The carrying capacity of the conductors must be at least: 1.25 × 27 amps, or 33.75 amps. The nearest size listed in Table 310–12 is No. 8 Type RHW, which has a carrying capacity of 45 amps. Table 1 of NEC Chapter 9 reveals that a ¾-in conduit is large enough for the 3 No. 8 conductors.

There is no listing for 27 amps in Table 430–146, so the next larger figure, 28 amps must be chosen. Since the code letter is unknown, it is not safe to assume that it will be higher than the F-to-V bracket. Column 5 provides ratings for F-to-V motors, and for non-code-letter motors drawing 30 amps or less, and which are auto-transformer-started. The motor could well fall within either of these classes. Here, the size of fuse and circuit breaker are both 70 amps. A 70-amp circuit breaker will be selected.

Upon arrival, the motor proves to have a nameplate rating of 30 amps and a code letter H. Referring to the 30-amp current listing in column 1, it may be seen that the maximum rating of a non-

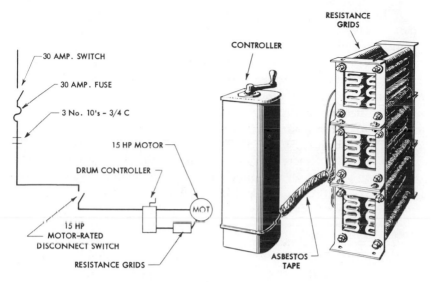

RESISTANCE
GRIDS

CONTROLLER

30 AMP. SWITCH

30 AMP. FUSE

3 No. 10's - 3/4 C

15 HP MOTOR

DRUM CONTROLLER

MOT

15 HP
MOTOR-RATED
DISCONNECT SWITCH

RESISTANCE GRIDS

ASBESTOS
TAPE

Fig. 16. Drum controller with 15-hp wound-rotor motor

adjustable overcurrent device is 40 amps, while that of an adjustable device is 37.5 amps. If a disconnect switch is used in addition to the branch-circuit circuit breaker, it must be a 10-hp motor-rated unit.

Wiring a 15 HP, Three-phase, 440-Volt, Wound-Rotor Motor

Primary Circuit

The full-load current for a 15 hp, 440-volt, wound-rotor motor, Fig. 16, is given in Table 430–150, as 20 amps. The conductor rating cannot be less than: 1.25 × 20 amps, or 25 amps. Type TW wire is to be used here, and Table 310–12 shows the nearest size to be No. 10, which has a carrying capacity of 30 amps. According to Table 1, NEC Chapter 9, a 3/4-in conduit is large enough for the three conductors. Column 7 of Table 430–46 gives a rating of 30 amps for either non-adjustable or adjustable branch-circuit protective device, a 30-amp fuse with a 30-amp switch being chosen in this instance.

The current rating stamped on the motor nameplate, 20 amps, agrees with the value stated in Table 430–150. Columns 2 and 3 of Table 430–146 list the same value, 25 amps, for either non-adjustable or adjustable running-overcurrent device.

The left-hand illustration in Fig. 16 shows the circuit for this motor. The controller and the grid-resistor are included. The controller is a drum type used for regulating motor speed. The illustration at the right shows a drum controller connected to a bank of resistors. The controller makes and breaks the circuit between line and stator of the motor, which represents the primary circuit. It also varies resistance included in the rotor or secondary circuit. The primary and secondary windings of the motor are entirely separated. Running, overcurrent devices are included in the primary circuit, but there are none in the secondary. The Code states that secondary circuits of wound-rotor motors, including conductors, controllers, and resistors, are considered as protected by motor-running overcurrent devices.

Secondary Circuit

Conductors between the secondary of a continuous-duty wound-rotor motor and its controller must have a carrying capacity not less than 125 percent of full-load secondary current. Where the secondary resistor is separate from the controller, as in the figure, the carrying capacity of conductors between controller and resistor shall not be less than the values given in Table 430–23 (exception). (*See App.*).

It will be assumed that the type of service here is continuous-duty. The carrying capacity of the wire between controller and resistor, under this condition, is given at 110 percent of full-load secondary current. The full-load secondary current is given on the nameplate of the motor as 32 amperes. The carrying capacity of the wire must be at least 1.10×32, or 35.2 amperes. The conductors must withstand considerable heat, sometimes as high as 200°C, so that only types A and AA are suitable here. Table 310–12 gives the carrying capacity of No. 12 as 40 amperes, which is more than enough for the purpose. The asbestos-insulated wires will be grouped or bundled, as indicated in the illustration, and will be taped together with asbestos tape in order to provide rigidity.

Use of Capacitors

Capacitors are sometimes employed to raise the power factor of a motor circuit, as indicated in Fig. 17. The subjects of "Power Factor" and "Capacitors" will be taken up in the next chapter. The NEC states three limitations upon the use of capacitors in this

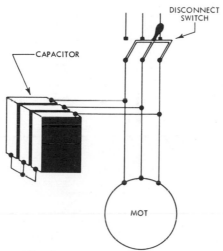

Fig. 17. Capacitor in motor circuit

connection: they must be wired according to rules governing capacitor installations, they must not be larger than the size needed to raise circuit power factor to unity, and the lowered value of motor current which results from their application must be used in determining the size of running-overcurrent protection.

For example, consider a 100 hp, 230-volt motor whose nameplate current rating is 250 amps. Columns 1 and 2 of Table 430–146 list a rating of 300 amps for a non-adjustable device, and 313 amps for an adjustable one. If a capacitor unit has the effect of lowering motor current to 210 amps, this value must be selected in column 1 of Table 430–146, so that the maximum rating of a non-adjustable protector becomes 250 amps, and that of an adjustable 263 amps.

Wiring a 7½ HP, 230-Volt, Direct Current Motor

The nameplate of the motor referred to in Fig. 18 shows a current rating of 31 amps. Table 430–147 (*See App.*) lists a current of 29 amps. The value given in the table, 29 amps, may be used for determining the size of conductor. Its carrying capacity cannot be less than: 1.25 × 29 amps, or 36 amps. Type R wire is to be used, and Table 310–12 shows the nearest size to be No. 8, with a current rating of 40 amps. Table 1 reveals that a ¾-in conduit is required for 2 No. 8 conductors. A third, No. 14, conductor runs from the rheostat to the motor field circuit.

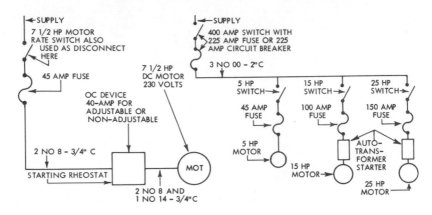

Fig. 18. Circuit for direct current motor

Fig. 19. Feeder supplying three induction motors

Because a notation for 29 amps is not shown in column 1 of Table 430–146, the next larger number, or 30 amps, will be used. Following across to column 7, a 45-amp fuse and a 50-amp circuit breaker are indicated as branch-circuit protective devices. A 45-amp fuse will be employed here in the $7\frac{1}{2}$-hp motor-rated switch that is to serve as disconnect as well as branch-circuit switch. Column 1 of Table 430–146 shows no designation for the 31-amp current stamped on the motor nameplate, so that the next larger one, 32-amps, shall be used. Columns 2 and 3 state that either 40-amp non-adjustable or 40-amp adjustable running-over-current device will be acceptable.

208-Volt Motors

A footnote to Table 430–150 states that full-load current values given for 220-volt motors must be increased by 6 percent to obtain full-load current ratings for 208-volt motors. In the case of a 15 hp, 208-volt motor, full-load current rating would be 106 percent of that given for the corresponding 220-volt motor, or; 1.06×40 amps, which gives 42 amps. This value would have to be used when checking branch-circuit requirements in Table 430–146.

Motor Feeders

Although the subject of Feeders will be reserved, generally, for a later chapter, a discussion of motor feeders seems appropriate at this time. In Fig. 19, a 5 hp, 230-volt, three-phase motor without code

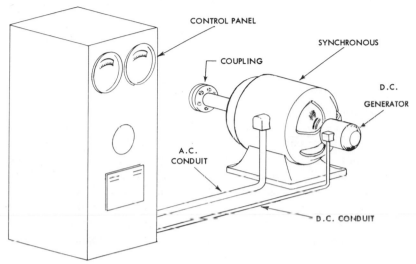

Fig. 20. Connection of synchronous motor

letter, a 15 hp, 230-volt, three-phase, auto-transformer-started, squirrel-cage motor with code letter **F**, and a 25 hp, 230-volt, three-phase, auto-transformer-started, squirrel-cage motor with code letter **D** are connected to the same feeder.

NEC 430–24 states that the carrying capacity of conductors supplying two or more motors shall have a current carrying capacity not less than 125 percent of the full-load current rating of the highest rated motor in the group, plus the sum of the full-load current ratings of the remainder. NEC 430–62 states that the rating of a feeder overcurrent device must not be greater than the largest rating of the branch-circuit protective device for any motor of the group, plus the sum of the full-load currents of the other motors.

Applying these rules, current ratings of the three motors taken from Table 430–150 are: 64 amps for the 25 hp, 40 amps for the 15 hp, and 15 amps for the 5 hp motor. The current carrying capacity of a Type R conductor must not be less than: (1.25 × 64 amps) + 40 amps + 15 amps, which equals 135 amps. Table 310–12 gives the nearest size conductor as a No. 00 which has a carrying capacity of 145 amps. Table 1 shows that 2-in conduit is required. The largest branch-circuit protective device for any motor in the group is determined from column 6 of Table 430–146 to be the 150-amp rating which applies to the 25 hp unit. Feeder-circuit protection cannot be greater than: 150 + 40 amps + 15 amps, or 205 amps. A 400-amp switch with a 225-amp fuse, or else a 225-amp circuit breaker can be used. Busway, discussed in chapter 1, is sometimes used as motor feeders.

Synchronous Motors

A synchronous motor has a stator like that of the induction motor, but its rotor is excited by direct current. Separate circuits run from control panel to stator and rotor, as indicated in Fig. 20. A direct current generator is often mounted on the end of the motor shaft for supplying the direct current needed by the unit. In any case, wires are run from both units as called for in blueprints furnished with the apparatus. The problem is not different from that of wiring other pieces of electrical equipment, except that allowance must be made for power factor in determining size of branch-circuit conductors.

Values of current given in Table 430–150, for synchronous machines, are based upon unity power factor. If the motor operates at some other power factor, such as .8, allowance must be made for the fact. For example, suppose that a 25 hp, 220-volt synchronous motor is to operate at a power factor of .8. Referring to Table 430–150, the current is listed at 54 amperes. But this value applies to a motor operating at unity. To determine the current at .8 power factor, the footnote should be consulted. It says that for motors operating at 90 percent and 80 percent power factor, the values given in the table must be multiplied by 1.1 and 1.25, respectively. Here, since the power factor is .8, the current must be multiplied by 1.25, so that the motor draws 1.25 × 54, or 67.5 amperes. Wire size, branch-circuit protection, and running overcurrent protection must be determined on this basis.

Motors Over 600 Volts

In addition to other code requirements, high-voltage installations are subject to certain special ones. NEC Article 430, Section J states that motors operating at potentials greater than 7,500 volts between conductors must be installed in fire-resistant motor rooms. Running, overcurrent protection shall consist either of a circuit breaker, or of overcurrent units integral with the controller, which shall open simultaneously all ungrounded conductors.

Each motor branch circuit and feeder of more than 600 volts

shall be protected against overcurrent by a circuit breaker, by high-voltage fuses approved for the purpose, or by a differential protective system. See NEC 430–124(c). The circuit breaker, or set of fuses, may constitute the disconnecting means if they comply with other requirements specified in connection with lower voltage installations.

GROUP-MOTOR AND SIMILAR INSTALLATIONS

Group Motors

NEC 430–53(b) states that two or more motors of any rating, each having individual, running, overcurrent protection, may be connected to one branch circuit under certain specified conditions. Each running overcurrent device must be approved for group installation, and each motor controller must be approved for group installation. The branch circuit shall be protected by fuses large enough to carry the starting current of the largest motor, plus an amount equal to the sum of the full-load current ratings of all other motors connected to the circuit. The fourth rule states that branch-circuit fuses must not be larger than allowed under NEC 430–40.

This section provides that thermal cutouts, thermal relays, and other devices not capable of opening short circuits, shall be protected by fuses or circuit breakers with ratings or settings not over four times the rating of the motor, unless these devices are especially approved for group installation and are so marked. Conductors to individual motors shall have the same current rating as the branch-

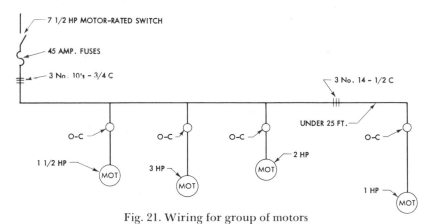

Fig. 21. Wiring for group of motors

circuit conductors unless they have a capacity not less than one-third that of the branch circuit, and are not more than 25 ft in length.

Fig. 21 shows such an installation, consisting of four motors, a 1 hp rated at 4 amps; a 1½ hp, rated at 5 amps; a 2 hp, rated at 6.5 amps; and a 3 hp, rated at 9 amps; all three-phase, 230-volt, squirrel-cage, and all driving parts of a single machine. The largest motor is the 3 hp. Its nameplate shows no code letter. The starting fuses for this motor, under Table 430–153, should be 300 percent of 9 amps, or 27 amps. The rating of the branch-circuit fuse will be equal to 27 + 6.5 + 5 + 4, or 42.5 amps. The nearest standard fuse is 45 amps. The rating of the single disconnecting means is determined with the aid of NEC 430–112 which states that the disconnecting means which serves a group of motors shall have a motor rating not less than that of the sum of the horsepowers. Here, the rating should be equal to 3 + 2 + 1½ + 1, or 7½ hp. The capacity of branch-circuit conductors must be equal to (1.25 × 9) + 6.5 + 5 + 4, or 26.75 amps. Table 310–12 shows the nearest size of type R conductor to be No. 10. The circuit conductors to each of the motors will be No. 14, since all come within 15 amps. These conductors are tapped directly to No. 10 branch-circuit wires. Three of the motors are grouped near the disconnecting switch, but the 1 hp is 15 ft away. It is permissible to use No. 14 here because its carrying capacity is more than ⅓ that of No. 10, and the length of conductor to the running overcurrent device does not exceed 25 ft.

It is assumed, in the present instance, that overcurrent devices connected in each motor circuit are approved for group installation. If not so approved, only the 3 hp unit comes within the rule of NEC 430–40. It states that devices for running, overcurrent protection shall be protected, in general, by fuses or circuit breakers with ratings not more than four times that of the device. In such case, individual switches with running-overcurrent devices would be needed ahead of each of the other three motors.

Metal-working machine tools having two or more motors are covered by NEC 670–4. This section merely rephrases provisions of NEC 430–24, with respect to the current-carrying capacity of conductors supplying this type of equipment.

Two or More Motors with One Controller

A single controller may be used for two or more motors, under

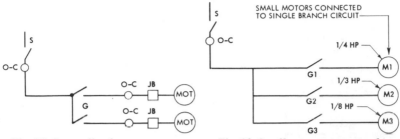

Fig. 22. Controller for two motors

Fig. 23. Small motors connected to single branch circuits

NEC 430–87, provided that the motors drive several parts of a single machine or piece of apparatus, or where the group is located in a single room within sight of the controller location. The term "in sight" means, of course, visible and within 50 ft. Fig. 22 illustrates the use of one controller with two motors.

Two or More Small Motors on One Branch Circuit

Under NEC 430–53(a), motors not exceeding 1 hp, and each having a full-load current not exceeding 6 amps, may be connected to a branch circuit which is protected at not more than 20 amps at 125 volts, or 15 amps at 600 volts or less. As indicated in the line diagrams of Fig. 23, which shows three small motors connected in this way, individual, running, overcurrent protection is not needed for each motor provided it is within sight of the circuit disconnecting means, and is not started automatically. NEC 430–42(a) points out that motors may be connected to 15-amp or 20-amp circuits along with lights and plug receptacles, provided the individual ratings do not exceed 6 amps.

SPECIFIC APPLICATIONS

Wiring a Hermetic Motor

The definition of a sealed refrigeration compressor is given in NEC 430–3 as a motor and compressor, both of which are enclosed in the same housing, with no external shaft or shaft seals, the motor operating in the refrigerant atmosphere. These hermetic type refrigerating units must be provided with a nameplate giving all necessary data, including a full-load current of the motor, as well as locked-rotor current in certain cases.

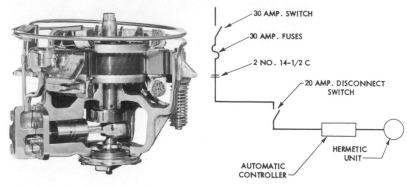

Fig. 24. Hermetic unit

Courtesy of Tecumseh Products Co.

Wire and Conduit

Fig. 24 shows a single-phase, 230-volt hermetic refrigeration unit at the left, and a line diagram of its circuit at the right. Locked-rotor current of single-phase motors having full-load currents greater than 9 amps at 115 volts, and more than 4.5 amps at 230 volts, is indicated on the nameplate. The locked-rotor currents of all polyphase motors is stated. If the unit has an integral protective device, the nameplate must be so marked.

In the present instance, it will be assumed that the nameplate shows a full-load current of 11 amps, 40°C rating, and a locked-rotor current of 55 amps. No protective device is indicated. Under NEC 430–6(b), the nameplate current of 11 amps is to be used as the basis for determining size of conductor. The carrying capacity of No. 14 is 15 amps. Since this is the smallest permissible size for branch-circuit conductors, two No. 14's will be installed in ½ in conduit.

Running Protection

NEC 430–32 provides that a running, overcurrent device shall be rated or set at not over 125 percent of motor full-load current. The nameplate value of a hermetic unit must be used here. For a current of 11 amps, the highest permissible setting is 1.25 × 11, or 13.75 amps. NEC 430–34 permits use of the next higher rating of overcurrent unit, not exceeding 140 percent of full-load value where the standard device is of a higher rating than the calculated value. In the present instance, the rating of the overcurrent device might

Fig. 25. Across-the-line starter with special overload devices

Courtesy of Allen-Bradley Co.

be increased to a maximum value of 14 amps.

Automatic Controller

An automatic controlling device, such as shown in Fig. 25, is used to start and stop the motor. NEC 430–83(Ex. 3) states that motor controllers rated in terms of full-load current and current-interrupting capacity shall be selected on the basis of both nameplate full-load current and locked-rotor current, respectively, of the com pressor. This section means that a controller marked in amps rather than in horsepower shall be able to carry full-load current of the motor, and shall be adequate to interrupt locked-rotor current of the unit as well. In the present case, for example, a device rated at 15 amps, with interrupting capacity of 45 amps, would not be acceptable. Although the carrying capacity here is great enough for controlling the unit under normal operating conditions, its interrupting capacity would be insufficient to permit breaking the circuit to a "frozen" compressor. If so used, electrical damage and fire may result.

The Code states, further, that for full-load current, the horse-power rating shall be selected from Table 430–148 (*See App.*) and for locked-rotor current, the horsepower rating shall be selected from Table 430-153 (*See App.*). Thus, if the controlling device is rated in horsepower, Table 430–148 shall be used to determine the horsepower corresponding to a given full-load current, and Table 430–153 (*See App.*) shall be used to determine the horsepower corresponding to a given locked-rotor current. The section continues, stating that where currents do not correspond exactly to current values stated in the tables, the next higher values of horsepower shall be selected. Finally, the section provides that if two different horsepower ratings are obtained by applying nameplate values to the tables, a rating at least equal to the larger of the two shall be selected.

In the present case, the full-load current of 11 amps does not correspond exactly with values given in Table 430–148. A $1\frac{1}{2}$ hp single-phase, 230-volt motor draws a current of 10 amps, and a 2 hp motor draws a current of 12 amps. Under the ruling, the controller must be rated at least 2 hp. Turning to Table 430–153, a locked-rotor current of 55 amps at 230 volts applies to a $1\frac{1}{2}$ hp motor. But the value obtained in checking full-load current is the greater of the two, and a 2 hp controlling device must be employed.

Disconnecting Means

The disconnecting means, also, must be selected on this basis. But NEC 430–109(b) permits a general-use switch for motors of 2 hp and less, provided its rating is twice the motor full-load current. Here, the disconnecting unit must be rated at 2 $\times$ 11, or 22 amps. In practice, a standard 30-amp, externally-operated knife switch would be installed.

The rating of the branch circuit protective device, as per NEC 430–52 and Table 430–153, should not exceed 175 percent of the full-load motor current marked on the nameplate. The rating may be increased to a maximum value equal to 225 percent of full-load current if the smaller device will not handle motor starting current. In the present case, an overcurrent device not larger than 17.5 amps should be selected. If it does not permit inrush of the required starting current, a 22.5-amp unit may be employed. A 30-amp branch circuit disconnect switch will be needed.

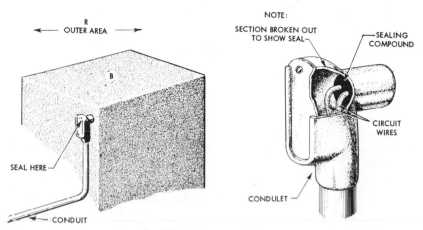

Fig. 26. Sealing conduit run

Sealing

In connection with refrigeration units, it may be well to mention a provision contained in NEC 300–6. It states that portions of raceway systems exposed to widely different temperatures, as in refrigerating and cold-storage plants, shall be arranged to prevent circulation of air from a warmer to a colder section. The reason for this rule is that warm air holds a larger quantity of water than cold air.

Referring to Fig. 26, suppose the temperature in refrigerating box *B* is 40°F, and that the temperature in surrounding area *R* is 65°F. A given volume of air in the *R* section holds more water than the same volume of air inside *B*. As air passes from *R* through the conduit into *B*, it will lose some of its moisture, depositing water inside boxes and fittings. After a time, the moisture will break down insulation on the wires and cause trouble. If a seal or block is installed at the point where the conduit emerges from the wall, as indicated at the left in the illustration, circulation of air will be prevented.

A method for sealing is shown at the right in the illustration. A condulet, installed in the conduit run at the outer wall of the box, is stuffed with duct seal or other approved material after the control, lighting, or motor circuit wires have been installed. An EYS fitting should be used where differences in temperatures is very

great, as, for example, when the temperature of the outer space is
65°F, and that of the box is 20°F.

WIRING CRANES AND HOISTS

Carrying Capacity of Wire

The Code lists special carrying capacities for rubber and ther-
moplastic-insulated wires used on crane and hoist circuits. The
smallest size of wire listed is No. 16 which is permitted for certain
motor and control circuits, where it is protected from physical
damage.

The short time duty under which these motors operate causes
less heating of conductors. For allowable carrying capacities of conductors having shorter duty cycles, values given in Table 610–14(a)
(*See NEC*), may be increased by 12 percent for the particular type
of insulation.

Disconnecting Means

NEC 610–31 calls for a disconnecting means between runway
conductors and power supply. This device shall be readily accessible
and operable from the ground. It must be within sight of crane or
hoist and the runway conductors. It must be arranged for locking in
the open position and must open, simultaneously, all ungrounded
conductors. It shall consist of a motor-circuit switch or circuit
breaker. The left-hand illustration in Fig. 27 shows this arrangement.

The disconnecting means may be a general-use switch, if a motor-
circuit switch or a circuit breaker is used in connection with a cab-
operated crane, and is placed within the cab or at one end of the runway within reach of the cab. This arrangement is shown in the right-
hand illustration.

The continuous ampere rating of the switch required here shall
not be less than 50 percent of combined short-time ampere ratings of
the motors, and shall not be less than 75 percent of short-time ratings
of motors required for any single crane motion.

Protection

Other points should be noted in connection with crane motors.
NEC 610–34 requires that limit switches be installed for upper limit
of travel on crane hoists. NEC 610–42 requires that if more than one
motor is employed on a crane, each motor shall have individual
overcurrent protection. When two motors operate as a single unit,

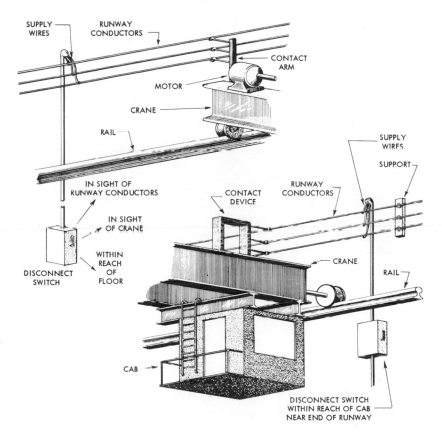

Fig. 27. Disconnecting means for crane

they may be protected by a single overcurrent device. NEC 610–51 provides that the entire crane or hoist structure shall be grounded.

WIRING ELEVATORS, DUMBWAITERS, ESCALATORS, AND MOVING WALKS

Service Classification

Elevators and dumbwaiters are classed as intermittent service applications. This means that elevator motors need no protection other than that offered by the branch-circuit overcurrent device. Branch-circuit conductors may be chosen on the basis of Table 430–22 (a-exception) (*See NEC*), which allows a capacity of 85 percent of full-

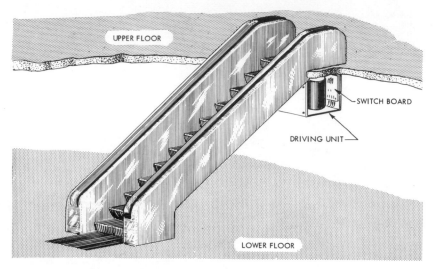

UPPER FLOOR

SWITCH BOARD

DRIVING UNIT

LOWER FLOOR

Fig. 28. Escalator - continuous service application

load nameplate value for 5-to-15-minute motors, and 90 percent for 30-to-60-minute motors.

Escalators, one of which is shown in Fig. 28, are classed as continuous service applications. Branch-circuit conductors must have a carrying capacity of 125 percent of full-load current, as required by NEC 430–22. Running protection for a 40°C motor, used in this connection, should be 125 percent of nameplate current. Provisions relating to escalators also apply to moving walks.

Wiring

Motor lead wires not over 6 ft in length may be carried directly to terminals on the control panel without regard to carrying capacity. Wires between control panels and motors may be cabled and taped, if not over 6 ft long, the group being supported at intervals not exceeding 3 ft.

A disconnect switch for the motor must be provided adjacent to, and visible from, the elevator machine. If the elevator is driven by a motor-generator, a disconnect switch in the control circuit of the driving motor will satisfy the requirement if it is adjacent to, and visible from, the elevator machine.

Under certain conditions, elevators driven by direct current motors may be subject to overspeed. NEC 620–91 and 620–92 require that measures be taken to insure that elevator speed may not attain a value greater than 125 percent of its rated up-direction speed at full load. All metal parts of an electric elevator shall be grounded, the metal raceways on elevator cars shall be bonded to the frame of the car.

Wiring in elevator shafts, which is not included in traveling cables, must be encased in rigid conduit, electrical metallic tubing, metal wireways, or MI cable, except short lengths of flexible conduit, armored cable, or approved rubber cord at gates and doors. Traveling cables must be special types E, EO, ET, or other approved types. The size of wire for operating and control circuits may be No. 20, and this size may be paralleled, in a cable, to equal a No. 14 conductor for a lighting circuit. The reason for this provision is to avoid the necessity for making up costly special cables with various sizes of wire. Lighting and power conductors may be run in the

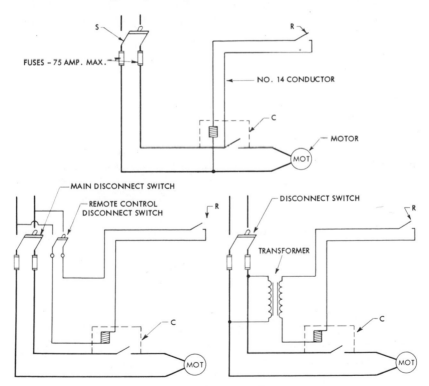

Fig. 29. Remote-control diagrams

same traveling cable. No. 16 and No. 18 control or operating circuit conductors are considered protected by a 20-amp fuse.

Clearances

In general, a clearance of 30 in must be preserved in front of an elevator panelboard, and 24 in behind it. Since these clearances are not obtainable in the case of escalators they may be waived, provided the control panel is connected with flexible leads which permit its removal from normal position for inspection and repair.

REMOTE-CONTROL CIRCUITS

General Rules for "Wired" Circuits

NEC 240–5 (Ex. 5) provides that conductors of remote-control circuits shall be considered, in general, as protected from overcurrent by devices that are rated or set at not more than 500 percent of their carrying capacity. At the top of Fig. 29 is a two line diagram of a single-phase motor circuit containing switch S, controller C, and motor M. There is also a pair of wires from remote-control device R for operating controller C, the circuit including the solenoid of controller C. If conductors of the control circuit are No. 14, with a carrying capacity of 15 amperes, the overcurrent device in switch S could be 5 $\times$ 15, or 75 amperes without violating the rule.

NEC 430–72 adds two more exceptions to the requirement for overcurrent protection. Such protection is not required if the whole control circuit and the controller are contained within the structure of a single machine or where opening of the control circuit by an overcurrent device would create a hazard, as for example, a fire pump.

NEC 430–74 requires that control circuits be disconnected from supply wires when the disconnecting means for the motor circuit is opened. But the disconnecting means may consist of two separate switches or devices, one of which cuts off the motor and controller, the other the control circuit. The two disconnecting devices must be immediately adjacent to one another, as indicated in the lower left illustration of Fig. 29. The section adds one further provision with respect to a transformer used to obtain a lower voltage for the control circuit. The transformer must be connected to the load side of the disconnecting means, as shown in the lower right illustration. Article 725 NEC permits No. 18 and No. 16 conductors for remote

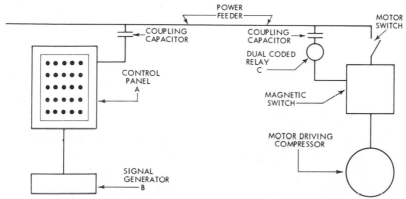

Fig. 30. Elements of high-cycle remote-control system

control circuits, if installed in raceway or cable, and protected by a fuse not larger than 20 amps.

"Unwired" Remote-Control Circuits

A comparatively new method of remote control is by means of high-frequency carrier waves that are transmitted over the existing wiring system. Motors driving pumps or air-conditioning apparatus may be started or stopped, lighting circuits may be turned on or off. There are three major components, as illustrated in Fig. 30, a control panel *A*, a signal generator *B*, and a number of dual-coded relays *C*.

Impulses at frequencies of 3510, 4200, 5000, or 6000 cycles originate in the signal generator. The control panel, which performs automatically under a programming mechanism, imposes the signal between one leg and ground of the supply feeder by means of capacitor-coupling. A relay coded for the particular signal being transmitted, receives the impulses and closes the circuit to a magnetic switch which controls a motor or lighting circuit. At the proper time, the relay causes the magnetic switch to drop out when another signal is transmitted. Panel *A* has indicating lights which flash to show that the distant unit has obeyed the signal.

BASIC MOTOR-CIRCUIT CONNECTIONS

Start-Stop Circuit

The wireman should be so thoroughly familiar with certain motor-circuit connections that he can sketch them off-hand. One of

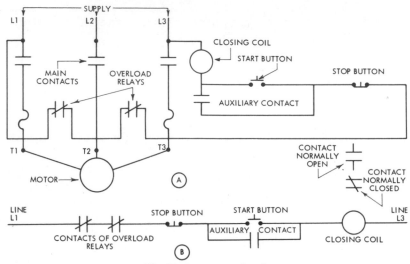

Fig. 31. Start-stop circuit

the more important is the stop-start circuit of Fig. 31. It is advisable to become acquainted first with the single-line diagram of Fig. 31B, observing the two symbols for normally-open and normally-closed contact pairs. After this one has become a routine exercise, the more complete drawing of Fig. 31A may be attempted.

Reversing Starter

The circuit of the reversing starter Fig. 32A need not be committed to memory. It is included at this point, to show how more complicated circuits may be analyzed by the method explained above. The limit switches, suggested by dotted outline, will not be used. Before going further, a small sketch of the rather involved start-stop assembly at the right side of the figure should be made, lettering each contact point as in view B.

A line diagram of the Forward circuit should now be made as in view C, identifying contacts of start and stop buttons by the letters marked on them in view B, and in the order they are passed through. When this sketch is finished, the path of the Reverse circuit should be drawn as in view D. It is possible, with the aid of such line diagrams, to analyze the most difficult control circuits, and to answer questions that come into the mind when looking at a strange blueprint. Here, for example, it may have been wondered at first glance, why contacts *c*, *g*, and *i* were connected together. Tracing through the sketches, the reason becomes quite obvious.

Lead Markings on Three-Phase Motors

The wireman should be familiar with connections for 9-lead dual-voltage motors. Connection diagrams are marked on name-

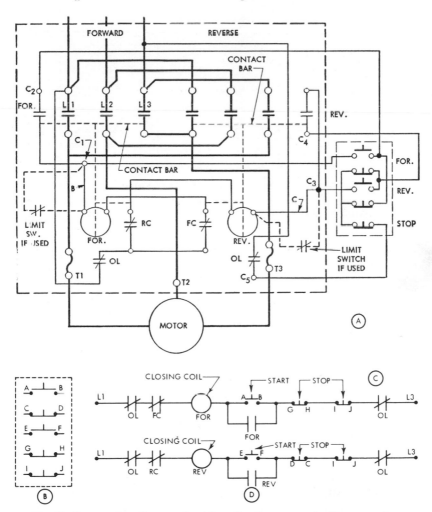

Fig. 32. Connection diagram for Allen-Bradley across-the-line reversing starter for three-phase squirrel-cage motor

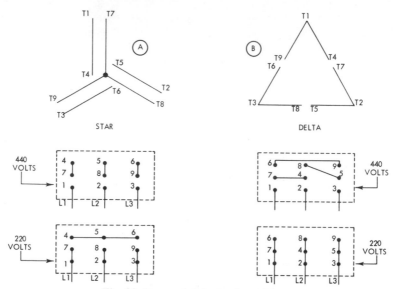

Fig. 33. Star and delta lead markings

plates of the newer motors, but not on older ones. And nameplates are sometimes lost or defaced. Figure 33A shows standard lead markings and groupings for star-connected stators. Figure 33B illustrates like arrangements for delta-connected stators. If the electrician doesn't know whether the winding is star or delta, he may soon learn with the aid of a test lamp. Only one set of three leads will light out in a star-connected winding, but there will be three sets of three in a delta-connected one.

Starter for Direct Current Motor

The left illustration of Fig. 34 shows a direct current rheostat, commonly known as a starting box. It consists of a metal enclosure which contains starting resistors, a set of contact buttons which are tapped to points along the resistor bank, and to a movable handle which is rotated slowly over the contact buttons. The circuit for this device is shown at the right, the contact handle being marked *H*, the resistors *R*, contacts *B*, retaining coil *E*, and overload device *O-C*.

As *H* is brought into contact with the left-hand button, current passes from circuit wire *1* through resistor *R*, retaining device *E*, overload contacts *O-C*, and armature *A* to circuit wire *2*. As the armature gains speed, the handle is moved to the next contact,

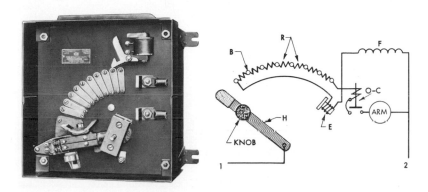

Fig. 34. Direct-current starting rheostat

Courtesy of Cutler-Hammer, Inc.

gradually passing across the full arc of the contacts until it touches against retaining device *E*. Here, an electromagnet attracts an iron "keeper" which is attached to *H*, holding the handle in this position so long as the unit is in operation. When the current is turned off, a spring returns the handle to the "off" position. It should be noted that a parallel circuit, which includes the field coils and retaining coil *E*, is maintained from the instant that contact arm *H* reaches the first contact button.

The motor is stopped by pressing a button which short-circuits coil *E*, or by tripping a latch which causes handle *H* to return to the "off" position. Under NEC 430–39 the motor controller may serve as the running overcurrent device, in a direct current circuit, if it is operative in both starting and running positions. Here, *O-C* is connected to operate in this manner. The reason for the requirement is to protect starting resistors from damage, and to prevent the handle from being moved too rapidly from one contact button to another.

Speed Regulator for Direct Current Motor

An adjustable-speed motor is one whose speed may be readily altered, and which maintains a fairly constant speed under varying load conditions. NEC 430–88 provides that an adjustable-speed motor, which is controlled by field regulation, shall be equipped and connected so that it cannot be started under weakened field unless the motor is especially designed for this service.

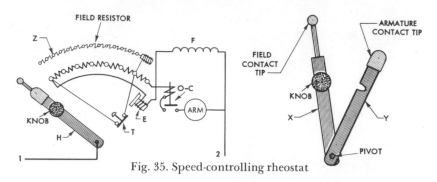

Fig. 35. Speed-controlling rheostat

The left illustration in Fig. 35 shows a line diagram of this unit. The rheostat is much like the one used for simple starting duty, except that it has an extra set of resistors which are connected into the field circuit. The motor is started in the usual way by moving handle *H* across the contact buttons. When the contact arm reaches the running position, the main portion of the handle, marked *Y* in the right-hand illustration, is held in this position by retaining device *E*. But portion *X* of the handle, which has a carbon contact at its upper end, is free to rotate backward over small contact buttons *Z*. As it does so, it causes resistance to be inserted in series with field coils *F,* increasing the speed of the motor.

A pair of contacts, *T,* short-circuit this field resistor until *Y* makes contact with the retaining device. At this instant, contacts *T* are forced open so that arm *X* may cause resistance to be inserted as explained above. When the arm swings back to the "off" position, contacts *T* again short-circuit the field resistor so that the motor cannot be started on a weak field. It is necessary to include this feature in connection with the standard adjustable-speed motor because its starting torque is greatly reduced under a weakened field, and the armature draws a heavy current which may damage the windings.

Safety Precautions in the Wiring of Motors

Motor wiring demands particular care on the part of the electrician, especially toward the finish of an installation, when it becomes time to throw the circuit switch. A first consideration is direction of rotation. The proper rotation should be learned from arrows marked on the equipment, from personal investigation or experience, or from inquiry where necessary.

If the unit is belt-driven, the belt should be removed for purpose of test. If it is direct connected, the coupling or drive gear should be loosened. In any event, the switch should be closed only momentarily to avoid possibility of damage in case of error. The second consideration is unusual noise. A low-pitched, growling sound may indicate magnetic abnormality due to a wrong voltage arrangement of the motor lead wires.

Finally, a workman should protect himself from inadvertent or accidental starting of a motor or its driven machinery. It is worth noting that the 1962 edition of the NEC has tightened the rule governing a motor not within sight of the controller. A manually-operable switch is now required within sight of the motor. Formerly, a locked button in the control circuit was deemed sufficient.

REVIEW QUESTIONS

1. What is the meaning of the abbreviation "Cont." on a nameplate?
2. What is the ambient temperature, expressed in Centigrade degrees?
3. Name the best code letter designation.
4. If the average squirrel-cage, induction motor is connected directly to the supply wires, what percentage of full-load current is it likely to draw?
5. What percentage of full-load torque is it likely to develop?
6. What is the most common starting method for medium-size, squirrel-cage motors?
7. Does the auto-transformer starter provide a closed-transfer?
8. Is an auto-transformer used for incremental starting?
9. Are intermittent motors used on escalators?
10. What is the rating of branch-circuit conductors in percentage of motor full-load current?
11. What distance does the term "within sight" include?
12. What is the maximum allowable branch-circuit protection in terms of full-load motor current?
13. What is the smallest percentage rating for a running-overcurrent device?
14. Do overcurrent requirements for hermetic motors parallel those for 50 degree motors?
15. Overcurrent requirements for D.C. motors parallel those for motors with what code letter?
16. Can the branch-circuit switch be used as the controller?
17. Is the current for a 208-volt motor greater or less than the value listed in the NEC motor tables?
18. Must the carrying capacity of a feeder be at least as great as 125 percent of the sum of all motor full-load currents?
19. What device picks up the high-frequency signal transmitted by the remote-control panel?
20. How many groups of three wires each will be found in a nine-lead, dual-voltage, delta motor?

Chapter Six

Transformers, Capacitors, and Generators

Definitions

A transformer is a device for changing the voltage of an alternating current supply to some other value which is desired by the user. Although power company employees deal also with those which change a lower voltage to a higher, the inside wireman is interested only in those which change the higher voltage to a lower one. The first type is known as a step-up transformer because it makes the voltage climb, or increase; the second type is termed step-down for the opposite reason. It is unnecessary for the interior wireman to learn technical details of transformer design. But he should possess a working knowledge of first principles, which are explained in the following section.

Nature of the Transformer

Fig. 1A presents a photograph of a modern distribution transformer. Outwardly it consists of a sheet metal case and two sets of terminals. One set is connected to the supply wires, the other to the consumer's service. The interior of the transformer, Fig. 1B, is also simple, having an iron core and two windings. The primary winding is designed for connection to the high-voltage circuit, current flowing through its turns setting up a magnetic flux which generates a voltage in the turns of the secondary winding.

As shown in the figure, the primary winding of a thousand turns of wire is connected to a supply line whose voltage is 2200. Flow of current in these one thousand turns results in the generation of 220 volts in the secondary winding which has one hundred turns of

146

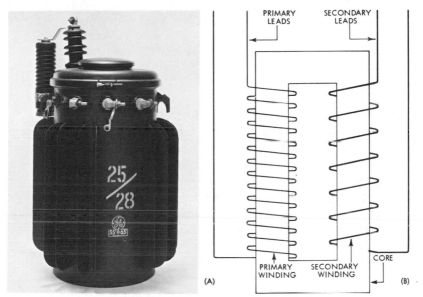

Fig. 1. Transformer

Courtesy of General Electric Co.

wire. This relationship between the number of turns in each wind-ing, and the voltage at its terminals, is a most important one. Since the number of primary turns is ten times the number of secondary turns, and since the voltage at the primary terminals is ten times that at the secondary terminals, it is clear that the relationship be-tween the two voltages is the same as that between primary and secondary turns. The first transformer rule may now be stated: The voltage ratio between primary and secondary winding varies di-rectly as the respective number of turns.

The only additional rule which needs to be learned is one con-cerning the relationship between primary and secondary currents. When the high-voltage winding is connected to the supply line, it causes a voltage to appear immediately at the secondary terminals. If a lamp, a motor, or any other load is attached to the secondary lead wires, current will flow through the circuit which includes the load and the secondary winding. This current generates a magnetic flux which opposes primary flux, and results in the primary wind-ing drawing more current from the supply line. Just enough cur-rent flows to counteract the effect of the secondary turns, and to maintain the transformer flux at the original value.

This state of balance continues. If the secondary requires more current, the primary current also increases. If the secondary current decreases, that of the primary does likewise. But the additional amount of current that flows in the primary is less than in the secondary. The reason is easily seen. The strength of magnetism created by a winding depends upon two things, the number of turns, and the current flowing through them.

Here, since the primary has ten times as many turns as the secondary, one one-tenth as many amperes need flow in order to counteract the magnetism of the secondary windings. If the load is 10 amps, the primary current needed to balance it is 1 amp, the turns multiplied by amperes being the same in each case. The second rule may now be stated: Current flow in primary and secondary windings varies inversely as their respective number of turns. It should be mentioned that the current needed to establish the original primary flux is so small that it may be neglected. In the present instance, it might be as low as $\frac{1}{2}$ amp.

Transformer Construction

The main problem in the operation of transformers is dissipation of heat created by flow of current through resistance of the windings. If insulation is to be maintained in a normally good condition, heat generated deep inside the turns of wire must be carried away before it builds up dangerous temperatures. Various methods are employed in this regard. With small units, the iron core and the surface of the coils may be exposed directly to the air. Heat is not removed fast enough, however, in many applications because the exposed area is too small. The area may be increased by enclosing the unit in a sheet metal box which is filled with epoxy resin. This material conducts heat rapidly to the metal cover, and prevents the interior from becoming too hot under rated load. In larger units, core and windings are surrounded by a sheet metal case through which air is forced under pressure, the heat being literally swept away by the stream of air.

Another common method is to fill the case with oil, the liquid penetrating the innermost crevices of the apparatus, and quickly transferring heat to the surface. Oil transformers are used for outdoor installations, such as on poles, or in ground-level pads. Here, the liquid tends to exclude damp air and moisture, as well as carrying on its main purpose. Oil is also used for extremely large units, known as power transformers. Cooling is often assisted in these by assemblies of metal radiator tubes through which the oil is caused to circulate while electric fans blow air through them. A non-inflammable liquid known as Askarel, is frequently substituted for oil, especially in medium-size units.

That type which is of particular interest to the wireman is the general purpose, or lighting, transformer rated at not over 600 volts. It may be dry, oil-filled, or Askarel-filled, but the dry type predominates. Such transformers are frequently grouped in rooms which contain necessary control panels and other equipment. Although pressure cooling methods are seldom employed, the rooms are ventilated.

Feeder conduits that enter transformer cases are often provided with some form of patented coupling, such as an Erickson, or a no-thread fitting, so that the transformer may be replaced, if necessary, with a minimum of labor. Like considerations also influence the placing of individual units.

Transformer Polarity

In order to properly connect banks of transformers with the least difficulty, the wireman must understand the difference between polarities. Transformer nameplates are usually marked to indicate whether the lead arrangement is such as to provide additive or subtractive polarity. If not so marked, he can readily determine the fact himself. The meaning of the term *polarity* will be explained with the help of Fig. 2.

Fig. 2A represents the top of a transformer whose primary lead wires are marked *H1* and *H2,* the secondary leads, *X1* and *X2.* Primary voltage is assumed to be at a particular instant, in a general direction as indicated by the arrow, from the lower-numbered terminal to the higher; that is from *H1* to *H2.* Primary current flow will induce, at this moment, a secondary voltage from *X1* to *X2.* Before current is turned on, a temporary jumper wire is connected from primary lead *H1* to the secondary lead on the same end of the transformer, *X2.* If a voltmeter reads 2200 volts from *H1* to *H2,* and the turns-ratio of the unit is 10 to 1, the reading from *X1* to *X2* will be 220 volts. When the meter is now applied to lead wires *H2* and *X1,* it will read 2420 volts. This lead arrangement, with *H1* and *X2* at one end of the transformer, and *H2* and *X1* at the other, is said to be additive.

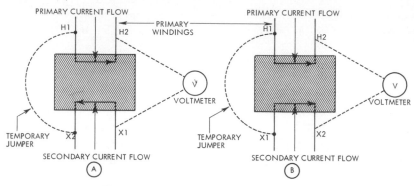

Fig. 2. Additive and subtractive polarity

Consider now the unit of Fig. 2B. Primary lead *H1* is connected temporarily to the secondary lead on the same end, which in this case is *X1*. When a test is made, the voltage between primary and secondary lead wires *H2* and *X2* on the other end of the transformer is less than that across the primary circuit, being equal to 2200 volts minus 220 volts, or 1980 volts.

The test may be performed more safely under low-voltage conditions. Instead of connecting the 2200-volt circuit to *H1* and *H2*, the low voltage wires may be attached thereto. With a turns-ratio of 10 to 1, secondary leads will show 22 volts. If the meter is connected across *H2* and *X1* as in Fig. 2A it will read 242 volts, and across *H2* and *X2* as in Fig. 2B, 198 volts.

Paralleling Single-Phase Transformers

When it is necessary to parallel two transformers that have no polarity indications, each set of primary wires should be marked *H1* and *H2*. A jumper should be installed between *H1* and the secondary lead wire on the same end of the unit. If the voltmeter shows a greater reading between *H2* and the remaining secondary lead, the arrangement is additive, and the secondary wires should be marked as in Fig. 2A. Should the meter give a lower reading when making the test, the secondary leads should be identified as in Fig. 2B.

Two additive transformers can be paralleled as in Fig. 3A. Both *H1* primary leads are attached to one of the supply wires, the *H2* leads to the other. On the opposite side, both *X2* leads are attached to one secondary wire, the two *X1* leads to the other. Subtractively

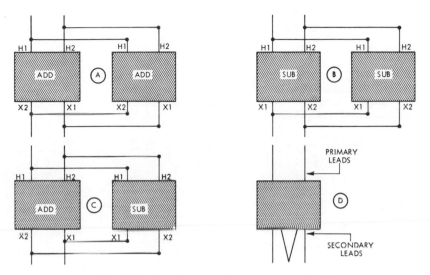

Fig. 3. Single-phase transformer connections

polarized transformers may be connected in a similar fashion, as in Fig. 3B. In either case, the $X1$ and $X2$ paralleling jumper wires follow the same pattern as the primary lead connections.

The paralleling of an additive unit with a subtractive one is done as in Fig. 3C. Here, it may be noticed that the secondary paralleling jumpers do not follow the same pattern as on the primary side. The inner terminals attach to one jumper, outers to the other. Only two primary lead wires are brought out ordinarily, but there are always four secondary leads. The two middle ones should be joined and taped, as in Fig. 3D, while the outers are treated as the ends of a single winding, during a test.

Connecting Three-Phase Transformers

Three-phase transformers may be connected in a number of ways, depending upon the primary and secondary voltages concerned. Three arrangements are shown in Fig. 4, star-star, delta-delta, and star-delta, the first word in each term referring to the primary, the other to the secondary.

In Fig. 4A, three additive polarity transformers are connected star-star, the $H1$ primary leads going to the supply conductors, the $H2$ leads joining to form the primary star. The $X1$ secondary leads connect to the feeder wires, and $X2$ leads make a secondary star.

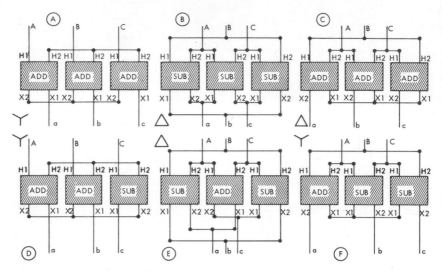

Fig. 4. Three-phase transformer connections

Each primary supply wire in the delta-delta scheme of Fig. 4B goes to an *H1* and an *H2* lead. Secondary feeder wires are handled in a similar way, each one attaching to an *X1* and an *X2* lead. The primary arrangement in the delta-star scheme of Fig. 4C is identical with that of Fig. 4B, but the *X2* wires of the secondary connect to feeder conductors, while the *X1*'s form a star.

All three methods can be varied in detail, so long as an orderly process is followed. For example, in Fig. 4A, the *H2* leads could be attached to supply wires, and the *H1* leads to the star. In Fig. 4B, the *H1* lead of the transformer on the left may connect to the *H2* lead of the middle one, the *H1* lead of the middle one to the *H2* lead of the transformer at the right, and the *H1* lead of this unit to the *H2* lead of the left-hand one. To avoid confusion, the pattern chosen for the high-voltage side in a delta-delta grouping, should be followed with respect to the secondary.

Fig. 4D, E, F repeat the connections illustrated in Fig. 4A, B, and C, except that two additive transformers are used with a subtractive in view D, two subtractives with an additive in view E, and two subtractives with an additive in view F. No difficulty will be experienced in handling these or similar groupings if secondary lead markings are carefully observed. In view D, lead wires of the subtractive secondary are crossed, as compared to the additives. The secondary leads of the additives in views E and F appear crossed as compared to those of the subtractives.

The star-star scheme of views A and D is used only with polyphase power or motors, rarely for lighting. Delta-Delta transformers, views B and E, are employed for either power or lighting. The delta-star connection of views C and F is, however, the most desirable one for both power and lighting. If a fourth wire is attached to the secondary star jumper, the popular network system results.

Transformer Impedance

Another matter which must be considered upon occasion when paralleling transformers, is impedance. Impedance is the opposition

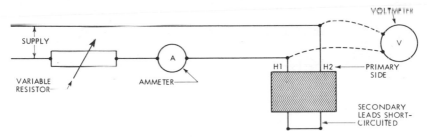

Fig. 5. Checking transformer impedance

that windings offer to flow of current. It is composed of resistance and reactance. Fig. 5 shows how its value may be determined. The secondary winding is short-circuited, and the primary is connected to a source of power which need not be more, usually, than about ten percent of normal supply voltage.

An ammeter and a variable resistance are placed in series with the high-voltage winding, and a voltmeter across its terminals. The resistance is adjusted until normal full-load current flows in the primary circuit. The voltage across *H1* and *H2* is read at the same time. Impedance is equal to rated voltage divided by the reading of the voltmeter. Thus, if normal voltage is 2200, and a test voltage of 132 produces full-load current, the impedance is equal to: 2200/132, or 6 percent.

When two identical transformers are to be paralleled, that is two of the same capacity, voltage, and manufacture, impedance is of no concern. If they are of different manufacture, however, it may be important. And where transformers are of different sizes, say a 37½

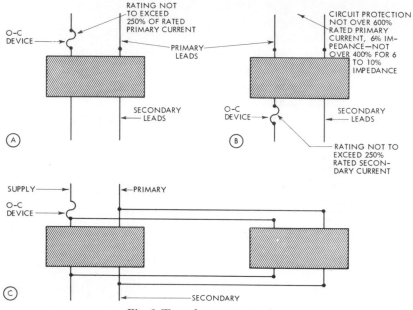

Fig. 6. Transformer protection

kva and a 15 kva, ammeter readings should be taken under load to see if they are providing current output in accordance with their individual kva capacities.

Overcurrent Protection

Under NEC 450-3, a transformer may be protected by an over-current device in the primary side, rated or set at not more than 250 percent of full-load current, as in Fig. 6A. Existing circuit protection, within this limit, is also acceptable. A secondary protective device may be substituted, Fig. 6B, for the primary one if rated at not over 250 percent of secondary current, and if certain conditions are satisfied.

In such case, the primary feeder overcurrent device can not be of higher rating than 600 percent of primary transformer current for a unit having up to 6 percent impedance, and not more than 400 percent for one having 6 percent to 10 percent impedance. This rule applies also to network transformers that are equipped with special circuit breakers. Transformers paralleled, or "banked," may be protected as a unit, Fig. 6C, if their impedances are such that they divide the load in proportion to their kva ratings.

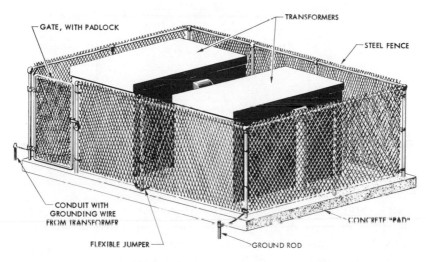

GATE, WITH PADLOCK

TRANSFORMERS

STEEL FENCE

CONDUIT WITH
GROUNDING WIRE
FROM TRANSFORMER

CONCRETE "PAD"

FLEXIBLE JUMPER

GROUND ROD

Fig. 7. Guarding and grounding

Grounding

The NEC provides that transformers shall be protected against physical damage and accidental contact. They shall, except in a few instances, be grounded. It is a good plan to ground them at all times. When they are supplied by wiring in metallic enclosures, the conduit or the cable sheath furnish such grounding automatically.

Transformers installed on outdoor pads should be guarded and grounded as in Fig. 7. Note that the cases and the wire fence are attached to driven grounding electrodes. Also observe that portions of the wire fence which must be removed upon occasion, are equipped with flexible bonding jumpers. The grounding conductor, when connected to a driven electrode, need not be larger than No. 6 copper wire. The grounding of transformer neutral conductors will be discussed in the next chapter.

Dry-Transformer Insulation

The kind of insulation employed in dry-type transformers is marked on nameplates. There are three grades: Class A, which is good for a temperature rise of 55 degrees above ambient; Class B, which retains its insulating qualities at temperatures up to 80 degrees above ambient; and Class H, which can safely withstand a temperature rise of 150 degrees above ambient. Ambient temperature, as with motors, is taken as 40 degrees Centigrade.

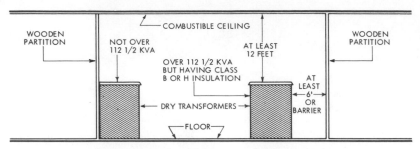

Fig. 8. Location of dry-type transformers

Location of Transformers

The NEC states clear details regarding permissible locations for the different types of transformers. Dry types rated at not over 600 volts, not over 112½ kva, and completely enclosed except for ventilating openings, can be installed anywhere indoors, even against a wooden partition. Those larger than 112½ kva must be installed in fire-resistant transformer rooms unless constructed with Class B or Class H insulation. They must also be separated from combustible material by an approved barrier, or by a distance not less than 6 ft horizontally and 12 ft vertically, as shown in Fig. 8. All transformers rated at more than 35,000 volts must be installed in approved vaults (*see NEC*).

Oil transformers not over 112½ kva capacity may be placed in less expensive vaults than the standard type, the dimensions being set forth in the NEC. A vault is not required for transformers of 600 volts or less, if suitable precautions are taken with respect to danger from oil fires. The total capacity cannot exceed 10 kva in a combustible location, or 75 kva in a fire-resistant structure. They may be installed in suitable detached buildings, without vaults, if accessible only to qualified personnel. When used outdoors, they must be so placed and guarded as not to endanger combustible structures, or to constitute a threat to fire escapes, doors, and window openings.

Mounting Transformers

Indoors, transformers are mounted on floors, walls, or ceilings, depending upon their size and construction, as well as the type of building. Small ones, generally, hang from walls or ceiling, while large ones rest on the floor. They should be handled carefully, not

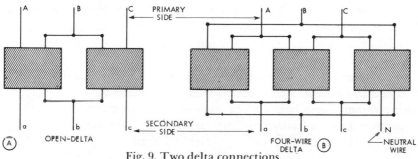

Fig. 9. Two delta connections

subjected to shock or dragged over uneven surfaces. Lugs or eye-bolts should be made use of when raising them.

The most common problem is the suppression of noise, this factor being more important with respect to offices or stores than with industrial locations. Characteristic 60-cycle hum, which is really 120 vibrations a second, is seldom objectionable in places where mechanical operations are in progress. If the noise level is fairly low, however, it becomes quite disturbing.

Various methods are available for combatting the trouble. Manufacturers can furnish suppressor pads that are effective in some instances. Floor mounted transformers can be set upon wooden strips. Units may be placed at an angle instead of being aligned parallel to a wall, and the best angle determined by trial and error. If noise is "telegraphed" out of the room along conduit runs that are attached to the transformer cases, short lengths of flexible conduit may be inserted in runs close to the units.

Additional Transformer Arrangements

There are three other common transformer connections in addition to the star and delta groupings already discussed in the study of polarity. Two of them are illustrated in Fig. 9. Fig. 9A shows open-delta transformers. The arrangement is really a three-phase delta pattern, but with a transformer missing. If a third unit were spanned across supply wires *C* and *A*, a completed delta would result. Power companies make use of the open-delta grouping because it saves equipment.

Where a single-phase transformer has been supplying lighting services, and a consumer in the area demands three-phase power to feed motorized appliances, it is customary to add a single small transformer to care for his needs. The original large transformer continues to furnish single-phase current to the lights, and with the help of the smaller unit, three-phase current to the motors.

A four-wire delta group is illustrated in Fig. 9B. The pattern is exactly the same as other delta connections examined before, except that a neutral conductor, N, has been attached to the middle tap of one transformer. Lamp loads may be connected between neutral conductor N and either (a) or (c). Three-phase power is supplied by conductors (a), (b), and (c). Wire (b), which does not carry any of the lighting current, is usually termed the "power leg."

The T-connection, whose principal use at one time had been in transformations from two-phase to three-phase, has enjoyed a revival the past few years in the field of three-phase transformation. It resembles the open-delta system to the extent that only two transformers are needed, but the similarity ends there. In principle, it is more like star-star. Fig. 10 shows the method. Two transformers are employed, the one on the left, M, being the main unit, the one on the right, T, being the teaser.

M is a standard transformer, with mid-point taps brought out on both primary and secondary. T is a special unit, its primary and secondary windings having approximately 86 percent as many turns as the respective primary and secondary coils of M. The secondary winding of T has a tap, N, which includes approximately 67 percent of the number of turns in the coil. This tap becomes the neutral feeder wire.

Connections between the transformers are made as shown, the H1 lead of T going to the mid-point, P, of M's primary, and the X1 lead of T going to the mid-point, (p), of M's secondary. Three-

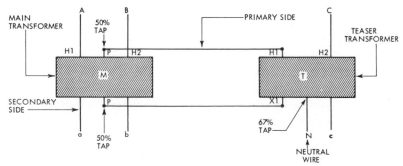

Fig. 10. T-Connected three-phase transformers

phase supply wires are attached to *H1* and *H2* of *M*, along with the *H2* lead of *T*. Power may be taken from secondary conductors (*a*), (*b*), and (*c*), while lighting circuits may be connected between neutral wire *N* and any or all of the other conductors.

The secondary output is exactly the same as that obtained from the network scheme. When lighting circuits are connected between any one of the three "phase" wires and neutral, without any load on the other two, neither primary nor secondary voltages are disturbed. Voltage relationships within the various connections will be discussed in the next two chapters.

Potential and Current Transformers

The term *potential transformer* is applied to small units which are employed in connection with electrical instruments for reducing line voltage to a safe value. Thus, a 20-to-1 potential transformer, Fig. 11A, may be used in connection with a switchboard installation for reducing a generated voltage of 2,300 to a value of 115 volts.

The NEC requires fuses in the primary circuits of potential transformers. It limits their value to 10 amps for voltages not exceeding 600, and 3 amps for those in excess of 600. The Code recommends a series resistor in the primary circuit to limit possible short-circuit current. The normal current is so small that voltage drop in the resistor is negligible. In case of a short circuit, however, the current is high and the voltage drop considerable.

Current transformers, Fig. 11B, are used to reduce a comparatively high feeder current to a value low enough for a recording

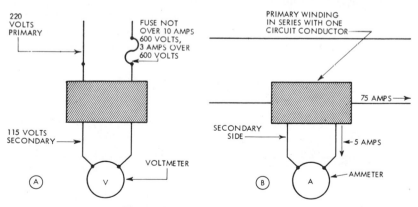

Fig. 11. Instrument transformers

meter. The usual ammeter or wattmeter has a 5-amp element. That is, its maximum carrying capacity is 5 amps. If the line current is 75 amps, a 15-to-1 step-down current transformer will be required.

CAPACITORS, RESISTORS, AND REACTORS

Power Factor

Capacitors, also known as condensers, are used to improve the power factor of a circuit. It may be well to define the term before going on. Power in a direct current circuit is equal to volts times amperes. The same rule holds good in alternating current circuits if voltage and current are exactly in step. If they are out of step, because of inductive reactance, volts times amperes do not equal watts, but volt-amperes. It is for this reason that alternating current apparatus such as generators and transformers, are rated in kva (kilovolt-amperes) instead of kilowatts. To obtain kilowatts, it is necessary to multiply the product of volts and amperes by a decimal number which is called the power factor. The value of this number depends upon how far apart the volts and amperes are; that is, how much inductance is present.

It should be mentioned at this point, that most alternating current devices possess inductance, the harmful effect of which is to require a larger current to produce a given amount of power. Larger alternators, larger supply transformers, and heavier conductors are needed. For this reason, generating plants charge a higher rate if a customer's power factor is too low. Steps are often taken to improve the condition.

The manner in which this can be done will be explained with the help of Fig. 12. The illustration shows both voltage and current as curves, or half-waves. In Fig. 12A, voltage half-wave *A-B* and

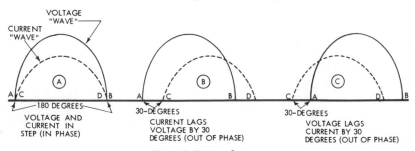

Fig. 12. Power factor

current half-wave *C-D* are exactly in step, the ends *A* and *C* together, *B* and *D* together. They are said to be in phase, the power being equal to the product of effective volts and effective amperes. In this case, the power factor is 1, or unity.

Voltage and current in Fig. 12B are no longer in step, but are said to be out of phase, inductance preventing the current half-wave from starting upward until the voltage half-wave has progressed some distance. A half-wave spans 180 electrical degrees. The distance between two half-waves can be expressed therefore, as a certain number of degrees, depending on the fraction of a whole width that it represents. Thus, if the space between *A* and *C* is ⅙ of a whole distance, they are: ⅙ × 180 degrees, or 30 degrees apart. That is, the current *lags* the voltage by 30 degrees. The power factor, here, would be .87 or, as it is often stated, 87 percent. If current lagged voltage by 60 degrees, the power factor would be .5, the value decreasing as the lag increased.

Capacitive reactance, or capacitance, has exactly the opposite effect, causing the voltage to lag the current as in Fig. 12C. If the right amount of capacitance is chosen the effect of inductance may be neutralized.

Use of Capacitors

Capacitors are used for the purpose of improving power factor. They are rated in kilovars, abbreviated kvars, instead of in kilowatts

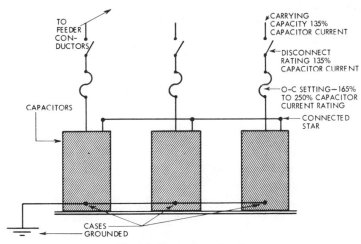

Fig. 13. Capacitor circuit

or kilovolt-amperes because their output is practically all reactive current. That is, the voltage lags the current by approximately 90 electrical degrees.

Article 460 of the NEC sets forth a number of rules applying to capacitors. As illustrated in Fig. 13, most of them state a 135 percent requirement. Conductors supplying a capacitor must have a carrying capacity not less than 135 percent of nameplate current. A disconnecting means is required, unless the unit is connected on the loadside of a motor overcurrent device, but it need not open all conductors simultaneously. It must have a pole in each ungrounded conductor, and must have a continuous current carrying capacity of 135 percent of nameplate value.

Transformers, which are sometimes employed to "couple" a capacitor to a higher-voltage circuit, must have a kva rating not less than 135 percent of capacitor kvar rating. An overcurrent device is required in each ungrounded conductor, its rating being as low as practicable. In practice, it has been found that this rating is between 165 percent and 250 percent of nameplate current, the exact setting depending upon the nature of short-time surges, or "spikes" that occur during normal operation. Cases must be grounded, and a means for draining the stored charge must be provided (*see NEC*). A unit which contains more than 3 gallons of combustible oil must be placed in a vault.

Capacitors are essential elements in static-magnetic voltage regulators, which also include transformers and reactors. These devices, which have no moving parts, are designed to maintain a steady voltage on a service or feeder, despite irregularities in the supply. They are needed upon occasion, where apparatus is particularly sensitive to voltage changes, for example, certain IBM installations.

Resistors and Reactors

Such devices in the immediate vicinity of ignitible substances should be immersed in oil, or enclosed in tight metal boxes. Resistors and reactors which are not mounted on switchboards, or in a manner to be described, must be separated from combustible material by a distance of not less than 1 ft.

If less than 1 ft from such materials, they must be attached to a slab or panel of noncombustible, nonabsorptive material such as slate, soapstone, or marble. It must not be less than ½ in thick and should extend beyond the edges of the device. Support is fur-

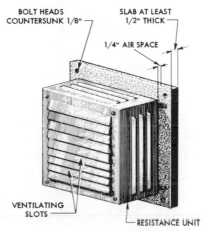

Fig. 14. Mounting resistor unit

nished by bolts countersunk at least $\frac{1}{8}$ in below the surface. These bolts are to be covered with insulating material.

When cabinets or cases which hold such devices are mounted on a plain surface, an airspace of at least $\frac{1}{4}$ in between case and surface, is required except at points of support. Such an installation is shown in Fig. 14. In general, wire with insulation suitable for 90°C operation shall be used. For motor starting service, other types of insulation are acceptable.

NEC 470–8 limits use of incandescent lamps. They may be employed as protective resistors for automatic controllers or as series resistors for other devices, where local authorities so permit. But they cannot be used to carry the main current, nor may they constitute the regulating resistance of the unit. Where incandescent lamps are used, they shall be mounted in porcelain receptacles. Today, lamps are seldom employed.

GENERATORS

Two-Wire Generators

Constant-potential generators, except alternating current generators and their exciters, must be protected from excessive current by circuit breakers or fuses. Alternating current generators Fig. 15A are exempted from need of overcurrent protection because their impedance limits short-circuit current to such a value that damage to windings is unlikely. Exciters for all generators, separately-excited

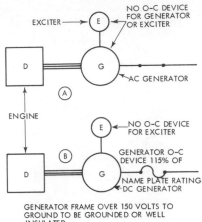

Fig. 15. Generator circuits

direct current as well as alternating current machines, are usually operated without overcurrent protection. It is considered better to risk damage to the exciter rather than have the generator shut down through operation of an exciter overcurrent device.

Conductors leading from a generator must have a carrying capacity, at least 115 percent of generator nameplate current rating, Fig. 15B. The frame of a generator operating at a terminal voltage in excess of 150 volts to ground must be grounded, or permanently and effectively insulated from ground.

A two-wire direct current generator may have the overcurrent device in only one conductor provided it is actuated by the whole load. A generator operating at 65 volts or less, and driven by an individual motor, is considered adequately protected by the motor overcurrent device if this unit will open the circuit when the unit is delivering not more than 150 percent of full-load current.

Balancer Sets and Three-Wire Generators

Balancer sets must be equipped with overload devices which disconnect the three-wire system in case of excessive unbalance. Three-wire direct current generators must be provided with overcurrent devices, one in either armature lead, which are arranged to disconnect the whole three-wire circuit in case of heavy overload or extreme unbalance. Fig. 16 shows a line diagram of a balancer set at the left, and a three-wire direct current generator at the right.

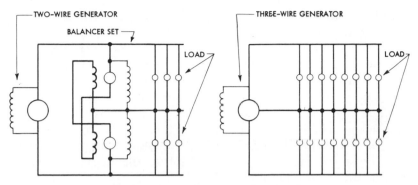

Fig. 16. Three-wire generating circuits

Emergency Generators—Motor Generator Sets

Small diesel- or gas-engine-driven generators that will carry a certain percentage of the total load have become common, not only for places of public assembly, but also for hospitals, department stores, and commercial buildings. Current for a low-voltage starting motor is supplied by a storage battery which is kept in a state of charge by either a tube type or a dry type rectifier. In the usual arrangement, the generator starts immediately upon occurrence of a power failure, an automatic throw-over switch connecting it to the desired circuits or feeders.

Motor-generator sets are frequently employed to generate direct current for special motors or machine tools. They are also used to provide high-frequency current that is required in the class of fluorescent lighting system discussed in Chapter Three.

Safety Measures in Connection with Transformers and Capacitors

The electrician should work on a "hot" transformer only when this becomes absolutely necessary. Terminals should be protected from accidental contact, in such case, especially those on the high-voltage side. When installing a new bank, secondary connections should be made first with temporary wires of small cross-section, unless the workman is certain that they are right. And, the secondary mains should not be connected to a parallel feeder until the voltage and phasing of the transformer bank are checked against those of the feeder.

The NEC takes special note of high-voltage transformers in section 710–10. Paragraph (a) sets forth precautions necessary with regard to transformers in public places; paragraph (b) deals with locations frequented only by employees; and paragraph (c) gives requirements for places accessible only to qualified persons.

The most important safety measure applying to capacitors is to avoid contact with open terminals until absolutely sure that it is safe to do so. After the capacitor disconnect switch has been opened, terminal lugs should be short-circuited with a piece of insulated wire whose ends have been exposed. Although the NEC requires that each capacitor be provided with a means for automatically draining stored charge, it is well to follow the suggested step in order to allow for mischance.

REVIEW QUESTIONS

1. What determines the voltage ratio of a transformer?
2. What other factor, in addition to the value of current, determines the strength of magnetism of a transformer coil?
3. What is the main problem in the operation of transformers?
4. Name the type of transformer of greatest interest to the inside wireman.
5. What letter is used to mark primary transformer lead wires?
6. Is the output voltage of a subtractive transformer less than that of a comparable additive transformer?
7. What instrument is used when making a polarity test?
8. Can additive and subtractive transformers be paralleled?
9. Could two additive and one subtractive transformer be connected star-star?
10. Is it ever advisable to connect the primary in delta and the secondary in star?
11. What effect does impedance have on flow of current?
12. Is impedance usually important when two identical transformers are to be paralleled?
13. Is it permissible to fuse the transformer primary at a value greater than 125 percent of rated current?
14. What factor must be taken into consideration when a transformer is to be fused only on the secondary side?
15. Name the three types of insulation used in dry type transformers.
16. Do 12,000-volt transformers have to be installed in vaults?
17. What is a common trouble connected with the setting of transformers?
18. How many transformers are required for a T-type three-phase transformation?
19. By what quantity must kilovolt-amperes be multiplied to obtain equivalent kilowatts?
20. In what terms are commercial capacitors rated?

Chapter Seven

Services —
Interior Distribution

Modern Trends

For many years, the established practice was to provide a single-phase service for commercial lighting. If elevators, ammonia compressors, or other large pieces of electrical equipment were present, a three-phase power service might be added. In many instances, however, the motor load was so small that it, too, could be handled by the single-phase supply. Industrial plants were often furnished with 440-volt or 575-volt, three-phase current for motor loads. But industrial lighting was usually taken care of with the conventional type of service.

Electrical power was generated at a number of different frequencies, ranging from 25 cycles to 133 cycles, with 60-cycle current predominating. Only a few years ago, one of the huge electrical generating concerns of the nation was supplying 50-cycle current to a large metropolis. Today, 60-cycle current is used far and wide. The same kind of progress has been made with respect to voltage and phase of current delivered to commercial and industrial users. The trend today is toward higher service potentials, and to three-phase supply. And there is widespread use of the customer's own transformers to produce on-the-spot voltages at particular locations on his premises. This chapter deals first with low-voltage services and distribution. Later on, it considers high-voltage applications.

SERVICES UP TO 600 VOLTS

Number of Services

The first important section in NEC Article 230 deals with the number of services permitted in a building, stating that a structure should be supplied through only one set of conductors. A number

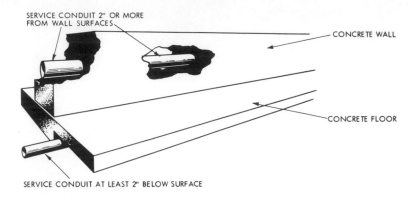

Fig. 1. Service conductors outside building

of exceptions are listed, two of which are of interest at this time. One declares that the requirement may be waived if capacity needs make this desirable. The other extends the waiver to buildings of large area.

Rapid growth of population, space-age needs, and soaring real estate values, have resulted in both horizontal and vertical expansion of business structures. Introduction of new methods and appliances, meanwhile, have witnessed a vast increase in electrical consumption per square foot of plant. These factors have created a need for enlarged supply facilities, and for multiple services.

Important NEC Sections

NEC 230–45 states that service conductors in conduit or duct which are under at least two inches of concrete beneath a structure, or encased in two inches of brick masonry or in concrete within a wall, Fig. 1, shall be considered outside the building. This rule is of great value when it becomes necessary to install service conductors between a street manhole and a point remote from property lines. It is worth noting, at this time, that the rule applies to high-voltage services as well as to those of 600 volts or less.

Where property under a single management consists of more than one occupancy, conductors supplying each unit must be provided with a readily accessible means within or adjacent to it, for disconnecting all ungrounded conductors. The main building in Fig. 2 is marked *"A"*. Feeder conduits run from it to B and C. This rule has given rise to much controversy, centered around the mean-

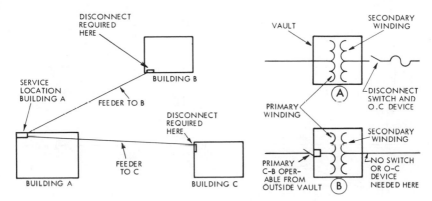

Fig. 2. Conductors supplying
additional buildings

Fig. 3. Service Overcurrent
protection

ing of the term "adjacent."

Some authorities would allow the feeder switches in *A* to satisfy the meaning of "adjacent" under all circumstances. Others claim to agree in this practice only if distances between units is "not too great," a very indefinite interpretation. It seems that the intent of the code is violated in either case. The Article says, further, that overcurrent protection may be located in the building served or in another on the same property. In other words, the disconnect switches in *B* and *C* may be unfused, the feeder overcurrent devices inside *A* satisfying the requirement.

Another section of Article 230 deals with overcurrent protection. Ordinarily, the service disconnect and overcurrent devices must be located in secondary leads from the supply transformer, as in Fig. 3A. An exception is made in the case illustrated by Fig. 3B, where the transformer, or bank, feeds a single main, and the primary circuit breaker is manually operable from a point outside the vault. In this event, the overcurrent device of the primary circuit breaker must protect the secondary conductors.

Service Switches

A service switch must have a blade, or pole, in each ungrounded supply conductor. Means for disconnecting the ungrounded conductor must be provided within the metal enclosure. For the latter purpose, the switch may either have an extra pole, or a connection block which may or may not be insulated from the metal surface.

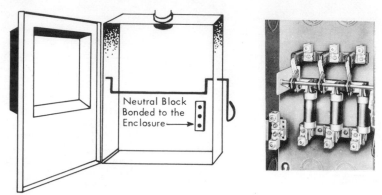

Fig. 4. Solid neutral service switch

Courtesy of General Electric Co.

This is the common "solid-neutral" switch of Fig. 4. Three types of general use switches are manufactured, HD, ND, and LD. These type letters mean: heavy-duty, normal-duty, and light-duty, respectively. The latter is not made in sizes larger than 200 amps.

Section 380 of NEC provides that knife switches rated at more than 1200 amps, 250 volts or less, and at more than 600 amps, 251 to 600 volts, shall be used only as isolating switches, and shall not be opened under load. Auxiliary contacts of a renewable, quick-break, or equivalent type, are required on all 600-volt knife switches designed for breaking currents over 200 amps. To interrupt currents greater than 1200 amps at 250 volts, or 600 amps at 251 to 600 volts, a circuit breaker or a switch of special design approved for such purpose, shall be used.

A special unit known as a bolted-pressure switch is approved for use up to 6000 amps. This switch has double-leafed blades which squeeze the stationary contacts when the switch is closed. Pressure is obtained by way of screw-thread construction at the hinge point and on both sides of the fixed member at the top of the switch, resulting in firm, low-resistance contact at either end of the blades.

Another device approved for low-voltage currents up to 4000 amps is the load interrupter switch of Fig. 5 (*left*). This unit has butt-type multiple contacts, along with arcing tips and current-limiting fuses, which will be discussed shortly. The mechanism, shown in Fig. 5 (*right*), is ruggedly constructed so that it will break up to twelve

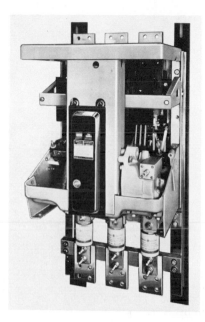

Fig. 5. High-current air break switches
Courtesy of General Electric Co.

times normal current without damage to itself.

Circuit-Breakers

The NEC states that the service disconnecting means can be a manually-operable circuit breaker. A push-button form of remote control circuit may be used in addition to the manual handle. The circuit breaker, in fact, can be of a type which is operated from a remote point by electrical, hydraulic, or pneumatic means, provided that it can also be closed and opened manually. As to construction, there are two general types, the rugged, steel-enclosed unit and the molded-case breaker. The steel unit is shown in Fig. 6.

Both types can be designed to open quickly under a short-circuit, and to drop out more slowly under simple overload. In the fully-magnetic unit, a mechanical time-delay feature such as an air or hydraulic plunger is introduced. Under moderate overloads, the plunger moves slowly toward the tripping mechanism. But if the current is several times normal, as when a short-circuit occurs, the plunger moves rapidly to strike the release catch. In the thermal-magnetic type, the magnetic element is not affected by ordinary overloads, the thermal element causing disconnection if the high

Fig. 6. Circuit breakers

Courtesy of (Left) General Electric Co.
(Right) I-T-E- Circuit Breaker Co.

current persists more than a few seconds. A current as great as ten times normal, however, causes the magnetic plunger to strike the tripping mechanism instantly.

Less expensive circuit breakers are made without this dual feature. One of the most important items connected with a circuit breaker is its short-circuit interrupting capacity. It depends to some extent upon size. This range varies from about 1000 amps for small breakers to over 100,000 amps for large ones, but it may be extended by the addition of current-limiting fuses. Some thermal-type breakers have temperature correcting elements which change the overload setting automatically, to compensate for higher or lower than normal ambient temperatures.

Safety Precautions in Connection with Switches and Circuit Breakers

When it becomes necessary to operate the service disconnect for purposes of repair or maintenance, it is wise to first open feeder switches or breakers. This is most desirable in the case of knife switches, in order to minimize burning of contact members.

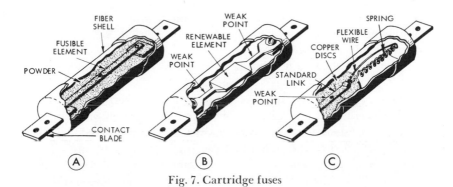

FIBER SHELL
WEAK POINT
SPRING
FLEXIBLE WIRE
FUSIBLE ELEMENT
RENEWABLE ELEMENT
COPPER DISCS
WEAK POINT
POWDER
STANDARD LINK
WEAK POINT
CONTACT BLADE
(A) (B) (C)

Fig. 7. Cartridge fuses

It might be well to note here, that one should never stand directly in front of a knife switch that is to be pulled. The workman should stand to the right of the device, manipulating the lever with his left hand. This is especially necessary when the switch is opened under emergency conditions. An arc caused by a short-circuit may be so violent as to burn through the metal switch cover, spewing hot metal in the immediate vicinity.

After work has been completed, the feeder circuit switches or breakers should not be touched until the main device has been closed. Then, they should be manipulated one at a time.

Cartridge Fuses

The standard non-renewable cartridge fuse is shown in Fig. 7A. The fusible element is soldered to the end pieces, and is surrounded by arc-quenching powder. It will carry 100 percent of rated current indefinitely when inside a switch enclosure, but will blow in a short time at a value slightly greater than this amount. On short-circuit, it will open immediately, although there is danger of destructive arcing, or even explosion, if the current exceeds 10,000 amps. This fuse is unsuited to applications where momentary overloads are to be expected, or where spiking may occur.

The renewable variety of Fig. 7B has weak points on either side of the central portion of the link. In the simplest form, it offers somewhat greater time-delay than the non-renewable fuse because the plate, washers, and screws that secure the link at the ends, absorb a certain amount of heat from a small-time overload. On short-circuit, the weak points melt quickly. Operating characteristics, generally, are similar to those of the non-renewable fuse. A similar time-lag device has a built-up central element which absorbs enough of the heat created by a moderate overload that an appreciable operating delay is introduced.

Figure 7C shows a dual-element type which combines a soldered portion with a short piece of standard link. The weak points melt quickly under short-circuit, but not from simple overload. The overload element, which is capable of a great number of variations in design, consists here of two copper discs that are soldered together. One is attached to the standard fuse link, the other by means of a flexible wire, to the end piece of the assembly. A coiled spring exerts tension on this half. With an overload, the solder melts, and the discs are pulled apart, breaking the circuit. The interrupting capacity of this fuse is sometimes as great as 100,000 amps.

Current-Limiting and High-Capacity Fuses

The general appearance of a current-limiting fuse is illustrated in Fig. 8A. Terminals and fuse clips are made non-standard in order to prevent substitution of ordinary types in applications designed for current limitation. The nature of this device will be explained with the help of the next illustration.

Figure 8B represents a half-wave of short-circuit current pro-

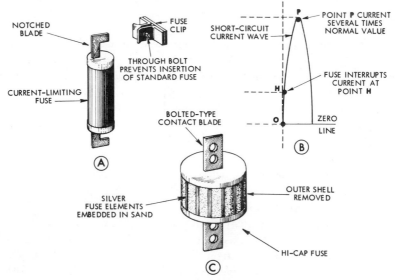

Fig. 8. Special fuses

duced by a fault which occurred at zero point of the circuit voltage wave. Current tends to rise to a peak value several times normal, creating effects similar to a lightning stroke. Lightning current flows the merest fraction of a second, but it wreaks tremendous destruction. Flow of short-circuit current, during two or three cycles, could wreck circuit breakers, switches, motor windings, and other equipment.

A current-limiting fuse must be able to withstand a flow of 200,000 amps in case of necessity, but the essential requirement is that it act swiftly enough to disrupt current flow before it rises to the peak represented by point *P* in Fig. 8B. Melting and arcing time of the element must be short enough to arrest the current at an intermediate point such as *H*. The resulting "let-through" current is then only a fraction of maximum possible value. Total destruction of equipment is prevented, and strains are reduced to harmless proportions.

The high-capacity, or hi-cap, unit of Fig. 8C is a low-resistance device with silver fuse elements. It is similar in many respects to the current-limiting fuse, being made in sizes up to 6000 amps, and having an interrupting capacity of 200,000 amps. The circuit is not broken with the same great speed, however, the "let-through" current being somewhat greater. These fuses are often employed in series with switches or circuit breakers that carry motor loads.

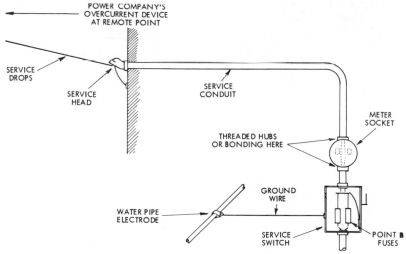

Fig. 9. Bonding service raceways

Grounding Service Raceway

Bonding of service raceways is illustrated here, by way of example. When a ground develops beyond point B, Fig. 9, which represents the service overcurrent device, fault current is readily interrupted before serious damage results. Should the ground occur in the service run ahead of B, however, there is nothing to limit flow of current except the power company's primary overcurrent unit, which may be quite remote from the service location.

It is for this reason that either a threaded hub or bonding must be relied on here. Resistance of the ground circuit must be made as low as possible, the object being to *incre*ase the rate of flow, if possible, so that the power company's remote protective device will operate to disconnect the supply wires. Connection between the service equipment and the grounding electrode should be as direct as possible, for a like reason.

Switchboards

The old job-fabricated switchboards are no longer found in modern commercial and industrial installations of any size. Free-

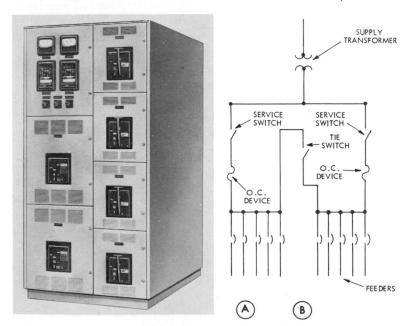

Fig. 10. Modern switchboards
Courtesy of I-T-E Circuit Breaker Co.

standing, totally-enclosed, factory-built units like the one shown in Fig. 10A are more compact and less expensive. They contain service, metering, and feeder control equipment.

On large projects, the double-end switchboard, illustrated by a line diagram in Fig. 10B, is widely accepted. Two bus-duct service runs emerge from the power company vault on the other side of a concrete wall. A pair of load-interrupter switches are employed, each feeding approximately one-half of the board. A tie circuit breaker makes it possible to connect the whole board to either service when desired.

Connection of bus-duct sections is largely a mechanical operation of assembling parts already engineered as to size and location. But the routing of conduits, pulling of wire, shaping and fastening it to lugs on the switchboard, still calls for individual initiative.

DISTRIBUTION SYSTEMS

Essential Components

The kind of distribution system in a given instance, is based of course upon the nature of the incoming service. It includes feeders, sub-feeders, and branch circuits, all of which have changed considerably in the course of a few years. Before analyzing them in detail, it is worth while investigating available forms of current supply. Their basic character was outlined in the chapter dealing with transformers. The matter of voltage between conductors, and that to ground, will now be considered.

Single-Phase, Three-Wire Circuits

Single-phase current is usually furnished from a transformer

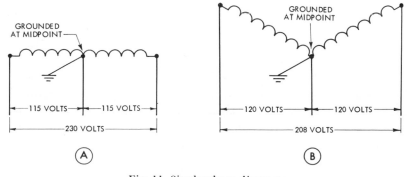

Fig. 11. Single-phase diagrams

whose secondary coils are joined outside the transformer case to form a center tap. Fig. 11A shows this connection, the midpoint becoming the grounded neutral conductor of the three-wire main. In this and following drawings, the primary winding is omitted in order to simplify. Potential between outer wires is 230 volts, that between either one and the neutral, 115 volts. This is also the voltage to ground.

Figure 11B represents a three-wire, single-phase circuit taken from the four-wire, three-phase, network system. Potential between the outer conductors is 208 volts. From either of them to the neutral conductor or to ground, it is 120 volts. Methods for calculating voltages in these diagrams will be explained in Chapter 8.

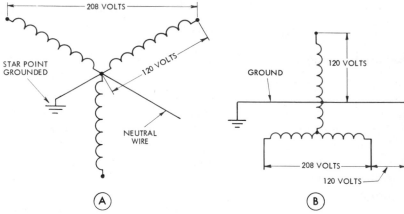

Fig. 12. Network and **T** connections

Three-Phase, 120-208-Volt Circuits

Potential between any two of the phase wires in Fig. 12A is 208 volts. That between any one of these wires and the neutral conductor is 120 volts. Ground potential, too, is of course 120 volts.

Figure 12B shows the T connection for obtaining four-wire, three-phase, 120-208-volt current, a main and a teaser transformer being used. The neutral conductor, which is grounded, is connected to a point ⅓ the distance from the midpoint of the main winding to the upper end of the teaser coil. Three-phase current may be taken from the outer wires at 208 volts, as in the network system, and single-phase current between any one of them and the neutral conductor, at 120 volts.

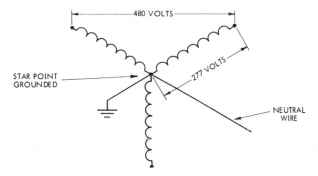

Fig. 13. 277-480-Volt star connection

Three-Phase, Four-Wire, 277-480-Volt System

The arrangement of Fig. 13 is similar to the original network system of Fig. 12. Note that the voltage to ground is higher, 277 volts instead of 120 volts. This system was popularized by the introduction of 277-volt fluorescent lighting. Motors are connected to the three 480-volt wires. Incandescent lighting and outlets for office machines must be supplied by single-phase 115-230-volt transformers or by three-phase 120-208-volt units. Variations of this connection are found upon occasion, such as the 240-416-volt and the 265-460-volt systems. Ground potentials in these cases are 240 volts and 265 volts, respectively.

Three-Phase, 480-Volt, Delta Connections

A three-phase, three-wire delta supply, Fig. 14A, is often found

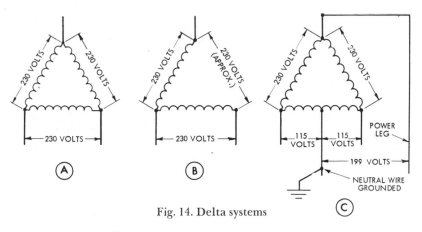

Fig. 14. Delta systems

in locations where there are a number of motors, and where load centers are established throughout the area for lighting and appliance panelboards. The open-delta connection of Fig. 14B is often used by power companies, as mentioned earlier, but it is seldom used in private installations.

The arrangement of Fig. 14C was also touched on in connection with transformer polarity. Four-wire services of this form are commonly provided where the motor load is small as compared to lighting requirements. The main point to note here is that the potential between the neutral conductor and either lighting wire is only 115 volts, whereas that between the neutral conductor and the power leg is 199 volts.

Feeder Systems

Fig. 15A shows the type of feeder commonly used in the past. Service wires at 115-230 volts, single-phase, connected to the main

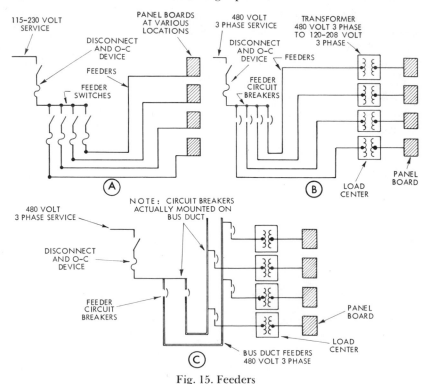

Fig. 15. Feeders

bus. Feeder switches extended overcurrent protection to individual feeders which supplied the various single-phase lighting and appliance panelboards.

The first significant change was the acceptance of 480-volt, three-phase supply from the power company, Fig. 15B. Polyphase feeders were run to load centers at various floors or locations, where step-down transformers converted the supply into the 120-208-volt, four-wire network system. This method has proven serviceable and economical in a majority of instances, because the original cost, including transformers, is not far different than the 115-230-volt system, and voltage regulation is far better.

Yet it lacks certain qualities that are desirable in the high-rise building, where runs are of considerable length, and where provisions for later expansion should be incorporated at the time of installation. Feeding upward from the basement and downward from the roof has been tried, because its effect is to reduce the height of the building by one-half. The two widely separated service locations, however, introduce complications.

The use of bus duct feeders, Fig. 15C, is the most recent change in high rise wiring. The duct occupies comparatively little cross-sectional space, and steps may be readily taken at the time of the original work to insure ease of future expansion. For example, floor chases can be made wide enough to accept paralleling runs of duct, and space allotted in electric rooms for additional distribution panels. Stab-in circuit breakers are inserted in the duct at each location to feed step-down transformers which, in turn, supply the panelboards.

Grounding Load-Center Transformers

A knotty problem connected with load-center distribution is the grounding of transformer secondary windings. The transformer case is grounded by the feeder conduit run. Some electricians also ground the neutral wire to the conduit, as in view A of Fig. 16. This is perhaps the most common method, but it is not a universally accepted one. The plan of using a ground bus which runs back to the service grounding electrode, Fig. 16B, is also followed. Another scheme is to ground it to the nearest waterpipe.

NEC 250–5 states that any wiring system operable at not more than 150 volts to ground must be grounded. Others should be grounded if operable at 300 volts or less to ground. Section 250–

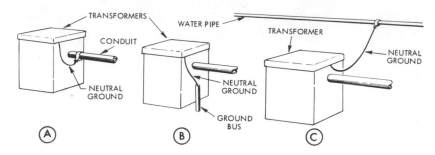

Fig. 16. Grounding transformers

112(a) requires that the neutral ground be made to a water pipe. This rule might seem to apply here, but the intent is clouded by Section 250–81 which speaks of a "metallic underground water piping system."

A load center is an isolated location, altogether remote from advantages to be gained from an underground network of piping. Faults occurring on circuits connected to the transformer should result in only "local" current flow. Any method which helps to thus restrict fault current would seem to be desirable. Certainly, a grounding bus which travels all the way back to a remote service location is not a reasonable answer.

One effective method is to bond conduits at a remote point, and to carry this "ground" back to the transformer. Since this is an expensive operation, the most practical solution is to rely on the conduit system, making certain that locknuts are tight and that crimping is properly done. If trouble eventually develops in this connection, code authorities will make definite provisions for correcting it.

Unprotected Taps

NEC 240–15 states that overcurrent devices shall be located at the point where a conductor receives current. It lists two important exceptions that are illustrated in Fig. 17. View A shows a No. 12 Type R conductor not over 10 ft in length, tapped to a No. 500 MCM Type R feeder. This method is acceptable if the carrying capacity of the No. 12 wire is not less than the sum of the allowable current-carrying capacities of other conductors which it supplies, the No. 12 conductor is encased in metallic raceway, and does not extend beyond the device to which it is connected.

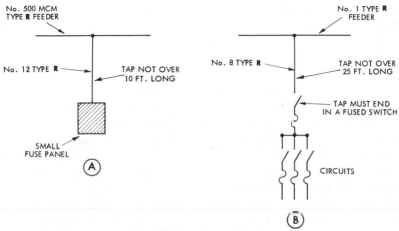

Fig. 17. Unprotected taps

The other exception is shown in Fig. 17B. A No. 8 Type R wire, not over 25 ft long, is tapped to a No. 1 Type R conductor. This practice is allowed provided that carrying capacity of the tap conductor is not less than one-third that of the larger conductor, and that it terminates in a single circuit breaker or set of fuses which limits flow of current to the allowable carrying capacity. In Fig. 17B, the carrying capacity of the No. 8 Type R conductor is 40 amps, while that of the No. 1 Type R conductor is 110 amps. The switch

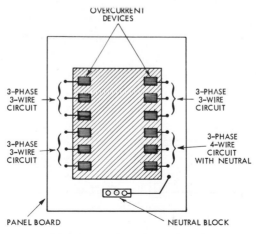

Fig. 18. Lighting and appliance panelboard

or circuit breaker may control a number of circuits or devices, as shown in the figure.

Panelboards

The NEC defines a lighting and appliance branch circuit panelboard as one having neutral conductors for at least 10 percent of its overcurrent devices which are rated at 30 amps or less. Fig. 18 shows a panelboard attached to a four-wire, three-phase feeder. There are three three-phase motor circuits and one three-phase lighting circuit; a total of 12 overcurrent devices. A neutral wire is associated with the lighting circuit, which has 3 overcurrent devices. Thus, 25 percent of them are provided with a neutral connection, and the panelboard falls within the above definition. Such a panelboard may not have more than 42 overcurrent devices, altogether, in a single enclosure.

NEC 384–16 states that a panelboard whose feeder has an overcurrent device larger than 200 amps ahead of it, shall be protected by overcurrent devices rated at a value not greater than that of the board. Fig. 19A illustrates this requirement. If the feeder is protected at 300 amps, and the panelboard is rated at 100 amps, a 100-amp overcurrent device will be needed. It should be noted, however, that if the panelboard were rated at 300 amps or more, no additional protection would be required.

Fig. 19B presents a variation of the rule, where the 115-230-volt

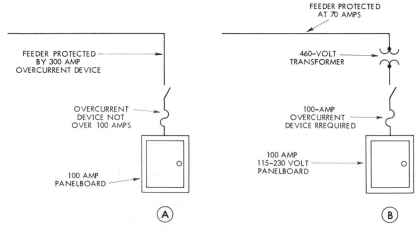

Fig. 19. Panelboard protection

panelboard is rated at 100 amps and the 460-volt supply transformer has 70-amp feeder protection. This panelboard must have a 100-amp overcurrent device directly ahead of it because the protection offered by the 70-amp fuse at 460 volts is equivalent to that of a 140-amp fuse at 230 volts.

Steady-Burning Loads

NEC 384–16 requires that overcurrent protective devices ahead of panelboards installed in commercial and industrial buildings where loads continue for long periods of time, shall have a rating not less than 125 percent of permissible circuit loading. This section merely calls attention to feeder and circuit limitations. Section 210–23(b) states that circuits for steady-burning loads shall not carry more than 80 percent of their current rating. Section 220–2 states that in such instances the unit loads specified in Table 220–2(a) (*See App.*) shall be increased by 25 percent.

Since these provisions are sometimes found confusing, an example is offered in Fig. 20. The office area supplied by the panelboard in the figure has an area of 4416 sq ft. Table 220–2(a) specifies a unit load of at least 5 watts per sq ft, or a total of: 4416 × 5 watts, which is 22,080 watts. NEC 220–2 requires that the feeder to the panelboard shall be large enough to handle 25 percent more than

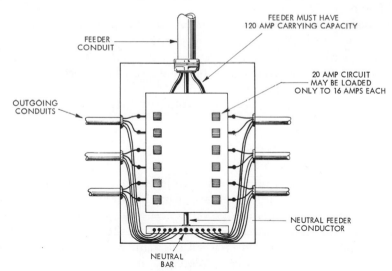

Fig. 20. Rules for steady-burning loads

this, or 27,600 watts. At 230 volts, the current equals: 27,600 watts/230 volts, or 120 amps.

There are twelve 20-amp circuits on the 3-wire, 115-230-volt panelboard. According to NEC 210–23(b), they cannot be loaded above 80 percent of 20 amps, or 16 amps. The total current that they can handle is equal to: 6 × 16 amps, or 96 amps on either side of the three-wire feeder. These lighting circuits will furnish the area with lighting power equal to 5 watts per sq ft, but they will be loaded to only 80 percent of their rating. The feeder, meanwhile, will be supplying current which loads the conductors to only 80 percent of their rating.

To allow for business machines and other electrical equipment, in addition to lighting, engineers often estimate load in a proposed office building at values from 7 watts per sq ft all the way up to 35 watts per sq ft. It is worth observing that under NEC 220–2(b) the current needed by each general use plug receptacle is assessed at 1½ amps.

Color Code

NEC 210–5 requires that color coding shall be followed. For three-wire circuits, the colors are: one black, one white, and one red. In four-wire circuits, the colors are: one black, one white, one red, and one blue. Wires of a given color must all be connected to the same feeder conductor. A green wire may be used only for grounding, and the white as an identified (neutral) conductor. Where more than one multi-wire circuit is carried through a single raceway, additional colors may be employed. This becomes necessary at times when 277-480-volt and 120-208-volt circuits are used in the same general area of the building.

HIGH-VOLTAGE PRIMARY SYSTEMS

Use of High-Voltage Circuits

High-voltage distribution has made rapid progress. Although limited mostly to industrial plants, it has been tried in commercial locations where considerable power is needed at points remote from the service location. In a number of instances, 4160-volt, three-phase feeders have been installed between the main switchboard and load centers throughout a building. Voltages up to 13.2 kv have also been used for this purpose. Services feeding industrial plants do not, ordinarily exceed 15,000 volts. Under NEC rules, service equipment shall be installed only in transformer vaults, or connected to approved metal-clad switchgear, when the voltage between conductors is greater than 15,000 volts.

Services

Modern high-voltage services are connected to unit substations, such as Fig. 21. Isolating switches or draw-out units are employed

Fig. 21. Unit substation and metalclad switchgear

Courtesy of I-T-E Circuit Breaker Co.

to disconnect the main circuit breaker or switch and the overcurrent devices, for repair or maintenance. The circuit breaker may be an automatic type, or it may be combined with approved fuses. An important precaution here, as with all switchboards, is to make certain that the frame is properly grounded.

INDUSTRIAL POWER DISTRIBUTION

Low-Voltage Radial System

Industrial power within a plant may be distributed in numerous ways. The simplest is the low-voltage radial system shown in the single-line diagram of Fig. 22. The plant consists of four buildings or distributing points. High-voltage service is obtained from the supply company at point S. A transformer or bank of transformers reduces the voltage for distribution to motors and lights. A separate low-voltage feeder is installed between the main switchboard and each distributing point. With this plan, failure of one low-voltage feeder will cut off power to its section of the plant.

This method has little to recommend it, aside from simplicity, for it requires a great deal of copper, and its constant losses are greater than in other systems. It is used, therefore, only in small establishments where distributing points are not too far removed from the service location. The supply could be single-phase if the load were predominantly lighting and small motors. But single-phase loads are rather uncommon with industrial plants. It will be

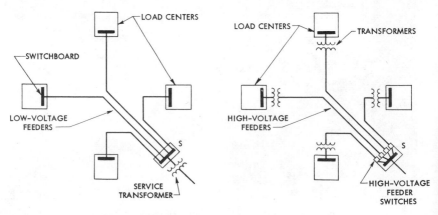

Fig. 22. Simple distribution system   Fig. 23. High-voltage distribution

assumed here that a single-line conductor represents a three-phase, four-wire feeder, and the single-line transformer, a bank of three-phase units.

High-Voltage Radial System

Fig. 23 represents a high-voltage radial layout. It is similar to the low-voltage arrangement except that high-voltage feeders are run to transformers at each distributing point. There, the voltage is reduced to its operating value. Copper losses are greatly reduced, but the initial cost of four small transformers is greater than that of a single large one.

Although this plan is superior, basically, to the first, it does not provide any greater assurance of continued service. If a feeder is damaged, its section is completely isolated from source of power, just as in the low-voltage scheme. A variation is sometimes employed, a single high-voltage feeder being extended from the service switch to a central location from which branches extend to each distributing point. Its only advantage is an initial saving in high-voltage cable.

Simple Loop System

Fig. 24 shows a layout which is superior, in certain respects, to the others. From the service location, a short feeder extends to point *T*, where it branches to a pair of circuit breakers which are connected to another feeder which makes a complete circle or loop. The loop taps off to each of the distribution centers *A, B, C,* and *D,* and

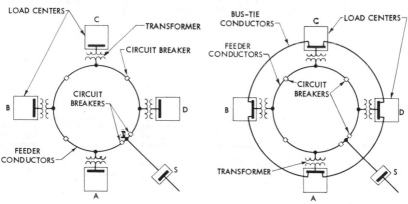

Fig. 24. Distribution loop   Fig. 25. System using bus-ties

it will be noted that a circuit breaker is inserted between each two distribution centers.

With this arrangement, any section of damaged feeder may be isolated from the others. If trouble develops in the transformer associated with section *A,* the nearest of the circuit breakers at *T* is opened, as well as the one between *A* and *B*. The remainder of the system will continue to operate. But electrical equipment in section *A* will be without power, as in the other two examples.

Loop System with Bus-Ties

Fig. 25 represents a system designed to eliminate complete shutdown of one part of the plant because of sectional feeder or transformer trouble. Fundamentally, it is similar to the plan of Fig. 24, but it has, in addition to the looped primary feeder, a loop connection between adjacent transformer secondaries. These connections, with circuit breakers at each switchboard location, form a continuous circle from *A* to *B,* to *C,* to *D,* to *A.*

There is considerable additional copper, but also complete as-

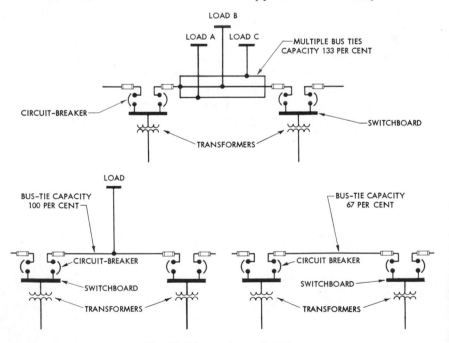

Fig. 26. Connection to bus-ties

surance that sectional primary faults will not isolate any section of the plant from a source of power. If the transformer in section A develops trouble, it may be cut out of the circuit and the section will continue to receive power from stations on either side by way of the secondary loop system.

Bus-Tie Conductors

These low-voltage loop connections are termed *secondary or bus-ties*. NEC 450–5 defines a secondary tie as a circuit operating at 600 volts or less between phases, and connecting two power sources or supply points such as secondaries of two transformers.

If loads are connected only at transformer supply points, and the bus tie is not protected by fuses limiting maximum current to 150 percent of conductor capacity, the current rating of the tie conductor shall not be less than 67 percent of full-load secondary current of the largest transformer. The lower right-hand illustration in Fig. 26 shows this system.

The carrying capacity of this same kind of tie must not be less than 100 percent of the rated secondary current of the largest transformer, if loads are also tapped from points other than at transformer locations. The lower left-hand illustration in Fig. 26 shows this tie.

A further variation is represented by the upper illustration. Here, the tie consists of multiple conductors per leg, with loads tapped to individual conductors between transformer locations. Unless such loads are tapped to every one of the tie conductors, the

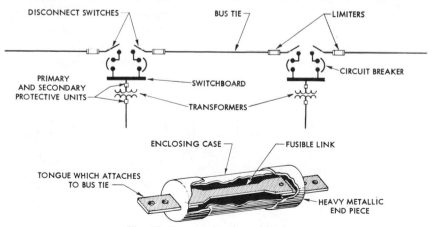

Fig. 27. Bus-tie circuit and limiter

combined capacity of the conductors between stations shall not be less than 133 percent of the rated secondary current of the largest transformer.

Limiters, Circuit Breakers, and Switches

Both ends of each tie conductor must be equipped with a protective device which will open under short-circuit conditions. This protection may consist of a fusible-link cable connector commonly known as a limiter, or an automatic circuit breaker set to operate under the same conditions. Secondary ties provided with limiters must have a switch at either end if the operating voltage exceeds 150 volts to ground.

In addition to these requirements for protection of tie conductors, transformers used in connection with these ties shall have, in the secondary circuit, an overcurrent device rated or set at not over 250 percent of rated current. And each transformer shall have a circuit breaker, actuated by a reverse-current relay, to disconnect the secondary winding if reverse current greater than rated, secondary current flows into the unit. The upper illustration in Fig. 27 shows a tie circuit with all the protection demanded by this section. The lower one shows a limiter.

Network Systems

A simple network system is represented at the left in Fig. 28. It

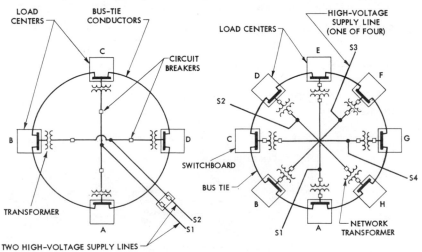

Fig. 28. Simple networks

has a secondary system identical with that of the preceding type, but the primary is somewhat different. Two primary feeders supply the transformers. Primary feeder *S1* is connected to the transformers which supply sections *A* and *C,* while *S2* is connected to those supplying *B* and *D.*

The illustration at the right shows a more complicated network which consists of eight distribution points fed by four primary feeders. The secondary circuits in both illustrations form a continuous circle of bus ties. This system provides the best guarantee of continued service and it is often employed in large plants.

The transformers used here are known as network units. They have secondary overcurrent devices, reverse-current relays, and co-ordinated, primary circuit, disconnects which remove the whole transformer from the line in case trouble develops within it or in the feeder circuit to which it is connected.

Cable and Conduit

Outdoors, high-voltage lines are protected by rigid conduit, duct like that in Fig. 29, or by the outer covering of direct-burial cable. Conduit runs should contain long sweeps rather than short bends, in order to reduce strain when drawing in cables. They should also be arranged to drain so that water pockets cannot form. Indoors, interlocked armored cable or approved unarmored cable may be placed in ladder-racks which are suitable for locations where direct physical hazards are unlikely.

Shielding

Nonleaded, fibrous-covered, rubber-insulated conductors used at voltages higher than a certain value shall be provided with a metal-

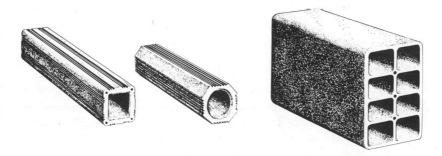

Fig. 29. Clay tile duct

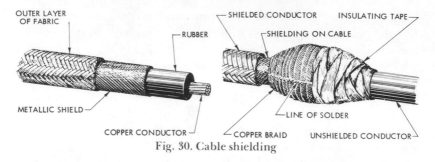

OUTER LAYER OF FABRIC — SHIELDED CONDUCTOR — INSULATING TAPE — RUBBER — SHIELDING ON CABLE — METALLIC SHIELD — LINE OF SOLDER — COPPER CONDUCTOR — COPPER BRAID — UNSHIELDED CONDUCTOR

Fig. 30. Cable shielding

lic or semiconducting shield which will confine the dielectric field. This shield is indicated at the left in Fig. 30. The term *dielectric field* refers to the static strain which is present in the air surrounding nonshielded high-voltage cables. This dielectric field breaks down oxygen in the air to form ozone and corona discharge which damage rubber insulation.

Shielding is required where conductors in damp locations are run in ducts or conduit, and where the voltage exceeds 2,000. In dry locations, shielding is not required unless the voltage exceeds 2,000 in a system with grounded neutral or 2,000 with ungrounded neutral. See NEC Table 710–5.

Stress Cone

The shielding material must be stripped back a safe distance where the cable terminates, such as in potheads or at joints. It is necessary to build a stress cone with rubber tape or other suitable insulating material, as indicated at the right in Fig. 30. Copper tape is wrapped over the insulation to a point about ¼″ from the middle of the cone. This wrapping is soldered together and to the shielding on the conductor. The purpose of the stress cone is to increase the length of leakage path at the end of the cable. Unless this is done, cable insulation often breaks down and carbonizes there.

Potheads

The code states that where cable conductors emerge from a metal sheath, and where protection against moisture or mechanical injury is necessary, the insulation of the conductors shall be protected by a pothead or other approved means. Fig. 31 illustrates a pothead. After cables are inserted, the body of the fitting is filled

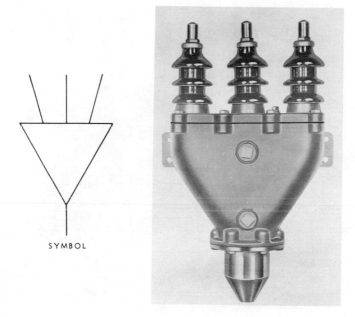

SYMBOL

Fig. 31. Pothead

Courtesy of G & W Electric Specialty Co.

with sealing compound. Although it is permissible to merely tape the ends of rubber or varnished-cambric cables, engineers usually specify that potheads be used in all cases, for terminating runs of cable.

Circuit Protection

High-voltage circuits may be guarded by circuit breakers or fuses of approved types. Figure 32 illustrates an oil-filled cutout which is made in sizes up to 300 amps and 7800 volts. Three of these units are connected to a gang-operating mechanism in the figure, so they may be used for disconnection, as well.

Motors

The code requires that motors operating at more than 7500 volts between conductors shall be installed in fire-resistant motor rooms. Motor branch circuit overcurrent protection may consist of a circuit breaker, suitable dry fuses, or oil-filled cutouts. A disconnecting means must be provided. If the branch circuit breaker

Fig. 32. High-voltage fuses
Courtesy of G & W Electric Specialty Co.

satisfies other code requirements as to location, it may serve in this capacity. The ganged oil-fuse cutout of Fig. 32 might be used in this way, too.

Running overcurrent protection may be a circuit breaker or a set of overcurrent units integral with the controller. Their rating is obtained from NEC Table 430–146, the same as for low voltage motors. Differential protection may be employed as running overcurrent protection. It consists of two or more sets of current transformers with associated relays.

REVIEW QUESTIONS

1. How far must a service conduit be from the inner surface of a wall in order to be considered outside the building?
2. On which side of a transformer are service disconnect and over-current devices usually placed?
3. Would a circuit breaker whose operation is fully automatic be approved as a service disconnect?
4. State the maximum interrupting capacity of a non-renewable cartridge fuse.
5. State the interrupting capacity expected of a current-limiting fuse.
6. Is a hi-cap fuse the same as a current-limiting fuse?
7. Is the T neutral connected to the junction of main and teaser windings?
8. What is the voltage between phase wires when the voltage to the star points is 277 volts?
9. What is the most recent type of feeder used in high-rise buildings?
10. A wiring system must be grounded if not over what voltage to ground?
11. State another name for an isolated center of distribution.
12. What is the longest permissible unprotected tap?
13. What is the minimum relative size of feeder and tap wire?
14. What size disconnect is required ahead of a panelboard which has 200-amp feeder protection?
15. What additional carrying capacity is required of a feeder that supplies a panelboard which serves steady-burning loads?
16. What steady-burning load is permitted on a 15-amp circuit?
17. What type of switchgear is used for high-voltage services?
18. In what kind of fitting should high-voltage cables be terminated?
19. What type fuse is required for a 15,000-volt circuit?
20. Does a 5000-volt motor require a special motor room?

Chapter Eight

Industrial and Commercial Calculations

Effect of NEC Rules

Discussion of commercial and industrial lighting in Chapter Four was based upon foot-candle intensities desired in certain locations. The NEC offers no recommendation as to the number of foot-candles, but Section 220-2(a), with its accompanying table, lists minimum values of watts per sq ft that must be supplied to a given area by its lighting feeder. Different "watts-per-sq-ft" ratings are assigned to several kinds of occupancies.

Although one type designated as an "Industrial Commercial (Loft) Building" is given a rating of 2 watts per sq ft, industrial locations are pretty much neglected. This treatment is to be expected, in the light of the countless, highly diversified industrial operations. Many commercial occupancies, on the other hand, are sufficiently standardized that specific values can be assigned them, for example: garages, restaurants, stores, and office buildings.

The minimum requirements for lighting power are usually exceeded today, especially in jobs which are properly engineered, because of emphasis on "easy seeing." In addition to carrying enough power for adequate illumination, feeders must provide energy for plug receptacles. The NEC contains no mandatory regulations dealing with them, except in respect to residential occupancies. This matter is left entirely to the discretion of the owner and his electrical representatives.

Chapter Plan

Calculations made necessary by the NEC rules will be explained in the early part of the chapter. This will be done largely by means of examples which include services, feeders, and circuits. The next

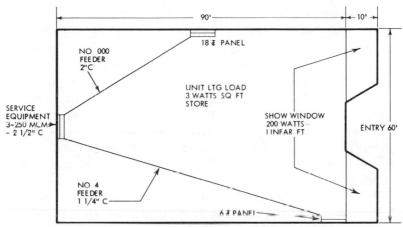

Fig. 1. Store building

section is concerned with principles relating to voltage, current, and power. Diagrams are made use of, and simplified mathematical methods are introduced. The final portion of the chapter is devoted to specialized items, some of which are constantly recurring in practice.

CIRCUITS, FEEDERS, AND SERVICES
SINGLE-PHASE LOAD

General Lighting

The interior of the store, Fig. 1, measures 60 ft by 90 ft, excluding the show window area, which is roughly 10 ft deep, its dimensions being noted on the illustration. The lighting service is 115-230 volts, single-phase. NEC Table 220–2(a) specifies a unit load of not less than 3 watts per sq ft for this occupancy. The floor area is equal to: 60 ft × 90 ft, or 5400 sq ft. Required lighting power is found by multiplying this area by 3 watts, giving a total of: 5400 × 3 watts, or 16,200 watts.

Store lighting usually falls within the classification of continuous-burning load, so that individual circuits may not furnish more than 80 percent of rated output. If 15-amp circuits are used for illumination, their maximum current is limited to: .8 × 15 amps, or 12 amps. This current will transmit power equal to: 12 amps × 115 volts, which is 1380 watts. The number of circuits to provide this wattage equals: 16,200 watts/1380 watts, or 11.7, which rounds out to 12.

Show Window Lighting

The minimum wattage for show window lighting is set forth in NEC 220–2(c) Ex. 2, which states that the amount can not be less than 200 watts for each linear foot of such window, measured horizontally along its base. This distance is equal to 29 ft for either one, or 58 ft in all. The minimum wattage is: 58 × 200 watts, which is 11,600 watts. It is worth noting here, that in some cases, depending upon circumstances, inspection authorities may class show-window lighting as continuous burning, so that the 80 percent and the 125 percent rules would apply. In the present case, it will not be considered so.

If 20-amp circuits are employed, they will each supply: 20 amps × 115 volts, or 2300 watts. The number of these circuits must be at least: 11,600 watts/2300 watts, which is 5+. Six fully-loaded circuits will include enough excess power to take care of lighting vestibule and entrance, the total load becoming: 6 × 2300 watts, or 13,800 watts.

Plug Receptacles

There are 80 general use plug receptacles in the building. NEC 220–2(b) designates these as "other outlets," and assigns a load rating of 1½ amps to each. Since they will be distributed by three-wire circuits, service and feeder must supply: 40 × 1½ amps, or 60 amps, which represents power equal to: 60 amps × 230 volts, or 13,800 watts. Plug receptacles are installed on 20 amp circuits, as a rule, each circuit furnishing power equal to: 20 amps × 115 volts, or 2300 watts. The required number will be not less than: 13,800 watts/2300 watts, which gives exactly 6. Customarily, at least two additional circuits would be provided to allow for expansion, but it will be assumed here that this factor was already taken account of in the large number of such outlets which are specified.

Feeders

The feeder to main panelboard *S*, Fig. 1, must have current carrying capacity equal to 125 percent of actual lighting requirements, in addition to the plug receptacle load. The lighting allowance is equal to: 1.25 × 16,200 watts, which is 20,250 watts. Adding 13,800 watts for plug receptacles, the power rating of the feeder is: 20,250 watts + 13,800 watts, or 34,050 watts. The current equals: 34,050 watts/230 volts, which is 148 amps.

Industrial and Commercial Calculations   201

NEC 220–4(d) states that the neutral feeder load shall be taken as the maximum unbalanced load. In other words, it is the greatest current to which the neutral conductor may be subjected if one of the main conductors were suddenly disconnected while the system was operating at full capacity. Here, such occurrence would find the neutral carrying a load of 148 amps, the same as the outer conductors. It must, therefore, be of the same size. Type RH-RW conductors are specified. Table 310–12 lists the nearest size of copper wire as No. 000, requiring a 2-in conduit.

The feeder to panelboard *W*, Fig. 1, which controls show window circuits, must have a carrying capacity not less than: 13,800 watts/230 volts, or 60 amps. Table 310–12 shows that No. 4 Type RH-RW conductors are satisfactory, while Table 1 lists the proper size of conduit as $1\frac{1}{4}$-in.

Service

Service conductors must be large enough to accommodate power supplied by the two feeders, the total amount being: 34,050 watts + 13,800 watts, or 47,850 watts. Their current rating must be equal to: 47,850 watts/230 volts, which is 208 amps. The nearest acceptable Type RH-RW conductor listed in Table 310–12 is No. 250MCM, which can be installed in $2\frac{1}{2}$-in conduit.

NEC 220–4(d) contains another provision which could be employed here if the situation warranted. The section states that a demand factor of 70 percent may be applied to that portion of the unbalanced load in excess of 200 amps. In the present instance, the excess is only 8 amps, which could be reduced to 6 amps by use of the factor. Such result is of no advantage because the neutral conductor must remain No. 250MCM, as before.

If the current had been 220 amps, however, requiring No. 300MCM main conductors, a smaller neutral could have been used. The excess over 200 amps of unbalanced load would be equal to: 220 amps − 200 amps, or 20 amps. When multiplied by the 70 percent demand factor, the excess is reduced to: .7 × 20 amps, or 14 amps. The neutral conductor would be considered as carrying: 200 amps + 14 amps, which is 214 amps, a value that falls within the capacity of No. 250 MCM Type RH-RW.

It should be noted that such demand factor may *not* be applied to any portion of load which consists of electric discharge lighting. The reason is that third harmonic current flows in neutral wires to which fluorescent units are connected. The subject of third harmonic current will be discussed later in this chapter.

Aluminum Conductors

Substitution of aluminum for copper in feeder and service conductors, will now be considered. A 148-amp conductor is needed as the feeder to Panelboard *S*. NEC Table 310–14 (*See App.*) lists the normal current carrying capacity of No. 000 Type RH-RW aluminum wire as 155 amps. However, a footnote to the table grants this conductor and a few others an increased carrying capacity when used for single-phase, three-wire, service and feeder runs. The No. 00 conductor, whose normal rating is 135 amps, is approved for 150 amps under the specified condition, and it may be used here. The conduit size remains 2-in, as before.

The feeder to panelboard *W* carries 60 amps. NEC Table 310–14 shows that a No. 3 conductor is satisfactory. In this case, also, the conduit size remains the same as before, 1¼-in. Current in the service conductors is 208 amps. Table 310–14 lists the carrying capacity of No. 350MCM conductor as 210 amps, making it the required size. Table 1 shows that 3-in conduit is necessary, one size larger than was needed for equivalent copper conductors.

THREE-PHASE LOAD

Survey of Location

The office location, Fig. 2, has an electric room in the Northwest corner. There is a data processing section at the Northeast end, a 120-208-volt panelboard in the Southeast corner, a 277-480-volt pan-

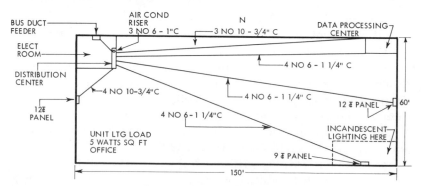

Fig. 2. Office building

elboard on the West wall, and a similar one on the East wall. The electric room receives power by way of a 480-volt, four-conductor, busduct riser. Most of the lighting is at 277-480 volts, fluorescent units being connected between phase wires and the neutral conductor. A small part of the lighting, and all plug receptacles, are connected to a 120-208-volt system obtained from delta-star transformers located in the electric room. The data processing center is also furnished with 120-208-volt power, except for a 15 hp, 400-cycle, motor generator to which a 480-volt, three-phase feeder runs from the electric room. Feeder switches for the 20 hp, 480-volt, three-phase air-conditioning system is also contained in the electric room.

277-480-Volt Lighting

The overall dimensions of the space are 60 ft by 150 ft, but the electric room takes up an area of 10 ft by 15 ft. Since the small room will be illuminated by a circuit taken from the secondary of the 120-208-volt transformer within the room, its area may be subtracted from the gross amount in determining lighting requirements. The office area is equal to: (60 ft × 150 ft) — (10 ft × 15 ft), which is 8850 sq ft. NEC Table 220–2(a) specifies a minimum unit load of 5 watts per sq ft, and Table 220–4(a) (see NEC) lists no demand factor for this type of occupancy. The necessary amount of lighting, therefore, is equal to: 8850 × 5 watts, or 44,250 watts.

All lighting will be at 277-480 volts, except for the space marked in dotted outline at the Southeast corner, which requires 120-208 volts for incandescent fixtures. The area of the section is 20 ft by 30 ft, a total of 600 sq ft. Its lighting needs represent: 600 × 5 watts, or 3000 watts. This amount can be subtracted from the total lighting power in order to find how much will be supplied at 277-480 volts. Taking 3000 watts from 44,250 watts, leaves 41,250 watts at the higher voltage.

It is customary to employ No. 12 as the smallest lighting conductor in large offices, despite the fact that the NEC permits No. 14. In some cases, 15-amp overcurrent devices are provided, even though No. 12 wire is used. Here, 20-amp circuit protection will be employed, the rating of the circuit being taken at 20 amps under provisions of NEC 210–3. Offices today, are generally continuous-burning loads, so that the circuits may not be loaded beyond the 80 percent point, which is equal to: .8 × 20 amps × 120 volts, or 1920 watts.

The number of 277-volt circuits will be: 41,250 watts/1920 watts, which gives 21+ or 22. This choice is subject to further modification, because the number of circuits in a standard, three-phase, four-wire panelboard is divisible by three. The nearest such figure in the present case is 24. Since the lighting is evenly divided between the two higher voltage panelboards, they will have 12 circuits each.

120-208-Volt Lighting and Power

The 120-208-volt system must take care of 3000 watts office lighting. If 20-amp circuits are employed, each may be loaded to 80 percent of capacity, which is 1920 watts. Two of them will be needed. There are 85 miscellaneous plug receptacles. At 1½ amps each, they will need: 85 × 1½ amps × 120 volts, which is 15,300 watts. A fully-loaded 20-amp circuit will provide 2400 watts, so that the number required for all will equal: 15,300 watts/2400 watts, or 6.4, which means 7. The 120-208-volt panelboard, therefore, will have 9 circuits.

The 120-208-volt transformers must also furnish 15 kva, three-phase, four-wire power to the processing center. A feeder will be run directly from the electric room to the location. The panelboard for this area is especially designed to handle the various machine circuits and the control equipment needed for the 400-cycle generating equipment.

Total required 120-208-volt power may now be determined by adding the various loads. The small panelboard takes: 3000 watts + 15,300 watts, or 18,300 watts. The data processing center needs 15 kva, which is a high-power-factor load that may be added directly to the lighting value. All that remains is the relatively small amount of power needed to illuminate the electric room, and which may be taken at 600 watts. Adding these amounts, the total cannot be less than: 18,300 watts + 15,000 watts + 600 watts, which is 33,900 watts.

Sub-Feeders

The size of the sub-feeder to the 120-208-volt panelboard is based upon: (1.25 × 3000 watts) + 15,300 watts, or 19,050 watts. Three-phase line current is equal to watts divided by the product of 1.73 and phase voltage. Phase voltage here is 208, which, multiplied by 1.73, gives 360 volts. Line current equals: 19,050 watts/360 volts, or 53 amps. NEC Table 310–12 shows the nearest size Type R wire as No. 6, with a carrying capacity of 55 amps. Table 1 shows that 4 No. 6 conductors may be installed in 1¼-in conduit. The next section of the chapter will give simplified methods for solving three-phase problems.

Each of the 277-480-volt panelboards must supply one-half of the total lighting load. Since this is a steady-burning application, the total load is equal to: 1.25 × 41,250 watts, or 51,560 watts. Each panelboard will require a feeder capable of supplying: $\frac{51,560}{2 \times 1.73 \times 480 \text{ volts}}$, or 31 amps. The nearest size of Type R wire listed in Table 310–12 is No. 8, whose current-carrying capacity is 40 amps. Three No. 8 conductors in ¾-in conduit will supply the West panelboard. Because of voltage drop (see later), the East panelboard is supplied by three No. 6's in 1¼-in conduit.

NEC Table 430–150 lists a current of 20 amps for the 15 hp, three-phase, 480-volt motor that drives the high-frequency generator. This value is to be multiplied by 1.25, as explained earlier, so that the rating of the conductor may not be less than: 1.25 × 20 amps, or 25 amps. No. 10 wire and ¾-in conduit are required.

The Table shows a current of 26 amps for the 20 hp, three-phase, 480-volt air-conditioning motor. This value, too, is multiplied by 1.25 so that the rating of the supply conductor can not be less than: 1.25 × 26 amps, or 33 amps. Table 310–12 shows the nearest size Type R conductor to be No. 6. Three of them require a 1-in conduit.

One sub-feeder remains, the 120-208-volt run from the electric room to the data center. The necessary power is 15,000 watts. Using the three-phase formula, current equals: 15,000 watts/360 volts, or 42 amps. Table 310–12 lists No. 6 Type R as the nearest size, and Table 1 indicates 1¼-in conduit.

Main Feeder

The power to be furnished by the main feeder is obtained by adding that supplied at 480 volts to that at 208 volts. First, it is advisable to change into watts the current and voltage for the 15 hp motor which drives the motor-generator, and the 20 hp motor which drives the air-conditioning system. This may be done in a way that is precisely the opposite to that for determining current from voltage and wattage. Line current and phase voltage are multiplied together, along with the factor 1.73.

The 15 hp motor requires 20 amps at 480 volts, the equivalent power being 1.73 × 20 amps × 480 volts, which is approx. 16,600 watts. Power for the 20 hp motor equals: 1.73 × 26 amps × 480 volts, which is 21,600 watts. A further adjustment is necessary. NEC 430–24 states that conductors supplying two or more motors shall have a carrying capacity equal to 125 percent of the full-load current rating of the highest rated motor plus the sum of full-load currents of the remainder.

NEC 430–25 carries the matter a step further, stating that when a feeder supplies a load which combines lighting and motors, an allowance equal to that required by NEC 430–24 shall be included in the feeder capacity. Taking 125 percent of motor current here, is the same as multiplying the above value of power by 1.25. Power for the larger of the two motors becomes: 1.25 × 21,600 watts, or 27,000 watts. Feeder capacity for both must be the sum of these two, or: 27,000 watts + 16,600 watts, giving a total of 43,600 watts.

Total feeder load equals: 43,600 watts + 51,560 watts + 19,050 watts + 15,000 watts + 600 watts, or 129,810 watts. This value may be used in determining current in the outer conductors. The only current in the neutral conductor will be from the 277-480-volt lighting. It may appear at first glance, that the 120-208-volt lighting power should be included, because the circuit has a neutral wire. The fact must be noted, however, that this conductor is entirely isolated from the main feeder, its current being obtained solely by way of transformation.

Current flowing in the outer conductors will equal: 129,810 watts/830 volts, or 157 amps. That in the neutral conductor will be: 51,560 watts/830 volts, or 62 amps. NEC 328–2 states that bare copper conductors in unventilated enclosures shall be permitted a continuous current-carrying capacity equal to 1000 amps per sq in of cross-section. For ventilated enclosures, the allowable capacity may be increased to 1200 amps per sq in. The duct will be classified as unventilated, so that the cross-sectional area of outer conductors will be: 157/1000 × 1 sq in, or .16 sq in. That of the neutral conductor will be: 62/1000 × 1 sq in, or .06 sq in.

Practical Observations

It is seldom necessary for the electrician to concern himself about the size of busduct conductor. This equipment is furnished under a manufacturer's nameplate, which states carrying capacity assigned it by the U-L Laboratories. Another practical fact is that a 150-amp busduct feeder would not likely be run from the service location to a single floor of a building. A more economical procedure would be to extend a 600-amp or larger duct to four or more floors of the building, with a circuit breaker tap connection at each electric room. This matter was discussed earlier, in connection with high-rise feeders.

Both installations analyzed here in detail, impose a balanced load on the phase conductors. That is, each of the three main feeder wires carries the same value of current. Such is the usual condition found on new projects, distribution layouts being designed with this object in view. It is not always possible to gain a perfect balance, however, where an existing plant is involved. For example, in the expansion of a huge manufacturing establishment, one of the buildings may have a large single-phase system which it is impractical to change. In this event, it is necessary to accept the unbalanced demand on the supply conductors and other equipment. Calculations relating to this sort of load will be considered in the next section of this chapter.

VOLTAGE, CURRENT, AND POWER

Three-Phase Chart

Two methods for determining three-phase voltage relationships are explained in this section. One makes use of diagrams or charts, which involve only measurement of distances. The other employs simple tables whose application requires no mathematical operations other than addition. Although the second plan gives more accurate solutions, the diagram scheme will be presented first because it clearly illustrates the principles involved.

The upper chart in Fig. 3 consists of two straight lines which meet at an angle of 120 degrees, each line being exactly 150 units in length. The scale shown underneath the chart is to aid in taking measurements. A length unit may represent any convenient number of volts. Thus, if each is taken as 2 volts, a whole line, measured from the zero point on the chart, would stand for 100 volts. Again, if it is desired to mark a point representing 120 volts, this would be done at the 40th division if each stands for 3 volts, or at the 30th if each stands for 4 volts. The only necessary precaution is to see that the same value is assigned to a unit of length throughout the whole process.

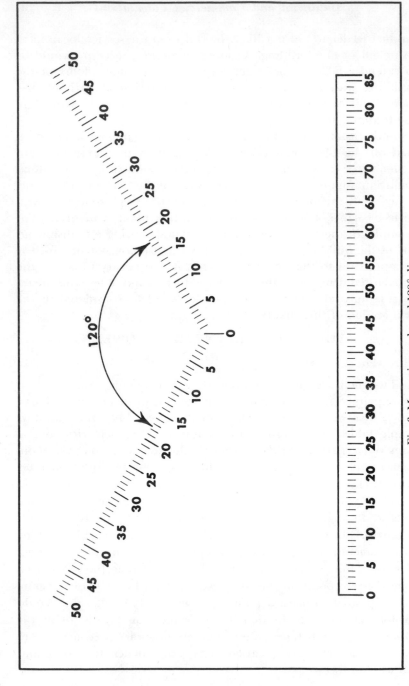

Fig. 3. Measuring scale and 120° diagram

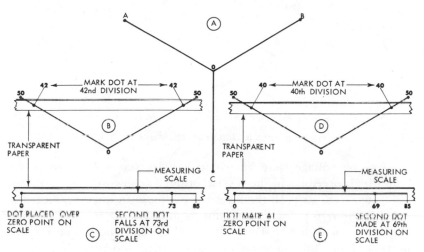

Fig. 4. Star or Y connection

Star Voltages

View A, Fig. 4 illustrates the usual Star diagram, which is both a symbol and a true sketch of voltage relationships existing in the circuit. Phases are designated as *A*, *B*, and *C*, one end of each meeting the others at the common, or star, point *O*. They may be considered as three primary or secondary windings of transformers, or as stator windings of an alternating current generator. Voltages between the outer ends and the star ends of the three phases are called star voltages. Those between the open ends, *A* to *B*, *B* to *C*, and *C* to *A*, are called line or phase voltages.

When either voltage is known, the other may be determined with the help of Fig. 3, which actually represents any one of the three triangular areas, *AOB*, *BOC*, and *COA* of Fig. 4. Suppose it is known that the star voltage is 126. To obtain phase voltage, proceed as in Fig. 4B, which is a small-scale drawing of Fig. 3.

If each division on the two legs of the figure equals 3 volts, 42 of them will stand for 126 volts. Lay a strip of transparent paper across the diagram as shown in Fig. 4B, and mark two such points, one for either leg. Transfer the paper strip to the measuring scale, as indicated in Fig. 4C, the lefthand dot coinciding with the zero point on the scale. The second dot will then fall on the 73rd division, and since each one is rated at 3 volts here, phase voltage is equal to: 73 × 3 volts, or 219 volts.

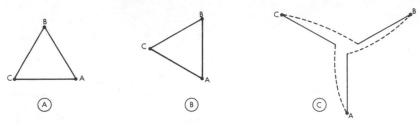

Fig. 5. Delta connection

If phase voltage were known to be 416, star voltage could be found by proceeding in the reverse order, as shown in Fig. 4D. Lay the transparent strip on the measuring line, as indicated, and mark a dot at the zero point. If each unit is allowed to represent 6 volts, 69 of them will denote 414 volts, a value sufficiently close for the purpose. Mark this point on the paper strip, and then place it on the angle diagram, Fig. 4E, adjusting the position until start and finish dots are evenly distant from center O. This will occur at the 40th divisions, so that star voltage is equal to: 40 × 6 volts, or 240 volts.

In order to simplify discussion, the paper strip and the measuring scale will be omitted from remaining illustrations. But the reader should understand that they are employed in all cases.

Delta Voltages

View A, Fig. 5, is the familiar delta symbol. Unlike the star diagram, it is merely a symbol, and does not illustrate the true relationship between phase voltages. In the figure, the angle between any two phase windings appears to be only 60 degrees. Actually, it is 120 degrees, just as in the star connection.

Views B and C, Fig. 5, will help explain the situation. Let the delta of view A be turned through a small angle to make the *B-A* leg vertical, Fig. 5B, the lettering remaining unchanged. Now, separate the three windings and arrange them as in Fig. 5C, each phase leg parallel to its original direction. Winding *A* is in the vertical position of *B-A* in Fig. 5B, winding *B* is parallel to *B-C* of Fig. 5B, and winding *C* is parallel to *C-A*.

The effect is exactly that of a star winding, except for the open star ends. If the line end of phase *B* (called *B*-line) is joined to the star end of phase *A* (called *A*-star), *A*-line to *C*-star, and *C*-line to *B*-star, as indicated by the dotted lines in Fig. 5C, a true representa-

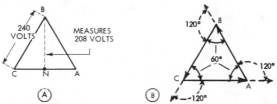

Fig. 6. (A) Finding voltage from power leg to neutral;
(B) Angular relationships in the delta connection.

tion of the delta connection is seen.

There is a single instance in which use of the charts is not recommended. This is in connection with the power-leg voltage of the four-wire, 120-240-volt delta arrangement discussed in Chapter 6. In order to find the voltage from power leg to neutral, the conventional delta diagram may be used, as shown in Fig. 6A. If the figure is drawn accurately to scale so that each side represents 240 volts, the voltage from the power connection *B* to the neutral point *N* will be found to measure approximately 208 volts.

This result may seem incorrect in the light of earlier paragraphs, since the conventional delta diagram, Fig. 6A, shows an angle of only 60-degrees between phase voltages instead of 120 degrees. Yet, the voltages of the three phase supply line are certainly 120 degrees apart.

Referring to Fig. 6B, the angular relationship may be seen by checking the angles outside the triangle which have been extended to show the 120 degree relationship with the delta symbol.

Voltages in Delta-Star Transformation

Fig. 7A illustrates a transformer whose primary windings are connected delta, and whose secondary windings are connected star, the turns-ratio between primary and secondary being 9 to 1. Primary phase voltage is the same as line voltage, which is 2500 volts. Since turns-ratio is 9 to 1, the voltage induced in each star leg of the secondary by the corresponding leg of the primary will be: $\frac{1}{9} \times 2500$ volts, or 277 volts.

This is the star voltage of the secondary winding. In order to find secondary phase voltage, the chart of Fig. 3 may be called upon, as shown in Fig. 7B. Allowing 6 volts for each division, 46 of them will equal 276 volts, which is sufficiently close here. Laying off 46 divisions on either leg, and then measuring between them,

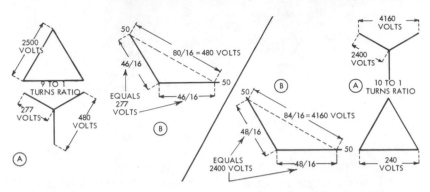

Fig. 7. Delta-star diagram   Fig. 8. Star-delta diagram

80 of the $\frac{1}{16}$ marks are included, showing that secondary phase voltage is: 80 × 6 volts, or 480 volts. Thus, when a pressure of 2500 volts is applied to the terminals of a 9 to 1, delta-star transformer, the secondary winding will produce 480 volts.

Voltages in Star-Delta Transformation

The transformer in Fig. 8A has star primary, and delta secondary windings. Primary phase voltage is 4160, and the turns ratio between primary and secondary windings is 10 to 1. Referring to Fig. 8B, which is of course Fig. 3 in miniature, an allowance of 50 volts per division on the measuring scale will require approximately 84 of the $\frac{1}{16}$-in marks for 4160 volts. Placing the scale on the diagram, the distances from center O are balanced at 48 on either leg, showing that star voltage of the primary winding equals: 48 × 50 volts, which is 2400 volts.

Since turns-ratio is 10 to 1, each primary coil will induce in its secondary coil a voltage equal to $\frac{1}{10}$ × 2400 volts, or 240 volts. In the delta connection, secondary winding voltage is also the phase voltage, so that phase or line voltage is 240. It is evident, then, that a star-delta, 10 to 1, 4160-volt transformer will have a secondary voltage of 240.

T-Voltages

It was stated in Chapter 6 that the method of obtaining the neutral voltage in the T transformer would be explained later. View A of Fig. 9 shows secondary main and teaser windings of a set of T transformers. Voltage across the terminals of the main winding is

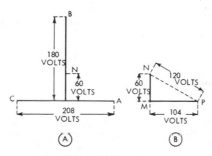

Fig. 9. T diagram

208, while that of the teaser winding is 180, the lower end of the teaser coil being connected to the mid-point of the main coil, as noted earlier. The neutral point is taken ⅓ the distance upward from the lower end of the teaser winding.

Figure 9B shows voltage relationships. The right triangle *MNP* is drawn to scale, base *MP* representing 104 volts, which is one-half that of the main winding. Vertical leg *MN*, drawn to the same scale as *MP* indicates 60 volts, which is ⅓ of 180 volts. Measurement of line *NP*, which indicates voltage between the neutral point and one end of the main winding, shows its value to be 120 volts. The same result will be obtained between the neutral point and the other end of the main winding. Also, the voltage from *N* to *B*, the upper end of the teaser winding, equals: 180 volts −60 volts, which is 120 volts. Between any one of the line wires and the neutral point, therefore, the voltage is 120.

Current in Star and Delta Windings

It is obvious that current flowing in each leg of the star windings of Fig. 10A, 69 amps, is exactly the same as that in the supply wire to which it is attached. This is not true of the delta connection of Fig. 10B, because current from any one of the line wires passes into two windings. The current in each delta leg is found to be: line current/1.73. Thus, if the supply current is 69 amps, the current per leg, or "coil current" as it is often designated, is equal to 69 amps/1.73, or 40 amps.

This same result might have been obtained with the aid of Fig. 3, as indicated in Fig. 10C. The 69th division mark is noted on the measuring scale. When the scale is laid on the diagram, and adjusted until the "end" marks are equally distant from point *O*, the

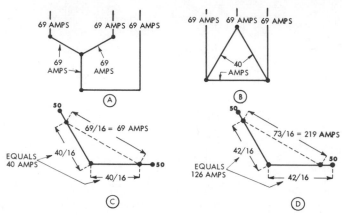

Fig. 10. Current relationships

readings are found to include 40 divisions, which means 40 amps per leg.

With current per delta leg given, line current may be obtained by the reverse process, Fig. 10D. Coil current here is 126 amps. Allowing 3 volts per division, 42 of them are marked on each leg of the diagram. Measuring between them, the number of divisions is found to be 73, which shows line current equal to approximately: 73 × 3 amps, or 219 amps.

Unbalanced Three-Phase Loads

In practice, unbalanced three-phase loads must frequently be considered. Fig. 11 shows this kind of circuit, the three elements of an industrial heating unit being of different sizes. The element connected between phase wires *A* and *B* draws 80 amps, the one between *A* and *C* draws 70 amps, and the one between *C* and *B* draws 60 amps. Current flowing in each of the line wires may be discovered with the aid of Fig. 3.

Views *B* and *C* of Fig. 11 illustrate how the current in each of the line wires is found. The chart of Fig. 3 is used, each unit representing 2 amps. Wire *A* supplies 80 amps to phase leg *BA* and 70 amps to leg *AC*. In Fig. 11B, 40 divisions are marked off on one leg of the figure, and 35 on the other, representing 80 amps and 70 amps respectively. Measurement shows the distance between them as 65 divisions, which means: 65 × 2 amps, or 130 amps.

Wire *B* furnishes 80 amps to *BA* and 60 amps to *BC*. Referring

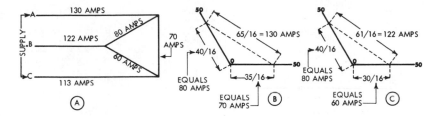

Fig. 11. Unbalanced delta

to Fig. 11C, 40 divisions representing 80 amps are noted on one leg of the figure, and 30 divisions for 60 amps, on the other leg. The distance between marked points is 61 units, so that current in *B* equals: 61 × 2 amps, or 122 amps. Line *C* furnishes 70 amps to leg *AC* and 60 amps to leg *BC*, requiring the notations 35 and 30. Here, the distance between is about 56-½ divisions, which are equal to: 56.5 × 2 amps, or 113 amps. (Draw sketch for current in wire C).

The above method can be employed in all cases of unbalanced three-phase circuits. For those who may prefer mathematical procedures, however, a not too complicated formula will be set forth:

$$L = \sqrt{b^2 + c^2 + bc}$$

L = line current
b = current in one leg
c = current in second leg

Thus, for line wire *A* in Fig. 11A:

$$L = \sqrt{80^2 + 70^2 + (80 \times 70)}$$
$$= \sqrt{6400 + 4900 + 5600}$$
$$= \sqrt{16,900} = 130 \text{ amps, the same value}$$

obtained by the use of Fig. 3.

Combining Single-Phase and Three-Phase Loads

In view *A*, Fig. 12, the current per leg of the delta-connected load is 40 amps, and the line current is approx. 69 amps. A single-phase heater which draws 40 amps is to be attached across phase wires *A* and *B*, view *B*, Fig. 12. It is common practice to add the single-phase current directly to existing three-phase current in order to find the new value of line current in supply wires *A* and *B*. Here, the current would equal: 69 amps + 40 amps, or 109 amps.

This solution is not exactly true, because the original three-phase current will be somewhat out of phase with the added single-phase

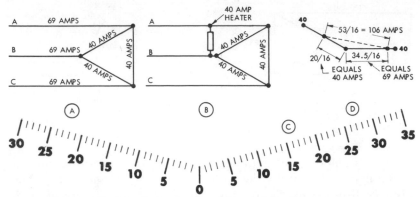

Fig. 12. Single-phase and three phase diagram

current. They must be combined as shown in Fig. 12C. The illustration is similar to Fig. 3, except that the legs of the diagram meet at an angle of 150 degrees instead of 120 degrees. As shown in the small view, Fig. 12D, where each $\frac{1}{16}$-in represents 2 amps, spaces representing 69 units and 40 units are laid off. When the distance between them is measured, line current is seen to be about 106 amps instead of 109 amps.

As shown here, the error is usually not great enough to warrant departure from the customary approximation. The facts are set forth, however, in order to give a fully rounded discussion. For those who prefer mathematical solutions, a formula similar to the earlier one is presented:

$$L = \sqrt{a^2 + b^2 + (1.73 \times a \times b)}$$

Substituting the figures:

$$L = \sqrt{69^2 + 40^2 + (1.73 \times 69 \times 40)}$$
$$= \sqrt{4761 + 1600 + 4775} = \sqrt{11136} = 105.5 \text{ amps.}$$

Power

The next section of this chapter includes certain tables which make the calculation of power a simple procedure. Before looking at them, however, standard formulas will be listed for reference:

Direct current power = Amps × Volts

Single-phase power at 100% power factor = Amps × Volts

Single-phase power at any power factor = Amps × Volts × P.F.

Three-phase power at 100% P.F. = 1.73 × Amps × Volts

Multiplier	115	120	208	230	240	277	416	440	460	480
1	115	120	208	230	240	277	416	440	460	480
2	230	240	416	460	480	554	832	880	920	960
3	345	360	624	690	720	831	1248	1320	1380	1440
4	460	480	832	920	960	1108	1664	1760	1840	1920
5	575	600	1040	1150	1200	1385	2080	2200	2300	2400
6	690	720	1248	1380	1440	1662	2496	2640	2760	2880
7	805	840	1456	1610	1680	1939	2916	3080	3220	3360
8	920	960	1664	1840	1920	2216	3328	3520	3680	3840
9	1035	1080	1872	2070	2160	2493	3744	3960	4140	4320

Table 1. Line voltage and star voltage, D C and single-phase power

Three-phase power at any P.F. = 1.73 × Amps × Volts × P.F. (*Note: The three-phase formula applies for either star or delta connection*)

TABULAR CALCULATIONS

Preliminary Explanation

With the aid of the three tables which follow, it is possible to determine direct current, single-phase, and three-phase power without performing any multiplications whatever. Also, the value of current for direct current, single-phase, or three-phase loads may be found without arithmetical division. All that is needed, aside from the tables, is a sheet of columnar paper. The method will be set forth by means of examples.

Problems Under Table 1

Example 1—The star voltage of a set of three-phase transformers

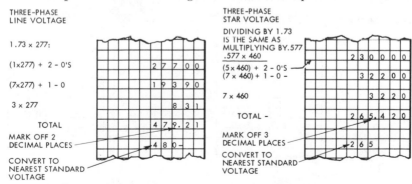

THREE-PHASE
LINE VOLTAGE

1.73 x 277:

(1x277) + 2 - 0'S

(7x277) + 1 - 0

3 x 277

TOTAL

MARK OFF 2
DECIMAL PLACES

CONVERT TO
NEAREST STANDARD
VOLTAGE

	2	7	7	0	0
	1	9	3	9	0
			8	3	1
	4	7	9	2	1
	4	8	0		

THREE-PHASE
STAR VOLTAGE

DIVIDING BY 1.73
IS THE SAME AS
MULTIPLYING BY.577
.577 x 460

(5 x 460) + 2 - 0'S
(7 x 460) + 1 - 0 -

7 x 460

TOTAL -

MARK OFF 3
DECIMAL PLACES

CONVERT TO
NEAREST STANDARD
VOLTAGE

	2	3	0	0	0
	3	2	2	0	0
	3	2	2	0	
	2	6	5	4	2	0
	2	6	5		

Fig. 13. Illustration for example 1　　　Fig. 14. Illustration for example 2

is given as 277 volts. What is line voltage? (See Fig. 13)

Since line voltage is equal to star voltage $\times$ 1.73, the procedure is as follows:

Find the column headed "277" in Table I.

Locate the first numeral of the multiplier which is 1 in the column which is headed, "Multiplier."

Follow across to the 277 column and set the result down on the squared paper, adding two zeros as shown in the illustration, Fig. 13.

Locate the second numeral of the multiplier, which is 7, and follow across to the 277 column, noting the amount shown there directly under the first notation, after adding one zero.

Locate the third numeral of the multiplier, which is 3, and follow across to the 277 column, noting the amount directly beneath the other two (with no zeros added in this last notation).

Total the columns, and mark off two decimal places (because there are two in the multiplier), obtaining the answer 479.21 volts, which is accepted in practical numbers as 480 volts.

Example 2—Line voltage is 460. What is star voltage? (Fig. 14)

Star voltage is equal to line voltage divided by 1.73. But, division by 1.73 is the same as multiplication by .577. This will be done here.

Proceed as before, locating the 460-volt column, and taking the numbers 5, 7, and 7, one after the other in the multiplier, noting the results on squared paper, as shown.

Add the numbers, and mark off *three* decimal places (because there are three in the multiplier), giving 265.4 volts, or the practical value of 265 volts.

Example 3—A direct current motor draws 125 amps at 230 volts. How much power does it consume? (See Fig. 15)

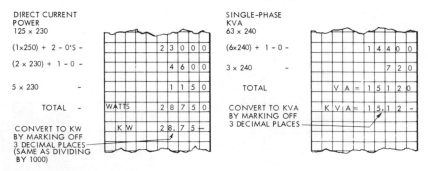

Fig. 15. Illustration for example 3   Fig. 16. Illustration for example 4

AMPS	VOLTAGE							
	2 0 8	2 2 0	2 3 0	2 4 0	4 1 6	4 4 0	4 6 0	4 8 0
1	3 6 0	3 8 1	3 9 8	4 1 5	7 2 0	7 6 1	7 9 6	8 3 1
2	7 2 0	7 6 2	7 9 6	8 3 0	1 4 4 0	1 5 2 2	1 5 9 2	1 6 6 2
3	1 0 8 0	1 1 4 3	1 1 9 4	1 2 4 5	2 1 6 0	2 2 8 3	2 3 8 8	2 4 9 3
4	1 4 4 0	1 5 2 4	1 5 9 2	1 6 6 0	2 8 8 0	3 0 4 4	3 1 8 4	3 3 2 4
5	1 8 0 0	1 9 0 5	1 9 9 0	2 0 7 5	3 6 0 0	3 8 0 5	3 9 8 0	4 1 5 5
6	2 1 6 0	2 2 8 6	2 3 8 8	2 4 9 0	4 3 2 0	4 5 6 6	4 7 7 6	4 9 8 6
7	2 5 2 0	2 6 6 7	2 7 8 6	2 9 0 5	5 0 4 0	5 3 2 7	5 5 7 2	5 8 1 7
8	2 8 8 0	3 0 4 8	3 1 8 4	3 3 2 0	5 7 6 0	6 0 8 8	6 3 6 8	6 6 4 8
9	3 2 4 0	3 4 2 9	3 5 8 2	3 7 3 5	6 4 8 0	6 8 4 9	7 1 6 4	7 1 7 9

Table 2. Three-phase KVA

Follow the same method as before, locating the 230-volt column, and using multipliers 1, 2, and 5 in turn. The answer is seen to be 28,750 watts, which may be changed, by marking off three decimal places, to 28.75 kw.

Example 4—A 240-volt, single-phase heater draws 63 amps. How many kva does this amount to? (See Fig. 16)

A point to note here is that only one zero is added to the first number written down, because there are only two figures in the multiplier. The answer to the example is 15.12 kva. If the power factor is unity, the power is also equal to 15.12 kw. This is true of all examples presented here.

Problems Under Table 2

Example 5—A small plant draws 127 amps, three-phase, at 460 volts. What is the kva input? (See Fig. 17)

Note that the values given in the columns are not simple multiples of the voltages at the top. As shown in the illustration, the pro-

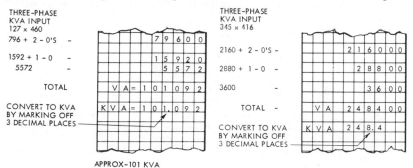

THREE-PHASE
KVA INPUT
127 x 460

796 + 2 - 0'S   -

1592 + 1 - 0   -
5572   -

TOTAL

CONVERT TO KVA
BY MARKING OFF
3 DECIMAL PLACES

APPROX-101 KVA

THREE-PHASE
KVA INPUT
345 x 416

2160 + 2 - 0'S -

2880 + 1 - 0   -

3600   -

TOTAL   -

CONVERT TO KVA
BY MARKING OFF
3 DECIMAL PLACES

Fig. 17. Illustration for example 5   Fig. 18. Illustration for example 6

220 Industrial and Commercial Wiring

Multiplier	KVA									
	1	2	3	4	5	6	7	8	9	10
1	1	2	3	4	5	6	7	8	9	10
2	2	4	6	8	10	12	14	16	18	20
3	3	6	9	12	15	18	21	24	27	30
4	4	8	12	16	20	24	28	32	36	40
5	5	10	15	20	25	30	35	40	45	50
6	6	12	18	24	30	36	42	48	54	60
7	7	14	21	28	35	42	49	56	63	70
8	8	16	24	32	40	48	56	64	72	80
9	9	18	27	36	45	54	63	72	81	90

Voltage	Multiplier
115	870
120	833
208	482
220	454
230	434
240	417
277	362

Voltage	Multiplier
208	278
220	262
230	251
240	241
416	139
440	131
460	126
480	120

Table 3. (A) single-phase and three-phase amps.
(B) single-phase. (C) three-phase

cedure is the same as with Table 1.

Example 6—A heavy lighting load draws 345 amps, three-phase, at 416 volts. What is the kva input? (See Fig. 18)

Problems Under Table 3

Two auxiliary tables are required in connection with Table 3, which gives the number of amps necessary to produce a certain value of kva or, in the case of D.C., kw. Table 3A lists multipliers for single-phase and D.C. Table 3B lists those for three phase.

Example 7—How much current will be needed to deliver 9 kva single-phase power at 230 volts? (See Fig. 19)

Referring to Table 3A, the multiplier for single-phase, 230 volts is 434. Proceeding as in the illustration, the current is found to be 39 amps.

Example 8—How much current is necessary to produce 10 kva at 208 volts, three phase? (See Fig. 20)

Table 3B shows the multiplier for 208 volts, three phase to be

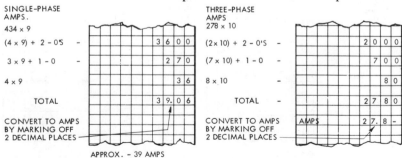

SINGLE-PHASE AMPS.

434 x 9

(4 x 9) + 2 - 0'5   —   3 6 0 0

3 x 9 + 1 - 0   —   2 7 0

4 x 9   3 6

TOTAL   3 9. 0 6

CONVERT TO AMPS BY MARKING OFF 2 DECIMAL PLACES

APPROX. - 39 AMPS

THREE-PHASE AMPS

278 x 10

(2 x 10) + 2 - 0'S   —   2 0 0 0

(7 x 10) + 1 - 0   —   7 0 0

8 x 10   —   8 0

TOTAL   —   2 7 8 0

CONVERT TO AMPS BY MARKING OFF 2 DECIMAL PLACES   AMPS   2 7. 8 -

Fig. 19. Illustration for example 7   Fig. 20. Illustration for example 8

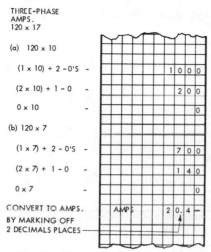

Fig. 21. Illustration for example 9

278. Following through, as in the illustration, the current is found to be 27.8 amps.

Example 9—How much current is needed to deliver 17 kva, three phase, at 480 volts? (See Fig. 21)

The first thing to notice in this example is that the table has no listing for 17 kva. In such case, it is merely necessary to select any two listings which add up to the desired amount. Thus, 10 kva plus 7 kva equals 17 kva. These two quantities may be chosen. Table 3B shows the multiplier for three phase, 480 volts to be 120.

The notations are recorded in two parts, (a) and (b). Those applying to the 10 kva portion are set down in the proper columns, followed by the ones for the 7 kva load. Adding the columns, and marking off the two decimal places, the current is found to be 20.4 amps.

ADDITIONAL CALCULATIONS

The Problem of Voltage Drop

The NEC has no mandatory requirements with respect to voltage loss in conductors. Section 215–3 recommends that feeder voltage drop to the final distribution point be limited to 3 percent for power or heating loads, and to 1 percent for lighting or combination loads. Voltage sensitive office equipment and the present trend in the direction of higher lighting intensities, however, are forcing consideration of this matter in the design of modern installations.

Voltage Drop Formulas

Voltage drop may be calculated by means of the simple formulas given below:

Single-phase, two-wire: $E = \dfrac{2 \times K \times L \times I}{Cir\ mils}$

Single-phase, three-wire: $E = \dfrac{1 \times K \times L \times I}{Cir\ mils}$
(balanced)

Three-phase, three-wire: $E = \dfrac{1.73 \times K \times L \times I}{Cir\ mils}$

Three-phase, four-wire: $E = \dfrac{1 \times K \times L \times I}{Cir\ mils}$
(balanced network)
K = 11.5 for copper

(Note: The value 10.4, commonly given in texts, does not take into account the normal operating temperature of insulated conductors)

K = 18.2 for aluminum

L = one-way length of feeder (in ft)

I = current in amps

Cir mils = circular mil area of wire as given in AWG wire Table.

Voltage Drop Calculations—Copper Conductors

Example 1—What is the voltage drop in a No. 10, two-wire, single-phase feeder that is 100 ft long, and which carries 25 amps?

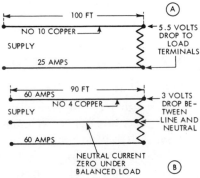

Fig. 22. Illustrations for examples 1 & 2

$$E = \frac{2 \times 11.5 \times 100 \times 25}{10380} = 5.5 \text{ volts (approx.)}$$

Example 2—What is the voltage drop between line and neutral conductor in a balanced single-phase, three-wire, No. 4 feeder that is 90 ft long, and which carries 60 amps?

$$E = \frac{1 \times 11.5 \times 90 \times 60}{41740} = 1.49, \text{ or } 1.5 \text{ volts.}$$

Only the resistance of one conductor is taken into consideration in Example 2, because the neutral carries no current under a perfectly balanced condition. If the circuit should become completely unbalanced, that is all lights on one side turned off, the voltage across each lamp on the side in use would be twice 3 volts, or 6 volts.

Example 3—What is the voltage drop per phase on a three-phase, three-wire, No. 1 feeder that is 70 ft long, and which carries 100 amps?

$$E = \frac{1.73 \times 11.5 \times 70 \times 100}{83690} = 1.7 \text{ volts approx.}$$

This is the voltage loss per phase, not per wire. If the voltage between any two line wires is 230 at the supply end, it will be: 230 volts — 1.7 volts, or 228.3 volts at the receiving end.

Example 4—What is the voltage drop in a balanced, three-phase, four-wire, No. 2 feeder that is 120 ft long, and which carries 85 amps of incandescent lighting?

$$E = \frac{1 \times 11.5 \times 120 \times 85}{66370} = \text{approx. } 1.8 \text{ volts}$$

This is the voltage drop between any phase wire and neutral,

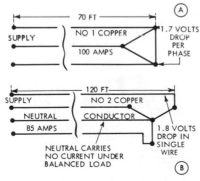

Fig. 23. Illustrations for examples 3 & 4

because the neutral conductor has zero current under balanced load conditions. If one phase is entirely inactive, the neutral will have the same load as each of the two phase conductors, but the current will be 60 degrees out of phase with that of the phase conductors. In this case, the voltage drop between phase wires and neutral will be less than twice that for one conductor. If two phases are inactive, the voltage drop between line and neutral in the remaining phase will be 2 times that for balanced load.

Skin Effect

In large sizes of wire, alternating current crowds to the outer layers of the conductor because of inductance, thus increasing apparent resistance. This tendency is called "skin effect." It need not be taken into account with sizes No. 0000 or smaller, but as diameters increase the added resistance becomes troublesome. For example, the A.C. resistance of No. 500MCM copper wire at 60 cycles is 13 percent higher than its D.C. value. Table 9 (*see NEC*) lists multiplying factors.

Short-Circuit Current

The fundamental nature of short-circuit currents was discussed under the heading of Current-Limiting Fuses. Although exact determination of available short-circuit current is a highly technical operation, the general method should be understood by the electrical worker. Fig. 24 shows a 112-½ kva, three-phase, four-wire, 120-208-volt transformer bank, consisting of three single-phase transformers, and supplying panelboard *L*, which is 100 ft distant. The feeder has four No. 500MCM copper conductors. A "dead" or "bolted"

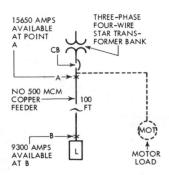

Fig. 24. Short-circuit current flow

short-circuit between a phase wire and neutral is assumed to have developed.

Suppose the fault to have occurred at point A, immediately beyond circuit breaker CB. In this case, the only impedance is that of the transformer, which is given as 2 percent. The normal current delivered by one transformer is equal to: 37,500 va/120 volts, which equals 313 amps. On short-circuit, the available current at this point is: 100/2 × 313 amps, or 15,650 amps. Circuit breaker CB would be subjected to this maximum value of current.

If the short-circuit had developed at point B, on or adjacent to panelboard L, the current would have a lower value, depending upon impedance offered by the transformer windings plus that of the feeder conductors. The resistance of 200 ft of No. 500MCM wire is .0046 ohm. Applying the correction factor of 1.13, from Table 9, the resistance or impedance becomes: 1.13 × .0046 ohm, or .0052 ohm. Impedance offered by the transformer is equal to: 120 volts/15,650 amps, which is .0077 ohm. Total impedance is: .0052 ohm + .0077 ohm, or .0129 ohm. Current flow under short-circuit at point B will have a maximum value of: 120 volts/.0129 ohm, or approx. 9300 amps, far less than was available at point A.

Where rotating equipment is present, as indicated by dotted outline in the figure, a somewhat greater current is available. Motors will supply to the fault, during a period of about 3 cycles, current equal to about four times their rated input, but the effect will quickly dissipate.

Third-Harmonic Current

A 60-cycle half-wave of current is shown at M in Fig. 25A. A

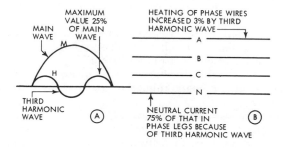

Fig. 25. Third harmonic

third-harmonic current, which has a frequency of three times 60 cycles, or 180 cycles, is shown at *H*. Third-harmonic current is generated by flux variations in transformers and in ballasts of fluorescent units. The small wave in the illustration is said to be a 25 percent harmonic because its maximum value is ¼ that of the main current wave.

Additional heating in the phase wires caused by the third-harmonic current, Fig. 25B, is only 3 percent greater than if it were not present. In the neutral conductor, however, which should be carrying zero current, the harmonics from each of the three phase wires add together, producing a heating effect equal to 75 percent of full-load, 60-cycle, current value. It is for this reason that the 70 percent neutral reduction factor is denied when fluorescent lighting is supplied. The third-harmonic current was taken here at 25 percent. It is often greater than this amount. If it were 33 percent of the main wave, it would heat the neutral conductor to the same point as if carrying full load 60-cycle current.

REVIEW QUESTIONS

1. What is the minimum requirement per linear foot for show-window lighting?
2. What is the load rating of a general use plug receptacle?
3. What demand factor is sometimes applied to neutral feeder load in excess of 200 amps?
4. What unit load does NEC specify for office locations?
5. How many amps per sq in are allowed a bare copper conductor in an unventilated enclosure?
6. Does the electrician usually calculate the size of busduct conductors?
7. What kind of load is represented when three feeder conductors carry the same current?
8. How far apart are star voltages in the three-phase diagram?
9. How many times star voltage is phase voltage?
10. Is star current less than phase current?
11. How many times coil voltage is delta phase voltage?
12. What is the secondary voltage of a delta-star, 4 to 1, 2300-volt transformer bank?
13. What is the secondary voltage of a star-delta, 4 to 1, 2300-volt transformer bank?
14. What is the voltage to neutral in a 208-volt, three-phase, T-connected transformer?
15. If the delta coil current is 10 amps, what is the line current?

16. Are unbalanced three-phase loads commonly found in practice?

17. Are single-phase amps usually added directly to three-phase amps?

18. In order to determine three-phase power at 100 percent P.F., volts times amps must be multiplied by what number?

19. What value is used for K in calculating voltage drop in copper wire?

20. What causes increased A.C. resistance of large conductors?

Chapter Nine

Special Applications
— Hazards

COMPUTING MACHINES

Description

During the past ten years, automated machinery has invaded the factory and the office, particularly the latter. Tasks once performed by great numbers of clerks are now done more rapidly and efficiently through devices supervised by a comparatively few technically trained employees. When a group of selected units is properly assembled and connected, as in Fig. 1, it may carry on involved operations that formerly needed a very large staff of workers.

These units are electro-mechanical in nature, but those which perform computations are almost entirely electronic. Until recently, electron tubes were employed throughout, but in the newer models tubes are replaced by transistors, germanium diodes, and magnetic cores. Power consumption has been greatly reduced, heat lessened. Nevertheless, considerable wattage is still needed for large installations.

Fig. 1. IBM Data processing system

Courtesy of IBM Corp.

228

Units are electrically joined, by means of signal and power cables, to carry out a sequence of operations. Various types of plugs and receptacles are employed in order to render unlikely an improper connection. Patented connectors such as Twistlock, L-slot, U-slot, and other special types of connectors are used.

Raised Floors

In order to avoid unsightly and potentially dangerous mazes of cables, raised floors such as in Fig. 2 have been adopted. The two basic types, pedestal and stringer construction, are illustrated. Cables are passed downward through suitable small openings directly under the machines into the space below, and extended to other units as desired. The floors consist of metal plates, plywood, or similar material. The chamber thus formed may be used as an air-conditioning plenum, or for concealing auxiliary equipment such as small air-compressors which supply pneumatic doors often found on the various units. Because individual sections of the raised portion may be easily removed, these devices are readily accessible.

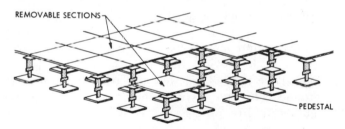

PEDESTAL TYPE RAISED FLOOR

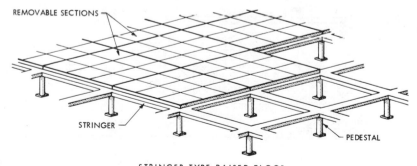

STRINGER TYPE RAISED FLOOR

Fig. 2. Pedestal and stringer raised floors

Cables and Feeders

The maximum length specified for a power cable is determined by the allowable voltage drop. The manufacturers recommend that cables up to 40 ft in length should be given a 125 percent "current factor." The term *current factor* means that the size of the conductors should be at least 125 percent of that required by the NEC tables. It is recommended, further, that for cables or feeders from 40 ft to 100 ft in length, the current factor should be 300 percent.

Power

Three-phase electrical power is generally used for data processing systems. Most of the equipment operates on 60-cycle current, but certain large units are designed for 400 cycles. When both types of units are present, separate 60-cycle and 400-cycle panelboards are employed.

SWIMMING POOLS

Safety Considerations

NEC 680, a new article, is devoted entirely to the consideration of *safety* in connection with swimming pools. Figure 3 emphasizes certain of these requirements, particularly those concerned with grounding. The Code provides that all metal which is part of the installation shall be bonded together and attached to an approved common ground. This rule includes the metal conduit, metal portions of lighting fixtures, piping systems, ladders, metal supporting

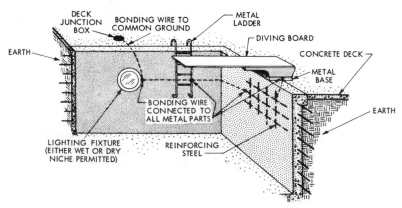

Fig. 3. Swimming pool

structure of the diving board, and also the reinforcing steel inside the concrete walls.

The maximum permissible voltage to lighting fixtures is 150. It is recommended that where the potential exceeds 30 volts, a ground-detector which automatically disconnects the circuit in case of trouble should be installed. The Code recommends also that isolating transformers of special design be employed. All metal parts of fixtures and a fixture supply conduit below grade level shall be of brass or suitable copper alloy. The same rule applies to junction boxes less than 4 ft from the perimeter of the pool, and less than 8″ above the concrete surface.

Transformers, unless approved for wet locations, shall not be installed less than 4 ft from the perimeter, 12″ from the concrete surface, or 12″ above maximum water level. No attachment receptacle is permitted within 10 ft of the inner walls of the pool unless it is an integral part of an approved lighting fixture.

An unbroken, insulated, No. 14 AWG or larger copper ground wire must be installed between the deck box and the grounding connection of the distribution panelboard. No service drops may be installed above the pool or within 10 ft horizontally of the pool or its accessory apparatus.

X-RAY EQUIPMENT

General Considerations

X-ray units are employed in foundries and machine shops for the purpose of inspecting metals, especially castings, for defects not visible on the surface. X-rays are not permitted in hazardous locations, nor on a supply voltage of more than 600. Although the code mentions guarding requirements for installations with open high-voltage wires, most jurisdictions will not permit such apparatus for industrial purposes. Completely enclosed units with shockproof cables are generally installed. In any case, noncurrent-carrying metal parts of tube stands, fluoroscopic devices, and other apparatus shall be grounded.

Both the radiographic and fluoroscopic type of units are found in industry. With the radiographic device, X-ray photographs of the material are taken. These photographs are then examined by men expert in such work. With the fluoroscopic type, the examiner views a screen on which is cast an X-ray shadow of the material. Fig. 4 shows an industrial X-ray unit.

Fig. 4. Modern X-ray unit

Courtesy of General Electric Co.

Installation

Section 660–15 states that transformers and capacitors which are parts of an X-ray device shall not be required to conform to general code requirements for transformers and capacitors. This permission avoids necessity for vaults. In view of the nature of the apparatus, and the limited amount of power which is involved, no fire hazard is incurred through this waiver of the general rule.

Means shall be provided to drain the capacitor charge automatically where the unit, or wiring thereto, are within 8 ft of the floor and accessible to other than qualified persons. If the equipment is within 8 ft of the floor, draining need not be provided for if it is enclosed in grounded metal or insulating material. In general, permanently connected X-ray units must be supplied by one of the usual approved wiring methods. NEC 660–3(a) permits the use of a suitable plug and cord for equipment supplied by branch circuits not larger than 30 amperes.

Portable apparatus of any capacity may be connected by cord and plug. A fused disconnecting means of adequate capacity (for at least 50 percent of the momentary rating) must be provided in a location readily accessible from the X-ray control area. For apparatus connected to a 115-volt supply line, and fused at 30 amperes or less, a plug and receptacle may serve as the disconnecting means.

Control

The low-voltage circuit of the step-up transformer used with stationary equipment must contain a circuit breaker which protects the radiographic circuit. If the circuit breaker is not manually operable, there shall be a manually-operable switch in this circuit, the switch being part of the equipment or directly adjacent to it.

With portable equipment, Section 660–4 waives the use of a circuit breaker when all high-voltage parts, including the X-ray tube, are within a single metallic enclosure which is provided with means for grounding. Industrial X-ray apparatus must be furnished with a switch that opens automatically except when held closed by the operator. Foot switches must be provided with a shield over the contact button in order to prevent accidental closing. Separate high-voltage switches are required where two or more pieces of apparatus are connected to the same high-voltage source.

METHODS OF UTILIZING ELECTRICAL HEAT

Conduction

Electrical heat for industrial processes may be obtained in a number of ways. The earliest method employs high-resistance conductors in the form of straight wires, coils, ribbons, or cast grids. The power expended in forcing current through the conductors shows up as heat. This type of heating is often found in electric ovens.

Fig. 5. Infrared oven

Courtesy De Vilbiss Company

Infrared Lamps

Another form of industrial heating which is quite popular to-day consists of banks of incandescent lamps which operate at temperatures somewhat lower than that of the ordinary incandescent lighting unit. Because of the low operating temperature, the lamp emits a high percentage of infrared rays which create heat in objects they fall upon. This form of heating is often employed for drying painted or lacquered objects, finding wide application in the automobile industry. Fig. 5 shows a modern oven.

Infrared heating lamps rated at 300 watts or less may be used with lampholders of the medium-base unswitched porcelain type, or other types approved for the purpose. But screw-shell lampholders shall not be used with infrared lamps over 300 watts rating unless the lampholders are especially approved for the purpose. Lampholders for infrared lamps may be operated in series on circuits of more than 150 volts to ground, provided the voltage rating of the lampholders is not less than circuit voltage. Each panel or strip carrying a number of infrared lampholders is considered as an appliance. Section 422–26(C) requires that infrared lamp heating appliances shall have overcurrent protection not exceeding 50 amps.

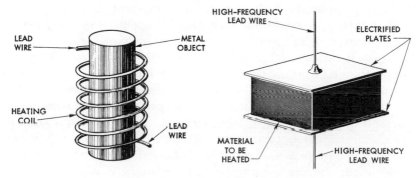

Fig. 6. Inductive and dielectric heating

INDUCTION AND DIELECTRIC
HEAT-GENERATING EQUIPMENT

Principles

In both these processes, heat is generated by high-frequency electric current. Induction heating is employed with metals or other conducting materials, while dielectric heating is used for nonconducting materials such as plastics. Induction heating is accomplished, as shown in the illustration at the left in Fig. 6, by placing the material inside an inductor coil. Dielectric heating is accomplished by placing the material between two electrodes. This scheme is illustrated at the right.

High-frequency current required for these purposes is sometimes obtained from motor-generators. But rotating apparatus cannot be used to generate frequencies in excess of 15,000 cycles per second. Other types of generators, therefore, are employed in the greater number of installations, mainly spark-gap converters, inverter-oscillators, or vacuum-tube oscillators.

For dielectric heating, the vacuum-tube oscillating units are employed almost exclusively. With these devices, current taken during heating periods is much greater than when the equipment is idling on the line. The idling current is termed *standby* current in the code.

Supply Circuits

Conductors for motor-generator equipment must conform to sections of the code already studied. For other than motor-generator equipment, Section 665–5(b) requires that the current-carrying capacity of conductors shall be determined by the nameplate rating. It shall be 100 percent of that rating for a single piece of equipment. Where two or more units are supplied, the carrying capacity must be equal to at least 100 percent of nameplate currents of all units, unless simultaneous operation is rendered impossible.

Where all units do not operate at the same time, the capacity of the feeder must not be less than 100 percent of the nameplate currents of the largest group of machines capable of simultaneous operation, plus standby currents of remaining machines. For example, the nameplate current of each of ten dielectric heating units is 10 amps, and the standby current 1.5 amps. If not more than four machines can operate at a given time, the size of feeder conductors should be based upon a current equal to $(4 \times 10) + (6 \times 1.5)$, or 49 amps.

Overcurrent Protection and Disconnecting Means

Overcurrent requirements for high-frequency motor-generators are no different than for general applications. For other generating devices, overcurrent protection for the unit must not exceed 200 percent of nameplate current. The disconnecting means must be readily accessible, and must have a current-carrying capacity at least 100 percent of nameplate current rating.

Fig. 7. Induction and dielectric heaters

Courtesy of Allis-Chalmers Manufacturing Co.

Output Circuits

Fig. 7 shows an induction heating unit on the left, and a dielectric heating unit on the right. The output circuits include all high-frequency components outside the generator, such as connecting leads and work applicator. Section 665–9 requires that connecting wires between generator and work applicator shall be enclosed or guarded with noncombustible material if more than 2 ft in length. It also directs that the generator output shall be at direct current ground potential. The direct current ground potential is that of the chassis of the electronic generating device, and may be a few volts higher than actual earth potential. The generator output often consists of a single-turn coil to which terminals of the heating coils or plates are attached. This output coil, under the requirement expressed here, must be grounded.

An exception to the rule is mentioned in Section 665-10 which states that commercial frequencies at not over 150 volts may be coupled to the output for control purposes, if they are limited to use only during periods of circuit operation. Other sections provide for additional safety measures, including bonding of noncurrent-carrying metallic parts, guarding of work applicators so they are not liable to inadvertent contact during "live" periods, locking or electrical interlocking of doors giving access to potentials greater than 500 volts, enclosing of generating apparatus in noncombustible housing, shielding of foot-switch contact buttons, and use of warning labels.

Remote-control switches or stations are required to be electrically interlocked. Capacitors of more than .1 Mfd. capacity are required to have bleeder resistors when installed on main circuits operating at voltages higher than 230, or on auxiliary circuits, regardless of voltage, and the maximum permissible R-F potential in a keyed oscillator circuit is limited to 100 volts.

Safety Measures with Respect to X-ray Units and Electronic Heating Devices

The first precaution with regard to X-ray and Electronic units is to avoid contacting exposed high-voltage terminals. If it is part of the electrician's duties to replace defective X-ray tubes, he should lock the circuit switch in the open position, and then make sure that capacitor units are in a discharged state. Only then, should he proceed to dismantle the covering element of the tube.

Electronic heating devices, both inductive and dielectric, are often employed in conjunction with hydraulic or pneumatic pressure machinery. The electrician should make certain that oil or air valves are shut off before venturing to place his hands upon working surfaces.

ELECTRIC WELDERS

Types

There are, in general, three kinds of electric welders, the transformer arc, the motor-generator arc, and the resistance welder. The first two perform welding operations through the medium of an arc drawn between the work and a metal rod, called an electrode. The resistance unit welds by virtue of an exceedingly heavy current which flows through the small area of materials which happens to be in contact at a particular instant.

In the arc types, material from the electrode rod is added to the weld. In the resistance type, no metal is added, and fusing is accomplished by pressing the two parts together as they reach the molten state. Manual as well as automatic welding is done with both types.

Transformer Arc Welders

Conductors. The current-carrying capacity of conductors for these units shall not be less than rated primary current times a duty-cycle factor, a table of which is provided in NEC 630–11(a). The term "duty-cycle" will be explained shortly. For a group of welders, the current-carrying capacity of the feeder may be less than the sum of current values as obtained above. Its rating should be determined, as per NEC 630–11(b), according to the use to be made of each welder, also taking into consideration the fact that all units may not be operating at the same time.

It is suggested in the NEC section, that conductor ratings based on 100 percent of the input value calculated for the two largest welders, 85 percent of that for the third, 70 percent for the fourth, and 60 percent for all others, should provide an ample margin of safety. The real basis, however, is actual field data obtained from identical or similar applications.

Overcurrent Protection. Each welder shall have overcurrent protection rated at not more than 200 percent of its rated primary current, except where supply conductors are already protected at a rating not in excess of this value. Overcurrent devices protecting conductors which supply one or more welders must be rated or set at not more than 200 percent of the conductor rating.

Disconnect. A disconnecting means is required in the supply connection of each welder that is not equipped with a disconnect mounted as an integral part of the welder. This switch or circuit breaker shall be large enough to accommodate the overcurrent device.

Example. A certain 220-volt, single-phase installation consists of nine transformer arc welders, all used on a 50 percent duty-cycle application. Two are rated at 100 amps, one at 75 amps, one at 60 amps, two at 50 amps, and three at 40 amps. It is necessary to determine the sizes of conductors and overcurrent devices, Type R copper wire being used for circuits and feeder.

The table in NEC 630–11(a) lists a multiplying factor of .71 for a 50 percent duty-cycle application. Applying this factor, the 100-amp welders may be assumed to draw 71 amps, the 75-amp welder 53 amps, the 60-amp welder 43 amps, each of the 50-amp welders 36 amps, and each of the 40-amp welders 28 amps. Under the method suggested in NEC 630–11(b), current for each of the two largest units will be 100 percent of 71 amps, or 142 amps for both. That drawn by the 75-amp unit will be 85 percent of 53 amps, or 45 amps. Proceeding in the same manner, current for the 60-amp welder is 70 percent of 43 amps, or 30 amps. Current for each 50-amp welder is 60 percent of 36 amps, or 22 amps, so that two of them draw 44 amps. Each of the 40-amp units will take 60 percent of 28 amps, or 17 amps, so that the three will draw 51 amps.

Feeder current is equal to the total: 142 amps + 45 amps + 30 amps + 44 amps + 51 amps, which equals 312 amps. Referring to NEC Table 310–12, a No. 500MCM Type R conductor with a carrying capacity of 320 amps is needed. The overcurrent device for this feeder should not be larger than 200 percent of 320 amps, or 640 amps. But the nearest standard fuse is 800 amps, and the nearest standard non-adjustable circuit breaker is 700 amps, either of which will be approved as per NEC 630–12. Overcurrent devices for each separate welder should not be larger than 200 percent of rated primary current, which means a 200-amp device for the 100-amp units, a 150-amp for the 75-amp unit, a 125-amp (nearest standard size) for the 60-amp welder, a 100-amp for each 50-amp welder, and an 80-amp for each of the 40-amp welders.

Nameplate. The nameplate must provide information as to both primary and secondary current, open-circuit secondary voltage, and the basis upon which the unit is rated.

Motor-Generator Arc Welders

Although these units are subject to the general rules covering motors and generators, there are certain additional rules. Section 430-22 provides that the carrying capacity of a conductor for a motor-generator, single-operator, arc welder may be 90 percent of nameplate current rating.

No motor overcurrent device is required for this condition of service. The branch-circuit overcurrent device is deemed sufficient protection for the motor if it does not exceed Table 430–152 or Table 430–153 values. Section 430-52, however, relaxes the rule somewhat, allowing the branch-circuit overcurrent device to be increased where necessary to a value not in excess of 400 percent of motor full-load current.

If a motor-generator arc welder is driven by a 10 hp, three-phase, 230-volt, code letter D, motor whose full-load current is 27 amperes, the carrying capacity of the conductor should not be less than .9 × 27, or 24 amperes. With type R wire, Table 310–12 shows that No. 10 is required. The branch-circuit overcurrent device, according to Table 430–152, should not be over 250 percent of 27 amperes, or 68 amperes. A 70-ampere fuse and a 100-ampere branch-circuit switch should be employed. The motor controller, or disconnect switch, is 10 hp.

Resistance Welders

Fig. 8 shows a resistance welder. Rated, current-carrying capacity of conductors for a single welder used on varying operation must not be less than 70 percent of rated primary current for seam and automatically fed welders, or 50 percent of rated primary current for manually-operated welders. The term "varying operation," here means unplanned or intermittent duty. Where the term "specific operation" is used, it means an operation which occurs and reoccurs according to a set plan.

Current-carrying capacity of supply conductors for a single welder whose actual primary current and duty cycle are known, must ot be less than the product of primary current and a multiplier which depends n duty cycle. This multiplier is given in Section 630–11(a), but it may be determined without reference to the ta-

Fig. 8. Resistance welder

Courtesy of Taylor-Winfield Corp.

ble, if occasion demands, by taking the square root of the duty cycle expressed in decimal form. Thus, if the duty cycle is given as 50 percent, it may be expressed as a .50 duty cycle. The square root of .50 is equal to .71, the value given in the table. If the duty cycle is 25 percent, or .25, the multiplier is equal to the square root of .25, or .5.

Duty Cycle. The term *duty cycle* expresses the percentage of time during which the unit is actually welding, or the percentage of time during which current flows through the work. If the supply is 60 cycles per second, and the device makes welds for only two 15-cycle periods per second, it is operating for a space of 30 cycles. Its duty cycle is equal to $\dfrac{30}{60} \times 100$, or 50 percent.

A 15-cycle period is only ¼ second, an interval too small for human determination. An electronic timer is used in conjunction with other automatic devices which move the work during the rest periods between welds.

Example. Consider a 12 kva resistance welder whose primary current is 65 amperes. If this welder is used on varying duty, the conductor size must be chosen on the basis of .7 × 65, or 45 amperes, which requires No. 6, type R wire. If used on manual duty, the conductor may be chosen on the basis of .5 × 65, or 33 amperes, requiring No. 8, type R wire. If applied to a specific operation employing four 3-cycle welds per second, the duty cycle is equal to $\frac{4 \times 3}{60}$ × 100 percent, or 20 percent. The multiplier for this duty cycle is found to be .45. The conductor, in this case, is chosen on the basis of .45 × 65, or 29 amperes, which calls for No. 10, type R wire.

Group of Welders. The rated current-carrying capacity of conductors which supply two or more welders shall not be less than the sum of the value obtained for the largest welder, plus 60 percent of that obtained for the remaining units. A certain installation consists of three resistance welders, the 12 kva unit referred to above, and two 6 kva units whose full-load primary currents are 32 amperes each. The three welders are used on specific operations, the large one on a 20 percent duty cycle, as before, and the small ones on a 30 percent duty cycle.

The rated current-carrying capacity of the feeder for the three units must be determined on the basis of 29 amperes already obtained for the larger welder, plus 60 percent of the value obtained for the smaller ones. Since the duty cycle is 30 percent, the multiplier is .55. The current used in determining carrying capacity for either of the small units is equal to .55 × 32, or 17.6 amps. But, only 60 percent of this amount is to be added, for each unit, to the 29 amperes required for the large unit. This value of current is .6 × 17.6, or 11 amps. The total current used in determining conductor size is equal to 29 + 11 + 11, or 51 amps. Table 1 shows that No. 6, type R, is required.

Overcurrent Protection. Each welder must have an overcurrent device rated or set at not more than 300 percent of rated primary current. For the 12 kva welder, the overcurrent device should be set at not more than 3 × 65, or 195 amps. For the 6 kva units, the overcurrent devices should be rated or set at not over 3 × 32, or 96 amps.

The feeder overcurrent device, must be rated or set at not more than 300 percent of conductor rating. In the above example, the rating of No. 6, type R, conductors is 55 amps. The rating of the feeder overcurrent device should not be greater than 3 × 55, or 165 amps.

Disconnecting Means. A switch or circuit breaker must be provided for each welder. The current-carrying capacity of the disconnecting means cannot be less than the rating of the conductors.

Nameplate Data. It should be noted that NEC 630–34 calls for the welder to be rated according to kva output at 50 percent duty cycle. If the device were used at some higher value of duty cycle, its kva capacity would be lowered proportionally. In practice, however, the 50 percent value is usually not exceeded.

ELECTRIC SIGNS AND OUTLINE LIGHTING

General Rules

Every outline lighting installation and every sign, other than portable, must be controlled by an externally-operable switch which opens all ungrounded conductors. It must be within sight of the sign, or able to be locked in the open position. Switches, flashers, and other devices controlling transformers shall have a current rating of not less than twice that of the transformers.

NEC 600–5 requires grounding, or isolating and insulating, of non-current-carrying parts of all but portable signs. Circuits which supply lamps, ballasts, and transformers, or combinations thereof, may be rated not to exceed 20 amps. Those supplying only electric discharge lighting transformers shall be rated not to exceed 30 amps. Cutouts and flashers are to be installed in separate compartments or in approved metal boxes. Outdoor enclosures should have drain holes.

Wood, used for external decoration, must not be closer than 2 in to the nearest lampholder or current carrying part. Metallic parts should be galvanized or otherwise protected. See NEC 600–8(e) for minimum thickness of metal enclosures.

Installations Over 600 Volts

Fig. 9 shows a neon sign. An exterior view is presented at the left, an interior view at the right. Conductors are required to be

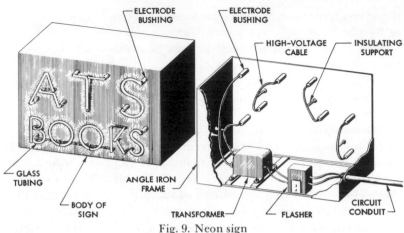

Fig. 9. Neon sign

of a type approved for purpose and voltage, and shall not be smaller than No. 14. Sharp bends in conductors should be avoided because the insulation tends to develop weak spots at such points. When run indoors, open conductors shall be mounted on noncombustible, nonabsorptive insulators which maintain a separation of at least $1\frac{1}{2}$ in between wires, and between wires and other surfaces. Exposed porcelain insulators shall be glazed.

Concealed conductors are governed by the same rule, except that separation may be reduced to 1 in for voltages of 10,000 or less. They must be installed in channels lined with noncombustible material. In damp locations, the insulation on all conductors must extend beyond the metal covering or raceway at least 4 in for voltages over 10,000, 3 in for voltages down to 5,000, and 2 in for voltages of 5,000 or less. In dry locations, the insulation shall extend not less than $2\frac{1}{2}$ in, 2 in, and $1\frac{1}{2}$ in, respectively.

Transformers. Where the transformer is at some distance from the tubing, as with outline installations, not more than 20 ft of cable from a single transformer shall be run in a metal raceway where potential between cable and raceway exceeds 5,000 volts. Transformers must be accessible, and their ratings cannot exceed 4,500 volt-amperes. The secondary voltage is limited to a nominal value of 15,000 for center-tapped transformers, or 7,500 volts for end-tapped transformers. The "tapping," here, refers to grounding point. High-voltage secondaries may not be connected in parallel nor in series, except to establish a mid-point grounding connection equivalent to that of a single unit.

Glass Tubing—Electrodes. Tubing should be supported on non-combustible, nonabsorptive supports which maintain a clearance of at least ¼ in from the nearest surface, where the voltage is greater than 7,500. Glass supports are employed for this purpose in connection with neon signs. Terminals of tubing must be separated from grounded metal and from combustible material by approved barriers or by 1½ in of air. Electrode receptacles shall be approved for the purpose.

When electrodes enter outdoor signs or indoor signs operating at more than 7,500 volts, they must have noncombustible, nonabsorptive bushings unless receptacles are provided, or unless the sign is wired with bare wire mounted on approved supports which maintain the tubing in proper position. Where bare wire is used, the conductor shall not be smaller than No. 14 solid copper.

SIGNAL SYSTEMS

Types

Under the broad head of signalling are included intercommunicating, fire-alarm, watchman's, paging, programming, nurse-call, burglar alarm, sprinkler, smoke detection, and loud speaker systems. Loud speaker systems consist of microphones or tape recorders, amplifiers, and speakers. Wiring connected with them will be touched upon in the following pages. Other types mentioned above have certain features in common. These will be set forth through investigation of two of them.

NEC Rules

Article 640 of the NEC presents regulations governing sound equipment used for public address or for music reproduction. It seems unnecessary to list all these provisions, but a few of the more important will be noted. Conductors in wireways and auxiliary gutters for general wiring cannot occupy more than 20 percent of the cross-sectional area. For sound-recording and reproduction, however, they may take up 75 percent of this area. Where power-supply conductors and sound conductors are grouped in the same enclosure, the sound conductors must have insulation at least equal to that of the power conductors unless the two are separated by a continuous metallic covering.

Article 725 deals with remote-control, low-energy power, low-voltage power, and signal circuits. It specifies two types of wiring: Class 1 and Class 2. Methods approved under Class 1, already mentioned in connection with remote-control motor circuits, are the same except in minor respects as for ordinary interior wiring. It should be mentioned here that amplifier output circuits carrying audio-program signals of 70 volts or less, and whose open-circuit voltage will not exceed 100 volts, may employ Class 2 wiring.

Transformers supplying low-voltage power circuits to coin-operated devices and similar equipment may not have ratings in excess of 1000 va and 30 volts. Those on low-energy power circuits for paging systems, signal lights, and such applications cannot have ratings in excess of 100 va. They must be protected by a fuse not larger than 20 amps. The kind of insulation on conductors for Class 2 systems need only be suitable for the particular voltage, but open conductors must be kept at least 2 in from lighting or power wires. Branch circuits connected to secondary leads of low-energy transformers need not be separately fused.

Nurse-Call System

There are two general classes of signal circuits, open-circuit, and closed-circuit. Programming, paging, and smoke-detection circuits are of the first type, which is illustrated by the nurse-call system shown in Fig. 10. Its main components are an annunciator, bedside pushes, and hallway signal lights. In the illustration, the supply conduit is shown entering the annunciator box. If the signal wiring is at reduced voltage, a step-down transformer will be found here, and cable will likely be run to signal lights and bedside pushes. If the circuit operates at supply voltage, the signal wiring will be run in conduit.

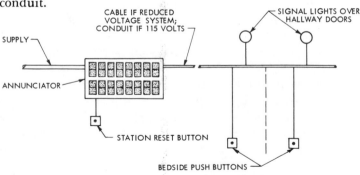

Fig. 10. Nurse-call system

When the patient uses the bedside push button or toggle switch, one of the annunciator drops will fall to uncover a white number, and a buzzer will sound. At the same time, the hallway light outside the patient's room will come on. The nurse at the annunciator station will observe the exposed number, and press the station reset button to restore the shutter and disconnect the buzzer. The light outside the patient's door will remain on, however, until she enters to reset the bedside push.

Fire-Alarm System

The circuit of Fig. 11 is characteristic of such applications as: burglar-alarm, sprinkler, and watchman's circuits. The control panel, which contains the necessary relays, is connected to 115-volt supply wires. A transformer and a rectifier convert the alternating supply current into reduced voltage direct current. The D-C circuit passes through break-glass sending stations which are connected in series. If someone breaks a glass to report a fire, a normally-closed switch inside the box opens, and current flow ceases. The D-C relay inside the control panel drops out, closing 115-volt contacts which ring the 115-volt alarm bells. If the 115-volt supply is interrupted for any reason, a low-voltage trouble bell rings. Signal lights are often combined with these systems.

HAZARDOUS LOCATIONS

Definitions

A hazardous location is one in which fire or explosion may occur unless special precautions are observed with respect to the nature and operation of electrical equipment. Locations associated with inflammable vapors, gases, or dusts are covered by this definition.

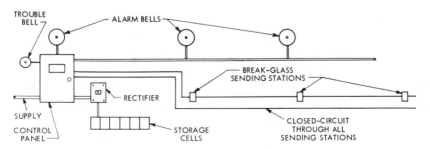

Fig. 11. Closed-circuit fire-alarm system

Article 500 of the National Electrical Code divides hazards into three classes and prescribes detailed measures for handling them. It would serve no purpose to repeat these details, but it is worth while noting important requirements and their application. A thorough treatment of hazards will be found in the author's *National Electric Code and Blueprint Reading.*

Classes of Hazards

Class I locations include those in which inflammable gases or vapors may be present in quantities sufficient to cause fire or explosion. A dyeing and cleaning establishment in which naphtha is used falls within this classification, as does a paint spray room operated in connection with a furniture manufacturing plant.

Class II locations are those in which combustible dust may be present. Grain mills and coal-pulverizing plants come under this heading.

Class III locations have ignitible flyings or fibers in the air. A bag factory or a hosiery mill come within the scope of this classification.

Each of the above classes is broken down into Divisions 1 and 2.

Types of Wiring and Equipment for Class I Locations

In general, Class I locations require special electrical equipment which is approved for operation in the hazardous areas. Explosionproof boxes and fittings are needed in Division 1 locations. Conduits must be sealed in both Division 1 and Division 2 classifications to prevent transfer of gas, vapor, or fire from one portion of the electrical installation to another. An EYS fitting, shown at the left

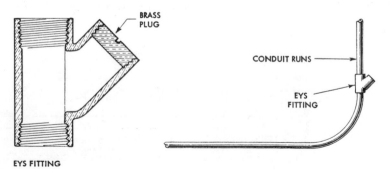

Fig. 12. Sealing of conduits

of Fig. 12, may be used for purposes of sealing. The fitting is inserted in the run of conduit, as indicated in the right-hand illustration, and is filled with an approved sealing compound after the conductors have been pulled in.

Rigid conduit is required in Division 1 locations, but electrical metallic tubing may be used in Division 2 areas. Although explosion-proof boxes with threaded hubs are not required in Division 2 installations, locknuts and bushings shall not be depended on for ground continuity. Bonding jumpers must be installed. Where rigid conduit is employed, it is deemed explosion-proof if at least five threads of the coupling are engaged.

Types of Wiring and Equipment in Class II Locations

Class II, Division 1 areas must be wired with rigid conduit and threaded boxes and fittings, the fittings having dust-tight covers. Electrical metallic tubing and dust-tight fittings may be used in Division 2. Sealing may be accomplished as in the Class I locations, or by a horizontal section of raceway not less than 10 ft in length. It may be accomplished between pieces of equipment by a vertical section of raceway not less than 5 ft long and extending downward from the dust-tight enclosure. The 10 ft horizontal length of conduit allows dust to settle before passing through to the other end.

Type of Wiring and Equipment in Class III Locations

Rigid conduit is required here in both Division 1 and Division 2 areas. Boxes and fittings shall have tight-fitting covers. No sealing of conduits or enclosures is required.

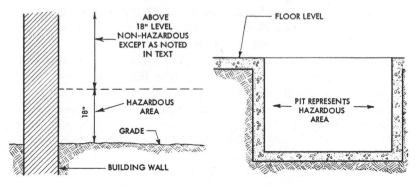

Fig. 13. Hazards in commercial garage

Commercial Garages

In general, the floor area of a commercial garage is considered a hazardous location to a level of 18 in above grade, as indicated at the left in Fig. 13. A pit below floor level, shown in the illustration at the right, is also a hazardous area. In order to comply with safety measures required by the 18 in rule, no wall plug receptacles should be installed in the area, nor should battery charging equipment be located in the room. Electrical equipment installed or used in a pit should be of the explosion-proof type called for in Class I locations.

Metallic conduit, type MI cable, or type ALS cable may be used in garages. Equipment less than 12 ft above the floor, and which gives off sparks or particles of hot metal, should be either totally enclosed or provided with protective screens. Portable lamps must be unswitched. When used in a hazardous area they must be of a type approved for this service.

Aircraft Hangars

Requirements for aircraft hangars parallel those for commercial garages, insofar as the 18 in and the pit rules are concerned. No battery charging is permitted within the hazardous space. In addition, the area within 5 ft horizontally of aircraft engines, fuel tanks, or aircraft structures which contain fuel, shall be considered Class I, Division 2 locations to the level of 5 ft above that of the upper surfaces of wings and engine enclosures.

Gasoline Service Stations

A dispensing island for gasoline is shown in Fig. 14. There are three electrically-driven pumps mounted in the dispensing area, a lighted canopy directly above the pumps, and a light standard with floodlight 15 ft away from the island.

The dangerous area includes all space within 20 ft, horizontally, of the dispensing area. At the pumps the hazardous area extends vertically to a height of 4 ft, and it must be treated as a Class I, Division 1 location. Beyond the island, the hazardous area extends upward to a height of only 18 in because gasoline vapor or fumes tend to settle near the ground level. This outer space must be treated as a Class I, Division 2 location.

Motors and junction boxes in bases of pumps must be of the explosion-proof type, and an approved seal must be provided in

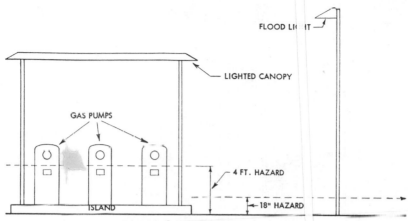

FLOOD LI(IT

LIGHTED CANOPY

GAS PUMPS

4 FT. HAZARD

ISLAND

18" HAZARD

Fig. 14. Gasoline dispensing area

each conduit entering a dispensing pump. No unic i, coupling, box, or fitting may be placed in the conduit between the s aling fitting and the point where the conduit leaves the Class I, Divi ion 1 area. Usually, a separate conduit is run from the panelboard ocation to each of the pumps.

It should be noted that the luminaires in the c nopy above the pumps are higher than the 4 ft limit of hazard. The efore, they may be ordinary lighting units. Although the lighting tandard at the right of the figure is within the 20 ft horizontal li it, the light is several feet above the 18 in height. An ordinary lug receptacle could not be placed at or near the base of the li ting standard unless it were more than 18 in vertically from grade evel.

Each circuit supplying equipment in or on a di ensing pump shall be provided with a means for disconnecting al conductors of the circuit from the source of supply. This provisi 1 is generally satisfied by using double-pole switches on circuits w ich enter the pumps, even though the supply is a 115-volt cir it with one grounded leg.

Outside area within 10 ft horizontally of any tank fill-pipe shall be considered a Class I, Division 2 location (unless, o course, it is already within a Class I, Division 1 area). Also, the sph rical volume within a 3-ft radius of a tank vent-pipe which disch ges upward shall be considered a Class I, Division 1 location. If he pipe discharges downward, the cylindrical volume below thi point, extending to the ground, shall be considered a Class I, D vision 2 lo-

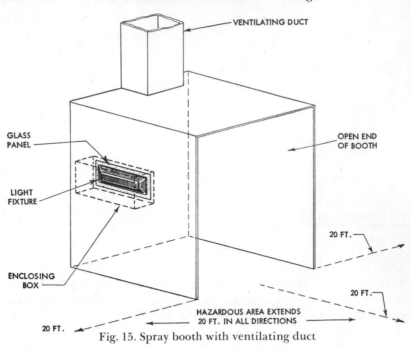

Fig. 15. Spray booth with ventilating duct

cation. This Division 2 rule also applies to the volume between the 3-ft radius and a 5-ft radius. In any case, the hazardous area does not extend beyond an unpierced wall.

Spray Booths and Spray Areas

Fig. 15 shows a spray booth with its ventilating duct. All area inside spray booth and exhaust duct must be treated as Class I, Division 1 hazards. Areas outside the booth, for 20 ft in every direction from the open face of the booth, must be treated as Class I, Division 2 hazards.

Class I, Division 1 treatment must be extended also to locations where spraying operations more extensive than "spot" or "touch-up" are conducted outside spray booths, and to all space within 20 ft horizontally from dip tanks and drainboards. Additional space within an open spraying area, beyond the 20 ft limit, is considered Class I, Division 2.

A spray booth may be lighted through glass panels provided the lighting fixtures are especially approved for the application. The glass panel must effectively isolate the hazardous area from the lighting unit.

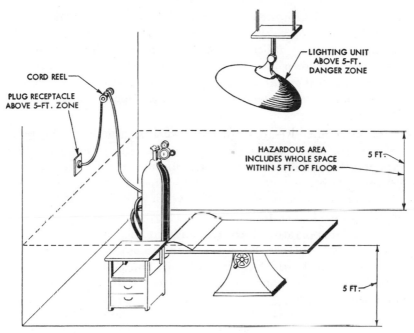

Fig. 16. Hazardous area in hospital operating room

Hospital Areas

The dangerous hospital areas, from standpoint of life or fire hazard, are the operating rooms where combustible anesthetics are given, and the rooms where such anesthetics are kept. Any room or space where combustible anesthetics or volatile disinfectants are stored must be treated as Class I, Division 1 location. Rules pertaining to operating rooms may be explained with the aid of Fig. 16.

The whole area within which the anesthetic is administered or used is designated Class I, Division 1 to a height of 5 ft. The reason for the 5 ft limit is that fumes tend to settle downward. All electrical equipment and devices installed within this 5 ft height limit must be suitable for Class I, Division 1 locations. Conduits installed within hollow walls or partitions come within the scope of this rule. It is customary to install plug receptacles and switches above this height. Conduits entering the hazardous zone must be effectively sealed.

Extension cords must be of the hard-usage type, and provided with cord reels or equivalent means for taking up surplus length. Portable lamps must be approved for Class I, Division 1 service. Plug receptacles used with these lamps must be polarized. Circuits entering the hazardous area shall be isolated from the general supply by transformers or by other methods. Normal conditions must be indicated by a green lamp which is lighted when the circuit is in use, and which is readily visible to those concerned. Wiring above the hazardous area may be in metal raceway, Type MI cable or Type ALS cable.

These circuits are controlled by switches, usually double-pole, which break all circuit conductors. Neither the primary nor the secondary voltage of an isolating transformer may be greater than 300 volts. Both case and core of a transformer used inside the operating room must be grounded. No overcurrent device may be installed within the hazardous area.

Electrical apparatus which frequently contacts bodies of persons, and which is used at a voltage greater than 8, are to be encased in a metallic case or sheath. All metal raceways and noncurrent carrying metal parts, except where the potential is 8 volts or less, shall be grounded. Resistors or impedances used in connection with apparatus must be approved for Class I locations, and so constructed that surface temperatures will not exceed 80 percent of the ignition point of the most volatile anesthetic.

X-ray apparatus and devices must be approved for Class I service, and arranged to prevent accumulation of electrostatic charges. This requirement is usually answered by use of high resistance grounds which remove static, or by conductive rubber floors.

TV apparatus employed within the operating room must conform to Class I requirements, and must be suitably guarded or screened against possibility of accidental hazards.

Motors in Class I Locations

In Class I, Division 1 locations, NEC 501–8(a) requires that motors, generators, and other rotating machinery shall be explosion-proof, positive pressure ventilated, or filled with inert gas. Flexible connections at motor terminals must also be explosion-proof.

In Class I, Division 2 locations, motors, generators, and other rotating electrical machinery in which centrifugal or sliding contact mechanisms are used shall be of the explosion-proof type, unless arcing and resistance devices are provided with enclosures approved for Division 2 areas.

Motors in Class II and Class III Locations

Electrical machinery used in Class II and Class III areas shall be totally enclosed, nonventilated; totally enclosed, pipe ventilated; or totally enclosed, fan-cooled and approved for such locations. Electrical equipment shall not be installed in locations where dust from production of magnesium, aluminum, or aluminum bronze powders may be present unless totally enclosed, or totally enclosed, fan-cooled, and specially approved for these locations.

REVIEW QUESTIONS

1. How are cables for IBM installations hidden from sight?
2. What current factor is recommended for a 75-ft cable?
3. Must X-ray installations comply with general code rules as to transformers and capacitors?
4. What is the rating of the largest branch circuit to which an X-ray machine can be plug connected?
5. What is the rating of the highest overcurrent device permitted with an infra-red-lamp heating device?
6. What percentage of nameplate current governs the carrying capacity of circuit conductors for a dielectric heater?
7. What percentage of nameplate current governs the maximum overcurrent protection for an electronic high-frequency generator?
8. What is the maximum allowable circuit protection for a 50-amp transformer type arc welder?
9. What size switch, rated in horsepower, is needed for a 100-amp, 230-volt, transformer arc welder?
10. What term expresses the percentage of time that a unit is actually welding?
11. State the maximum rating of an overcurrent device allowed with a 100-amp resistance welder.
12. State the maximum rating of a branch circuit for an electric sign.
13. What is the smallest size of conductor allowed inside a high-voltage electric sign?
14. Name a common type of seal fitting used in conduit runs entering or leaving a hazardous area.
15. To what height from the floor is a Class 1 hazard assumed to exist in a hospital operating room?
16. What types of motors are permitted in a Class 1 hazardous area?
17. How is the buzzer silenced in a nurse-call system?
18. How is the hallway signal light extinguished in a nurse-call system?
19. What type of circuit is used in a fire-alarm system?
20. Does the trouble bell on the fire-alarm system studied here, operate on A-C or on D-C?

Appendix

Tables in the Appendix from the National Electrical Code are reprinted by permission of the National Fire Protection Association. The National Electrical Code is published by the National Board of Fire Underwriters and single copies may be obtained from their offices listed below:

85 John Street, New York 38, N.Y.
222 West Adams Street, Chicago 6, Ill.
465 California Street, San Francisco 4, Calif.

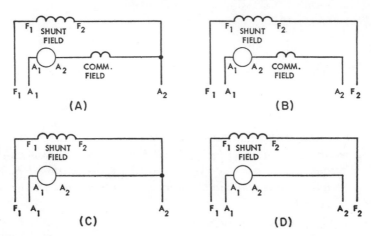

Connection diagrams for direct current shunt motors. (A) Nonreversing, commutating-pole type; (B) Reversing, commutating-pole type; (C) Nonreversing, without commutating poles; (D) Reversing, without commutating poles.

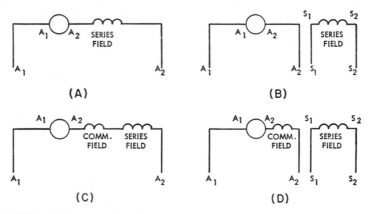

Connection diagrams for direct current series motors. (A) Nonreversing type; (B) Reversing type; (C) Nonreversing commutating-pole type; (D) Reversing commutating-pole type.

Luminaire Mounting Height for Systems with 40% or More of Fixture Output Downward†

Ceiling Height for Systems with Less than 40% of Fixture Output Downward†

Width (feet)	Length (feet)	8 / 10½	9 / 12	10 / 13½	11 / 15	12 / 16½	13 / 18	15 / 21	17 / 24	19 / 27	23 / 33	27 / 39	33 / 48	43 / 63	53 / 78
8	10	0.8	0.7	0.6	0.5	0.5									
	14	0.9	0.8	0.7	0.6	0.5	0.5								
	18	1.0	0.9	0.7	0.7	0.6	0.5								
	25	1.1	0.9	0.8	0.7	0.6	0.6	0.5							
	30	1.2	1.0	0.8	0.7	0.7	0.6	0.5							
	40	1.2	1.0	0.9	0.8	0.7	0.6	0.5	0.5						
10	10	0.9	0.8	0.7	0.6	0.5	0.5								
	14	1.1	0.9	0.8	0.7	0.6	0.6	0.5							
	18	1.2	1.0	0.9	0.8	0.7	0.6	0.5							
	25	1.3	1.1	1.0	0.8	0.8	0.7	0.6	0.5						
	30	1.4	1.2	1.0	0.9	0.8	0.7	0.6	0.5	0.5					
	40	1.5	1.2	1.1	0.9	0.8	0.8	0.6	0.6	0.5					
12	12	1.1	0.9	0.8	0.7	0.6	0.6	0.3							
	16	1.3	1.1	0.9	0.8	0.7	0.7	0.6							
	20	1.4	1.2	1.0	0.9	0.8	0.7	0.6	0.5	0.5					
	30	1.6	1.3	1.1	1.0	0.9	0.8	0.7	0.6	0.5					
	50	1.8	1.5	1.3	1.1	1.0	0.9	0.8	0.7	0.6	0.5				
14	14	1.3	1.1	0.9	0.8	0.7	0.7	0.6	0.5						
	20	1.5	1.3	1.1	1.0	0.9	0.8	0.7	0.6	0.5					
	30	1.7	1.5	1.3	1.1	1.0	0.9	0.8	0.7	0.6					
	40	1.9	1.6	1.4	1.2	1.1	1.0	0.8	0.7	0.6	0.5				
	60	2.1	1.8	1.5	1.3	1.2	1.1	0.9	0.8	0.7	0.6	0.5			
	80	2.2	1.8	1.6	1.4	1.3	1.1	1.0	0.8	0.7	0.6	0.5			
16	16	1.5	1.2	1.1	0.9	0.8	0.8	0.6	0.6	0.5					
	20	1.6	1.4	1.2	1.0	0.9	0.9	0.7	0.6	0.5					
	30	1.9	1.6	1.4	1.2	1.1	1.0	0.8	0.7	0.6	0.5				
	40	2.1	1.8	1.5	1.3	1.2	1.1	0.9	0.8	0.7	0.6	0.5			
	60	2.3	1.9	1.7	1.5	1.3	1.2	1.0	0.9	0.8	0.6	0.5			
	80	2.4	2.1	1.8	1.6	1.4	1.3	1.1	0.9	0.8	0.7	0.5			
18	20	1.7	1.5	1.3	1.1	1.0	0.9	0.8	0.7	0.6					
	30	2.1	1.7	1.5	1.3	1.2	1.1	0.9	0.8	0.7	0.6				
	40	2.3	1.9	1.7	1.5	1.3	1.2	1.0	0.9	0.8	0.6	0.5			
	60	2.5	2.1	1.9	1.6	1.5	1.3	1.1	1.0	0.8	0.7	0.6	0.5		
	80	2.7	2.3	2.0	1.7	1.6	1.4	1.2	1.0	0.9	0.7	0.6	0.5		
	100	2.8	2.4	2.0	1.8	1.6	1.5	1.2	1.1	0.9	0.7	0.6	0.5		
20	20	1.8	1.5	1.3	1.2	1.1	1.0	0.8	0.7	0.6	0.5				
	30	2.2	1.8	1.6	1.4	1.3	1.1	1.0	0.8	0.7	0.5				
	40	2.4	2.1	1.8	1.5	1.4	1.3	1.1	0.9	0.8	0.7	0.5			
	60	2.7	2.3	2.0	1.8	1.6	1.4	1.2	1.0	0.9	0.7	0.6	0.5		
	80	2.9	2.5	2.1	1.9	1.7	1.5	1.3	1.1	1.0	0.8	0.7	0.5		
	100	3.0	2.6	2.2	2.0	1.8	1.6	1.3	1.2	1.0	0.8	0.7	0.6		
	120	3.1	2.6	2.3	2.0	1.8	1.6	1.4	1.2	1.0	0.8	0.7	0.6		
25	30	2.5	2.1	1.8	1.6	1.4	1.3	1.1	0.9	0.8	0.7	0.6			
	40	2.8	2.4	2.1	1.8	1.6	1.5	1.2	1.1	0.9	0.8	0.7	0.5		
	60	3.2	2.7	2.4	2.1	1.9	1.7	1.4	1.2	1.1	0.9	0.7	0.6		
	80	3.5	2.9	2.5	2.2	2.0	1.8	1.5	1.3	1.2	1.0	0.8	0.6	0.5	
	100	3.6	3.1	2.7	2.4	2.1	1.9	1.6	1.4	1.2	1.0	0.8	0.7	0.5	
	120	3.8	3.2	2.8	2.4	2.2	2.0	1.7	1.4	1.3	1.0	0.8	0.7	0.5	
30	30	2.7	2.3	2.0	1.8	1.6	1.4	1.2	1.0	0.9	0.7	0.6	0.5		
	40	3.1	2.6	2.3	2.0	1.8	1.6	1.4	1.2	1.0	0.8	0.7	0.6		
	60	3.6	3.1	2.7	2.4	2.1	1.9	1.6	1.4	1.2	1.0	0.8	0.7	0.5	
	80	4.0	3.4	2.9	2.6	2.3	2.1	1.7	1.5	1.3	1.1	0.9	0.7	0.5	
	100	4.2	3.6	3.1	2.7	2.4	2.2	1.9	1.6	1.4	1.1	0.9	0.8	0.6	0.5
	120	4.4	3.7	3.2	2.8	2.5	2.3	1.9	1.7	1.5	1.2	1.0	0.8	0.6	0.5
	140	4.5	3.8	3.3	2.9	2.6	2.4	2.0	1.7	1.5	1.2	1.0	0.8	0.6	0.5
35	40	3.4	2.9	2.5	2.2	2.0	1.8	1.5	1.3	1.1	0.9	0.8	0.6		
	60	4.0	3.4	3.0	2.6	2.3	2.1	1.8	1.5	1.3	1.1	0.9	0.7	0.6	
	80	4.4	3.8	3.3	2.9	2.6	2.3	1.9	1.7	1.5	1.2	1.0	0.8	0.6	
	100	4.7	4.0	3.5	3.1	2.7	2.5	2.1	1.8	1.6	1.3	1.1	0.9	0.6	0.5
	120	4.9	4.2	3.6	3.2	2.9	2.6	2.2	1.9	1.6	1.3	1.1	0.9	0.7	0.5
	140	5+	4.3	3.7	3.3	3.0	2.7	2.2	2.0	1.7	1.4	1.1	0.9	0.7	0.6
40	40	3.6	3.1	2.7	2.4	2.1	1.9	1.6	1.4	1.2	1.0	0.8	0.7	0.5	
	60	4.4	3.7	3.2	2.8	2.5	2.3	1.9	1.7	1.5	1.2	1.0	0.8	0.6	0.5
	80	4.9	4.1	3.6	3.1	2.8	2.5	2.1	1.8	1.6	1.3	1.1	0.9	0.7	0.5
	100	5+	4.4	3.8	3.4	3.0	2.7	2.3	2.0	1.7	1.4	1.2	0.9	0.7	0.6
	120	5+	4.6	4.0	3.5	3.2	2.9	2.4	2.1	1.8	1.5	1.2	1.0	0.7	0.6
	140	5+	4.8	4.1	3.7	3.3	3.0	2.5	2.1	1.9	1.5	1.3	1.0	0.8	0.6
50	50	4.5	3.9	3.3	2.9	2.6	2.4	2.0	1.7	1.5	1.2	1.0	0.8	0.6	0.5
	70	5+	4.5	3.9	3.4	3.1	2.8	2.3	2.0	1.8	1.4	1.2	1.0	0.7	0.6
	100		5+	4.5	3.9	3.5	3.2	2.7	2.3	2.0	1.6	1.4	1.1	0.8	0.7
	140		5+	4.9	4.3	3.9	3.5	2.9	2.5	2.2	1.8	1.5	1.2	0.9	0.7
	170			5+	4.5	4.1	3.7	3.1	2.7	2.3	1.9	1.6	1.3	1.0	0.8
	200			5+	4.7	4.2	3.8	3.2	2.8	2.4	2.0	1.6	1.3	1.0	0.8
60	60		5+	4.0	3.5	3.2	2.9	2.4	2.1	1.8	1.5	1.2	1.0	0.7	0.6
	80		5+	4.6	4.0	3.6	3.3	2.7	2.4	2.1	1.7	1.4	1.2	0.9	0.7
	100		5+	5.0	4.4	4.0	3.6	3.0	2.6	2.3	1.8	1.5	1.2	0.9	0.7
	140			5+	4.9	4.4	4.0	3.4	2.9	2.5	2.1	1.7	1.4	1.0	0.8
	170				5+	4.7	4.2	3.6	3.1	2.7	2.3	1.8	1.5	1.1	0.9
	200				5+	4.9	4.4	3.7	3.2	2.8	2.3	1.9	1.5	1.1	0.9
80	80			5+	4.7	4.2	3.8	3.2	2.8	2.4	2.0	1.6	1.3	1.0	0.8
	140					5+	4.9	4.1	3.5	3.1	2.5	2.1	1.7	1.3	1.0
	200						5+	4.6	3.9	3.5	3.2	2.3	1.9	1.4	1.1
100	100					5+	4.8	4.0	3.5	3.0	2.4	2.0	1.6	1.2	1.0
	150						5+	4.8	4.1	3.6	2.9	2.5	2.0	1.5	1.2
	200							5+	4.6	4.0	3.3	2.7	2.2	1.7	1.3

Room Ratio Table

Reprinted from "General Lighting Design" by permission of General Electric Company

Appendix

Table 1. Maximum Number of Conductors in Trade Sizes of Conduit or Tubing

Derating factors for more than three conductors in raceways, see Note 8, Tables 310-12 through 310-15

Types RF-2, RFH-2, R, RH, RW, RH-RW, RHW, RHH, RU, RUH, RUW, SF and SFF
Types TF, T, TW, THW and THWN
(See Section 300-17, 300-18, 346-6 and 348-6)

Size AWG or MCM	Maximum Number of Conductors in Conduit or Tubing (Based upon % conductor fill, Table 3, Chap. 9, for new work)											
	½ Inch	¾ Inch	1 Inch	1¼ Inch	1½ Inch	2 Inch	2½ Inch	3 Inch	3½ Inch	4 Inch	5 Inch	6 Inch
18	7	12	20	35	49	80	115	176				
16	6	10	17	30	41	68	98	150				
14	4	6	10	18	25	41	58	90	121	155		
12	3	5	8	15	21	34	50	76	103	132	208	
10	1	4	7	13	17	29	41	64	86	110	173	
8	1	3	4	7	10	17	25	38	52	67	105	152
6	1	1	3	4	6	10	15	23	32	41	64	93
4	1	1	1	3*	5	8	12	18	24	31	49	72
3		1	1	3	4	7	10	16	21	28	44	63
2		1	1	3	3	6	9	14	19	24	38	55
1		1	1	1	3	4	7	10	14	18	29	42
0			1	1	2	4	6	9	12	16	25	37
00			1	1	1	3	5	8	11	14	22	32
000			1	1	1	3	4	7	9	12	19	27
0000				1	1	2	3	6	8	10	16	23
250				1	1	1	3	5	6	8	13	19
300				1	1	1	3	4	5	7	11	16
350				1	1	1	1	3	5	6	10	15
400					1	1	1	3	4	6	9	13
500					1	1	1	3	4	5	8	11
600						1	1	1	3	4	6	9
700						1	1	1	3	3	6	8
750						1	1	1	3	3	5	8
800						1	1	1	2	3	5	7
900						1	1	1	1	3	4	7
1000						1	1	1	1	3	4	6
1250							1	1	1	1	3	5
1500								1	1	1	3	4
1750								1	1	1	2	4
2000								1	1	1	1	3

*Where an existing service run of conduit or electrical metallic tubing does not exceed 50 ft. in length and does not contain more than the equivalent of two quarter bends from end to end, two No. 4 insulated and one No. 4 bare conductors may be installed in 1-inch conduit or tubing.

Table 1. National Electrical Code

Table 8. Properties of Conductors

Size AWG	Area Cir. Mils	Concentric Lay Stranded Conductors		Bare Conductors		D. C. Resistance Ohms/M Ft. at 25°C, 77°F.		
		No. Wires	Dia. Each Wire Inches	Dia. Inches	*Area Sq. Inches	Copper		Aluminum
						Bare Cond.	Tin'd. Cond.	
18	1624	Solid	.0403	.0403	.0013	6.510	6.77	10.9
16	2583	Solid	.0508	.0508	.0020	4.094	4.25	6.85
14	4107	Solid	.0641	.0641	.0032	2.575	2.68	4.31
12	6530	Solid	.0808	.0808	.0051	1.619	1.69	2.71
10	10380	Solid	.1019	.1019	.0081	1.018	1.06	1.70
8	16510	Solid	.1285	.1285	.0130	.641	.660	1.07
6	26250	7	.0612	.184	.027	.410	.426	.674
4	41740	7	.0772	.232	.042	.259	.269	.423
3	52640	7	.0867	.260	.053	.205	.213	.336
2	66370	7	.0974	.292	.067	.162	.169	.266
1	83690	19	.0664	.332	.087	.129	.134	.211
0	105500	19	.0745	.373	.109	.102	.106	.168
00	133100	19	.0837	.418	.137	.0811	.0844	.134
000	167800	19	.0940	.470	.173	.0642	.0668	.105
0000	211600	19	.1055	.528	.219	.0509	.0524	.0837
	250000	37	.0822	.575	.260	.0431	.0444	.0708
	300000	37	.0900	.630	.312	.0360	.0371	.0590
	350000	37	.0973	.681	.364	.0308	.0310	.0506
	400000	37	.1040	.728	.416	.0270	.0278	.0443
	500000	37	.1162	.814	.520	.0216	.0225	.0354
	600000	61	.0992	.893	.626	.0180	.0185	.0295
	700000	61	.1071	.964	.730	.0154	.0159	.0253
	750000	61	.1109	.998	.782	.0144	.0148	.0236
	800000	61	.1145	1.031	.835	.0135	.0139	.0221
	900000	61	.1215	1.093	.938	.0120	.0124	.0197
	1000000	61	.1280	1.152	1.042	.0108	.0111	.0176
	1250000	91	.1172	1.289	1.305	.00864	.00890	.0142
	1500000	91	.1284	1.412	1.566	.00719	.00740	.0118
	1750000	127	.1174	1.526	1.829	.00617	.00636	.0101
	2000000	127	.1255	1.631	2.089	.00539	.00555	.00884

*Area given is that of a circle having a diameter equal to the overall diameter of a stranded conductor.

The values given in the table are those given in Circular 31 of the National Bureau of Standards except that those shown in the 8th column are those given in Specification B33 of the American Society for Testing Materials.

The resistance values given in the last three columns are applicable only to direct current. When conductors larger than No. 4/0 are used with alternating current the multiplying factors in Table 9, Chapter 9 should be used to compensate for skin effect.

Table 8. National Electrical Code

Table 220-2(a). General Lighting Loads by Occupancies

Type of Occupancy	Unit Load per Sq. Ft. (Watts)
Armories and Auditoriums	1
Banks	2
Barber Shops and Beauty Parlors	3
Churches	1
Clubs	2
Court Rooms	2
*Dwellings (Other Than Hotels)	3
Garages — Commercial (storage)	½
Hospitals	2
*Hotels, including apartment houses without provisions for cooking by tenants	2
Industrial Commercial (Loft) Buildings	2
Lodge Rooms	1½
Office Buildings	5
Restaurants	2
Schools	3
Stores	3
Warehouses Storage	¼
In any of the above occupancies except single-family dwellings and individual apartments of multi-family dwellings:	
Assembly Halls and Auditoriums	1
Halls, Corridors, Closets	½
Storage Spaces	¼

*All receptacle outlets of 15-ampere or less rating in single-family and multi-family dwellings and in guest rooms of hotels [except those connected to the receptacle circuits specified in Section 220-3(b)] may be considered as outlets for general illumination, and no additional load need be included for such outlets. The provisions of Section 220-2(b) shall apply to all other receptacle outlets

Table 220-2 (a) National Electrical Code

Table 430-7(b). Locked Rotor Indicating Code Letters

Code Letter	Kilovolt-Amperes per Horsepower with Locked Rotor
A	0 — 3.14
B	3.15 — 3.54
C	3.55 — 3.99
D	4.0 — 4.49
E	4.5 — 4.99
F	5.0 — 5.59
G	5.6 — 6.29
H	6.3 — 7.09
J	7.1 — 7.99
K	8.0 — 8.99
L	9.0 — 9.99
M	10.0 — 11.19
N	11.2 — 12.49
P	12.5 — 13.99
R	14.0 — 15.99
S	16.0 — 17.99
T	18.0 — 19.99
U	20.0 — 22.39
V	22.4 — and up

The above table is an adopted standard of the National Electrical Manufacturers Association.
The code letter indicating motor input with locked rotor must be in an individual block on the nameplate, properly designated. This code letter is to be used for determining branch-circuit overcurrent protection by reference to Table 430-152, as provided in Section 430-52.

Table 430-7 (b) National Electrical Code

Table 430-23 (Exception)

Resistor Duty Classification	Carrying Capacity of Wire in Per Cent of Full-Load Secondary Current
Light starting duty	35
Heavy starting duty	45
Extra heavy starting duty	55
Light intermittent duty	65
Medium intermittent duty	75
Heavy intermittent duty	85
Continuous duty	110

Table 430-23 (Exception) National Electrical Code

Notes To Tables 310-12 through 310-15.

Current-Carrying Capacity. The maximum, continuous, current-carrying capacities of copper conductors are given in Tables 310-12 and 310-13. The current-carrying capacities of aluminum conductors are given in Tables 310-14 and 310-15.

1. Explanation of Tables. For explanation of Type Letters, and for recognized size of conductors for the various conductor insulations, see Sections 310-2 and 310-3. For installation requirements see Section 310-1 through 310-7, and the various Articles of this Code. For flexible cords see Tables 400-9 and 400-11.

2. Application of Tables. For open wiring on insulators and for concealed knob-and-tube work, the allowable current-carrying capacities of Tables 310-13 and 310-15 shall be used. For all other recognized wiring methods, the allowable current-carrying capacities of Tables 310-12 and 310-14 shall be used, unless otherwise provided in this Code.

3. Aluminum Conductors. For aluminum conductors, the allowable current-carrying capacities shall be in accordance with Tables 310-14 and 310-15.

4. Bare Conductors. Where bare conductors are used with insulated conductors, their allowable current-carrying capacity shall be limited to that permitted for the insulated conductors of the same size.

5. Type MI Cable. The temperature limitation on which the current carrying capacities of Type MI cable are based, is determined by the insulating materials used in the end seal. Termination fittings incorporating unimpreg- nated organic insulating materials are limited to 85°C. operation.

6. Ultimate Insulation Temperature. In no case shall conductors be associated together in such a way with respect to the kind of circuit, the wiring method employed, or the number of conductors, that the limiting temperature of the conductors will be exceeded.

7. Use of Conductors With Higher Operating Temperatures. Where the room temperature is within 10 degrees C of the maximum allowable operating temperature of the insulation, it is desirable to use an insulation with a higher maximum allowable operating temperature; although insulation can be used in a room temperature approaching its maximum allowable operating temperature limit if the current is reduced in accordance with the Correction Factors for different room temperatures.

8. More Than Three Conductors in a Raceway or Cable. Tables 310-12 and 310-14 give the allowable current-carrying capacities for not more than three conductors in a raceway or cable. Where the number of conductors in a raceway or cable exceeds three, the allowable current-carrying capacity of each conductor shall be re-

Notes to Tables 310-12 through 310-15 National Electrical Code

duced as shown in the following Table:

Number of Conductors	Per Cent of Values in Tables 310-12 and 310-14
4 to 6	80
7 to 24	70
25 to 42	60
43 and above	50

Exception — When conductors of different systems, as provided in Section 300-3, are installed in a common raceway the derating factors shown above apply to the number of Power and Lighting (Articles 210, 215, 220 and 230) conductors only.

Where single conductor or multi-conductor cables are stacked or bundled without maintaining spacing and are not installed in raceways, the individual current-carrying capacity of each conductor shall be reduced as shown in the above table.

9. Where Type RH-RW rubber insulated wire is used in wet locations the allowable current-carrying capacities current carrying capacities shall be that of Column 2 in Tables 310-12 through 310-15. Where used in dry locations the allowable current-carrying capacities shall be that of Column 3 in Tables 310-12 through 310-15.

10. **Overcurrent Protection.** Where the standard ratings and setting of overcurrent devices do not correspond with the ratings and settings allowed for conductors, the next higher standard rating and setting may be used.

Except as limited in Section 240-5.

11. **Neutral Conductor.** A neutral conductor which carries only the unbalanced current from other conductors, as in the case of normally balanced circuits of three or more conductors, shall not be counted in determining current-carrying capacities as provided for in Note 8.

In a 3-wire circuit consisting of two phase wires and the neutral of a 4-wire, 3-phase WYE connected system, a common conductor carries approximately the same current as the other conductors and is not therefore considered as a neutral conductor.

12. **Voltage Drop.** The allowable current-carrying capacities in Tables 310-12 through 310-15 are based on temperature alone and do not take voltage drop into consideration.

13. **Deterioration of Insulation.** It should be noted that even the best grades of rubber insulation will deteriorate in time, so eventually will need to be replaced.

14. **Aluminum Sheathed Cable.** The current-carrying capacities of Type ALS cable are determined by the temperature limitation of the insulated conductors incorporated within the cable. Hence the current-carrying capacities of aluminum sheathed cable may be determined from the columns in Tables 310-12 and 310-14 applicable to the type of insulated conductors employed within the cable. See Note 9.

Notes to Tables 310-12 through 310-15 National Electrical Code

Table 310-12. Allowable Current-Carrying Capacities of Insulated Copper Conductors in Amperes

Not More than Three Conductors in Raceway or Cable or Direct Burial (Based on Room Temperature of 30° C. 86° F.)

Size AWG MCM	Rubber Type R Type RW Type RU Type RUW (14-2) Type RH-RW See Note 9 Thermoplastic Type T Type TW	Rubber Type RH RUH (14-2) Type RH-RW See Note 9 Type RHW Thermoplastic Type THW THWN	Paper Thermoplastic Asbestos Type TA Thermoplastic Type TBS Silicone Type SA Var-Cam Type V Asbestos Var-Cam Type AVB MI Cable RHH†	Asbestos Var-Cam Type AVA Type AVL	Impregnated Asbestos Type AI (14-8) Type AIA	Asbestos Type A (14-8) Type AA
14	15	15	25	30	30	30
12	20	20	30	35	40	40
10	30	30	40	45	50	55
8	40	45	50	60	65	70
6	55	65	70	80	85	95
4	70	85	90	105	115	120
3	80	100	105	120	130	145
2	95	115	120	135	145	165
1	110	130	140	160	170	190
0	125	150	155	190	200	225
00	145	175	185	215	230	250
000	165	200	210	245	265	285
0000	195	230	235	275	310	340
250	215	255	270	315	335	....
300	240	285	300	345	380	....
350	260	310	325	390	420	....
400	280	335	360	420	450	....
500	320	380	405	470	500	....
600	355	420	455	525	545	....
700	385	460	490	560	600	....
750	400	475	500	580	620	....
800	410	490	515	600	640	....
900	435	520	555	...	....	....
1000	455	545	585	680	730	....
1250	495	590	645	....	....	....
1500	520	625	700	785	....	....
1750	545	650	735	....	....	....
2000	560	665	775	840	....	....

CORRECTION FACTORS, ROOM TEMPS. OVER 30° C. 86° F.

C.	F.						
40	104	.82	.88	.90	.94	.95	....
45	113	.71	.82	.85	.90	.92	....
50	122	.58	.75	.80	.87	.89	....
55	131	.41	.67	.74	.83	.86	....
60	140	....	.58	.67	.79	.83	.91
70	158	....	.35	.52	.71	.76	.87
75	167	....	....	.43	.66	.72	.86
80	176	....	....	.30	.61	.69	.84
90	194	....	....	....	.50	.61	.80
100	212	....	....	....	....	.51	.77
120	248	....	....	....	....	....	.69
140	284	....	....	....	....	....	.59

†The current-carrying capacities for Type RHH conductors for sizes AWG 14, 12 and 10 shall be the same as designated for Type RH conductors in this Table.

Table 310-12 National Electrical Code

Table 310-14. Allowable Current-Carrying Capacities of Insulated Aluminum Conductors in Amperes

Not More than Three Conductors in Raceway or Cable or Direct Burial (Based on Room Temperature of 30° C. 86° F.)

Size AWG MCM	Rubber Type R, RW, RU, RUW (12-2) Type RH-RW Note 9 Thermoplastic Type T TW	Rubber Type RH RUH (14-2) Type RH-RW Note 9 Type RHW Thermoplastic Type THW THWN	Paper Thermoplastic Asbestos Type TA Thermoplastic Type TBS Silicone Type SA Var-Cam Type V Asbestos Var-Cam Type AVB MI Cable RHH†	Asbestos Var-Cam Type AVA Type AVL	Impregnated Asbestos Type AI (14-8) Type AIA	Asbestos Typ A (14) Type AA
12	15	15	25	25	30	30
10	25	25	30	35	40	45
8	30	40	40	45	50	55
6	40	50	55	60	65	75
4	55	65	70	80	90	95
3	65	75	80	95	100	115
*2	75	90	95	105	115	130
*1	85	100	110	125	135	150
*0	100	120	125	150	160	180
*00	115	135	145	170	180	200
*000	130	155	165	195	210	225
*0000	155	180	185	215	245	270
250	170	205	215	250	270	....
300	190	230	240	275	305	....
350	210	250	260	310	335	....
400	225	270	290	335	360	....
500	260	310	330	380	405	....
600	285	340	370	425	440	....
700	310	375	395	455	485	....
750	320	385	405	470	500	....
800	330	395	415	485	520	....
900	355	425	455	....	....	....
1000	375	445	480	560	600	....
1250	405	485	530	....	....	....
1500	435	520	580	650	....	....
1750	455	545	615	....	....	....
2000	470	560	650	705	....	....

CORRECTION FACTORS, ROOM TEMPS. OVER 30° C. 86° F.

C.	F.						
40	104	82	.88	.90	.94	.95	....
45	118	.71	.82	.85	.90	.92	....
50	122	.58	.75	.80	.87	.89	....
55	131	.41	.67	.74	.83	.86	....
60	140	....	.58	.67	.79	.83	.91
70	158	....	.35	.52	.71	.76	.87
75	167	....	....	.43	.66	.72	.86
80	176	....	....	.30	.61	.69	.84
90	194	....	....	....	.50	.61	.80
100	212	....	....	....	....	.61	.77
120	248	....	....	....	....	....	.69
140	284	....	....	....	....	....	.59

*For three wire, single phase service and sub-service circuits, the allowable current-carrying capacity of RH, RH-RW, RHH, RHW, and THW aluminum conductors shall be for sizes #2-100 Amp., #1-110 Amp., #1/0-125 Amp., #2/0-150 Amp., #3/0-170 Amp. and #4/0-200 Amp.

†The current-carrying capacities for Type RHH conductors for sizes AWG 12, 10 and 8 shall be the same as designated for Type RH conductors in this Table.

Table 310-14 National Electrical Code

Table 430-146. Overcurrent Protection for Motors
(See Tables 430-152 and 430-153)

These values are in accordance with Sections 430-6, 430-22, 430-32, 430-34, 430-52, 430-59, except as follows: The current values in Column 1 are to be taken from Tables 430-147 through 430-150, including footnotes, but the values shown for running protection in Columns 2 and 3 must be modified if nameplate full load current values are different, as provided in Section 430-6. The current values shown in Columns 2 and 3 must be reduced by 8 per cent for all motors other than open type motors marked to have a temperature rise of not over 40°C. as required by Section 430-32. For certain exceptions to the values in Columns 4, 5, 6, and 7, see Sections 430-52, and 430-59. See Section 430-53 for values to be used for several motors on one branch circuit. For running protection of motors, see Section 430-32. For setting of motor-branch-circuit protective devices, see Tables in Sections 430-152 and 430-153. For grouping of small motors under the protection of a single set of fuses, see Section 430-53.

Col. No. 1	2	3	4	5	6	7
	For Running Protection of Motors		Maximum Allowable Rating or Setting of Branch Circuit Protective Devices			
Full load current rating of motor amperes	Maximum rating	Maximum setting	With Code Letters: Single phase, squirrel cage and synchronous. Full voltage, resistor or reactor starting, Code letters F to V inclusive. Without Code Letters: Same as above.	With Code Letters: Single phase, squirrel cage and synchronous. Full voltage, resistor or reactor start, Code letters B to E inclusive. Auto transformer start, Code letters F to V inclusive. Without Code Letters: (Not more than 30 Amperes) squirrel cage and synchronous, auto transformer start, high reactance squirrel cage.*	With Code Letters: Squirrel cage and synchronous auto transformer start, Code letters B to E inclusive. Without Code Letters: (More than 30 amperes) Squirrel cage and synchronous auto transformer start, high reactance squirrel cage.*	With Code Letters: All motors code letter A. Without Code Letters: DC and wound rotor motors.

Table 430-146 National Electrical Code

No.	of non-adjustable protective devices. Amps.	of adjustable protective devices. Amps.	Fuses	Circuit Breakers (Non-adjustable Over-load Trip)	Fuses	Circuit Breakers (Non-adjustable Over-load Trip)	Fuses	Circuit Breakers (Non-adjustable Over-load Trip)	Fuses	Circuit Breakers (Non-adjustable Over-load Trip)
1	2	1.25	15	15	15	15	15	15	15	15
2	3	2.50	15	15	15	15	15	15	15	15
3	4	3.75	15	15	15	15	15	15	15	15
4	6	5.0	15	15	15	15	15	15	15	15
5	8	6.25	15	15	15	15	15	15	15	15
6	8	7.50	20	15	15	15	15	15	15	15
7	10	8.75	25	15	15	15	15	15	15	15
8	10	10.0	25	20	20	20	20	20	15	15
9	12	11.25	30	20	20	20	20	20	15	15
10	15	12.50	30	30	25	20	20	20	15	15
11	15	13.75	35	30	25	30	25	30	20	20
12	15	15.00	40	30	30	30	25	30	20	20
13	20	16.25	40	40	30	30	30	30	20	20
14	20	17.50	45	40	35	30	30	30	25	30
15	20	18.75	45	40	35	30	30	30	25	30
16	20	20.00	50	40	40	40	35	40	25	30
17	25	21.25	60	50	40	40	35	40	30	30
18	25	22.50	60	50	45	40	40	40	30	30
19	25	23.75	60	50	45	40	40	40	30	30
20	25	25.00	60	50	50	40	40	40	30	30
22	30	27.50	70	70	60	50	45	50	35	40
24	30	30.00	80	70	60	50	50	50	40	40
26	35	32.50	80	70	70	70	60	70	40	40
28	35	35.00	90	70	70	70	60	70	45	50

*See note at end of table.

Table 430-146 National Electrical Code (*Continued*)

Col. No. 1	2	3	4		5		6		7	
	For Running Protection of Motors		Maximum Allowable Rating or Setting of Branch Circuit Protective Devices							
	Maximum rating of nonadjustable protective devices.	Maximum setting of adjustable protective devices.	With Code Letters Single phase, squirrel cage and synchronous. Full voltage, resistor or reactor starting, Code letters F to V inclusive. Without Code Letters Same as above		With Code Letters Single phase, squirrel cage and synchronous. Full voltage, resistor or reactor start, Code letters B to E inclusive. Auto transformer start, Code letters F to V inclusive. Without Code Letters (Not more than 30 Amperes) squirrel cage and synchronous, auto transformer start, high reactance squirrel cage.*		With Code Letters Squirrel cage and synchronous auto transformer start, Code letters B to E inclusive. Without Code Letters (More than 30 amperes) Squirrel cage and synchronous auto transformer start, high reactance squirrel cage.*		With Code Letters All motors code letter A. Without Code Letters DC and wound rotor motors.	
Full load current rating of motor amperes	Amps.	Amps.	Fuses	Circuit Breakers (Non-adjustable Over-load Trip)	Fuses	Circuit Breakers (Non-adjustable Over-load Trip)	Fuses	Circuit Breakers (Non-adjustable Over-load Trip)	Fuses	Circuit Breakers (Non-adjustable Over-load Trip)
30	40	37.50	90	100	80	70	60	70	45	50
32	40	40.00	100	100	80	70	70	70	50	50
34	45	42.50	110	100	90	70	70	70	60	70
36	45	45.00	110	100	90	100	80	100	60	70

Table 430-146 National Electrical Code (*Continued*)

38	50	47.50	125	100	100	100	80	100	60	70
40	50	50.00	125	100	100	100	80	100	60	70
42	50	52.50	125	125	110	100	90	100	70	70
44	60	55.00	125	125	110	100	90	100	70	70
46	60	57.50	150	125	125	100	100	100	70	70
48	60	60.00	150	125	125	100	100	100	80	100
50	60	62.50	150	125	125	100	100	100	80	100
52	70	65.00	175	150	150	125	110	125	80	100
54	70	67.50	175	150	150	125	110	125	90	100
56	70	70.00	175	150	150	125	125	125	90	100
58	70	72.50	175	150	150	125	125	125	90	100
60	80	75.00	200	175	175	125	125	125	90	100
62	80	77.50	200	175	175	125	125	125	100	100
64	80	80.00	200	175	175	150	150	150	100	100
66	80	82.50	200	175	175	150	150	150	100	100
68	90	85.00	225	175	175	150	150	150	110	125
70	90	87.50	225	175	175	150	150	150	110	125
72	90	90.00	225	200	200	150	150	150	110	125
74	90	92.50	225	200	200	150	150	150	125	125
76	100	95.00	250	200	200	175	175	175	125	125
78	100	97.50	250	200	200	175	175	175	125	125
80	100	100.00	250	200	200	175	175	175	125	125
82	100	102.50	250	225	225	175	175	175	125	150
84	110	105.00	250	225	225	175	175	175	150	150
86	110	107.50	300	225	225	200	200	200	150	150
88	110	110.00	300	225	225	200	200	200	150	150
90	110	112.50	300	225	225	200	200	200	150	150
92	125	115.00	300	250	250	200	200	200	150	150
94	125	117.50	300	250	250	200	200	200	150	150
96	125	120.00	300	250	250	200	200	200	150	150
98	125	122.50	300	250	250	200	200	200	150	150
100	125	125.00	300	250	250	200	200	200	150	150
105	150	131.50	350	300	300	225	225	225	175	175
110	150	137.50	350	300	300	225	225	225	175	175
115	150	144.00	350	300	300	250	250	250	175	175
120	150	150.00	400	300	300	250	250	250	200	200

Table 430-146 National Electrical Code (*Continued*)

Col. No. 1	2	3	4 Maximum Allowable Rating or Setting of Branch Circuit Protective Devices		5		6		7	
Full load current rating of motor amperes	For Running Protection of Motors		With Code Letters Single phase, squirrel cage and synchronous. Full voltage, resistor or reactor starting, Code letters F to V inclusive. Without Code Letters Same as above.		With Code Letters Single phase, squirrel cage and synchronous. Full voltage, resistor or reactor start, Code letters B to E inclusive. Auto transformer start, Code letters F to V inclusive. Without Code Letters (Not more than 30 Amperes) squirrel cage and synchronous, auto transformer start, high reactance squirrel cage.*		With Code Letters Squirrel cage and synchronous auto transformer start, Code letters B to E inclusive. Without Code Letters (More than 30 amperes) Squirrel cage and synchronous auto transformer start, high reactance squirrel cage.*		With Code Letters All motors code letter A. Without Code Letters DC and wound rotor motors.	
	Maximum rating of nonadjustable protective devices. Amps.	Maximum setting of adjustable protective devices. Amps.	Fuses	Circuit Breakers (Nonadjustable Overload Trip)	Fuses	Circuit Breakers (Nonadjustable Overload Trip)	Fuses	Circuit Breakers (Nonadjustable Overload Trip)	Fuses	Circuit Breakers (Nonadjustable Overload Trip)
125	175	156.50	400	350	350	250	250	250	200	200
130	175	162.50	400	350	350	300	300	300	200	200
135	175	169.00	450	350	350	300	300	300	225	225
140	175	175.00	450	350	350	300	300	300	225	225

Table 430-146 National Electrical Code (*Continued*)

145	200	181.50	450	400	400	300	300	300	225	225
150	200	187.50	450	400	400	300	300	300	225	225
155	200	194.00	500	400	400	350	350	350	250	250
160	200	200.00	500	400	400	350	350	350	250	250
165	225	206.00	500	500	450	350	350	350	250	250
170	225	213.00	500	500	450	350	350	350	300	300
175	225	219.00	600	500	450	350	350	350	300	300
180	225	225.00	600	500	450	400	400	400	300	300
185	250	231.00	600	500	500	400	400	400	300	300
190	250	238.00	600	500	500	400	400	400	300	300
195	250	244.00	600	500	500	400	400	400	300	300
200	250	250.00	600	500	500	400	400	400	300	300
210	250	263.00	800	600	600	500	450	500	350	350
220	300	275.00	800	600	600	500	450	500	350	350
230	300	288.00	800	600	600	500	500	500	350	350
240	300	300.00	800	600	600	500	500	500	400	400
250	300	313.00	800	700	800	500	500	500	400	400
260	350	325.00	800	700	800	600	600	600	400	400
270	350	338.00	1000	700	800	600	600	600	450	500
280	350	350.00	1000	700	800	600	600	600	450	500
290	350	363.00	1000	800	800	600	600	600	450	500
300	400	375.00	1000	800	800	600	600	600	450	500
320	400	400.00	1000	800	800	700	800	700	500	500
340	450	425.00	1200	1000	1000	700	800	700	600	600
360	450	450.00	1200		1000	800	800	800	600	600
380	500	475.00	1200		1000	800	800	800	600	600
400	500	500.00	1200		1000		1000		600	600
420	600	525.00	1600		1200		1000		800	700
440	600	550.00	1600		1200		1000		800	700
460	600	575.00	1670		1200		1000		800	700
480		600.00	1600		1200		1000		800	800
500		625.00	1600		1600		1000		800	800

*High-reactance squirrel-cage motors are those designed to limit the starting current by means of deepslot secondaries or double-wound secondaries and are generally started on full voltage.

Table 430-146 National Electrical Code (*Continued*)

Table 430-147. Full-Load Currents in Amperes Direct-Current Motors

The following values of full-load currents are for motors running at base speed.

HP	120V	240V
¼	2.9	1.5
⅓	3.6	1.8
½	5.2	2.6
¾	7.4	3.7
1	9.4	4.7
1½	13.2	6.6
2	17	8.5
3	25	12.2
5	40	20
7½	58	29
10	76	38
15		55
20		72
25		89
30		106
40		140
50		173
60		206
75		255
100		341
125		425
150		506
200		675

Table 430-147 National Electrical Code

Table 430-148. Full Load Currents in Amperes Single Phase Alternating Current Motors

The following values of full-load currents are for motors running at usual speeds and motors with normal torque characteristics. Motors built for especially low speeds or high torques may have higher full-load currents, in which case the nameplate current ratings should be used.

To obtain full-load currents of 208- and 200-volt motors, increase corresponding 230-volt motor full-load currents by 10 and 15 per cent, respectively.

The voltages listed are rated motor voltages. Corresponding nominal system voltages are 110 to 120, 220 to 240, 440 to 480.

HP	115V	230V	440V
⅙	4.4	2.2	..
¼	5.8	2.9	..
⅓	7.2	3.6	..
½	9.8	4.9	..
¾	13.8	6.9	..
1	16	8	..
1½	20	10	..
2	24	12	..
3	34	17	..
5	56	28	..
7½	80	40	21
10	100	50	26

Table 430-148 National Electrical Code

Table 430-150. Full-Load Current*
Three-Phase A.C. Motors

HP	Induction Type Squirrel-Cage and Wound Rotor Amperes					Synchronous Type †Unity Power Factor Amperes			
	110V	220V	440V	550V	2300V	220V	440V	550V	2300V
½	4	2	1	.8					
¾	5.6	2.8	1.4	1.1					
1	7	3.5	1.8	1.4					
1½	10	5	2.5	2.0					
2	13	6.5	3.3	2.6					
3		9	4.5	4					
5		15	7.5	6					
7½		22	11	9					
10		27	14	11					
15		40	20	16					
20		52	26	21					
25		64	32	26	7	54	27	22	5.4
30		78	39	31	8.5	65	33	26	6.5
40		104	52	41	10.5	86	43	35	8
50		125	63	50	13	108	54	44	10
60		150	75	60	16	128	64	51	12
75		185	93	74	19	161	81	65	15
100		246	123	98	25	211	106	85	20
125		310	155	124	31	264	132	106	25
150		360	180	144	37		158	127	30
200		480	240	192	48		210	168	40

For full-load currents of 208- and 200-volt motors, increase the corresponding 220-volt motor full-load current by 6 and 10 per cent, respectively.

*These values of full-load current are for motors running at speeds usual for belted motors and motors with normal torque characteristics. Motors built for especially low speeds or high torques may require more running current, in which case the nameplate current rating should be used.

†For 90 and 80 per cent P. F. the above figures should be multiplied by 1.1 and 1.25 respectively.

The voltages listed are rated motor voltages. Corresponding nominal system voltages are 110 to 120, 220 to 240, 440 to 480 and 550 to 600 volts.

Table 430-150 National Electrical Code

Table 430-151
Locked-Rotor Current Conversion Table
As Determined from Horsepower and Voltage Rating
For Use Only With Sections 430-83, Exception No. 3, and
430-110(b)

Max. H.P. Rating	Maximum Motor Locked—Rotor-Amperes					
	Single Phase		Two or Three Phase			
	115V	230V	110V	220V	440V	550V
½	58.8	29.4	24	12	6	4.8
¾	82.8	41.4	33.6	16.8	8.4	6.6
1	96	48	42	21	10.8	8.4
1½	120	60	60	30	15	12
2	144	72	78	39	19.8	15.6
3	204	102	—	54	27	24
5	336	168	—	90	45	36
7½	480	240	—	132	66	54
10	600	300	—	162	84	66
15	—	—	—	240	120	96
20	—	—	—	312	156	126
25	—	—	—	384	192	156
30	—	—	—	468	234	186
40	—	—	—	624	312	246
50	—	—	—	750	378	300
60	—	—	—	900	450	360
75	—	—	—	1110	558	444
100	—	—	—	1476	738	588
125	—	—	—	1860	930	744
150	—	—	—	2160	1080	864
200	—	—	—	2880	1440	1152

Table 430-152. Maximum Rating or Setting of Motor-Branch-Circuit Protective Devices for Motors Marked with a Code Letter Indicating Locked Rotor KVA

Type of Motor	Per Cent of Full-Load Current		
	Fuse Rating (See also Table 430-146, Columns 4, 5, 6, 7)	Circuit-Breaker Instantaneous Type	Setting Time Limit Type
All AC single-phase and polyphase squirrel cage and synchronous motors with full-voltage, resistor or reactor starting:			
Code Letter A	150	...	150
Code Letter B to E	250	...	200
Code Letter F to V	300	...	250
All AC squirrel cage and synchronous motors with auto-transformer starting:			
Code Letter A	150	...	150
Code Letter B to E	200	...	200
Code Letter F to V	250	...	200

For certain exceptions to the values specified see Sections 430-52 and 430-54. The values given in the last column also cover the ratings of non-adjustable, time-limit types of circuit-breakers which may also be modified as in Section 430-52.

Synchronous motors of the low-torque, low-speed type (usually 450 RPM or lower), such as are used to drive reciprocating compressors, pumps, etc., which start up unloaded, do not require a fuse rating or circuit-breaker setting in excess of 200 per cent of full-load current.

For motors not marked with a Code Letter, see Table 430-153.

Table 430-151 National Electrical Code

Table 430-153. Maximum Rating or Setting of Motor-Branch-Circuit Protective Devices for Motors not Marked with a Code Letter Indicating Locked Rotor KVA

Type of Motor	Per Cent of Full-Load Current		
	Fuse Rating (See also Table 430-146, Columns 4, 5, 6, 7	Circuit-Breaker Setting	
		Instantaneous Type	Time Limit Type
Single-phase, all types......	300	....	250
Squirrel-cage and synchronous (full-voltage, resistor and reactor starting)...............	300	....	250
Squirrel-cage and synchronous (auto-transformer starting) Not more than 30 amperes.............	250	....	200
More than 30 amperes...	200	....	200
High-reactance squirrel-cage Not more than 30 amperes...............	250	....	250
More than 30 amperes...	200	....	200
Wound-rotor.............	150	....	150
Direct-current Not more than 50 H.P...	150	250	150
More than 50 H.P.......	150	175	150
Sealed (Hermetic Type) Refrigeration Compressor* 400 KVA locked-rotor or less	**175	....	**175

For certain exceptions to the values specified see Sections 430-52, and 430-59. The values given in the last column also cover the ratings of non-adjustable, time-limit types of circuit-breakers which may also be modified as in Section 430-52.

Synchronous motors of the low-torque low-speed type (usually 450 R.P.M. or lower) such as are used to drive reciprocating compressors, pumps, etc., which start up unloaded, do not require a fuse rating or circuit-breaker setting in excess of 200 per cent of full-load current.

For motors marked with a Code Letter, see Table 430-152.

*The locked rotor KVA is the product of the motor voltage and the motor locked rotor current (LRA) given on the motor nameplate divided by 1,000 for single-phase motors, or divided by 580 for 3-phase motors.

**This value may be increased to 225 per cent if necessary to permit starting.

Table 430-153 National Electrical Code

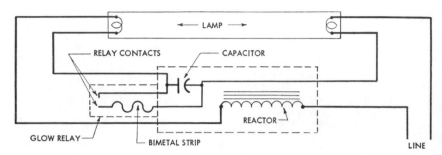

Wiring diagram of fluorescent lamp using glow relay starter

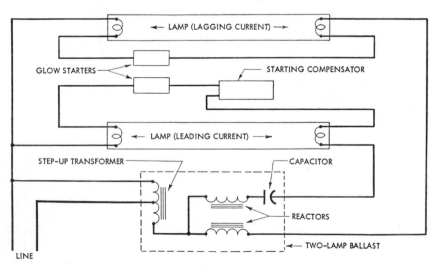

Wiring diagram of two-lamp fluorescent unit

INDEX